The
Last Love
Song

Also by Lucinda Riley

Hothouse Flower
The Girl on the Cliff
The Light Behind the Window
The Midnight Rose
The Italian Girl
The Angel Tree
The Olive Tree
The Love Letter
The Butterfly Room
The Murders at Fleat House
The Hidden Girl

The Seven Sisters Series
The Seven Sisters
The Storm Sister
The Shadow Sister
The Pearl Sister
The Moon Sister
The Sun Sister
The Missing Sister

By Lucinda Riley and Harry Whittaker

Grace and the Christmas Angel
Bill and the Dream Angel
Rosie and the Friendship Angel
Alfie and the Angel of Lost Things
Atlas: The Story of Pa Salt

The Last Love Song

LUCINDA RILEY

writing as Lucinda Edmonds

MACMILLAN

Previously published as *Losing You*

This revised and updated edition first published 2025 by Macmillan
an imprint of Pan Macmillan
The Smithson, 6 Briset Street, London EC1M 5NR
EU representative: Macmillan Publishers Ireland Ltd, 1st Floor,
The Liffey Trust Centre, 117–126 Sheriff Street Upper,
Dublin 1 D01 YC43
Associated companies throughout the world

ISBN 978-1-0350-7207-1 HB
ISBN 978-1-0350-7208-8 TPB

1 3 5 7 9 8 6 4 2

A CIP catalogue record for this book is available from the British Library.

Typeset in Sabon LT Std by Palimpsest Book Production Ltd, Falkirk, Stirlingshire
Printed and bound in the UK using 100% Renewable Electricity
by CPI Group (UK) Ltd

Visit **www.panmacmillan.com** to read more about all our books
and to buy them.

Foreword

Dear Reader,

Thank you for picking up this Lucinda Riley novel. I'm Lucinda's son, Harry Whittaker. If you know my name, it will no doubt be from *Atlas: The Story of Pa Salt*, the conclusion to Mum's Seven Sisters series, which became my responsibility after her death in 2021.

I wanted to explain how *The Last Love Song* has come to be published in 2025. To do so, I must provide a potted history of Mum's work, so I hope you'll indulge me.

From 1993 to 2000, Mum wrote eight novels under the name Lucinda Edmonds. Her career was seemingly cut short by a book called *Seeing Double*. The fictional plot suggested that there was an illegitimate member of the British Royal Family. The recent death of Princess Diana and subsequent monarchical turmoil meant bookshops deemed the project too much of a risk. Consequently, Lucinda Edmonds orders were cancelled, and her contract was voided by her publishers.

Between 2000 and 2008, Mum wrote three novels, all of which went unpublished. Then, in 2010, she had a breakthrough. Her first book as Lucinda Riley – *Hothouse Flower* – hit the shelves. Under this new name, she went on to become one of the world's most successful writers of female fiction, having sold seventy million books at the time of writing. Alongside her brand-new novels, Mum rewrote three 'Edmonds' books: *Aria* (which became *The Italian Girl*), *Not Quite an Angel* (which became *The Angel Tree*) and the aforementioned *Seeing Double* (which became *The Love Letter*). As for the three unpublished novels, all have now been released with great success.

There's no doubt that Lucinda has always been one of the world's best storytellers, but her authorial voice naturally matured over her thirty-year career. She conducted extensive work on her three 90s rewrites: changing plots, adding characters and amending her style. Consequently, I have undertaken the role here, refreshing and updating the text, helping to turn the 'Edmonds' into a 'Riley'. I performed the same task for *The Hidden Girl* in 2024.

The Last Love Song was originally published in 1997 under the title *Losing You*. For me, this book is particularly special due to its setting. Many readers will know that although she was born in Lisburn, Mum always felt that Ireland's West Cork was her spiritual home. Shortly after my birth in the early 1990s, we moved from England to Clonakilty. My favourite childhood memories are embedded in the breathtaking coastal landscape – namely in the hidden coves of Inchydoney beach, where Mum would tell me stories of the naughty sprites that lived within. Afterwards, we would warm ourselves in one of Clon's welcoming pubs, and hope for a performance from a fiddler or flautist. The local tonic of music and myths set my imagination whirring, and it's no wonder Ireland boasts some of the finest literary minds.

The Last Love Song is, in many ways, a tribute to West Cork. I shan't divulge too much of the plot, but it's clear that the bright lights of London's Carnaby Street pale in comparison to the Wild Atlantic Way and the (fictitious) Ballymore.

The text is instantly recognisable as Lucinda's work. In these pages you will discover passionate love, tragic loss and, of course, a devastating secret from the past which threatens to destroy the future. I wrote in my foreword to 2024's *The Hidden Girl* that 'the (editorial) process has been challenging' due to the book's difficult themes. I faced no such challenge here. Working on *The Last Love Song* has been a total joy. Although, as a new father of twin girls, I must admit that meeting deadlines has been *much* harder!

To Lucinda's returning readers, Mum is waiting for you like an old friend, ready to pull you into the past. As for new readers, welcome! I'm thrilled you have chosen to spend some time with Lucinda Riley.

Harry Whittaker, 2025

Prologue

London, June 1986

There were always day-old newspapers lying around in the television room, but she never bothered reading the news items. Sometimes she'd collect them and make her way through the crosswords. It helped ease the boredom. Gathering up the tea-stained copies of *The Sun* and *The Mirror*, she put them under her arm and made her way back to her cell. Thankfully, it was empty. Muriel had gone to the showers.

She settled herself onto her bunk and took the first newspaper off the pile. Searching for the puzzles page, she found a familiar face staring out at her. Steeling herself to ignore it, she turned over the page.

The man was still a huge star. His status had reached cult proportions due to his disappearance all those years ago. The odd picture in the papers was inevitable.

She tried to put the past to the back of her mind. Finding the crossword, she took out a biro from her jumpsuit pocket. Chewing it, she slowly began to fill in the letters. But, inevitably, her concentration was shot.

Eventually, she gave up, turned the pages back over and began to read.

COME HOME, CON!

It has been announced today that sixties sensation The Fishermen will reunite at London's Wembley Stadium during

1

the upcoming sell-out Music for Life concert. Stars past and present have pledged their support to sing for Africa this weekend, but the question on everybody's lips is . . . will Con Daly turn up? The Fishermen's lead singer famously hasn't been seen in public for over a decade.

She lay back, the newspaper still open on her lap. She'd learnt to numb herself against emotion. That was the only way to survive in here. Lying there, staring at the crack in the ceiling that she had watched grow from an inch to over a foot long, a small smile crossed her face.

Was it pleasure she was feeling?

No, not really.

She'd stopped believing in fate a long time ago. But it was a happy coincidence that, if all went well in front of the parole board in two weeks' time, she would be emerging from prison just before The Fishermen made their historic reunion performance at Wembley.

That night, as the light in the cell flashed three times to indicate the minutes before lights-out, she went over to the sink and brushed her teeth. Then she took the four pills the screw had just given her out of her dressing-gown pocket and dropped them into the rushing water. She watched as they swirled around before disappearing down the plughole.

When she turned around, Muriel was watching her in horror.

'Gawd, love, why on earth did you do that? You won't get no more now. You know what they're like.'

She climbed silently up onto her bunk.

'That's fine, Muriel. I don't need any more. Goodnight.'

A few seconds later, the lights went out.

Instead of quickly falling into her usual drugged, unrestful sleep, she felt wide awake.

It would take a while for the previous dose to leave her system and her brain to clear, but she could handle it. She *had* to.

She allowed herself to plunder her memory, to bring the anger back up to the surface. The pain would give her strength and feed the need for retribution.

Part One

Preparation

1

West Cork, Ireland, April 1964

The village of Ballymore nestled neatly into the rugged West Cork coastline. Its bright pink-, yellow- and blue-painted houses were a cheering sight on bleak, grey winter days, as storms beat relentlessly in from the Atlantic. The fifteen hundred residents were used to the rain, which had been known to fall continuously for three months without respite. They only endured the long winters knowing that a glorious summer would follow. The sky would become azure, and young and old alike would spend long days on the golden beaches for which the area was famed. They knew that, for those few short weeks, there was no better place to be on God's earth.

Sorcha O'Donovan followed the rest of the village out of the church and into the bright April air.

''Tis a beautiful morning!' smiled Mary O'Donovan. 'I think spring has arrived at last.'

'Yes, it's grand altogether, Mammy,' nodded Sorcha, eager to be gone. 'Mammy, can I go over to Maureen's before lunch? I promised I'd help her with her maths.'

Mary had spotted a friend and was waving to her.

'Yes, but be sure to be back for one o'clock. You know how particular your daddy is.'

'Yes, Mammy.'

Sorcha watched as her mother turned and started to make her way through the crowd towards her friend. Then she retrieved her bicycle from the side of the church and set off through the gates in the direction of Maureen's house. When she was out of sight of the crowd outside the church, she turned a corner and pedalled as fast as she could along the path that led away from the village towards the sea.

Fifteen minutes later, having cycled the two and a half miles to the beach, she hid her bicycle in a hollow, then perched on a sand dune to catch her breath and smooth her wind-strewn hair. It wasn't more than a few seconds before she heard the sound of Con's guitar and the mellow tone of his voice drifting closer to her. Sorcha leapt to her feet and searched about her.

'Con, Con, it's me!' she shouted, competing with the sound of the waves as she ran joyfully through the dunes, covering her mass dress in sand. 'Con! Where are you?' An edge of confusion had crept into her voice. 'Con? I—'

There was a friendly roar from behind her. Sorcha didn't even have time to turn before she was jumped upon. The pair fell softly onto the beach, rolling over and over until they came to rest in a hollow.

Sorcha looked up at him lying on top of her, his huge blue eyes set under a pair of full dark eyebrows, framed by lashes so long and curly they were almost feminine. His skin was still tanned from the sea air even after a long winter, and his thick black hair fell in waves to his shoulders. She knew she'd love him for the rest of her life, whatever the cost.

'Hello, Sorcha-porcha. Have you missed me?' He smiled down at her, giving her a trademark wink. 'I've certainly missed you.'

A lump came to her throat. She nodded, then stroked his cold cheek with her finger. 'Oh yes, Con. Oh yes.'

His lips came down hard onto hers, and she felt his hand slowly creeping up her thigh. She enjoyed the sensation for a few seconds before her conscience won out.

'Con, you promised me!' She wriggled away from him and lay on her side.

'I'm mad for you, Sorcha-porcha. I think of nothing else, I swear. I even wrote a song for you last night.' Con gently caressed her hair. 'I'm going to get my guitar and sing it for you.' He jumped up and raced over a dune.

Sorcha lay still, her eyes closed, wanting to record every second they shared so she could think about it when she was alone at night without him.

He was back.

'I've called it "My One True Love".'

She turned over and watched him as he began to sing to her.

'Ah, Con, 'tis a beautiful melody. Did you really write it for me?' Sorcha asked when he'd finished.

'Yes. And I meant every word.' He reached over to her and planted another kiss on her lips. 'Must you go?'

Sorcha was brushing the sand from her dress and straightening her hair.

'You know I have to. Daddy will be fierce cross if I'm not back in time for dinner.'

His arms enveloped her. 'Ah, Sorcha. Come live with me and be my love,' he quoted. Then he tipped her face up to his. 'You know we can't go on like this. You're seventeen in a few months. Then no one can stop us.'

'They can. You know they can.' She nestled into his chest.

'Not if you come with me across the sea. I can't stay here much longer. It's only you that keeps me from leaving immediately.'

'Please, Con, don't say that.'

'I'm sorry, but it's the truth. You're going to have to decide, Sorcha-porcha.'

'Yes, yes, I know. I'll come on Wednesday, after school.'

9

'I'll be in my hut, waiting for you.' He kissed her once more. 'Goodbye, my love.'

'Goodbye.'

Reluctantly, she left his arms and began scrambling across the dunes. Sorcha shivered as the wind whipped around her bare legs. The weather was changing, suddenly and dramatically, as it was prone to do in West Cork. She turned and saw Con gazing out to sea at the storm that was brewing. She perhaps had ten minutes before the heavens opened, and consequently serious problems explaining her soaked clothing to her mammy and daddy. Sorcha wheeled her bicycle onto the road, climbed on and began to pedal for home.

The figure who had watched the two of them for the past forty minutes scurried away unseen.

'Mary, mother of God! You're drenched, child! How did you manage that on a two-minute cycle from Maureen's? Get upstairs with you and change. I'll be putting the dinner on the table in three minutes.'

'Yes, Mammy.' Sorcha hurried up the stairs. She headed for the bathroom and locked the door behind her. Then she climbed into the bath and began to undress, shaking each of her garments thoroughly. When she was naked, she climbed out of the bath and ran the taps, swirling the tell-tale golden sand away down the plughole.

When Sorcha reappeared downstairs, her father was already sitting at the highly polished mahogany table in the dining room. It was always cold in there, and there was a musty smell because it was never used more than once a week.

'Sit down then, Sorcha,' said her father.

Sorcha obeyed, as her mammy brought in the piece of beef which had been cooking since seven this morning. Mary placed it in front of her husband.

'I hope you'll find 'tis tender, Seamus,' she said nervously as he picked up the carving knife.

The two women sat in silence as Seamus pedantically cut the joint into perfect slices. Only when he'd cut all three portions was Mary allowed to fill the plates with vegetables.

All that hard work, thought Sorcha, lifting her fork. *And by the time we get to eat it, it's no more than lukewarm.*

No one spoke. Seamus did not approve of chat during dinner. After the food was finished, the plates were cleared away by Sorcha while Mary brought in a perfect apple pie from the range in the kitchen.

Sorcha watched her daddy as he ate. She wondered whether he'd been born with a frown, or had frowned so often his face was simply frozen that way. Whichever the reason, he always looked cross. Sadly, everyone said Sorcha resembled him. She certainly had his thick, curly, auburn hair and green eyes. She was tall, too. Her friends at school called him handsome and said how lucky she was to have such a fine-looking father, but Sorcha often prayed at night that she hadn't inherited his personality. When she'd been small, she'd been afraid of him and his readiness with the back of his hand, but now . . . she despised him.

'Can we have the radio on, Mammy?' she asked.

'You know your daddy won't want to be disturbed after lunch.'

'Quietly?'

Mary shook her head as Sorcha knew she would. 'Maybe later.'

Sorcha began to dry the wet dishes.

'Mammy, can I ask you something?'

'Of course.'

'Do you love Daddy?'

'Sorcha!' Mary blessed herself. 'What a question to ask! Surely you know I do.'

11

'I suppose. I . . . well, I've been reading a book for English lessons. It's called *Wuthering Heights*. It's about love and . . . passion.'

'I see.' Mary continued to wash up.

'Were you ever madly in love with Daddy? I mean, so bad that you couldn't sleep at night, that it was grand just to be near him, that when he kissed you, you thought you would burst with happiness?'

Mary stopped washing up and studied her daughter. Sorcha's eyes were alight, her face flushed.

'I . . . yes.' She nodded. 'I was once mad for someone . . . I mean your daddy, in the way you describe. But Sorcha, that kind of feeling can't last. A few months, maybe; in rare cases a couple of years. But then life gets in the way, real life.' Mary gazed out of the window at the raindrops plopping heavily onto the pane. 'In all honesty, it's rare you marry the man you really love.'

'But you did.'

Mary looked at her daughter and smiled weakly. 'Of course I did. Now, have you your homework to finish?'

'Yes.'

'Then get along with you up to your room. I'll do the rest of this.'

Sorcha kissed her mother's soft cheek. 'Thank you, Mammy.'

Upstairs in her spacious, comfortable bedroom, Sorcha reached for her satchel, unloaded her textbooks, paper and writing equipment onto her desk and sat down. Once she was comfortable, her fingers felt for the envelope at the bottom of her pencil case and she drew it out. It was crumpled, the small photograph inside even more so. She laid it in front of her and traced the contours of his face, as she'd done a thousand times before. Sorcha could see her fingerprints all over it.

'Con . . . Con,' she murmured as she stared at her love. The picture was terrible, out of focus and missing a left ear because of the way she'd cut it from the flyposter advertising his band's latest gig. But that hardly mattered.

Closing her eyes, Sorcha cast her mind back to the very first night, three months ago now, when she had first kissed him . . .

2

January 1964, three months earlier

'There's a band playing at the GAA hall Saturday week,' Mairead informed the girls as they filed out of the hall after morning prayers.

Her three friends raised their eyebrows as they walked down the corridor towards their classroom.

'I heard they're meant to be fierce good,' Mairead continued. 'They've put up posters in the town. You'll see after school.'

'What sort of band?' asked Katherine O'Mahoney as they entered the classroom. 'And who's in it?'

'A proper band, with guitars and drums. Con Daly's the lead singer.'

All four girls sat down at their desks and opened their satchels.

'He's a bad 'un,' imparted Maureen McNamara gravely.

'With his daddy having been a drunken eejit and his mammy dying when he was small, what chance did he have?' asked Katherine. 'Living in that godforsaken hut all alone on the beach. I'd say he needs to be pitied.'

'You always did have a soft heart, Katherine O'Mahoney. My brother says Con has a grand voice, though. He heard him in a bar in Clonakilty a while back,' Mairead concluded.

Sister Benedict's heavy footsteps echoed down the corridor.

'Well, I'm on for going,' whispered Mairead. 'Who'll join me?'

There was no time for further discussion as Sister Benedict entered the classroom.

The four girls reconvened after school. On the walk down the hill into Ballymore village they discussed the situation.

'All the St Joseph's boys will be there. My brother Johnny.' Mairead nodded in Katherine's direction. She blushed. 'Tommy Dalton.' Mairead looked at Maureen who studied her feet. 'And for you, Sorcha, any boy who takes your fancy.'

'And how are we meant to be getting out of our houses on a Saturday night to watch a band?' asked Sorcha.

'Don't worry your heads about that. I have it all worked out,' Mairead added confidently.

'Go on then,' challenged Katherine.

Mairead looked smug. 'Well, my mammy and daddy are going up to Milltown on Saturday morning to see my auntie. They won't be back until Sunday lunchtime. Johnny's meant to be looking after me. So, you can tell your parents you're all coming to stay the night. They don't need to know Mammy and Daddy are away. As long as we're all there for mass on Sunday morning, they'll not be suspicious at all.' Her eyes shone with pride. 'There now, what do you think?'

The three girls looked at each other.

'And what if they found out where we'd been? Jesus, Mary and Joseph! I'd be crucified!' said Maureen.

'They won't, though, will they? They'd never think that their sweet little daughters would be dancing the night away with boys!' giggled Mairead.

Sorcha shook her head uncertainly as they came to her turning on the road. 'I'm not sure, so, Mairead.'

'Well, you think about it, Sorcha O'Donovan. Most of us are nearly seventeen. We're not babies any more. So what if they do find out? Will they put us in Cork city jail and throw away the key? I doubt it!'

Sorcha blushed. 'You're right, Mairead. I'll think about it. See you tomorrow.'

She waved and walked down the narrow winding street into the large Georgian McCurtain Square. In the centre, enclosed within iron railings, was a formal garden with a small fountain that gurgled meekly. The professional people of the town resided here, in terraced, four-storey houses that were the envy of many. Sorcha crossed the square and approached her front door. On the left-hand side was a shiny brass plate that read:

SEAMUS O'DONOVAN, SOLICITOR

Her father used the three large downstairs rooms for his practice. The family lived above on the next three floors. Sorcha turned the key and headed for the stairs.

'I'm home, Mammy,' she called, divesting herself of her hat, blazer, gloves and scarf. She walked down the corridor and opened the kitchen door. A wonderful smell of bacon filled her nostrils as she went to the scrubbed oak table and kissed her flour-covered mother.

'Hello, darling. Did you have a good day? There's a hot drop in the pot.'

'Thank you. I did have a good day. Do you want a cup of tea?'

'No, thank you. I need to finish this pie. Helen is coming for supper.'

Sorcha bristled. 'Oh, Mammy, does she have to?'

'Yes, you know she does. Poor thing, with no parents to love her. It's the least we can do. And don't be forgetting that she's a distant cousin of your daddy's, Sorcha.'

Helen McCarthy was in Sorcha's class at the convent, even though she was almost eighteen. Her parents had died in a car accident when she was five, leaving their large house and fortune to their only daughter. Since their death, Helen had been taken care of by an elderly aunt.

Sorcha never mentioned Helen's monthly visits to her schoolmates. Helen's mother had been English and a Protestant, uninvolved in the church community in the village. The family had always kept themselves separate; as a small child Helen had gone to a private primary school in Bandon, only joining the convent at the age of twelve. As she had a larger frame than most of her classmates, wore glasses, and was slower academically, she was an easy target for bullies.

Once a month, Helen came to the O'Donovans' for supper. Seamus managed Helen's trust and his practice took care of matters relating to the ten-bedroom mansion and two hundred acres which would come to Helen on her eighteenth birthday, as stipulated in her parents' will.

Sorcha often confessed to Father Moynihan that she'd been cruel and thoughtless and would try to talk to Helen in the future, or join her for lunch in the refectory where she sat in a corner alone every day. But she never quite managed it.

'Try and be friendly, Sorcha,' begged her mother. ''Tis only a few hours, one evening a month. She is in your class, after all.'

'Mammy, I'll do my best, I swear.'

'Like the good girl that you are. Off with you and finish your homework before Helen arrives.'

Supper was as difficult and uncomfortable as it always was. Helen sat there, focused on her food and little else.

'So, Helen. Any thoughts on what you're going to do when you leave school?' asked Seamus in his friendliest voice.

'I'm not sure,' replied Helen, looking momentarily lost, before returning her attention to the plate.

'Well, I'll be wanting to have a talk with you very soon. It'll be only a few months before the Lissnegooha estate is in your control.'

'Yes,' said Helen as she absentmindedly tore a piece of bread apart.

Pudding seemed interminable. When Mary stood up and began to clear away the dishes, Sorcha followed her.

'I'll help you.'

'No, I'm grand by myself. You take Helen up to your room for a while.'

Sorcha gave her mother one of her special looks, then gritted her teeth and said, 'Come on, Helen. Let's go upstairs.'

Helen followed up the stairs behind Sorcha and took a seat on the edge of her bed. Sorcha pulled out her desk chair and sat on that.

She couldn't think of a thing to say.

Helen's hand began to tap nervously on her leg. She summoned her courage and spoke.

'Are you going to hear the band at the GAA hall on Saturday night?' she ventured.

'How did you know about that?'

'I've seen the flyposters in town and I heard you discussing it in the classroom this morning.'

Sorcha guiltily shook her head. 'No, of course not.'

'Oh,' said Helen. She looked down at her hands and twiddled her thumbs. Sorcha could see her nails were bitten to the quicks. 'That Con Daly is in it.' Helen reached into her pocket and brought out a crumpled flyposter, unfolding it carefully. 'He's . . . well, he's very handsome, don't you think?' Helen blushed to the roots of her unbrushed hair.

'Yes, I suppose.' Sorcha hadn't really thought about it.

'I talk to him sometimes, when I'm out riding on the beach. I can see his hut from my bedroom window. Wouldn't it be grand to be like him, Sorcha? Living by yourself with no one telling you what to do.'

Sorcha watched Helen in amazement. It was more than she'd ever heard the girl say.

'I think it would be lonely and cold in that hut. There's not even a lavvy.'

'People like Con and me, well, we get used to our own company. It comes from being different. We're probably the same, in many ways.'

'Except you're going to be very rich with a big house and Con Daly has nothing except a shack he only borrows since his daddy died and they took away his house to pay the debts.'

Helen looked downcast. 'Yes, I suppose.' She folded the poster carefully and put it back in her pocket. Sorcha watched her visibly retreat into her shell. They sat in silence until Mary knocked on the door five minutes later to say Seamus was ready to give Helen a lift back home.

'Bye then, Sorcha.'

'Bye, Helen.'

She nodded and left the bedroom. Five minutes later, Sorcha went into the bathroom to begin her nightly ablutions. Then she got into bed, pulled the covers over her and thought about the concert on Saturday week. If she went, it would be the first time she'd ever told a lie to her parents. Besides, what would she wear? Her mass dress? Sorcha giggled at the thought of such a thing, turned over and closed her eyes. She would sleep on it and see how she felt in the morning.

'Mammy, Mairead has invited Katherine, Maureen and me to stay over at her house next Saturday night. Will it be all right if I go?' Sorcha's fingers were crossed behind her back.

Mary was busy scrubbing the kitchen floor. 'I don't see why you shouldn't, if all your homework is done before you leave.'

'It will be, I swear.'

'Then you may tell Mairead that you'll be there.'

'Grand.' Sorcha stood there, amazed it had been so easy.

Mary looked up at her. 'Is there anything else you want, Sorcha? Would you like to help me scrub the floor?'

'I . . . no. Thanks, Mammy.'

Sorcha skedaddled before she gave herself away.

'Come in before they see you,' Mairead whispered as she opened the kitchen door.

'But they're *meant* to see us, remember?' giggled Sorcha.

'Yes, of course they are,' Mairead laughed. 'I've had to pay my brother Johnny not to tell. He's coming to the concert with some of his friends.'

'And he won't say anything?'

'No. He's after liking Katherine, so he'll not tell,' said Mairead, smiling. 'Did you bring something to wear?'

'Yes. My mass dress.' Sorcha followed Mairead up the stairs to her small bedroom.

'No! You couldn't.'

'I'm teasing. I'll show you in a minute.'

Katherine was sitting in her underwear on the floor amid heaps of clothing.

'It's no good! Everything looks dreadful! I'm going home to spend the night in bed.'

'Don't be an eejit!' scolded Mairead. 'You look grand in your riding jodhpurs and black sweater. They show off your figure.'

'I can't wear my riding breeches to a concert!' wailed Katherine.

'Of course you can. You know it said jodhpurs are the new

20

fashion in that magazine Maureen got from her aunt in London.'

Sorcha dumped her bag on the floor. 'I don't know why you're worrying,' she said. 'You know how the boys all swoon when you walk past. You don't even have to try with that lovely long blonde hair and your big blue eyes.'

'Get along with you,' said Katherine. 'You're the envy of every girl in the class with your red curls and long legs. You're just as pretty as any of those models in Maureen's magazine.'

'When each of you has finished telling the other she should enter a beauty pageant tomorrow, perhaps we can get down to business.' Mairead raised an eyebrow. 'Maureen's late. She said she'd be here by half past four. It's gone five o'clock now.'

'She'll be here,' said Sorcha, nodding. 'I saw her in town earlier.'

'Right. Well.' Mairead picked up a brush and comb, brandishing them at the girls. 'Who's first in my salon?'

An hour and a half later, the transformation was complete. Sorcha surveyed her reflection with wonderment.

'I can't believe it's me.' She made an exaggerated 'O' with her painted scarlet lips. Her eyelids felt heavy with the false eyelashes her friend had applied. Sorcha touched her hair, which Mairead had teased into a neat twist, then fastened with kirby grips onto the top of her head. The old kilt she'd found languishing at the back of her wardrobe had taken well to being shortened seven inches. She'd altered the side seams so that it hugged her thighs and showed off her long, slim legs.

Katherine was also admiring herself. 'Mairead, you ought to open your own salon. You're a genius,' she smiled.

Mairead shrugged modestly and folded away the picture of the model from the magazine she'd been copying from. 'It was nothing. Now, it's time for me. Will you ring Maureen while I'm in the bathroom?'

Sorcha hardly took her eyes off the mirror. 'If she's not here in ten minutes, I will.'

'Grand. Tidy up a little, will you?'

'We'll try,' sighed Katherine, sitting gingerly on the bed so as not to disturb her golden locks, which Mairead had brushed until they shone. 'You know, I don't think our mammies would recognise us even if they found where we were tonight.'

'No. I can only imagine what my daddy would say if he saw my painted face and short skirt.'

'Do you think it will happen tonight for one of us?' asked Katherine.

'What do you mean, "it"?' asked Sorcha.

'That we might get kissed.' Katherine tucked her long legs under herself.

'Who knows?'

The two girls sat in silence, pondering the enormity of such an event.

There was a knocking from downstairs. Katherine jumped up. 'That'll be Maureen. I'll go let her in.'

Two minutes later, Katherine appeared back in the bedroom with a flushed Maureen.

'Jesus, Mary and Joseph! I thought I'd never escape. Shane is sick and Mammy made me mind him while she was out. How much time have I got to get ready?'

'Plenty if we all help you,' Katherine reassured her.

Half an hour later, the four girls were sitting on the bed nervously contemplating their deception.

Maureen, looking uncomfortable in an emerald-green dress she'd stolen from her mother's wardrobe, shook her head. 'I don't know whether we shouldn't forget this, make some sandwiches and put our pyjamas on.'

'Just stop panicking. Here.' Mairead produced a small bottle of whiskey from under the bed. 'We all need some courage.' She took the top off, put the bottle to her lips, threw her head back and drank.

The other girls watched as Mairead's eyes began to water.

'Quick, your mascara will run.' Sorcha offered her a handkerchief.

'Who's next?' Mairead offered the bottle as she dabbed at her eyes.

The three girls looked at each other uncertainly.

'Jesus, well, you three are full of the spirit of adventure, aren't you!' Mairead shook her head and rolled her eyes.

'Give it here.' Sorcha grabbed the bottle and took a sip. 'You next, Katherine.'

Katherine closed her eyes and took a healthy slug. Her eyes shone as she passed the bottle to Maureen. 'I like it.'

'Do you now?' laughed Maureen, taking a swig. She had to be slapped hard on the back as she coughed and spluttered helplessly.

'Right, are we ready?' asked Mairead.

The other three nodded solemnly.

'Then we'll put on our coats, get on our bicycles and go.'

'What if we see anyone we know?' asked Katherine.

'We wave at them and smile. We're only out to enjoy an evening bicycle ride.' Mairead shrugged.

'What, in the dark?' giggled Sorcha.

'Come on, let's go.'

The four girls filed out of the bedroom.

It was a fifteen-minute cycle ride up to the GAA hall. Breathing a collective sigh of relief that most folks were huddled inside by the fire on this cold January night, the girls hid their bicycles around the back of the hall and went to take their places in the short queue that had formed outside.

'Give me your money and I'll pay for all of us,' said Mairead.

Sorcha turned around and saw a handful of boys studying them appreciatively. She nudged Katherine and winked. Mairead paid for the tickets and the four girls filed into the ladies' for a quick repair job.

As Sorcha carefully replenished her lipstick, she could hear the band warming up in the hall next door. A shiver of excitement ran through her.

'You're growing up at last,' she whispered to her reflection.

By nine o'clock, the hall was full to bursting.

'See, they've come from other villages. It's so crowded we'll never be spotted,' Mairead reassured the others as they pushed their way over to the bar. 'Now, what'll we order?'

'Lemonade.'

'Shall I make that four?'

There was a collective nod.

An amplified voice echoed across the crowd. 'And now, ladies and gentlemen, will you all give a big hand for Con Daly and his band!'

The announcer left the stage. The girls stood on tiptoe to watch as the five members took their places. Con Daly strolled casually forward to the microphone.

'Evening, all, and a big welcome from me and the boys. We hope you'll enjoy yourselves. Let's rock!'

Con turned around, counted his band in, and suddenly the hall was filled with the sound of a rich, deep voice, backed by a languorous guitar rhythm.

The girls stood watching him.

'You know, I would hardly recognise him. He's handsome when he cleans himself up, isn't he?' whispered Mairead.

'Now I look at him, he is a fine figure of a man. That black hair and those big blue eyes remind me of Elvis. Don't you think, Sorcha?' said Katherine.

Sorcha didn't answer. She was staring, transfixed, at Con Daly.

'What a grand voice,' put in Maureen. 'It's as good as anything you hear on the radio.'

'Sorcha, take your lemonade. Sorcha!' Mairead nudged her.

'Yes, sorry.' Sorcha took the bottle, put the straw in her mouth and sucked without taking her eyes off the stage.

'Er, I . . . would you be wanting to dance, Katherine O'Mahoney?'

A tall, painfully thin young man with a bad case of acne was standing behind Katherine. They all knew him. He was in the same year as Johnny, Mairead's brother.

'Well now, I might want to dance,' nodded Katherine, turning around, 'but not with you, Ryan O'Sullivan.'

The girls giggled as Ryan slunk away, his head bowed in embarrassment.

'Ah, now, you shouldn't be so cruel,' admonished Maureen.

'Maybe I'm waiting for Johnny to come over and ask me,' smiled Katherine.

The girls found an empty table on one side of the hall and sat down. They watched the band and those who had begun to dance. Sorcha could hardly drag her eyes away from Con Daly.

The group finished a lively number to rapturous applause, and Con spoke gently into the microphone.

'You're a grand audience, thank you. Now, we'll lower the tempo. Take your partners, girls and boys. This is a ballad I wrote as I was looking over the beautiful bay of Ballymore.'

Johnny sidled up to the table.

'Do you fancy a dance, Katherine?' he enquired confidently.

Katherine blushed and nodded. She stood up and took Johnny's outstretched hand.

'And you, Sorcha, would you have a dance with me?'

It was Angus Hurley, a young man whom Sorcha had known since childhood. His parents ran the cotton factory outside the village.

Sorcha nodded and Angus led her onto the floor. He put his arms loosely round her waist and Sorcha hooked hers over his shoulders. They swayed awkwardly to the music.

'I'm surprised your parents let your group come tonight,' he said.

'They don't know we're here. And if you breathe a word, Angus Hurley, none of us will ever speak to you again.'

'I'll say nothing, Sorcha, you know I won't.'

Sorcha put her head back over Angus's shoulder and watched Con Daly. As she looked at him, his eyes seemed to focus on her. For a good ten seconds the two of them stared at one another. She reluctantly dragged her gaze away.

'Sorry, Angus. I was miles away. What was it that you were saying?'

'I . . . well, I was asking you . . . That is, I . . .' Angus blushed. 'I was thinking maybe we could go to the flicks in Bandon next week. You . . . you look beautiful this evening, Sorcha. And I've always liked you, as I'm sure you know.'

'It's kind of you to ask me. Could I think about it and let you know?'

'Okay,' Angus nodded.

The ballad finished and Sorcha returned to the table. Maureen was sitting there alone, looking dejected.

'Where's Mairead?'

'Oh, some gorgeous man came and whisked her away. Katherine's still dancing.'

Sorcha looked to the dance floor and saw her friend's arms

26

wrapped tightly around Johnny's neck. She smiled. 'It's grand to see those two together after all this time. They've liked each other for months.'

'And what about you and the handsome Angus?'

'Oh, he asked me to the cinema next week and I said I'd think about it.'

'You did what? Sorcha, you know very well that Angus is the catch of the town. He'll have that factory one day and the big house on the hill. Plus, he looks like a film star.'

'Well now, that's your taste, Maureen. Personally, I think Con Daly is better looking.'

'No!' Maureen baulked. 'He's probably not had a bath for months!'

Sorcha rolled her eyes. 'You're terrible.'

'Well, all I can say is that you should be grateful you have a boy who likes you. I don't know why I bothered coming. Who'd want to dance with me when I'm so fat and ugly?'

Sorcha looked at her best friend's heart-shaped face, her nose sprinkled with freckles, and the small curls of ginger hair escaping from the pleat Mairead had painstakingly pinned on the back of her head.

'You're beautiful, Maureen, so you are,' Sorcha replied honestly.

'Then why am I sitting here like a wallflower while everyone else dances?'

'You won't be for much longer, I promise. Excuse me, I need to go to the ladies'. Back in a minute.'

Sorcha stood up just as the band announced they were taking a ten-minute break. She headed for Angus, who was standing by the bar at the back of the hall.

'Angus, I'll go to the flicks with you next week.'

'You will?' He broke into a relieved smile. 'That's grand altogether, Sorcha!'

'On one condition.'

Angus held his hands up. 'Anything.'

'That you buy my friend Maureen a lemonade, talk to her for a while, and when the band starts up, you ask her to dance.'

Angus shrugged. 'All right. I'll pick you up from your house at seven next Friday. We can go in the new car I'll be getting for my eighteenth birthday.'

'Grand. I'll see you then, as long as you keep your promise.'

'I'm on my way for the lemonade now.'

Sorcha smiled, then headed in the direction of the ladies', tucked inside the entrance hall. She stood in front of a small cracked mirror, tidied her hair and replenished her lipstick. She was just coming out of the door when an arm caught her and pulled her outside, causing her to audibly gasp.

'Hush! I won't hurt you, I swear.'

She recognised the voice and smelt the pleasant aroma of manly aftershave. An electric tingle fizzed through her as Con Daly's body pressed close behind hers.

'Sorcha O'Donovan, I've seen you and your friends hanging around the beach from my place and I've always thought you were beautiful. Tonight, you are the loveliest sight I've ever seen. In all honesty, I want to marry you right here and now . . .' He swung her round to face him. It was dark but she could see he was grinning widely at her. 'Or at least, come for a hot drop at my place next week.' Sorcha stared up into his eyes, words failing her.

'Will you?'

'Will, will . . . will I what?'

'Come to my place next week?'

'I—'

'Of course you will. You know where I live?' She nodded. 'Then I'll expect you. Now, come here and kiss me.'

He pulled her gently towards him and planted a small kiss

on her lips. Then he took her lightly by the shoulders and stared down at her.

'Sorcha-porcha.' He winked. 'I'll be waiting for you.'

Sorcha watched as he made his way inside. She leant against a wall, breathing heavily. Her legs felt like cotton wool and her head was spinning.

Con Daly was no better than a tinker living in his shack on the beach. Before tonight she would have probably crossed the street to avoid him, and never would have dreamt that she'd accept his physical affection . . .

Sorcha blessed herself and asked God to forgive her – not only for the kiss, but because she had enjoyed every moment of it.

Would she go to see him next week?

Sorcha pushed herself away from the wall as the band began to play.

Walking inside, she observed Angus dancing with Maureen, Katherine smooching Johnny and Mairead being held very close by a boy she'd never seen before.

Then she looked up to the stage.

He smiled at her.

She knew something had begun tonight that could change her life completely.

3

Helen McCarthy saddled up her horse, Davy, checked the girth, then swung herself onto his back. She turned him out of the stable yard, trotted along the winding drive, out of the gate, and pointed Davy in the direction of the beach.

On her own two feet, Helen was ungainly. Yet from a distance, sitting comfortably on the tall stallion, her seat so assured . . . girl and horse made a perfectly elegant picture.

It was the only time Helen felt in control.

Three minutes later, they'd reached the long stretch of white sand.

'Giddy-up!' Helen tapped Davy's bottom and the horse began to canter. The wind whipped around her face, the crash of the waves deafening her. As was often the case, Helen began to sob loudly, her wails matching those of the seagulls up above her.

She rode until she reached the far end of the beach. She slowed Davy to a trot, and they carefully picked their way through the rocky outcrop onto the sheltered sandy cove Helen had come to regard as her own private haven. She came here when things were bad. Consequently, it was where she spent most of her time.

Dismounting Davy, she tethered him to a rock that stuck out of the sand, then walked slowly towards the waves.

For a few moments, and not for the first time, Helen contemplated continuing to venture right out until the waves brushed her thighs, her stomach, her neck, then eventually closed over her head, bringing peace and silence.

Tears began to trickle out of her eyes once more, stinging her salty cheeks. She shook her head. She was too scared of water to drown herself.

Helen turned and walked back, climbing onto the rock that gave the best view of the coast. As she surveyed the scene, her eyes fixed on the blinking of the Galley Head Lighthouse, shrouded in mist.

School had been more miserable than usual, if that was possible. She had heard Sorcha and her cronies giggling about the fun they'd had at the concert at the GAA hall last Saturday night. Helen was filled with hurt at the way they stopped talking immediately when they noticed she was behind them.

The rejection of Sorcha O'Donovan was particularly painful. The girl was very pretty, bright and popular, with a mother and father who loved her. In short, Sorcha had everything Helen herself longed for.

She looked up to the sky. In forty minutes or so the day would end and blackness would descend. After a night of respite, the sun would rise and Helen would have to endure the humiliation of rejection once again.

'Oh, Mother, why did you and Daddy leave me?!' she wailed. How many other children in the village had lacked a comforting arm around their shoulder when they'd tripped and fallen? How many had missed their bedtime story, or the kiss with a rough male cheek that spoke silently of love and security as the light was switched off?

'I have nothing, nothing!'

Helen knew her last statement was dramatic and far from

true. There was one thing she was going to have very soon, and lots of it.

She wiped her eyes with a none-too-clean hanky and tried to order things in her mind.

'Will I spend my whole life crying?'

'You might.'

Helen jumped and turned around. The elegant figure of Con Daly came into view. He stood on the rock, towering over her. She blushed an unsightly red colour.

'Isn't this view grand?'

Helen sniffed and wiped her nose. 'It is.'

'It might be my favourite spot.'

'Mine too.'

'I know.' He came and crouched on the rock beside her. 'The perfect place for useless articles like you and me to come and be alone.'

Helen guffawed. 'You're not useless. All the girls at school were raving about you and your band.'

'Were they now?' Con raised an eyebrow. 'Any girl in particular?'

'Should there have been?'

Con shrugged. 'Maybe.'

'Oh.' Helen's shoulders sagged a little.

'I didn't see you there,' he said.

'No. I didn't want to go by myself.'

Con exhaled deeply. 'Ah, Helen, what it is to be living on the edge of society like us. Tolerated, but never accepted. I'm all for leaving as soon as I can.'

'Lucky you.' Helen ground her riding boot into the sand.

'You have nothing to keep you here either.'

'I have fear to keep me here, Con.'

'Yes, 'tis a powerful thing, fear. But never forget that loneliness gives you strength. You can spend your life observing others, on the outside looking in. You end up learning a lot about human nature that way.'

'I've learnt that it stinks,' she replied bitterly.

'Come on now, life isn't that bad. You have that grand mansion and the land around it. Plenty of money to make your dreams happen. The world is your oyster.'

'I'd trade it all to be popular. And as pretty as Sorcha O'Donovan.'

Con grinned. 'I think everyone would like to be as pretty as her. But you can buy yourself a new hairstyle and a set of friends.'

Helen sighed. 'I suppose so.'

Con stood up. 'I'm off. I have an assignation at my palace over there.' He indicated the hut.

'You do?'

'Yes.' He put a finger to his lips. 'But it's a secret. Goodbye, Helen.' Con reached out and put a reassuring hand on her shoulder. Helen's heart began to beat faster and her body was filled with an indescribable warmth. 'You know where I am if you want a chat.'

'Thanks, Con,' she choked.

Helen watched him step easily over the rocks and disappear.

She thought about what he had said. Despite his reputation as an unwashed layabout, Con was a clever man. The conversations they'd had over the years were infrequent but memorable. He was the one person she knew who did not treat her as if she had no brain in her head.

Plus, he seemed to become more handsome every time she saw him.

For want of any other man to think of, she thought about Con. She supposed she was a little in love with him, but aware that her feelings would never be reciprocated.

What man could ever love her?

She pulled her scarf up around her ears. The wind was starting to bite. Con had just voiced an idea that had been dancing around Helen's head more and more insistently in recent times. Seamus O'Donovan had assured her she'd be a very wealthy young lady. Helen wasn't quite sure exactly how rich she'd be, but it was a simple matter of asking. She knew her lawyer thought her dense, that she'd never be able to grasp her financial situation or cope with the responsibility of running the estate. Maybe he was right. She certainly struggled at school, unable for some reason to make sense of words written on the page, even though she understood the meaning in her mind. But numbers were no problem. She had always been excellent at maths.

And this large amount of money that would soon be hers . . . as Con had said, it could buy her an escape. She could go anywhere she wanted – somewhere where she could start again. But where? She'd hardly been out of Ballymore. Did she have the courage to leave a life that might be difficult, but was at least safe and familiar?

Helen looked out over the darkening skyline. There was no more time for thinking. She had to ride home before the light was lost completely.

She mounted Davy. As she trotted along the beach, she saw a glow emanating from Con's hut.

Drawing closer, Helen heard the sound of laughter coming from within. She called her horse to a halt and watched for a moment. Con's silhouette appeared in the small grimy window. He was joined by a second silhouette. Their mouths met and they shared a kiss.

Helen blushed bright red, hating herself for spying, but unable to avert her gaze. Eventually, the door of the hut opened and a slim figure emerged. It wasted no time in scampering off across the dunes before Helen had a chance to see who it was.

She continued to watch as Con came out and stood in the doorway. A match flickered and Helen saw the red glow of a cigarette. It was almost completely dark now. Davy huffed in impatience.

Helen cantered away along the beach.

4

May 1964

'So, will you come with me, Sorcha?'

She looked at Con, lying full-length on the battered couch he ate and slept on. She shivered and moved nearer to the small fire that was burning in the stove. Even though it was the beginning of May, the nights could still be sharp.

'Con Daly, where would we go? What would we live on? I have no money, and neither do you.'

'I have my guitar, Sorcha. We wouldn't starve, even if I have to sing on street corners with my hat placed on the pavement for silver. And I know it won't be long before I'm getting gigs, and after that, a record deal.' Con pointed away from the ocean. 'London's where the music scene is happening. That's where I have to be.' He reached in his pocket and drew out a battered cigarette. Then he moved over to the stove and lit it on the hot coals. He took a drag. 'Want some?'

Sorcha shook her head.

Con put an arm around her and pulled her towards him. He kissed her, his lips tasting of the tar he'd just inhaled. He stroked her hair lovingly.

'Ah, Sorcha-porcha, I'm a man whose passion is inflamed. You won't let me make love to you, you won't say if you'll come with me to England . . . I'm beginning to wonder if you love me at all.'

Her eyes filled with tears. 'Con, you know I love you. It's

fierce. I think of nothing else. Even Sister Benedict has asked me if I've any trouble at home because my marks are slipping at school. It's just that . . . I . . . I'm scared, Con.'

'What of, Sorcha? My love? Me?'

He tipped her face up to look at him, his eyes gentle.

'No. I . . . well, I've always thought I'd leave school, attend a secretarial college in Cork and take a job in my daddy's office. Then I'd . . .'

'Wait until a suitable man wants to marry you. Don't you know that there's a world out there waiting to be explored? This tiny corner of the earth will be the same for the next fifty years. I thought you'd be after excitement, Sorcha. Don't you want to *live*? Don't you want *me*?'

'I . . .' Sorcha looked at him helplessly.

'Atch!' Con stood up, threw his cigarette onto the stove and banged its door closed. He ran a hand through his hair. 'Sorcha, it's been three months now that we've been together. I understand that you're young and are protected by that mammy and daddy of yours. I want you to come with me, be part of my future. I've sworn to take care of you, marry you if you wish, but I can't be sitting here wasting time trying to convince you. I'm going to London, Sorcha, with or without you, in a month's time. I have enough money to pay for your passage too, if you want to come. There, that's how it is,' he sniffed. 'Now I suppose you'd better be leaving. Otherwise Mammy and Daddy might call the guards and I'd be accused of kidnapping you.'

Con moved towards the door and opened it.

Fighting back tears, Sorcha looked around for her jacket.

'Behind you.' Con indicated the arm of the couch. Sorcha picked it up and moved to the open door in silence.

'Goodbye, Con. When shall I see you again?'

He shrugged his shoulders.

Sorcha walked through the door and out into the bracing night air. The door was shut behind her with a bang.

Sorcha scrambled along the path through the dunes, her eyes blinded by tears, her sobs echoing around her. She wished she could go to church, ask His advice, but she knew running away with a man and leaving her family behind to enjoy what would soon become pleasures of the flesh was not the kind of operation He would be happy to deal with.

'Ouch!' Sorcha stumbled and lay in the sand waiting for the pain in her ankle to lessen. She turned over and looked up at the sky. It was a beautiful clear night and she could see the stars twinkling brightly in their constellations.

If she let him go without her, wouldn't she regret it for the rest of her life? What was she leaving here? She wasn't a child any more. And the thought of a future without Con was unbearable.

That evening, Sorcha took her seat at the O'Donovan family dining table as her mother scooped out mountainous dollops of colcannon onto the plates. Once Seamus had delivered his lengthy grace, dinner was its usual tense affair. When her mother had finished clearing the crockery, Sorcha plucked up enough courage to engage her father in conversation.

'Daddy?'

'Sorcha.'

'You're always asking Helen McCarthy what her plans are for her future.'

He stared at her unblinkingly. 'Did you intend to ask a question, or merely make a statement?'

Sorcha blushed. 'Sorry. I just thought, as I'm getting on to be seventeen, that we could discuss my future?'

Seamus seemed to soften a little. 'Yes. That sounds like a prudent conversation.' He crossed his arms. 'Now, as much as I love you as a daughter, I need the quality of work you produce to be top class.'

Sorcha knew exactly where this conversation was heading.

'Therefore, before I take you on at the firm as a typist, I will need you to obtain the highest secretarial qualification. Cork has a number of institutions that will be suitable, but my recommendation would be—'

'Daddy?' Sorcha dared to interrupt. Seamus raised a curious eyebrow. 'I know that you want me to work in your offices, and that'd be grand altogether, but . . .' Sorcha's mother reappeared at the table with a steaming bread pudding.

'Please, finish your sentence, Sorcha.'

Sorcha was flustered. 'I have heard that there are lots of opportunities in London.'

'London?' Seamus queried. 'Who's put ideas in your head about that?'

'No one, I just—'

Seamus straightened his back. 'No daughter of mine is to go gallivanting off to England.'

'I understand, Daddy, but I really think that I could make something of myself there. There's not as many opportunities here at home.'

Sorcha's eyes crossed to her mother, who was stiffly filling three bowls with the beige-brown pudding, visibly anxious.

'Not many opportunities here?' Seamus leant in across the table towards his daughter. 'And what, pray tell, do you believe the opportunities to be in London?'

Sorcha stared blankly down at the table. 'Well . . .'

'Precisely. You don't have an answer. Whichever silly little friend of yours has mentioned this to you clearly hasn't been thinking about the realities of life. You'll go over there with nothing. How will you afford accommodation?'

'I . . .'

'Bills? Food?'

'I don't know.'

'Because you won't have any help from me. None at all.'

'I wouldn't expect any.'

'Oh, wouldn't you? That's about the only logical conclusion you've been able to draw this evening. If your plan is to go over there and find some fancy millionaire man to marry, it's a foolish one. There's a lot more women to choose from in England, that come from better stock than you.'

Sorcha observed her mother's eyes shoot daggers at her father, unseen by Seamus.

'You've a much better chance here, with someone we deem suitable.'

Sorcha felt an anger simmering within her. It was in danger of bubbling over. 'What if I don't want to get married? What if I want to have a career?'

Her father guffawed. 'It's a career you want, is it? Are you hearing this, Mary? Our daughter wants a career!' His laughter sent a tidal wave of shame washing over Sorcha. 'You'll make a fine typist and an even better wife and mother. No man will want his woman working outside the marital home.'

'Daddy, please just listen to—'

'Enough!' Seamus banged his fist on the table. 'Your mother and I have raised you to represent the O'Donovan family. I will *not* have my child flouncing off to England only to have you come crawling back with an expectation that I will fix everything for you. You will *not* embarrass this family, Sorcha. That is the end of it.'

Pudding was consumed in total silence.

That night, Sorcha cried silent tears in bed. Seamus had worn her down. Whether she liked it or not, going to London with Con was an impossibility. Travelling across the Irish Sea would mean cutting ties with her family entirely, and no matter how her father made her feel, Sorcha wasn't sure she could make such a life-changing decision at such a young age.

If Con truly loved her, as he said he did, then surely a life together in Ballymore was enough?

That said, her next task was to convince her father that Con was more than just the local reprobate. Perhaps if Seamus could appreciate his talent, he would see that Con could be a provider.

With all his ability, how could he fail?

Of course, announcing her relationship brazenly over breakfast tomorrow morning would not be the wisest move. It might just give Seamus a heart attack. That was a problem for a different day.

Sorcha dried her tears on her pillowcase and thought about Con's shimmering eyes.

Con was strumming morosely on his guitar when he heard the tap on the door. It opened before he reached it.

Sorcha stood there shivering with cold and emotion. 'I love you, Con. I never want to be without you.'

'You'll come with me to London then?'

Sorcha steeled herself. 'No, Con. I can't just leave everything behind. This is where my life is.'

Con shook his head and cast his eyes to the floor. 'Oh, God, Sorcha. How will I cope without you?'

She took his hands in her own. 'You don't have to, Con Daly. Stay here, with me.'

'You know that will never work. Your father won't allow us to be together.'

'That's my problem, Con, and one I will solve . . . with time.'

He freed his hands and rubbed his eyes. 'I can't give up my music. You know I can't.'

'I do. But I was thinking that you could go to Dublin, and try and get someone in the business to notice you there.'

Con seemed unsure. 'They want folk singers in Dublin. I'm a rocker.'

'Yes. But all you need is a chance. Then you can be whatever you want, Con. When you're successful, with thousands of pounds and three houses, Daddy will see that you're the man for me.' She gave him a reassuring smile. 'And then, who knows? Maybe we'll both end up in London just like you want.'

Con looked genuinely torn. 'Jesus, I love you, Sorcha-porcha. I just . . .' Sorcha took his head in her hands and kissed him gently, then more passionately. After a few minutes, desire took over. He pulled her down on the sofa and his hands began to roam Sorcha's body. He waited for them to be removed from her breasts, but met no resistance. His fingers travelled up her legs and caressed the soft flesh of her inner thigh, still waiting to be checked. But her eyes were closed, her lips turned up in a faint smile.

Small sighs of pleasure left her.

'Sorcha . . . is this . . . can we?'

She opened her eyes and smiled up at him.

'Yes. Just promise me one day we'll be married. Then I can think that this won't be a mortal sin.'

'We're married now in our souls. Love is no sin in God's eyes, Sorcha.'

'No. Then love me, Con.'

Two hours later, Sorcha was back home, soaping herself in a hot bath. She felt a little sore, but it was a nice pain, because it was where she and Con had been joined. She'd cycled like a madwoman all the way home, terrified her mother might have called Maureen's to find out why she was so late, only to discover Sorcha hadn't been there at all. But when she arrived home, her mother was in bed with a migraine and her father was still out at a meeting in the community hall.

Slipping her nightgown over her head, Sorcha climbed into bed. She looked at the almost hairless teddy that usually kept her company in bed. Grabbing him, she tossed him out of bed.

Teddies were for children.

And now she was a woman.

After tonight, Sorcha knew that she and Con completely belonged to one another. All would have to be well.

She would make sure of it.

5

'So, Helen, you can see from the figures that the investments your trustees have made have been rather successful. Your money has more than doubled. Now, it's obviously your decision, but I would recommend you keep the investments as they are and live off the interest. I'd say there will be enough to provide for the upkeep of the house and grounds, and also keep you very comfortable.'

Helen looked across the desk at the papers sat in front of Seamus O'Donovan. There were columns of upside-down figures relating to her financial future – figures she must grasp and understand if she was to take control of her life.

'May I take those home with me, so I can look through them?'

Seamus raised an eyebrow. 'Why of course, Helen. But without wanting to seem rude, it's doubtful you'll be able to make sense of them.'

'I'm sure you're right, Seamus, but I'll take them just the same.'

'Grand job. Now, Helen, I need you to decide whether you wish me and the other trustees to carry on managing your money for you. As I said before, I'm also prepared to continue to manage the house and grounds. We would have to come to some kind of financial agreement for my trouble but I would not be greedy.' Seamus tidied the papers in front of him, slid them into an envelope and handed them to Helen.

'Thank you, Seamus. I appreciate all your help and I'm grateful to you and the other trustees for managing my money so well for the past fourteen years.'

''Twas nothing, Helen. Good luck with those figures. I'm happy to help if you want anything explained.'

Helen stood up. 'Can we meet again next week?'

'Of course.' Seamus walked her to the door. 'Come on Wednesday for your usual supper with us. Arrive a little early and we can talk before we eat. And, Helen?'

'Yes, Seamus?'

'In three weeks' time you'll be a very wealthy young lady. Until then I am still a trustee of your estate. Therefore I feel justified in giving you a few words of warning. Trust no one. There are a lot of people out there who will want to take advantage of your, er, youth – and money.'

Helen smiled at him. 'Thank you, Seamus. I'll be careful.'

'Grand. Goodbye then.'

'Goodbye.'

Helen opened the heavy entrance gates to the drive that wound up to the house. As she walked she looked at the land around her with new appreciation. The formal gardens were small, with most of the acreage in the farmland surrounding the house. This was rented out to local farmers for grazing. As the house came into view, she studied it. She'd always thought it ugly, its solid greystone walls built to withstand the salt air, rain and high winds that came from living so close to the sea. It was always cold inside. The six formal rooms downstairs were never used. Aunt Betty gave them a once-a-year spring clean, then the dustsheets would be replaced over the antique furniture, all in immaculate condition due to the lack of use. She and her aunt lived mainly in the kitchen, where the range burnt night and day.

Apart from the large black-and-white-tiled bathroom, the only other room Helen visited was her bedroom. Ignoring the grand, high-ceilinged bedrooms on the first floor, she had tucked herself up in one of the cosier attic rooms, originally used by the servants. A large window seat allowed her to view the village of Ballymore on one side and the beach on the other. She spent a lot of time sitting there, gazing out at the world.

Helen let herself in through the side door that led through a lobby into the kitchen. There was a note from her aunt saying she'd retired early. A pot of overcooked stew was simmering on the range. Helen helped herself to a bowl, then sat down at the large wooden table and took her papers out of the envelope.

Two hours later, the bowl of stew was untouched and congealed beside her.

It had taken her a while to work out what the columns meant and what needed to be added together to produce the grand total.

Helen whistled. If she'd got it right, then 'grand' was the right word.

'A fortune,' she breathed. Certainly enough, she thought, to see her comfortably through the rest of her life.

Helen stared into space. Where was that life to be? Here? Where she was so unhappy? Or should she take her money and start afresh somewhere else?

Helen shook her head. She was a coward. She could see herself staying here for the rest of her days. If she had someone to go with her, a friend maybe, then it might be an option.

She yawned. It was almost midnight. Tomorrow, thanks be to God, was Sunday, which meant no school.

Helen folded her papers away in the envelope and made her way upstairs to her attic bedroom.

* * *

She woke to a beautiful sunny morning. Knowing how quickly the weather could change and not wanting to waste a minute of it, she threw on some clothes, said a quick good morning to her aunt as she passed through the kitchen and saddled up Davy. She loved riding on summery Sunday mornings: the beaches were deserted as the rest of the town was at mass.

A good canter along the shore left Helen feeling exhilarated and ready for breakfast. As she trotted homeward, she saw a distant figure running away from the beach. She watched as the figure retrieved a bicycle from a hollow in the dune and dragged it onto the road.

'Sorcha O'Donovan,' she breathed, wondering what she was doing out here when every other God-fearing Ballymore citizen was in church.

Sorcha waved at someone behind Helen, then pedalled off at high speed towards the village.

Helen turned and saw Con Daly perched on top of a sand dune. He was only a few feet away from her.

'Morning to you, Helen. And isn't it a beauty?' he smiled at her.

A sob choking her throat, she could only nod in his direction.

With a click of her heels, she rode off along the beach.

The following Wednesday, Helen sat in Seamus O'Donovan's office.

'There.' She passed him the envelope full of papers.

'Thank you. Did you manage to grasp the situation?'

'Yes, I think I did. At least I know now how much money I have and how the investments work.'

'And do you wish to keep them going as they are?'

'For the present, yes.'

'Good. I suggest you open a bank account and then I can pay in a monthly amount. Do you have plans for the future, Helen?'

'I . . . not at the moment.'

'Well now, you have enough money to take your time and decide.' Seamus looked at his watch. 'Time we were going upstairs. Mary will have our supper ready.'

After supper, rather than wanting to delay the moment the two of them would adjourn to her bedroom, Sorcha could hardly wait to get Helen alone.

'You saw me on the beach last Sunday, didn't you?'

'Yes, I did. Meeting Con Daly.' Helen studied her bitten fingernails.

'No! Whatever gave you that idea? I had a terrible headache. I wanted some fresh air, Helen, that's all.'

'Oh. I thought I saw you waving to him?'

'He . . . he's a friend. I see him when I walk on the beach sometimes.'

Helen swallowed hard before speaking. 'Do you always let your friends kiss you?'

'I . . .' Sorcha studied Helen's pallid face. Her eyes kept darting around Sorcha's bedroom, as if she was terribly nervous. 'You have it wrong, Helen, really you do.'

'I've seen you before, Sorcha, at night once. You were definitely kissing Con Daly.' Helen plucked up the courage to meet Sorcha's gaze. 'I heard you laugh.'

Sorcha pulled out the chair from her desk and sank down into it.

'So, Helen, you've seen me. Will you tell?'

'I don't see any reason why I should.' Sorcha didn't believe her. 'So, tell me all about it. Are you in love?'

Sorcha bit her lip. 'Helen, you swear you won't tell? No one knows, not even Maureen.'

Helen nodded. 'If you trust me, I swear I won't.'

It looked like Sorcha had no choice and, besides, she was bursting to tell someone. 'All right then.'

Sorcha stood up and opened her bedroom door to check no one was lurking on the landing outside, then sat down on the bed next to Helen.

'There's not much to say, really. I love Con Daly and he loves me.'

Helen sat in contemplation. 'Will you marry him?'

'One day, yes.'

'He wants to leave Ballymore. Will you go with him?'

Sorcha looked surprised. 'How do you know that?'

'Oh, Con and I talk sometimes,' she said coolly. 'Don't you worry that one day you'll go to his hut and he'll be gone?'

'No. He understands that I can't leave Ballymore at the moment. He's going to go to Dublin and get a record deal and then my daddy will see that he can take care of me.' She knew she was saying too much, but she couldn't help herself.

'He must really love you to stay.' The back of Helen's eyes began to sting with tears. She fought them, hard.

'Yes. But *please*, Helen, if Mammy and Daddy knew any of this now, then . . .' Her voice trailed off.

Helen stared at her for longer than was comfortable. 'I'm good at keeping secrets when I want to. Do you think Con will make it?'

'Oh yes. He has a fierce good voice, Helen. And he writes all his own songs.'

'What if your parents find out?'

'They'll rant and rave but I'm nearly seventeen. One day I hope that Con will become famous and make lots of money and we can come back to Ballymore and everyone will be pleased to know us.'

Sorcha sounded out of breath. Helen realised she wasn't as confident as she seemed.

There was a knock at the door. 'Seamus is ready to drive you home, Helen.'

'I'm coming, Mary.' Helen stood up.

'You swear you won't say anything?' Sorcha pleaded.

Helen gave her a half-smile. 'I swear.'

Sorcha eyed her. 'If you did, Helen McCarthy, God forgive me, I think I'd kill you.'

Helen nodded slowly. 'I know.' Sorcha followed her out of her bedroom and down the stairs. Seamus was waiting in the hall.

'Thank you for supper, Mary. Bye, Sorcha.'

'Bye, Helen.'

Helen followed Seamus out of the front door.

That night, Helen gazed out of her bedroom window. She could see the small oil lamp twinkling in Con Daly's hut on the beach. She sighed. Why was life so unfair? Not only was Sorcha popular and pretty, but she had Con Daly. There was no doubt that Con would make it. They would run away from Ballymore and start a new life together.

It seemed Sorcha had everything Helen wanted.

She sat staring out of the window for a long time.

6

On Friday afternoon, the last day of term, the girls were going off to celebrate. As usual, their plans did not include Helen. She watched as Sorcha and her friends linked arms and marched off down the hill to the village. There was a big party at Katherine's house.

Her frustration at the injustice of her life increased.

On Sunday morning, she came downstairs to find Aunt Betty had planned a special birthday breakfast for her.

'There you are, Helen. Enjoy it.' Betty smiled at her niece. 'There's a parcel for you.'

Helen opened the tightly wrapped package and found a leather-bound copy of *The Complete Works of Shakespeare*. A lump came to her throat. She found it hard enough to read a comic, let alone Shakespeare. Still, her aunt had obviously taken a great deal of trouble to buy her something nice. Helen stood up, walked around the table and kissed Betty on the cheek.

'Thank you, Aunt,' she nodded. 'It's a grand present and I'll treasure it always.' Helen sat back down and tucked into the eggs, bacon and sausages. Betty finished her own breakfast and studied her niece.

'So, Helen, today you come of age. The house is yours and you're an adult. You won't be needing me any more.' Helen looked up and realised her aunt was eyeing her nervously. 'Do you intend to keep the house, or will you be selling it?'

'I'll be keeping it, of course. I hope things will continue just the same as they always have done.'

'So, you won't be minding if I stay on here, Helen?'

'Of course not. It's your home too. Why should I mind?'

'Well, maybe I'll stay until you find yourself a husband and then, of course, you must be mistress here and I can find a cottage in which to see out the rest of my days.'

'Aunt, I would never turn you out. You've always been here to look after me. You're the only family I have.'

'Thank you. I appreciate it, Helen.' Betty stood up and hurriedly began to clear away the breakfast plates.

This morning, Helen had become a very wealthy woman. And now she would make the first significant decision of her adult life.

She returned to her bedroom and sat on her window seat. It was wet with condensation. The rain lashed against the panes and the gale-force winds made them rattle.

There was no doubt about it, the weather was perfect.

Helen looked down at her well-bitten nails, and began to peel the cuticles away. She was even more apprehensive than anticipated.

As she took Davy out for a ride later that morning, small white balls of flotsam were blown up onto the path from an angry sea. Used as he was to the harsh weather, Davy was still unsettled by the wind. She cut short her ride and went inside.

Before lunch, Aunt Betty and she each had a glass of sherry to toast her coming of age. Helen kept an eye on the clock as her aunt served up roast beef. After lunch, Helen went upstairs and stationed herself on her window seat.

Would she come today? Helen wasn't sure she could endure the stress of waiting much longer.

The time ticked on.

And then she saw her, in sou'wester and mac, pedalling towards the dunes. The bicycle went into the hollow as usual and she scrambled over the dunes towards the hut. The door opened and she disappeared inside.

Helen's heart thudded against her chest. It was no less than she deserved.

She went downstairs to make a telephone call. As she picked up the receiver, she hesitated for a moment. Was she really capable of doing this? Helen closed her eyes, thought of the future, and dialled the number.

'Where are you going, dear?' asked Mary as Seamus shrugged on his coat.

'That was Helen on the telephone. She saw Sorcha cycling to the beach, but hasn't seen her return. Helen's concerned because of the gale. The tide is very high out there today.'

'Sorcha told me she was going to visit Maureen this afternoon.' Mary looked puzzled.

'Well, Helen's insistent she saw Sorcha pedalling towards the beach. I ought to investigate.'

'But sure, Sorcha has been on that beach since she was a baby. She knows the sea.'

'I'm sure you're right, but Helen sounded worried.'

'Well, I suppose that wind is fierce bad. If she *is* on the beach, she'll be drenched.'

'Don't worry, I'll find her.' Seamus put on his hat. 'See you later.'

After stopping at Maureen's house and finding that Sorcha wasn't there, Seamus drove his car down to the beach. The wind was almost strong enough to knock him off his feet. He stood on a dune and looked across the sand. It was deserted. Picking his way across the dunes, the wind roaring in his face, Seamus saw Con Daly's hut. If he was home, maybe he'd seen Sorcha.

Seamus walked to the front door and was about to knock when something moving inside caught his attention. He stared through the salt-smeary pane of glass. On the floor, a pair of naked bodies were writhing together. As the couple rolled, Seamus found himself staring at his daughter's face.

He stumbled back from the window, crouched down and gagged several times.

'Jesus, Mary and Joseph!'

Wiping the saliva from his chin, Seamus stood up and marched into the hut.

'You bastard!' He dragged Con up by his hair and threw him against the wall. 'I'll have the guards on you!'

Sorcha's eyes shot open in surprise. Fear followed instantly. Grabbing Con's shirt, she dragged it on and watched helplessly as her father punched and kicked her lover until he slid down the wall and lay in a foetal ball at his feet. 'You bastard, you *bastard*!' Seamus shouted as Con tried to shield himself.

Sorcha eventually found her voice.

'Stop it, Daddy! Stop it! You'll kill him!'

She stood up and threw herself on top of Con. 'Stop it, Daddy, please!'

Seamus could no longer kick his victim without landing serious blows on his daughter's body. Breathing heavily, his face red, his eyes glazed with rage, he stared down at her.

'Say he forced himself on you, and we will go to the guards and have him arrested.'

Sorcha shook her head. 'No, Daddy, he didn't. I love him.'

'I'll try again. Say he made you do this, and we can go home and this bastard can be locked up where he belongs.'

'No! Daddy, can't you understand? I love him! You can't stop us being together. I'm almost seventeen.'

'You refuse to admit he forced you?'

'Yes. He didn't. I wanted him to.'

He slapped her brutally across the cheek. 'You disgust me! You're no better than a common whore! And no daughter of mine!'

'We're going to be married.'

'Married! Ha! Is that what he promised you? And do you really think any priest would marry you after what you've done?'

Sorcha's defiance left her and she began to sob. Con stirred beneath her and put an arm out to comfort her.

'Sorcha, I will ask you one more time. Admit he gave you no choice, and we can go home. If you refuse, then I will denounce you as my daughter. I will never allow you in my house again. In my eyes you will be dead.'

'Oh, Daddy! Oh, Daddy, *please*, I can't. I love him.'

Seamus stared at his daughter for a few seconds.

'Goodbye, Sorcha. May you and this tinker you profess to love rot in hell!'

The door slammed and Seamus was gone.

On the way home, Seamus stopped at a bar in the town. He knocked back four whiskeys in ten minutes. Fellow drinkers stared at him in amazement. No one could ever remember seeing Seamus O'Donovan taking a sniff of alcohol in a bar before.

'Where in God's name have you been? I've been frantic with worry!'

A pale Mary greeted her husband at the front door. Immediately she smelt the whiskey on his breath.

'Where's Sorcha, Seamus?'

Seamus hiccupped. 'Your darling daughter is at present sitting in a hut on the beach with the tinker Con Daly. Probably they are both naked.'

'Seamus!' Mary blessed herself. 'Jesus, Mary and Joseph, it's a sin to say such a thing!'

'It's also a sin to lie, Mary, isn't it?' Seamus hung his coat on the peg and swayed towards the stairs. 'I'm going to bed. Sorcha is banned from this house. She will never come home again. And if I hear you have been anywhere near her, you too will be out on the streets. Do you understand?'

'I . . . Seamus, the least you could do is explain. Please, I——'

'Shut up, woman!' he roared. 'I've had enough of pleading females today. I've told you as much as you need to know. Now, goodnight!'

Sorcha held a bloodstained rag to Con's eyebrow. He flinched as she pressed it.

'I'm sorry, but we must stop the bleeding.'

'For a solicitor, your daddy knows how to punch. Oh, Sorcha-porcha, what a terrible thing.'

Sorcha did not reply. She was trying hard not to think, just to get on with the practical business of tending to Con's wounds.

'How did your daddy know where to find you?' Con mused. 'Is there anyone else you told of us? Friends at school?'

Sorcha blushed. 'Helen McCarthy. She was the only one that knew. She can see the beach from her house. I'd bet she saw me coming and telephoned my daddy.'

'Helen McCarthy? Why would she be doing such a thing?'

'She's an evil, malevolent witch. She's always hated me. And she's had a fierce crush on you for ages.'

Con looked nonchalant. 'Has she?'

'Oh yes. She probably couldn't stand the thought of us together. Well, she's gone and done it now. There, you look better. You're going to have a shiner by tomorrow. Your eye is fierce swollen.'

'Pass the whiskey from the cupboard over there. I think we could both do with a drink.'

Sorcha fetched the bottle of whiskey, sat down next to Con and handed it to him. He undid the top and swigged straight from it.

'Want some?'

Sorcha took a slug.

'So, Sorcha-porcha, where do we go from here?'

Sorcha put her head in her hands. 'It seems now I really have no choice. I can't go home, so I guess I'm coming with you. Con?' She turned to him.

'Yes?'

'We're going to London.'

Con struggled to suppress a smile. 'Really?'

Sorcha shrugged. 'I don't see that there's any other way. As you know, my life here is over.'

Con wrapped a tight arm around her. 'I suppose you're right.'

Sorcha looked up at his beaten face. 'On one condition.'

'Name it,' he replied.

'That we go tomorrow. I don't want to stay in Ballymore for a moment longer than necessary. Maybe we could find a guesthouse in Dublin for a couple of nights and stay there until our boat sails for England.' Sorcha's face fell. 'Oh no, I've thought of something terrible!'

'What?'

'My post office savings. I withdrew them in case you needed help getting to Dublin.' Con suddenly looked deathly guilty. 'They're in an envelope in my room. I'd nearly a hundred pounds.'

'Oh, dear me, now . . . that is a great shame,' sighed Con, his eyes skirting about the hut.

'Unless . . . unless I telephoned my mother and begged her to bring the money to me. Then I could say goodbye to her and . . .' Sorcha bit her lip as tears welled in her eyes.

Con put a comforting hand on her knee.

'I know, I know. I swear I'll never forget what a sacrifice you made for me today. I'll do anything I can to make it up to you,' Con comforted her.

He kissed her gently and she tasted the coppery flavour of blood on his lips.

'I love you, Sorcha.'

'I love you too, Con.'

7

Her mother reminded Sorcha of a sinner entering Heaven, looking left and right as if she might be struck down at any minute.

'Can we close the curtains, Sorcha, just in case?'

'There are no curtains, Mammy.' Sorcha shrugged. 'Don't worry. Daddy would never come back here if it was the Blessed Virgin herself commanded it.'

'I brought your envelope.' Mary handed it over. 'And the bags of clothes you asked for.'

'That's grand, Mammy. I'm very grateful.'

Mary glanced around the hut uncertainly. 'Sorcha, please, your daddy won't tell me what happened yesterday. He came home drunk. I've not seen him like that before. He says he never wants you to set foot in our house again. Of course, he's exaggerating. You must come home. You are our daughter. Once he calms down, he'll see sense.'

'No, Mammy, he won't.'

'Then tell me what happened!'

'He found me and Con here together in the hut. We were . . . kissing.'

Mary studied her daughter's face. 'Was that all, Sorcha O'Donovan? Your daddy might be a puritan, but even *I* cannot see him banning you from our house for *kissing* Con Daly.'

'I . . .' Sorcha blushed and hung her head. 'No, Mammy. That's not all.'

She sank onto the couch and stared at the bare floorboards.

Mary sighed. 'I see. Well now, it's no good me telling you what a stupid girl you've been, is it?' Sorcha shook her head. 'Have you been to confession?'

'Oh really, Mammy. As if that'll help me and Con.'

'Sorcha! I'm doing my best to stay on your side, but I won't tolerate that kind of talk! It's best I leave.'

'Don't go! I'm sorry, Mammy, really I am. I meant nothing by it but I just couldn't tell Father Moynihan. Besides, Con and I are leaving for England tomorrow.'

Mary swallowed hard. 'Are you now?'

'Yes. I don't think we have a choice. Daddy will never forgive us. Con is already ostracised in the village and even if we married, it would make things no better.'

Mary stared at her daughter, her face a mask of sadness. 'What will you live on?'

'Con has some money saved, and I have a little in the envelope you brought me. As soon as we get to England, Con will find a job. He has a grand voice. He's hoping he'll be able to get a recording contract.'

Mary nodded. 'Well, 'tis true there will be more opportunities for him in London. He has no future here.'

'Oh, Mammy, I'm so sorry. I never meant for this to happen. I can hardly believe it has.'

Mary paused. 'Sorcha, are you pregnant?'

'No, Mammy.'

'Well, I suppose that's one blessing we must count.'

'Yes.'

'So, you love Con Daly, do you?'

'Yes.'

'And you think he loves you?'

'I know he does, Mammy. He tells me all the time. As soon as we get to England, we'll be married.'

Mary watched as Sorcha's eyes shone with happiness. She shrugged. 'I hope you're right. And I only hope Con Daly realises the sacrifice you're making for him.'

'You think I've ruined my life, don't you?'

Mary sighed, then sat down next to Sorcha on the couch and took her daughter's hand in hers.

'I'd not be much of a mammy if I wasn't feeling scared for you, Sorcha. You're so young. I could scream and shout at you, tell you what a silly girl you've been, but what is the point? Your daddy's already done that and you're leaving anyway.'

'We have no choice, Mammy, really, not now.'

'No, I suppose you don't, Sorcha.' Mary stared off into the distance. 'I once loved someone very much when I was about your age. He too went away but I wasn't brave enough to go with him. Ah well.' Mary smiled. 'I got your daddy instead.'

'Do you love him?'

'Of course I do,' Mary replied briskly, visibly pulling herself out of her reverie. 'Does he know of your plans?'

'No. No one does, except you. Do you think he'll ever forgive me?'

'I think it's doubtful. He worships you, always has done since you were small. He still sees you as his baby, which will make the hurt worse. But never mind Seamus for a moment. When you're settled you must write to me with an address.'

'Of course I will, Mammy.'

'Best to send any letters to Maureen's house. She can pass them on to me. Your daddy collects the post every morning and I wouldn't trust him not to tear a letter from you up.'

'Will you explain to Maureen what has happened?'

Mary nodded, then looked at her watch. 'I must go. Your

daddy will be expecting his dinner on the table.' She stood up and Sorcha followed suit. 'Take care of yourself.'

'I will.'

Mary reached out and pulled her daughter to her. She kissed her on the forehead. 'If there's ever anything you need, I'll try and get it for you.'

'Thank you, Mammy.'

Mary's eyes were bright with tears as she headed for the door. 'Ah well, Sorcha, there's half of me that envies you. Goodbye, my darling. May God go with you.'

Mary was just about to shut the door when Sorcha remembered the question that had been nagging at the back of her mind.

'Mammy, how did Daddy know where I was yesterday?'

'Helen McCarthy telephoned us to say she was concerned because she thought she'd seen you on the beach earlier and the storm was very bad.'

'Oh.'

'Why?'

'No reason.' Sorcha went to the door and gave her mother a hug. 'I'll miss you, Mammy. Goodbye.'

Sorcha sat on a dune and stared out at the sea. The day was hot and the water was a perfect Mediterranean blue. The sound of the waves hit her senses as though she was hearing them for the first time.

She realised then how lucky she'd been to grow up in such a beautiful place. Her mind turned to the long lazy summer days she'd spent on this beach with her friends. And all the winter nights she'd scuttled home in the lashing rain to find a plateful of steaming stew and a warm fire to dry herself against.

Her life in Ballymore. A life that had seemed so dull while

she was living it but now seemed so perfectly safe and secure. She felt like crying, but steeled herself not to. There was no turning back.

Con placed his hand on her shoulder. 'Ready?'

Sorcha nodded. 'Yes.'

'Good. I've not bothered locking the hut.' He smiled.

'No.'

Con sat down next to her. 'Are you sure you're all right?'

'Yes.' Sorcha nodded. She stood up. 'Come on, Con. I have a call to make on our way.'

Helen heard the doorbell ring, but, knowing her aunt would answer it, lay where she was on her bed.

'Helen, it's for you.'

She swung her legs off the bed and went onto the landing. 'Who is it?'

'Sorcha O'Donovan.'

'Oh, I . . .' She stood reluctantly at the top of the stairs.

'Come on, Helen,' said her aunt irritably. 'Sorcha's waiting.'

Helen made her way slowly down the long oak staircase. Sorcha was standing in the hall.

'Shall I put the kettle on?' asked Betty.

'No, thank you. I only have a few minutes,' Sorcha replied brusquely.

'I'll be in the kitchen if you change your mind.'

As Helen reached the bottom step, Betty turned and walked down the hall. Sorcha watched her, waiting for the click of the kitchen door. Helen saw she was pale, but perfectly composed.

'Hello, Helen. I came to say goodbye.'

'Oh, I—'

'I came to thank you for telling my father where I was yesterday.'

'I . . . I was worried. The storm, I . . .'

'Don't waste your breath on lies, Helen. You knew where my father would find me. You wanted him to.'

'No. I—'

'Con and I are leaving for England today.' Helen said nothing. 'I just wanted to ask you why, that's all. You gave your word you wouldn't tell.' Helen found she could not speak. Eventually, Sorcha gave a small smile. 'You expected my father to find me in the hut, then take me home and ban me from ever seeing Con Daly. And like a good little girl, I'd settle down again in Ballymore, Con would disappear and I'd have lost my chance of escape, and Con too. That's what you planned, isn't it now?'

Helen stared guiltily past Sorcha at the man stood behind her.

'And what you have succeeded in doing is the opposite. My father refuses to let me ever set foot in his house again. So I say thank you. What you did has made it impossible for me to stay. Con and I *have* to leave.'

Helen had nothing to say.

'Maybe it's good there'll be a sea between us, Helen. I knew you were jealous, but I didn't know you hated me so much. I shall try and forgive you, because you deserve pity. You may have lots of money but you don't have a single friend. I hope I never lay eyes on you for as long as I live.'

'I . . .' Helen tried to retort but nothing came out. A large tear plopped onto her cheek.

Con moved closer to the open doorway.

'Sorcha, we must go,' he said softly.

'Yes, I've said what I came to say.' Sorcha turned and walked towards Con, then she turned back to Helen. 'Well, you've succeeded in one thing. Now I have no family either, just like you. But I do have Con, and he loves me. I doubt you'll ever know how that feels. Goodbye, Helen.' Sorcha turned on her heel, and began to storm away from the McCarthy manor. When Con did not immediately follow, she whipped around to observe the pair sharing a protracted, lingering look. Helen was staring at Con with intensity, and Sorcha noted her shifting uncomfortably from side to side. 'Con! It's no good intimidating her. Let's go.'

Helen shut the door, then immediately turned and ran upstairs to her bedroom. She threw herself on the bed and sobbed.

'It's so unfair, it's so unfair,' she repeated over and over. Eventually she stood up and dried her eyes, the sting of Sorcha's words still burning in her mind. Why did she feel like the villain? Sorcha and her friends had been just as cruel to her over the years.

She opened the top drawer of her bedside cabinet and took out the freshly opened bank account book. Sitting down on her bed, she studied the amount that had been deposited only yesterday. She brushed her hand across the figure written in ink.

This was the only legacy from her parents. Her life had to change. And if no one would help her change it, she would have to find the courage and the strength to change it by herself.

Twenty-four hours later, Sorcha was standing looking over the railing at the fast-disappearing coastline of her native land. Con's arms were wrapped around her, sheltering her from the strong sea breeze. He turned her in towards him.

'Well, Sorcha-porcha, we've gone and done it. Scared?'

She looked up at him, his face dim in the approaching dusk. 'A little.'

'Me too.' He pulled her close. 'But we have each other, whatever we have to face. And that's all that matters.'

'Yes.'

Con looked over her head and whispered a silent goodbye.

'I promise you one thing. The next time I return home, the whole country will know I'm coming.'

Two months later, another figure stood in almost exactly the same spot on the deck of the boat. Up for a breath of fresh air from her stuffy cabin, Helen refused to let herself shed a tear.

Ireland had done her no favours. She hoped the country in which her mother had been born would.

8

London, October 1964

Sorcha woke to the smell of boiled cabbage. Not the sweet, mouth-watering aroma that used to emanate from her mother's kitchen when she cooked the very same vegetable in a pot with bacon, but a rancid, stomach-churning smell that heralded the start of another day in the hell-hole where she and Con resided.

Plop. Plop. Plop.

Sorcha sighed. It was raining. Through the ceiling. She sneezed, then searched under the pillow for a hanky with which to blow her nose. Her throat felt like sandpaper. Maybe a hot drink would help. She rolled over two inches and as good as fell out of the narrow single bed. Con grunted and stretched out, his body relieved to have some space. Sorcha ran quickly to the fireplace and lit the couple of sticks she'd saved from last night to generate some warmth. Then she poured on the remaining coal and covered it with slack to keep it burning longer.

It was freezing. And only the end of October. Jesus only knew what it would be like here in January.

Come on, Sorcha, come on, she chided herself as she headed for the kitchenette and turned on the one-ringed Baby Belling stove to heat the kettle. By January there was every chance that Con would be famous and they would be living in a beautiful house like the ones she had seen on the edge of Hampstead Heath.

It was a thought that was beginning to seem more unrealistic as each day passed.

Sorcha grabbed Con's big sweater and pulled it over her nightdress. She hopped from foot to foot as she waited for the kettle to boil.

Her lover was still sleeping. He looked so peaceful, as if he'd not a care in the world. The kettle whistled. Sorcha grabbed it and poured the water into the teapot.

She had no regrets. She was with the man she loved. It didn't matter if they lived in a mouse-infested attic room and were reduced to rationing themselves to one inadequate meal a day. Or that, after three and a half months away, she was fiercely homesick for Ballymore. Londoners were so brusque, so rude. Everything moved at such a frenetic pace here, and Sorcha longed for the sound of the gentle voices of her homeland.

And more than anything, Sorcha missed the space and openness of Ballymore. She stared disconsolately out of the attic window and saw only row upon row of smoky grey chimney pots.

She felt tears scorch the back of her eyes as she thought of the beach, at this time of year majestic in its wild, windswept beauty. And the air, so fresh you felt as if your lungs had been given a spring clean every time you breathed in.

Stop it, Sorcha, stop it. Remember, when you were there you couldn't wait to leave.

She poured some tea into a tin mug and took it to the fire. She hated it without milk, but there was none left and no money for more.

The worst thing of all was that soon even this place would be a luxury they could not afford. They had one more month's rent in the tin in the cupboard. Sorcha knew there'd be no mercy from their landlady. If they were more than a few days late with the cash, they were out.

And then what?

Of course, neither of them had had any idea just how hard it would be. On arriving in London they'd gone to a guesthouse, bought a newspaper and looked through the 'Flats to Rent' section. They'd quickly moved on to 'Rooms to Rent' when they'd seen the size of the weekly asking prices. They were young, Irish and unmarried (though they soon learnt to lie about their matrimonial status), and had no references to offer a prospective landlord. They'd got the room they had now only because it was unfit for human habitation and the land-lady had agreed to waive the usual formalities.

Con had roamed the clubs and bars of Soho trying to persuade the owners to hear him sing, but to no avail. Sorcha had begged him to let her look for work in one of the big shops in the West End, but he would not hear of it.

In desperation, Con had started busking in Carnaby Street. Sorcha would go with him, stoically walking the four miles from their room in Swiss Cottage to save money. Some days, he'd do well enough for them to go into one of the nearby bars and have a drink. For those few evenings, life was grand. They were in the most happening city in the world, part of a new generation of youth who would not be playing by their parents' rules.

Then, at other times, when the rain poured down as they struggled back home silently, a few sixpences in Con's pocket, depression would set in for the rest of the night.

She looked out of the window and prayed the rain would stop soon, as busking in Carnaby Street on a wet day was pointless. No one wanted to stand listening to a dripping singer. So, on rainy days it was down into the tube station, playing until an officious ticket collector was sent to move you on, or, even worse, the police. Con had an instinctive hatred and fear of the force. The subterranean days were not happy ones.

Sorcha sipped her tea. Feeling strange, she threw off Con's jumper. Bizarrely, sweat seemed to be pouring off her. She sighed loudly. How could they go on like this? Yes, they were still close, but the tension of living on such a knife edge was starting to affect their relationship. A nagging fear was beginning to eat away at Sorcha. What if Con grew tired of her, of this life? Maybe he didn't want to marry her any more. Maybe—

'Good morning, Sorcha-porcha. How did you sleep on our shared bed of nails?' Con's arms wrapped around her shoulders.

She'd begun to shiver again. 'Not well. I found another bedbug in the night. It climbed up my thigh.'

'Ah, 'tis not the Ritz, that's for sure. But who knows what today might bring?'

'The rain, Con.' Her legs felt shaky as she went to the kitchenette to pour him some tea.

He smiled at her as she handed him his tin mug.

'Are you getting tired of this life, my Sorcha? Not what my little princess is used to, is it?'

'No decent human being should have to get used to living like this,' she snapped, then immediately regretted it. 'I'm sorry. I'm worried, that's all. And I don't feel very well.' Sorcha staggered suddenly as the world spun around her. Con caught her and put a hand to her forehead.

'Jesus, you're burning up, Sorcha! Get back into bed. I'll make you some milky tea.'

'There isn't any milk, Con. We finished it last night.'

'Then I'll go out to get some. Come on, into bed with you. There'll be no busking for me today. We have to get you well.'

Sorcha let Con lead her back to bed and tuck her in. She watched as he pulled on his worn jeans and sweater.

'I'll be off to get some milk and some medicine for that temperature. You stay put now.'

She nodded limply. 'Sorry, Con.'

'Don't you apologise, Sorcha. 'Tis this hell-hole of a life I'm treating you to that's to blame.'

After he'd left, Sorcha lay with tears of self-pity trickling out of her closed eyes. She dozed off and began to have nightmarish dreams . . . She was stuck up on a roof in the pouring rain. Con was trying to reach her before she slipped down into infinite blackness . . . but he was only reaching out with one hand because he held his guitar with the other and wouldn't let it go . . . She slipped. As she fell she called out his name . . .

'Con! Con! *Con!*'

'I'm here, Sorcha, I'm here beside you. It was a dream, a bad dream, that's all.'

She opened her eyes and looked up at him. He was pale, his face concerned. She looked around and realised the room was almost in darkness, with just one candle shining a light.

'There now.' He gently smoothed her sweat-matted hair. 'Thanks be to God, I think the fever has finally broken.'

'I . . . how long have I been sleeping?'

'Well, it's about three in the morning. I couldn't wake you when I got back from the shops so I called the doctor. He told me to sponge you down and to send for him again if your temperature hadn't lowered in a few hours. You have influenza, Sorcha. Would you like some water?'

Her throat felt parched. She nodded.

Gently, Con put the glass to her lips.

'What have I brought you to?' he sighed. 'London, the big city, and we live no better than peasants during the Famine.'

Sorcha stretched out her hand and rested it on Con's.

'We mustn't lose sight of our dream. You are talented, you *will* be discovered. We just don't know the right people, that's all.'

'And how do you get to know the right people, Sorcha? No.' Con shook his head. 'I'm only an itinerant from Ireland. I was above myself to think things would be different.'

71

Sorcha gave a weak sigh. 'Please don't say that.'

'While you were lying there looking as though you might be after taking your last breath, I made a decision. We can't go on living like this. I'm going to give it to the end of this week and then on Monday I'll start looking for work as a labourer, along with all the other Paddies. We can't live on what I earn as a busker. You know we can't.'

'But *I* must be able to find a job, Con. There has to be somewhere in London that wants a willing pair of honest hands.'

'It's *my* job to provide for *you*, especially after I took you away from your home.'

'I'll not see us starve because of your male pride. If I can find work, then I'll take it.' Sorcha coughed violently.

'Well, now is not the time or place to have such a discussion. Let me do the worrying and you concentrate on getting better. Close your eyes, my love. I'll sit here until you're asleep.'

Too exhausted to argue further, Sorcha did as she was told.

9

It was a beautiful, bright October day. Music was blaring from the West End boutiques and bars, with the customers and staff dressed in carnival colours. The atmosphere was electric.

'Carnival colours, carnival colours,' he hummed, stopping in the middle of Carnaby Street, taking out his notebook and chewing his pencil.

The most noticeable thing about Derek Longthorne was his height. Or lack of it. Although during his teens he'd measured himself every day, he reckoned he'd not grown since two months after his thirteenth birthday. He'd begged his mum to take him to a specialist to see if he could have a massive injection of growth hormone to give him a few extra inches. She'd laughed, ruffled his hair and told him his dad had been the same; that women had only noticed his handsome face and big baby-blue eyes, and it hadn't stopped them falling at his feet.

The trouble was, thought Derek, if women were to fall, they'd probably end up in direct eye contact with him. Chortling inwardly at his own sarcasm, he set off in the direction of the shoe shop and the promised four inches that were to be his for the exchange of a ludicrous amount of money. Surely, after this height extension, Peggy couldn't fail to go out with him?

He entered the shop and caught the eye of a stick-thin assistant who was puffing on a cigarette at the back.

'Hi, the name's Derek Longthorne. I've come for my boots.'

The assistant put down her smoke. 'I'll go and see if they're ready.'

'They are, they must be. I mean, I telephoned this morning and—'

'Keep your 'air on. I'll go and 'ave a look-see.'

Derek waited in an agony of suspense. He *had* to have them today. Eventually, the girl came back with a large box.

''Ere. Wanna try 'em?'

'Yes, please.'

'Sit down then.' The girl indicated a red plastic-covered pouffe.

He sat down and watched as she slid the boots out of the box. They were made of soft shiny brown leather. Derek removed his brogues.

'It's okay, I can put them on.' He reached out a hand to take them from her.

'Suit yourself.' She shrugged and ambled off to finish the cigarette still burning in the ashtray.

Derek slid on the boots and fastened the zips running up the inside of his ankle.

He staggered a little as he stood, feeling unbalanced. Then he walked carefully across to the mirror.

Five foot seven. At last, the unattainable dream. Derek smiled at the mirror, ran a comb through his blond hair, blew a kiss at his reflection, paid and left the shop.

He was in no rush to go home. He bought a new pair of trousers and sauntered down Carnaby Street imagining Peggy opening her front door and falling into his arms.

He'd loved her for the past six years, ever since her family had moved from the North down to London, and Peggy had joined his class at school. Even his cousin Todd, usually not given to superlatives about women, had thought Peggy was 'cute'. Peggy had immediately become very popular, joining the 'in' gang of girls while his male classmates queued up to take her out.

Derek knew he didn't really stand a chance. He'd dreamt about Peggy at night and contented himself with that. Until . . . he'd met her on the way to school and discovered she lived at the end of his road. Derek began to engineer their morning meetings. He'd linger behind a hedge until he saw Peggy emerge from her front gate, then walk behind her for a while and hail her. She'd turn around, and he'd take in her big blue eyes, huge in her lovely face.

'Hi, Derek,' she'd say, and wait for him to catch up with her. Then they would walk the fifteen minutes to school together. Derek had lived for these morning interludes. At school, he was known as 'Little Del' – even some of the teachers had picked up on it – yet Peggy made him feel special.

The first Christmas, Derek had presented her with a bottle of perfume. She'd opened it, flung her arms around his shoulders and kissed him.

'Derek, you really are the sweetest guy I know.'

This had taken his passion on to newer, dizzier heights. In January, when school had resumed, Derek had plucked up the courage to ask Peggy out. To his amazement, she'd said yes. He'd taken her to the pictures to see Elvis in *Jailhouse Rock*, and they'd shared a bag of popcorn. Derek had spent the entire film trying to pluck up the courage to put an arm round Peggy's shoulder.

'It's been lovely,' Peggy had said, as Derek escorted her to her front door, 'to go out with a boy to a film and know he won't jump your bones the minute the lights go down.' Then she had kissed him gently on the cheek. 'Goodnight, Derek. You're a really good friend.'

It hadn't been so easy when he'd discovered that Peggy was

going out with Mikey Doolan, the class hunk. Derek shuddered as he remembered being picked up from the police station by his white-faced mum, having been caught red-handed after throwing a brick through Mikey's parents' kitchen window. Following a couple of other similar incidents, Derek had been referred to a psychologist. The doctor had told Derek's mother that he had developed an obsession, probably caused by his teenage hormones going wild. She was assured he would grow out of it. Of course, Derek had pretended this was the case, but inside, he knew that his love for Peggy would never, ever leave him.

Derek decided he fancied a drink. He went into one of the noisy bars, sat up on a stool and ordered a beer. He sighed. All that was five years ago now. He'd done as the psychologist and the police had ordered him to, and stayed away from Peggy. He knew she wasn't *really* intimidated by how intensely he loved her. She had only said that to cover up her real feelings for him. She knew, deep down, that he was the man for her.

Derek was biding his time. These days, Peggy lived above a chip shop, only a few hundred yards down the road from him. He knew she went into the West End every day to some college or other, because he had once sneaked onto the same bus and watched where she had got off.

Derek took a sip of his beer. He comforted himself that Peggy would love him when he was famous. He remembered all the talk in the boys' changing room about the groups they would form when they left school. Most of them had since taken apprenticeships in the local shoe factory and a lot of them were unemployed. Whereas he, Derek Longthorne, a.k.a. 'Little Del', was rhythm guitarist in a proper band. He would engineer a meeting between the pair of them soon. But the timing needed to be right. Derek had to *impress* her.

Todd, his cousin on his dead dad's side, was someone Derek idolised. When he'd started at the same school as Todd, he'd been mercilessly bullied due to his stature. Todd, three years older, had looked out for him, sorted out the bullies and made sure Derek was left alone. He'd gone to a really famous music college when he'd left school, and had told Derek to keep practising his guitar, as one day he would want to form a band. Derek had taken his cousin at his word. He practised for hours every night, nearly driving his mum mad, but finding that the concentration drove thoughts of Peggy from his mind.

Then, sure enough, Todd had come to see him the summer Derek had left school and asked him if he'd be interested in becoming part of the new group he was forming. In spite of their being cousins, Derek had to audition. His years of solid practice, combined with a natural ability, had made it easy for Todd to offer him a place.

Derek drained the rest of his beer from the glass. That had been three years ago. Fame was taking longer than expected. 'Todd Bradley and the Blackspots' got regular gigs and had a small following, but it was hardly megastardom. Worst of all, they had just lost Norman, their bass guitarist, to another group, which had further demoralised them.

Derek checked his watch. There was no need to rush home tonight. Auntie Marge was coming round for tea, and Derek knew how she and his mum liked to be left alone for a nice chat. He stood up and decided to take a wander down Carnaby Street.

Con suppressed a yawn as he hauled his guitar onto his shoulder and played a few chords. Trying to find a spot where his instrument wasn't drowned out by records blaring from the shops was becoming more and more difficult. He checked what he'd made so far. Almost ten shillings. If he was honest, it wasn't enough to keep a dog alive.

This was it. The last day. On Monday he'd find himself a proper job, paying decent money. Sorcha and he would soon be out on the streets. She deserved better. He owed her a good life, after everything. There was no alternative.

'Ah well,' he sighed out loud to no one in particular. 'No one can say I didn't try.'

As he strolled along, Derek thought of the song he'd half composed earlier today. He might show it to Todd when it was ready, to see if they could play it at one of their gigs.

Suddenly, Derek became aware of a melodious sound coming from the other side of the street. It was in such contrast to the rest of Carnaby's hectic cacophony that he turned around to look. The busker was tall – Derek no longer resented him for that – and extremely good-looking. The song he was singing was not one he had heard before, so he presumed it was an original. Although simple, it had a haunting melody. Derek slowly ambled across the road to watch for a while. There was no doubt the chap was a proficient guitarist, and he liked his deep, mellow voice.

When the busker stopped, Derek reached into his pocket and pulled out some shillings. He threw them into the open guitar case.

'Play another one.'

Con stared at the young man. He'd watched him cross the street towards him. His gait was unusual, his knees occasionally bowing out to the sides, as if he was unbalanced. With his blond hair and big blue eyes, he reminded Con of an overgrown choirboy. Age-wise, he could have been anywhere between sixteen and thirty. Con glanced down at the four shillings that had been thrown into his guitar case.

'Any requests?'

'Play another of your own.'

Con gave him a courteous grin. 'Okay.'

He played a more uptempo number that he'd composed as a fourteen-year-old and which was still one of his favourites.

When he'd finished, the young man clapped. 'That was great. Do you play bass by any chance?'

'I have been known to.'

He walked forward and offered his hand. 'Derek Longthorne. Pleased to meet you. Fancy a beer?'

Con arrived home two hours later. He was lurching between happiness and uncertainty. Having made up his mind that his music career was over, he'd been offered a tenuous step in the right direction.

'Hello, sweetheart. Something smells good.' Con sniffed the air as he crossed the room to hug Sorcha, who was standing stirring the contents of a saucepan. 'And you *look* good enough to eat.' He wrapped his arms around her waist and kissed her, staring into the saucepan. 'What's with the bacon? And the mini-skirt?'

She turned to face him. It was the first time he'd seen her wearing make-up in a while.

'Con, I . . .' Her eyes sparkled. 'We're having a celebration.'

'Are we? Have I forgotten an anniversary or a birthday?'

'No. I need you to promise you won't be cross.'

'Sorcha, with you looking like that, I'm putty in your hands.'

'Okay. I've got a job. I'm starting on Monday and I'll be paid five pounds a week.'

Con dropped his hands from around her waist. 'Now, I was thinking we'd been through this before.'

'Con, we have. But things are desperate.'

'I know, I know,' he sighed. 'Well now, what exactly is it you'll be doing?'

'Something very ladylike. I'm going to be working on the perfumery counter in Swan and Edgar's.'

'Isn't that a match company?' He sat himself on the flat's one threadbare chair.

'No, eejit,' Sorcha giggled, relaxing a little. 'It's a grand department store in Piccadilly Circus. Oh, Con, say you're pleased?'

'Come here.' Con patted his knee.

Sorcha walked over to him and sat down, winding her arms round his neck.

'I think,' he said as he kissed her neck, 'that I can't think' – he kissed her shoulder – 'until I've made love to you.'

Afterwards, they lay on the narrow bed, limbs entwined. 'So, my precious princess has to go and earn a crust for her useless article of a lover. I never thought it would come to this.' Con stroked the silken skin of Sorcha's inner thigh.

'It won't be for long. Something will turn up for you, I'm sure.'

'Well, as a matter of fact, something happened to me today.'

'What? A good something?'

'Could be.'

Sorcha's eyes lit up. 'Tell me, Con.'

'I've met a man who says he's a member of a group. Their bass player has just left. He heard me busking, took me for a beer and asked me to go along to some pub in Camden Town tomorrow night to try out.'

'As what?'

'Their bass player.'

'Oh, I see.'

'You don't sound very excited.'

'I'm sorry. I just thought you wanted your own group. A bass player?' Sorcha wrinkled her nose. 'You're worth more than that.'

'And you're worth more than flogging perfumes to fat,

wealthy women.' Con sprang out of bed and searched in his jeans for his tin of tobacco and cigarette papers.

'I'm glad for you, Con, really. I just always imagined you would be fronting the band.'

'Sorcha, we both imagined a lot of things that haven't happened since we got here. Anyway, I've just decided not to do it. I'll be much better off looking for steady work as a labourer.' Con lit his roll-up and sucked on it morosely.

'No, I didn't mean it like that. Of course it's a start. Of course I'm pleased. Tell me about them. What kind of music do they play?'

Con shrugged. 'Modern rocky stuff. They do covers and some of their own songs.'

'Are they well known?'

'I've never heard of them,' he grinned. 'But 'twould be a start.'

'Con, it's grand news. You must go tomorrow night.'

'I'll be thinking about it,' he said eventually. 'Now, how about some of that bacon?'

The Queen Victoria pub on Camden High Street was noisy and very smoky. There was an eclectic mix of drinkers, from old men sitting round a table playing cards to the young, brightly coloured mob huddled down at one end of the bar watching the band set up their gear on the small dais.

'Hey,' whispered Sorcha as they stood a few yards away, 'looks as though they have a following. That's something.'

Con did not reply. He was watching the scene with interest.

'Hi! Glad you could make it.' Derek slapped Con on the back. 'And who is this vision of loveliness?' His eyes turned to Sorcha.

'My lady, Sorcha O'Donovan.'

'Derek Longthorne. Rhythm guitarist with the Blackspots.

Pleased to meet you, Sorcha.' He smiled at her. 'Right, step this way and I'll introduce you to the rest of the group. I had a word with Todd and he thinks it best if you listen for the first set to get an idea of our style, then come up and join us after the break.' He steered Con towards the dais. Sorcha followed meekly behind, feeling awkward.

'Oh, Sorcha, why don't you go and join Lulu at the table in the corner? She's Todd's girlfriend. She'll fill you in on who's who. Now, Con, as I was telling you yesterday, the style is very . . .'

Sorcha looked in the direction that Derek had pointed. Sitting at a table smoking a cigarette was a beautiful girl. She had long, straight, ebony hair reaching almost to her waist. Her locks were in total contrast to her skin, which was the colour of pale alabaster. The woman's eyes were heavily lined with black kohl, and her lips a startling red against her white skin. She was dressed in a beautifully tailored blue suede suit with matching boots.

Feeling horribly dowdy in her mac and tweed mini, Sorcha moved slowly over to the table.

'Hello. Derek said I should come over.'

The huge doe eyes focused on Sorcha. They swept her from top to bottom so piercingly that Sorcha could feel herself blushing.

'Then sit.'

'My name's Sorcha O'Donovan. I've come with Con Daly. He's trying out as bass guitarist for the band.'

'Bully for him,' Lulu drawled, taking another drag of her cigarette. 'I wouldn't hold out much hope, darling. They've tried out twelve in the past month. This isn't some little hick end-of-the-pier outfit, you know. Todd Bradley and the Blackspots are going places.'

'I'm sure they are.'

'Todd is a classically trained musician. He knows what he's talking about.'

'Which one is Todd?'

'He's standing by the mic.'

Sorcha glanced at Todd. With his glasses and short back and sides, he certainly didn't look like a sweaty rock-and-roller.

'He's the cleverest man I've ever met. Introduced me to Proust and Freud. He can quote poetry for hours on end. The man has a vast brain. I find him so stimulating. Every one of his songs is meaningful, a poem set to music.'

Sorcha stared at Lulu, half of her now hoping Con would not come up to scratch. She could hardly see a blossoming friendship before her.

'So, er, Sonia, what do you do with yourself?'

'My name's Sorcha actually. Next Monday I start on the perfumery counter of Swan and Edgar's.'

'Really? How fascinating. I'm an actress. You might recognise me? I've done loads of films.' Lulu turned her penetrating stare back to Sorcha, challenging her.

'I . . . yes, I'm sure now that I do.'

'I have a test next week for Hammer.'

'Who?'

'*Who*? Hammer Pictures of course. I'm testing for a bride of Frankenstein.'

'Oh, I'm sure that the part would suit you very well.'

'Thank you.' Sorcha was glad that Lulu took it as a compliment.

'Okay, chaps.' Todd had taken the microphone. There was a surge of applause from the audience. 'Thanks for coming along. We'll start with an old favourite. This is "Time Slips By".'

Sorcha watched with interest as the band began to play. She was no expert when it came to music, but they produced a decent melodious sound and Todd had a pleasant voice. She saw Con studying them intently. At one point he turned around and winked at her. She winked back. Lulu was sitting with her head resting on the banquette, eyes shut, mouthing the words. Sorcha made a concerted effort to listen to the lyrics. They certainly made sense, but the 'poetry' eluded her.

Twenty minutes later, the band announced they'd take a short break. Todd stepped easily off the podium and made his way towards Lulu.

'Superb as always, my lovely.' She kissed him on both cheeks.

'Thanks. Who's this?'

A pair of intelligent eyes gazed at Sorcha with interest from behind the glasses.

'Sorcha, Con's girlfriend.'

'Ah, our possible bassist, discovered languishing in Carnaby Street by Derek.' Todd smiled. 'Good to meet you, Sorcha. I really hope Con works out. The band can't move forward until we have a fourth member who's as committed as the rest of us. I'll catch you later, sweetheart. I want to chat to Con and let him have a tinker with our bass guitar. Bye, Sorcha, great to meet you.' Todd blew a kiss to Lulu and left.

'That man just oozes sex, doesn't he?' murmured Lulu.

Fifteen minutes later, Todd was back behind the microphone.

'Right, let me introduce you to Con Daly, recently arrived from the Emerald Isle, though we'll try not to hold that against him,' Todd chuckled, 'and fresh from fronting his own successful band over there. As always, I want you to help us decide if Con is our new man. Con Daly, ladies and gents!'

Con climbed onto the stage, gave an embarrassed wave, then put the bass guitar strap over his neck.

'Good luck, Sonia,' Lulu cooed. 'This crowd can be tough.'

'Thanks,' Sorcha replied through gritted teeth. This was hideous. Con, who could knock the lot of them into a cocked hat with his talent, was being treated like some dumb apprentice.

'We're gonna play "Can't Buy Me Love"! We all know that one.' Todd smiled, and counted the band in.

'Come on, Con, show them what you can do,' muttered Sorcha under her breath.

The audience whooped and cheered. Todd led them straight into another Beatles hit.

'Now, not only can this man play bass, he tells me he can also sing. I give you Con Daly!'

Con came forward and stood in front of the microphone.

'Thanks,' he said, and began to play the haunting, familiar guitar riff that signalled the start of 'House of the Rising Sun'.

Sorcha watched as Lulu suddenly sat up straight and stared at Con. The song was a perfect fit for her man. A wave of pride washed over her.

As the band brought The Animals' hit to a close, applause rained around the pub. Con bowed and took his place behind Todd.

'So what do we think?'

'Yes! Yes!' came the reply from the audience.

'Well, Con, looks like you're in. Welcome to Todd Bradley and the Blackspots.'

'With a bit of training your guy could really sing.' Lulu was looking at Sorcha with new respect.

'I think he's after doing okay without the training.'

Lulu furrowed her brow. 'Don't get defensive. He's good. Anyway, he'll only be backing. Todd's the singer in the group.'

'Sure,' replied Sorcha morosely.

An hour later, after declining an offer to join the rest of the band at a club in Soho due to lack of funds, Sorcha and Con went strolling through Regent's Park on their way home to Swiss Cottage.

Con was on a high.

'We'll be rehearsing three afternoons a week. They've got over a dozen gigs in pubs lined up for the next month. Todd's dead set on going to the top. Your man has a really professional attitude, Derek's shit-hot on rhythm guitar and Ian, the drummer, is exceptional. I really think it could happen for them. Well, us!'

Sorcha nodded silently.

Con stopped.

'You've been so quiet since we left. Are you not a little happy for me?'

'Of course I am, Con. It's just that when you stepped forward and sang, the stage came alive. I know I'm biased, but the audience felt it too. As Todd's girlfriend said, you'll only be playing bass and singing backing. Todd Bradley is the star and . . . well, I just know he won't give you a look-in.'

Con stopped and took Sorcha's hands. 'Don't you think I know that? But, Sorcha, so what if I have to play second fiddle to Todd for a while? It's a start. If I'm good, I'll be noticed whether I'm singing lead or backing. It's better than nothing, that's the way I see it.'

'Of course.'

'Ah, Sorcha.' Con took her in his arms and hugged her tightly. 'Always looking out for me, aren't you now?' He kissed her on the forehead. 'You know it won't pay very much. Todd was saying that the fee split between four doesn't go far. He's said I can borrow his bass guitar for now but I'll have to buy my own eventually.'

'Then it's grand that I have a job. I'm happy to support you until things start to take off, as long as you can stand me stinking of six different types of perfume when I come home.'

'I wouldn't want to be living off you for long, but let's give it a couple of months and see how it goes.'

'Grand.'

Con looked down at her. 'No matter what we go through, we'll always be together.'

'Always,' she repeated as his lips came down to meet hers.

10

Helen yawned and gazed out over the London skyline. The room was stuffy, the number of bodies crammed into it and the old gas heater making the air unpleasant to breathe.

What had she been thinking, signing up to do a business course? It had all been a terrible mistake. She was finding the coursework impossible and was aware she was falling behind. The sums were okay, but then they always had been. She'd already decided she'd leave at the end of this term and rethink her future.

'Miss McCarthy, could I ask that you give me the answer to the question sometime today? The class is hanging on your every word. Miss McCarthy?'

Helen suddenly became aware the tutor was addressing her. Blushing, she glanced down at the figure, neatly written at the bottom of the page.

'Yes, I'm sorry. The company would be left with approximately thirty-five thousand, having paid seven thousand, five hundred pounds and fifteen shillings to the Revenue.'

'Well done. Okay, class, for your home assignments this weekend, I want you to answer the questions on page forty-seven of the *Bookkeeping Practices for Beginners* textbook. I'll see you on Monday at nine thirty sharp. Have a nice weekend.'

There was an audible sigh of relief as the fifteen students

packed away their pens, notepads and textbooks and began chatting about their plans for the following two days.

Helen put away her things, stood up and moved towards the door.

'Miss McCarthy, can I have a word?'

She nodded resignedly and walked towards the tutor. He waited until the last student had left the room, shut the door behind him, then perched on the table he used as a desk.

'Sit down a minute, would you, Miss McCarthy.'

Helen sat, her mind slipping back to the days when the nuns had held her back and castigated her for her dreadful work.

'I wanted to talk to you about the work you've been handing in.'

'I . . . I know it's sometimes not up to scratch. I'll try harder in future, Mr Bryant. I . . .'

A well-rehearsed litany of excuses and promises to do better poured out of her. Mr Bryant held up his hands.

'Helen, please – may I call you Helen?'

'I . . .' She looked up at him. His eyes were kind. She realised for the first time that he didn't look at all cross. 'Yes.'

'First of all, I think you should remember that you are no longer at school. Myself and the other tutors here are paid by the students. How much or how little work you actually do while you're here is really up to you. We are salaried to teach, advise and assist you. Therefore, any comments I make are only meant as constructive criticism, to help you attain the qualification you are paying the school to receive. Do you understand?'

'Yes.' It all amounted to the same thing, whichever way he chose to cloak it. He was about to tell her that her work was terrible.

'Helen, some of your written work is abysmal,' he chuckled. Helen could not help visibly shrinking away from him. '*But* your work with numbers is, frankly, absolutely superb. You are by far and away the brightest in the class.'

She looked up at him, puzzled.

'Helen, do you ever read books?'

'Sometimes. I . . .' Then she shook her head. 'No, I don't.'

'Why not?'

'Because . . .' Her hands twisted round on each other.

'Because you find it almost impossible to make out the words on the page?'

'Yes,' she said, and burst into tears.

'Okay, okay. Here, take this.' Tony Bryant offered her a hanky.

'Thank you.' Helen blew her nose hard. 'I do try, Mr Bryant, really I do. I'm just stupid and that's all there is to it.'

Tony Bryant shook his head. 'Is that what the teachers at your school led you to believe?'

'It's what you believe, isn't it?' she snuffled.

'God, no. I've been marking your homework for almost two months now. Your written work is virtually unintelligible . . . and yet I've never corrected a single sum. Therefore, you clearly have a very mathematical brain. This leads me to deduce that you are not in the least bit stupid. Far from it, in fact.' Helen was hanging on his every word. 'However, all this does make me think you might have an issue that requires attention.'

'What kind of issue?'

'Helen, have you ever heard of something called dyslexia?' Helen shook her head. 'It's a learning difficulty which means that one finds it very tricky to make out words on a page.'

'Oh. Well, that does sound a bit like me.'

Tony held his hands up. 'Now, I'm no expert, but I have had a couple of students with similar struggles. Both were diagnosed with dyslexia.'

A small ray of hope was beginning to illuminate Helen's world. 'You . . . you really think this may be my problem?'

'I do. I'd like you to go and see an acquaintance of mine. He'll be able to tell you if my theory is right. The only thing is . . . he doesn't come cheap.'

'Money's no problem,' Helen replied quickly.

'Fine.' He wrote a name and address on a pad. 'Dr Allen's based in Harley Street. I don't know his telephone number offhand, but why don't you drop by on your way home tonight? It's only a ten-minute walk from here. His receptionist can book you in for an appointment.'

Tony Bryant smiled at her. Helen began to understand why the other girls in her class found him so attractive.

'Thank you.' She took the piece of paper and stuffed it into her coat pocket.

'Don't thank me, Helen. I hope I'm right. I just wish someone had picked up on this before now.' He gave her a warm smile. 'It must have made things very difficult for you.'

Helen swallowed the lump in her throat. 'It has.'

'Right then.' He stood up. 'Time to go. Doing anything nice over the weekend?'

'No, I—'

'Good, good. Do let me know the upshot of your meeting with Dr Allen.'

'I will.'

With a small wave, he disappeared down the steps.

It was fifteen minutes before Helen was composed enough to leave the Baker Street school and make her way to Harley Street.

The address that Tony had given her turned out to be one of the many white stucco-fronted houses in Harley Street. She rang the bell by the door several times to no reply, then saw a notice that Dr Allen's surgery was closed at five every evening. It was now twenty past. Helen scribbled down the telephone number on the front of one of her exercise books, walked back down the steps and made her way into Oxford Street. Christmas lights had been erected in the past few days and there were shoppers scurrying in and out of the big department stores. She found the right bus stop to take her home to Wimbledon and walked to the end of a very long queue.

Forty-five minutes later Helen let herself in to number seven Wimbledon Park Grove. The building was a double-fronted Victorian house which had been divided into flatlets some years ago. Helen's was on the top floor. She checked on the table to see if there had been any post. Aunt Betty wrote every two weeks and Seamus O'Donovan kept in contact about her finances.

Today there was nothing. She looked at the mail for the other residents, none of whom she had managed more than a brief 'hello' with.

As she climbed the stairs, Helen mused how different people here were from those in Ballymore. Four of them all living under the same roof, sharing the same front door, and yet knowing nothing about each other. At home, you could live five miles up the road from someone but they would still know your business before you did.

She turned the key in the lock and switched on the light in the tiny corridor, before hanging up her coat and making her way into her sitting room-cum-bedroom.

The room was cold. Helen went across to the electric fire and plugged it in. Then she closed the curtains around the big bay window.

Although she had seen several larger flats when she'd been looking for somewhere to live, Helen had chosen this one for two reasons. First, there was a beautiful cherry-blossom tree outside her window. She knew in the spring it would bloom into a riot of pinky-white. And secondly, the flat included that most rare of private modern conveniences, her own bathroom.

An hour later, Helen emerged from the en suite wrapped in her cosy new velour dressing gown. She emptied some baked beans into a saucepan and put two pieces of bread underneath the grill, then switched on her prize possession: a new black-and-white television.

'Timed perfectly,' she smiled, as the theme music to *The Avengers* played from the small speaker. This was Helen's favourite programme. Emma Peel was her heroine and she thought Diana Rigg the most beautiful girl she'd ever seen.

After sitting glued to the screen, Helen looked down as the credits rolled and realised she'd forgotten to eat her beans on toast. Hungry, but without the energy to make herself anything else, she tipped her congealed supper into the bin, brushed her teeth, then threw back the candlewick bedspread and climbed into bed.

It was only half past eight, but it didn't matter. She was tired and, besides, she wanted to think about Tony Bryant. Tony . . . Helen shuddered involuntarily at the thought of his name. He'd been so kind . . . and the way he'd looked at her with his big brown eyes . . .

11

'Okay, guys, let's try it. On the count of four.'

The four members of Todd Bradley and the Blackspots began to play. The draughty, deserted warehouse with its magnificent view of Tower Bridge echoed to the sound of Todd's latest composition. Con plucked along on his bass, coming in with Ian the drummer and Derek for the harmonies as Todd provided the lead vocal.

'Stop!' Todd put his hand up. 'You're all coming in a beat too late on the *ah, ahs*. And soften it a little. You're drowning me, boys. Let's go again.'

An hour and a half later, Ian lit a joint and offered it around.

'So,' Todd said as he took a drag and passed it to Derek, who inhaled too much and began to cough. 'Are we all fit for tomorrow night?'

'Sure, yeah.' There was a general nodding of heads.

'Good. We'll meet at seven to set up.'

'I've called the A and R guy at Pirate Records,' interjected Derek. 'You never know, he might show.'

'Hey, man, you always call him before our gigs and he never turns up,' smiled Ian affably.

'One day he might. You never know who's in the audience,' Derek answered defensively. 'I do my best, you know.'

'We know you do.' Todd checked his watch. 'I've got to fly. I'm meeting Lulu in half an hour. See you guys tomorrow.'

Con and Derek helped Ian pack up his drum kit and carry it to the ancient van used as the band's 'wheels'.

'Man, I wish we had a permanent base. Shifting this stuff is wearing me out.'

'One day we'll have our own studio, Ian. You wait and see,' said Derek.

'And Harold Wilson will be stoned in the Houses of Parliament,' quipped Ian. 'I'm off. There's a party in Soho tonight. You guys want to come? There'll be chicks and a lot of good gear.'

Con and Derek shook their heads. Ian shrugged. 'Suit yourselves. I'd give you a lift but there's no room. See you tomorrow.'

'Yeah, and this time don't forget where, Ian.'

After several attempts to start the van, Ian waved and chugged off down the street. Con and Derek followed him and turned right to walk over Tower Bridge.

'Smoke?' Derek offered a packet.

'Cheers.' Con took an Embassy out of the packet and both men lit up.

'What are you doing for Christmas?'

'Staying at home with Sorcha. You?'

'Oh, I have to keep my mum happy and spend it with her,' said Derek with a shrug. 'I'm all she has. You know what families are like.'

Con didn't reply.

'So, you've been with the band almost a month now. What do you think of us?'

'I think you're all grand,' said Con generously.

'I'm not asking about personnel. I want to know what you think of the sound.'

'Well now, I think Ian's a fierce good drummer when he's not whacked out of his head. Todd can write . . . interesting songs, and you're more than a bit nifty on the rhythm guitar. How's that?'

'It's a cop-out, Con, that's what it is. I know the problems we have. We don't have a strong enough identity. We're like a thousand other groups all trying to be the Beatles or the Stones. Yet the reason those two bands are doing so bloody well is that they are *different*.'

The pair reached the other side of Tower Bridge.

'Listen, fancy a bevvy, Con?' asked Derek.

'Ah, sure, I'd love to but I can't. I have to meet Sorcha from work in twenty minutes and Piccadilly's a fair walk from here, so it is.'

'Okay.' Derek shrugged. 'I'll see you tomorrow evening. Bye.'

Con watched him as he walked off. There was something sad about Derek, but he couldn't quite put his finger on what it was. Con turned and began to walk quickly in the direction of Piccadilly Circus.

She was already waiting for him in their usual coffee place in Archer Street.

'Hello, beautiful.' He kissed her and sat up at the bar next to her. 'Good day?'

'Not bad. It's fierce busy with all the Christmas shoppers. We've had to employ two extra girls to help out. What about you?'

Con took out his tobacco tin and began to roll up a cigarette. 'Ah, 'tis fine.'

'Did you play Todd your new song? You said you were going to?'

Con took a drag of his cigarette. 'I know I did, but I feel like I'm treading on his toes. He writes the songs for the band and that's the way he wants it to stay.'

Sorcha brushed a piece of lint off Con's collar. 'Well, did you at least ask if you could have a number to sing? He couldn't begrudge you one song, surely?'

'Thanks,' Con said as the waitress passed him his cappuccino. 'Well now, I reckon he might. He has a mighty big ego. Ah, Sorcha, let's leave it until after the festive season. We have ten gigs in the next two weeks. That'll mean some extra money to see us through for a while. I don't want to jeopardise that by stirring things up. Besides' – he kissed her on the nose – ''tis the season of goodwill to all men, and that includes egotistical singers, stoned drummers and short rhythm guitarists.'

'Fine, I'll let it be. As a matter of fact, I have some good news of my own.'

'And what might that be?'

'One of the girls who works in gloves and handbags knows of a bedsit in her house in Hampstead that's empty. 'Twould be a fair bit more than we're paying, but the roof doesn't leak and Bridget says it's quite spacious.'

'How much more?'

Sorcha pursed her lips. 'With my Christmas bonus, we could afford the deposit. Okay, it'll mean having to cut back on extras, but can you imagine having a nice comfortable room? Could we at least go and see it, Con, please?'

Con kissed her cheek. 'Of course, Sorcha-porcha, whatever you say.'

They moved into the bedsit in Arkwright Road three days before Christmas. It consisted of a large, newly decorated airy room which opened onto a small kitchenette.

Sorcha had four days' leave from work, and they spent the Christmas break settling in. On Christmas Eve, Sorcha received a Christmas card with three pounds in it from her mother. With that, she went shopping in Berwick Street market just as the stallholders were packing up, and managed to buy a small tree, a turkey and a big spray of holly.

While Con was out at his gig, Sorcha busied herself making

the room festive. She stuffed the turkey and peeled the vegetables ready for the following day, then hummed along to the
carols on the radio as she wrapped Con's present: an expensive
aftershave she'd bought at Swan and Edgar's with her staff
discount.

'*Silent night, holy night.*' Sorcha placed Con's present under
the tree, then went to the window and opened the curtains.
The night was still and crisp, with hardly a breeze blowing.

The bells on the radio rang out to herald the arrival of
midnight.

'Merry Christmas, Mammy,' she murmured.

The following morning, Con and Sorcha exchanged their
presents. Sorcha opened a velvet box. Inside was a ring. Sorcha
held it up to the light and saw how the small emerald sparkled
in its cluster of diamonds.

'Con, 'tis beautiful,' she breathed. 'However did you afford
it?'

'You're not to concern yourself with that. I've been well paid
in the last week.' Con knelt beside her, reaching for the ring
and the third finger of her left hand. He slid it on. 'There. It's
a little large, but the man in the jeweller's said he could alter
it.'

She looked up at him, her eyes shining. 'Is this meant to
be . . . ?'

'Yes. An engagement ring. I only wish 'twas a wedding ring
I was placing there. As soon as I've earned enough money to
give you the day you deserve, I promise I'll be meeting you in
front of the altar.'

Sorcha kissed him. 'I love you, Con. And this ring means
the world to me.'

Later, after a good dinner, a few too many whiskeys and a
walk over the heath, Sorcha snuggled up to Con contentedly.

'It's been a grand Christmas Day, just the two of us in our new home,' she said.

'You didn't think back to Christmases in Ballymore?'

'A little. Did you?'

'No, Sorcha, I didn't. My daddy would get so wrecked on whiskey on Christmas Eve that most times he'd not be out of bed until the afternoon and then he'd sulk because the bars were shut on Christmas night,' Con chuckled.

'Well, now you have me, and I'm your family. And I promise I'll never leave you or hurt you, ever.'

He stroked her hair gently. 'And I promise that one day I'll make you proud of me.'

'I know you will, Con, I know it.'

12

'Well, Helen, Tony Bryant was right. I believe you are dyslexic.' Dr Allen, a middle-aged Englishman, glanced at her over his half-moon glasses.

'That . . . that's wonderful,' breathed Helen.

'Upon my word, I don't think I've ever heard a patient go into paroxysms of delight when I've diagnosed them.'

'Sorry. It means that I've finally found a reason why I find it hard to read and why I did so badly at school.'

'Yes. I can see what you mean. However, dyslexia can be a persistent little problem. It's going to take a lot of patience and determination to overcome it.'

'I'm very determined.'

'Good, that's the spirit. It might interest you to know that we believe one in four children who have experienced learning difficulties at school have dyslexia. However, many are never treated. The tests I've subjected you to this morning have given me an idea of the level of your problem. You can distinguish colours and have no issue with numbers. It seems words jump off the page at you.' Helen nodded. 'You muddle up the letters when you write, even though you know where they should go. It's not uncommon, and I've definitely come across worse. I really do think with time and patience, you can learn to manage the problem. I'm going to start you off with some worksheets.'

Dr Allen handed Helen a sheaf of papers. 'I want you to copy exactly the word above the space, over and over again. It's boring and repetitive, but it's been proven to work. Slowly you will train your brain to recognise the shapes. I also want you to be brave and read as much as you can. Start off with magazines. The sentences are usually short and there are always pictures to give you the gist. I cannot stress enough the importance of practice.'

'Yes, Dr Allen. I'll do anything to get better, I really will.' Helen meant it.

'Jolly good. My receptionist will make your next appointment. I'll see you in a week and we'll go through the worksheets and discuss any problems you've encountered.'

'Thank you, Dr Allen. I'm very grateful.'

They both stood up and Helen held out her hand.

'Good show, good show. Take care in that snow out there. Looks perilous.'

'I will. Goodbye.'

Even though the pavements were treacherous, Helen walked along with a spring in her step.

I'm not stupid, I'm not stupid, she thought to herself, smiling. Even a half-hour wait for a bus that broke down at Wimbledon Hill could not dampen her spirits. She arrived home soaked to the skin, but feeling happier than she could ever remember.

The fortnight break for the Christmas holidays was initially something that Helen had been dreading. She had briefly contemplated going home to Ballymore, but had decided Christmas with her aunt in that big, empty house was an even more depressing prospect than spending two weeks by herself in London.

As it turned out, Helen did not feel the slightest bit low.

On Christmas Eve, she went out shopping on Wimbledon

High Street. She bought a small turkey, vegetables, a bottle of wine and a huge box of chocolates. Then she went into a newsagent's and purchased a large pile of women's magazines. Not only would reading the editorials give her the practice Dr Allen had stressed she needed, but she could enjoy the lovely glossy photographs of the models wearing the latest fashions.

Her shopping done, she staggered home under the weight of her bags.

Christmas morning was spent producing a fine lunch. *What a shame it's only for me*, thought Helen, pondering how wonderful it would have been if Tony Bryant had been sitting opposite her.

Having watched the Christmas night film, Helen slipped into bed to have her 'ten minutes of Tony' fantasy. Afterwards, she picked up a pile of magazines from the bedside cabinet. Jean Shrimpton, Twiggy and a raft of nameless, beautiful women assailed her vision as she turned over the pages. With a sigh, Helen lay back on her pillows and stared at the ceiling.

Come on, Helen, get real. Tony could never find you attractive. You're just a four-eyed nobody with no friends.

Tears of self-pity began to fill her eyes. Yet this time, rather than indulging in her sorrow as she'd done in the past, Helen felt rather revolted by it. Wiping her eyes, she climbed out of bed and went to stand in front of the full-length mirror inside the wardrobe door.

First, she inspected her face. Her skin was somewhat sallow and a little spotty. She remembered reading in one of the magazines that, if you cut out chocolate and drank silly amounts of water, you could improve your complexion.

Next, she took off her glasses and studied her eyes. There was no doubt they were her best feature: oval-shaped and an unusual aqua-green. Helen sighed. Unless she wanted to spend all day bumping into things, there was no way she could go without her glasses. There was, however, a chance that she might be able to find a pair of more flattering frames.

'Eeee,' she mouthed at the mirror. Her teeth were nice: pearly and straight with no unsightly gaps.

Helen ran a hand through her hair. *It really is the dullest colour. Ditchwater meets dead mouse,* she thought. But it was thick, and there was a lot of it.

Taking a deep breath, Helen removed her pyjamas and braced herself to objectify her naked body for the first time in her life. What had that magazine said? Fifteen minutes of exercise a day combined with a sensible diet and it was possible to shed pounds if one wished to do so. She buttoned up her pyjamas and climbed back into bed. Then she flicked through another magazine, tracing the slim, lithe bodies of the models.

Surely it was worth a try?

Settling down under the sheets, she reached and turned off the bedside light. There were ten days before she went back for the start of the new term. Ten days in which, if she could not completely alter herself, she could at least make a start.

'There you go, darling. What do you think?' The hairdresser held up a mirror so she could see the back of her head.

Helen swung her head from side to side and smiled. 'I love it.'

'The difference is incredible.' The hairdresser ran his fingers proudly through the shiny, sharply cut bob. 'As I said, take a bottle of our special shampoo for unloved hair and wash it twice through at least three times a week. The style is easy to maintain.' He pulled the cape from around Helen's shoulders. 'See you again, darling.'

Helen walked out into the bright January sunshine. The sales were on, and Regent Street was crowded. She fumbled in her handbag for her *London A–Z.* Getting her bearings, she began to walk in the direction of Carnaby Street. She'd read about it in one of her magazines and knew it was the place to go if one wanted 'hip threads'.

'Can't Buy Me Love' blared out from some speakers in front of a boutique. The next shop along was playing the new Rolling Stones single. Further down the street were a couple of buskers strumming their guitars. It was packed with young people, the cacophony of noise and colour overwhelming Helen. She'd never seen anything quite like it.

Her new hairstyle giving her a little more confidence, she took a deep breath and walked into one of the new boutiques.

Back in her flat, Helen straightened the tweed mini-skirt and pulled the black polo-neck sweater down over her hips. She turned to the side and surveyed herself in the mirror. Okay, she wasn't Twiggy, but her concerted attempt to look after her body in the past ten days was beginning to show some dividends. In her black tights and dark patent boots, Helen's legs looked shapely. Plus, the make-up routine she'd practised obsessively definitely gave her features definition.

She grabbed her new leather three-quarter-length jacket and put it on, then picked up her schoolbag. There was no doubt about it. For the first time in her life, Helen was proud of what she saw in the mirror. Unthinkingly, she blew her reflection a kiss, opened the door to her flat and closed it behind her.

As she had hoped he would, Tony kept her back after class.

'Helen, I wanted to enquire how things are going with Dr Allen.'

'Oh, very well, thank you.' She nodded. 'I've really been working hard and I think my reading and writing are getting better. Dr Allen said he was very pleased with me at my last appointment.'

'Good! I'm sure I'll start to notice an improvement in your work very soon.'

'Thank you, Mr Bryant. For everything,' she said shyly as she began to walk towards the door.

'Oh, and, Helen?'

'Yes, Mr Bryant?'

'I think your new hairdo looks smashing.'

Helen almost skipped home. The time, money and effort she'd put in over ten days . . . it was all worthwhile to hear those few simple words from the mouth of the man she loved.

13

'Bye, sweetheart. I'll meet you tonight at the Victoria. I might be a little late as the dragon's called a floor meeting.' Sorcha kissed Con on the cheek.

He grabbed her and pulled her down on top of him.

'Con! Let me go! It took me hours to style my hair!'

'Be off with you then to your myriad of smells,' he said, releasing her. She smiled down at him as she straightened her hair.

'Don't forget to buy some milk. I'm late. I'll have to run all the way down Fitzjohns Avenue.'

'It'll keep you fit, Sorcha-porcha.'

'The cheek from a man still lazing in bed!' Sorcha headed for the door and opened it. 'Bye-bye.'

'Bye, sweetheart.'

The door shut behind Sorcha and Con sat up, crossed his arms behind his head and gazed out of the window. It was a lovely, bright March morning. All around the city daffodils were starting to peep through hedgerows, forcing their golden heads through the dead detritus of winter.

Con reached for his old guitar, which lay on the chair next to the bed. Sitting further upright, he began to strum it.

'And I have loved you more than . . .'

He played a loud discord and put the guitar back on the chair.

There was no doubt about it, his days with the Blackspots were coming to an end. Sorcha had been right. With Todd Bradley in charge, there was no way he was ever going to get a look-in. He'd presented the man with a number of songs he thought might be suitable for the band to try.

'Great, Con, I'll look at them,' was the usual response. And then, inevitably, they would never be mentioned again.

Con jumped out of bed and began to search for his tin of tobacco. The Blackspots were going nowhere, and the lead singer had a serious case of megalomania.

He could do better. He'd tell them at the gig tonight.

'God, Con, looks like you're going to have to help me out this evening.'

Todd was very pale and a scarf was wrapped tightly round his neck. He was knocking back port and lemon in large gulps.

'Is it the flu?'

'Yes. Lulu had it last week. I wish I'd given her a bit more sympathy now. It's painful to talk. I'll introduce us as usual, then you come forward and sing with me.'

'Okay.'

'Derek, can you and Ian put more welly into those backing harmonies? You won't have Con to rely on tonight.'

'Sure, man, no hassle,' Ian said, and nodded in their general direction.

'What the hell is he on tonight? He looks completely out of it,' croaked Todd.

Con shrugged. 'Maybe you should have a word. He's getting worse. The other night he fell asleep halfway through a number.'

Todd held up his hand. 'Sure, Con, when I'm up to it. Will you test the sound level on the amps, please?'

'Yes, Todd. Anything you say, Todd,' mumbled Con.

* * *

Freddy Martin was driving home to his comfortable flat in Belsize Park when he was suddenly beset by the urge for a pint. He pulled off Camden High Street, parked his car up a side alley, bought an evening paper and went into the Victoria Arms.

He ordered his pint, drew up a stool and sat by the bar.

'Good evening, ladies and gents. Nice to see you here again. Apologies for my cold. Luckily for you, Con has promised to help me out.'

Glancing up at the dais in the corner, Freddy saw it was the regular band, a foursome with a dreadful name whom he remembered as fairly uninspiring. As they began to play their first song, he opened his newspaper and began to read.

'Con, you're going to have to take over, mate. I can't hack it, there's nothing left,' stage-whispered Todd dramatically after the third number.

Con nodded.

'Do you know the words well enough?'

'Yes, sure I do.'

'Okay.' Todd nodded. 'Begin with "Fields of Glory".'

'Good evening, folks. I'll be taking Todd's place for the rest of the evening. Our man's gone down with flu.'

An 'ah' came up from the audience. Con nodded at the band. 'Right, let's go.'

Freddy was reading that the Cavern Club in Liverpool, the venue where the Beatles had begun, was in danger of being taken over by the Official Receiver. He had played there in the early days and felt a surge of nostalgia for what used to be.

'*Fields of glory, as they march on . . .*'

He looked up at the dais as the voice drifted into his consciousness. He was struck by what he saw.

Now that's what I call a good-looking bloke, thought Freddy, *and he can sing.*

'One day we'll win, oh yes, oh yes, we will.'

'Sack the lyricist,' muttered Freddy under his breath. But he was interested enough to put down his paper for the next number.

'You're good,' mumbled Freddy, 'very good.'

The band had doubtlessly improved since he'd last seen them. This new member seemed to have finally brought some cohesion to the group. The sound was much more polished.

Freddy ordered another pint as the band climbed off the dais at the end of the first set. He was tempted to go over and introduce himself, but decided against it. He was interested, but needed to hear more.

Freddy watched for another half an hour, mulling over the band's look. He concluded that the boys were all attractive in their own ways. At the end of the day, sex appeal was what sold records in their truckloads.

'What the hell,' sighed Freddy. He'd been bored out of his mind in the past six months. He needed a challenge.

Slipping off the bar stool, he went over to say hello.

'Hi, chaps, caught the act. Enjoyed it.'

'Thanks,' croaked Todd, bent over an amplifier with his back to Freddy. 'Not the best night to catch us, though. I've got the flu and—' Todd stood up and turned around, his face flushed with exertion. Before him was a tall man with a chiselled jaw and a blond side parting. His suit was immaculate.

'I . . . er . . . Good evening, Mr Martin,' he stuttered.

'Listen, Todd, isn't it?'

'I . . . yes.'

'Here's my card. Give me a bell and let's meet up. I'd like to have a chat with you. Don't leave it too long, okay.'

'Okay, Mr Martin.'

'Right. See you, lads. Thanks for the music.'

Freddy Martin waved a hand in their general direction and made his way out of the pub. All four band members stared after him.

'Bloody hell.'

'Bugger me.'

'I'll be blowed.'

'Would someone tell me who your man was?' said Con in confusion.

'That, Con, was Freddy Martin. He was a huge rock-and-roller in the fifties, always at number one. I mean, his music's gone out of fashion nowadays, but blimey, I have his entire single collection up in the attic.' Derek was awed.

'So, he was a well-known singer.' Con glanced at Ian and Todd, who were looking as impressed as Derek.

'Con, he's now a manager. He was the guy who discovered The Tin Men. He launched them.'

'Apparently there was some heavy disagreement and they disbanded six months ago,' Derek continued.

Todd sneezed and pulled out a well-used hanky. 'Excuse me. Anyway, maybe Freddy is looking for a new group to manage. I tell you, that guy knows everybody in the music business.'

Derek had begun hopping up and down with excitement.

'Hey, chaps, this could be it, this could be the big one. Who's for a drink?'

'Todd, I need to go home.' Lulu's voice cut into the excitement. 'I'm shooting at Elstree tomorrow and I have to be there for six.' She rose imperiously from her seat.

'Sure, Lulu. Listen, chaps, I'll love you and leave you. I've got to go home and nurse this flu. I'll call Freddy Martin tomorrow morning. I'll be in touch with you all when I've spoken to him.'

Todd and Lulu left and Derek went to get some drinks from the bar. Sorcha squeezed Con's hand as he sat down next to her.

'You were grand up there,' she whispered. 'No wonder Freddy Martin thought the band was good.'

'Thanks.' Con kissed her. 'Back into the ranks tomorrow, of course. Ah, Derek, good man yourself.' Con looked up as his bandmate put the drinks on the table.

'Well, here's to Todd Bradley and the Blackspots. Let's hope this time next year that name will be on everybody's tongue.' Derek raised his glass.

'I'll drink to that.'

'The first thing that has to go is the band name. It's awful. Coffee, anyone?'

Freddy looked around at the four young men sitting nervously in his spacious sitting room. They all nodded. Freddy poured the steaming black liquid into four china cups.

'Help yourself to milk and sugar. The point is, you have to have a short, sharp name that's easily remembered. Anyway, that's something we can put our thinking caps on about if we decide we're going to work together. Who writes the songs?'

'I do.' Todd sat up, ready for praise.

'I'm going to be brutally honest with you, Todd, from what I heard a couple of evenings ago, they're not quite hitting the mark. The melody lines are unusual, which I think is a positive . . . but your lyrics stink. Does anyone else in the band write?'

'I do,' Derek put in.

'Fine. Let me have a look at your stuff.'

'And I do,' said Con quietly.

'Great. Ditto for you, Con. Ideally, you'll write your own material. It makes life much simpler and gives you a definitive sound. We *can* employ a songwriter if needs be, but let me see what you can come up with first.'

Con shot a glance at Todd. His face was red with humiliation.

'Now, as for your image . . . or rather lack of it . . .' chuckled Freddy. 'You're all good-looking boys but you're not doing yourselves justice. I'd consider new haircuts and fresh wardrobes an absolute essential before we let you out in public again.'

The four boys silently sipped their coffee. Eventually, Con spoke.

'Mr Martin, I'm not wishing to be rude, but you don't like our name, our music, our hair or our clothes. Would you be so kind as to tell us what you do like?'

'My apologies, Con. You'll have to get used to the fact that I say exactly what I think. It cuts out the crap. You're sat here, aren't you? It means I think you have potential. The four of you look good together on stage. Two blonds and two brunettes is an appealing combination. Musically, you have a nice sound. Aside from that you have . . .' Freddy searched for the right word. 'You have a *charisma* that's raw at the moment, but could be developed. I reckon with a bit of time, effort and money, we could put together something special.' He gave the boys a wide grin.

'Not being presumptuous, Mr Martin, but what exactly is it you're offering us?' Todd enquired.

'Todd, don't rush me. I was coming to that. More coffee, anyone?' Freddy poured himself another cup as the four boys shifted nervously in their seats. 'I'm sure you know that I used to be a performer myself. For the past few years I've managed a very well-known group. For reasons I do not wish to go into, that group are now no more. What I'm thinking about offering you boys will be the same deal as I offered them, many moons ago. Personal management.' Freddy stood and began to stroll around his sitting room. 'As you can imagine, my connections in the music business are widespread and well established. Any group that I take on is going to get through the door of a record company on my recommendation alone. I would personally fund demo tapes and all expenses incurred before such time as I secure you a deal. I would also pay you all a living wage that would then be clawed back out of your first contract. For the privilege of having me as your manager, the band would pay me twenty per cent of your gross earnings. That, Mr Bradley, is the deal.'

'I see,' nodded Todd.

The other boys stared in silence at Freddy.

Freddy crossed his arms and walked back over to the band, towering over them. 'There is one thing you would have to understand before we go any further. I am a reasonable man, but if I've learnt anything from managing the last lot, it's that there's only room for one chief. I need hardly say who that would be.' Freddy looked at his watch. 'I'm afraid I'm going to have to call a halt to this meeting. I have a lunch in Soho in half an hour. Why don't you boys go away, have a chat amongst yourselves and see how you feel?' He stood up and his guests followed him to the front door. He solemnly shook their hands one by one.

'Goodbye. Call me in a couple of days and we'll reconvene.'

Freddy shut the door, allowed himself a small smile at the recollection of their glazed expressions, then ran upstairs to find his car keys.

Out on the pavement, the four boys looked at each other.

'Pub?' they agreed in unison, and set off along the road until they found one.

'Did you see that gaff? Man, that's serious spondulicks.' Ian lit up a smelly joint as Derek and Todd came back with the beers.

Todd coughed and waved away the smoke. 'Ian, do you have to? That's the third since breakfast.'

'Hey, Todd, it's way better for you than ciggies,' Ian replied good-naturedly, taking another drag.

'So.' Todd took a sip of his pint. 'What did everyone think?'

'He's a powerful man,' said Con.

'Knows a lot of people,' put in Derek.

Todd sniffed and pursed his lips before offering his opinion. 'Well, I thought he was a first-class, out-and-out tosser,' he sneered. 'We don't need him, boys. All he did was tear our music to shreds and suggest a haircut.' Todd shook his head. 'I'm sorry. He may be Mr Big Shot, but I loathed him.'

'That's because he said your lyrics stink, Todd,' smiled Ian peaceably. 'Maybe he was right,' he shrugged.

'Oh really, Ian? Well, maybe if you weren't stoned out of your skull day and night you might try putting pen to paper and writing some stuff. Then you'll know how difficult it is to—'

'Boys, boys.' Con held up his hands. 'This is not the time to be arguing. We've been given a proposal and we need to consider it seriously.'

'He talked about a living wage,' breathed Derek incredulously.

'Yeah, depends what sort of "living" he was talking about, though,' Todd said morosely.

'Well, let's be honest, it's got to be better than what we're all trying to survive on at the moment,' said Derek.

'So you'd sell your artistic integrity for the sake of a few pounds a week, would you?'

'We have to eat, Todd,' put in Con. 'And there's nothing wrong with wanting to make money. I thought he was straight-talking. No messing. I liked that.'

'That's only because he thought the sun shone out of your arse.' Todd shook his head.

'Well, man, it was something he liked. Don't knock it,' said Ian, searching his pockets for a box of matches and relighting his joint.

Todd looked like he was going to launch himself at Ian, so Derek put a fraternal hand on his shoulder. 'You know how hard it is to get anyone from a record company to come to a gig. Freddy Martin would have them along in a blink of an eye. He also said he'd be paying for demo tapes, something we could never do, Todd.'

Todd shrugged off his cousin's hand. 'Yeah, Derek, and then he'll claw the money back when we get our first deal and then take twenty per cent of all we earn for the privilege.'

'But that's business, Todd,' Derek shrugged. 'Any manager will want to take his cut. We can be the best band in the world, but if we have no money to put into our development, then it's pointless. We could stay as we are for years.'

'He may have insulted us, but hey, man, he must think we have *something*. It's his reputation on the line too. Anyone for a drag?' Ian waved his joint around.

'No thanks,' said Con. 'Freddy Martin knows what he's talking about. I admit he's not perfect, but what else do we have? There are a hundred bands in London who would jump at a chance like this. If we don't take it, then another group will.'

'Hear, hear,' said Derek. 'Guys, you know what I suggest?'

'Pray tell us,' droned Todd.

'That we take a vote on it.'

'What if it's a split decision?' asked Ian. 'There are four of us.'

'Then we'll toss a coin or something,' Derek smiled. 'Okay, I'll go first. I say we go with Freddy Martin.' Derek shrugged as Todd shot him a venomous look.

'I say I leave the band if the rest of you vote in favour,' said Todd.

'Con?' Derek turned to him.

'I'm with you, Derek. I'm thinking that a new haircut and a sissy suit is preferable to possible failure and probable starvation.'

'Ian?' Derek asked.

'I'm with you too. I'm looking forward to the screaming groupies.' He smiled.

'Well, chaps, looks like the decision's been taken. We're giving Freddy Martin a shot. Sorry, Todd,' said Derek.

Todd stood up, a look of disgust on his face. He silently left the pub.

'You've done what?!'

Lulu stood in the centre of her Chelsea sitting room, staring down incredulously at her boyfriend.

Todd poured another glass of whiskey from the already half-empty bottle. He took a slug and shrugged. 'Yep, I've left.'

'You stupid, arrogant little shit!' Lulu picked up a cushion from the sofa and threw it at him.

'Lulu, I thought you'd be on my side? You've always said how much you love my lyrics. Freddy Martin said they stank!'

He looked like a hurt little boy. Lulu knew she must try a different approach.

'Darling, I do love your songs. I think you're wonderfully talented. It's just that after all this time, the break has come. Freddy Martin, *the* Freddy Martin, ex-manager of one of the most famous groups in the country, has offered to manage you. And you say you're leaving. You must understand that I'm surprised.'

'Look, Lulu, you don't know, you weren't there. Freddy insulted me. I'm the lead singer of the Blackspots, yet there was Freddy Martin kissing Con Daly's arse and telling him how wonderful *his* voice was. Seems to me that I'll be consigned to supporting cast in *my own* group. No thanks. I'll start another, better group. I'll beat Con Daly at his own game.'

Lulu sank into a chair and sighed. She pushed her thick black hair back from her face. 'So this is about jealousy more than anything else. You think Con's stolen your limelight.'

Todd clenched his fists. 'I bloody hate him, Lulu, and his gentle Irish charm. He has the rest of the band and Freddy Martin taken in, but not me.' Todd put his head in his hands. 'Behind that calm exterior is steel. Con is as determined to make it to the top as I am.'

'And is that wrong?' Lulu shook her head. 'Now you *are* sounding spoilt and jealous. Con's a nice guy, Todd. Yes, he's talented, and good-looking. But surely those are the qualities a group needs to make it?'

Todd shot a steely look at Lulu. 'You're talking as if you fancy Con Daly.'

Lulu rolled her eyes. 'No, but I can see why a lot of women would find him attractive.'

'Great. Just boost my ego, why don't you.' Todd hiccupped suddenly.

'Todd, darling, you know it's you I love. What I'm saying is that Con *is* an asset. That's how you should think of him. There's room for both of you! Look at Lennon and McCartney – both brilliant musicians, singers and songwriters. I'll bet there's been fireworks between those two at times. But the more ability you have in a group, the more potential there is for massive success. Work with Con. Don't make an enemy of him.'

'You're certain I shouldn't leave then?'

'Absolutely.'

'Shit.' Todd rubbed his eyes and stifled a yawn. 'I'm a bit pissed.'

'I know.' Lulu stood up and went to sit next to him. 'Trust me, Todd, darling. My instincts tell me you must stay.'

'Okay,' Todd sighed, after a long pause, 'but I can never like that Con Daly.'

'You don't have to like him; you just have to *work* with him. Come on, I'm going to put you to bed.'

Todd rose slowly to his feet. He took a tress of Lulu's hair and twirled it round his finger. 'You think I'm better than Con, don't you?'

Lulu took his hand and led him to the bedroom. 'Yes, darling.' Without putting the lights on, she began to unbutton his shirt.

'Hi, Con, I . . . I was just passing and I wondered if I could pop in for a chat.'

Todd lived in Chelsea. Con thought it unlikely he had just been 'passing' Arkwright Road in Hampstead at nine thirty in the morning.

'Sure. Come in.'

Todd followed Con up three flights of stairs to a large airy room.

'This is pleasant.' Hands in pockets, Todd looked out of the window.

'Ah, 'tis Sorcha. She has the touch.'

'Yes. Um . . . look, Con, I thought we ought to have a chat.'

'Of course. I was just making myself some coffee. Want some?'

'Great. I seem to have one hell of a hangover this morning. I would have slept it off except Lulu gets up at five to go to the studios and for such a feminine creature she clomps around like a baby elephant. Subsequently I can never get back to sleep.' Todd knew he was rambling out of nervousness. 'Look, Con, what I said yesterday . . . I was in a state, angry at the way Freddy Martin spoke to me. You know how you feel about your own songs. It's hard to be told they stink, especially when you've studied for years at music college.'

'Of course.' Con filled two mugs with instant coffee powder and hot water. 'We're out of milk.'

'That's fine. I take it black anyway.'

'Grand job. There you are.' Con handed one of the mugs to Todd, perched on the arm of the sofa and waited expectantly.

'The thing is that you and I are the strength in the band, both as singers and songwriters. Ian and Derek look good and will support the group well musically, but it's us who are going to make the magic happen.'

'It's generous of you to say so.' Con took a sip of his coffee, his calm gaze never wavering from Todd's face.

'So, to that end, I was thinking last night that we should maybe . . .' – the conversation seemed to be paining Todd – '. . . pool our resources on the writing front. I know you tend to go for a more melodic, slower sound, whereas I like as many noisy riffs as I can get in.' Con nodded. Todd held his hands up. 'And I admit some of my lyrics can be a bit self-indulgent, whereas, excuse me for saying, yours can verge on the sickeningly romantic. Maybe together we could curb each other's excesses.'

Con gently swirled the coffee in his mug. 'That all makes sense. Does this mean that if we're talking about the future, you've changed your mind about leaving?'

'Yes, of course. I founded the damned band, didn't I? Yesterday was a heat-of-the-moment thing, that's all. I calmed down and realised I'd overreacted.'

Con was definitely impressed by Todd's new attitude. 'He was hard on us all.'

'Well, I have a feeling there'll be worse to come from Mr Martin. We'd better get used to the fact that he doesn't keep his opinions to himself.'

'So, you're happy to go with him then?'

'As you all pointed out, it's better than starvation.'

Con nodded and reached for his tin of tobacco. 'So, you want to have a go at writing some stuff together?'

'Yeah. We should give it a shot.'

'I'm open to that.'

'Good. I think it's very important we work as a team. Did the rest of you decide when you were going to give Freddy Martin the news that we'd accepted his offer?'

'Derek was going to ring him this afternoon. We'd better let him know you're back in.'

Todd nodded, a trifle humbly. 'Sure.'

14

'Hello, Derek! Fancy meeting you here. You're looking well.'

'Thanks.'

Even though he was shaking inside his lifts, he tried to radiate a calm confidence.

'You, er . . . seem to have grown.' Peggy studied him.

'Do I?' He prayed he wasn't blushing. 'Two haddock and chips, please, love, one with salt, one with salt and vinegar.' The server nodded and prepared the order. 'Thanks.' Derek reached over the counter and took the warm parcel of newspaper from the woman.

'Next.'

'Oh, one cod and chips and two pickled onions, please,' requested Peggy. 'So, Derek.' Peggy turned to face him and gave a polite smile. 'What are you doing with yourself these days?'

Derek tried to lean nonchalantly against the chip shop wall, but misjudged the angle and tripped backwards awkwardly. 'I'm actually in a group.'

'Oh. A group of what?' she enquired innocently.

'A band. A rock band.'

'Are you? Still playing your guitar then?'

'Yep, still strumming away on that bloody thing, hahaha!' The laugh was too aggressive, and caused Peggy to take a step back.

Save it, Derek. 'As a matter of fact, Freddy Martin has just signed us up,' he said, as casually as possible.

Peggy did a double-take. 'You mean, *the* Freddy Martin?'

Bingo. She was impressed. 'Yes. It's early days yet, but things are looking good.'

'Here's your order, miss.'

'Thanks.' Peggy took her parcel from the woman behind the counter and the two of them moved towards the door of the chippy.

'What do you do with yourself these days then?' Derek asked, knowing full well.

'Oh, I'm at college in the West End, doing a boring business studies course. And I share the flat above this chippy with a friend of mine.'

'Ah, right. You moved out of home, did you?'

'Yes. Well, you know how overprotective my dad was. You still at home?'

Derek shuffled awkwardly. 'Yeah. I couldn't leave Mum. She depends on me.'

'Of course. How is she?'

'Oh, the arthritis is pretty bad now. She can't get out unless she's in a wheelchair. She can just about manage to make herself a cup of tea.'

'I'm sorry to hear that, Derek. But it sounds as though you're doing really well. Do you play many gigs? Oh, er, sorry.' She realised there was a queue of people waiting to get out of the chip shop. 'We seem to be forming a bottleneck.'

Derek pushed the door open and the two of them stepped out onto the pavement.

'Oh yes, all over the place. But we'll probably be in the studio for a while. Freddy wants us to do some demos.'

'Gosh. It all sounds awfully exciting.'

Derek continued to play it as coolly as possible. 'I guess it is, yeah.'

'Look, Derek, I have to go or the chips will get cold.' Peggy looked at him. Derek had always been very sweet to her. Something about his boyish appearance was so innocent, which she liked. Of course, he'd become intense and obsessed when she had made it clear that she saw him only as a friend . . . but that was a long time ago now. Peggy took a chance. 'Let me know where you're playing and maybe I can come and see you.'

Derek nodded. 'Will do.' He acted out a thought coming into his mind: 'Actually, we'll be playing tomorrow night at the Queen Victoria in Camden Town. It's only fifteen minutes from here.'

'Oh, well, I might make it. Nice to see you again.'

'And you, Peggy.'

She appeared taken aback. 'Goodness, no one's called me *that* for years. Not since school actually. Anyway, bye, Derek.'

She waved as she walked off. Derek suddenly felt faint. He went and perched on the edge of a graffiti-covered bench to try to stop his head from spinning.

That had gone better than he could have ever imagined.

She'd looked pretty impressed. No. *Very* impressed. She'd also looked extremely beautiful.

She might come along tomorrow night, to see him play.

Derek stood up, realising the chips he'd bought for him and his mum were now stone-cold. He threw them in the bin by the bench and went back inside the chippy to queue again for two fresh portions.

He'd been right all along. He and Peggy were meant to be together.

* * *

123

Sorcha's counter had been particularly busy for the past month. She supposed it was because spring was in the air. Even though she was on her feet from first thing in the morning until the store closed at six in the evening, she enjoyed the work. The other girls who worked in the store were friendly and she enjoyed their lunchtime chats, full of gossip about who was seeing whom.

Even though Con had recently told her that he would soon be earning enough to keep the both of them, she doubted whether she'd want to give up the job. After all, what would she do with herself in their room in Hampstead all day? Sorcha knew how Con felt about her working. But this was 1965. Lots of girls earned a living, particularly here in London. There might be an argument, but she would stand her ground. Besides, any extra money helped at the moment.

Sorcha hummed to herself as she dusted the bottles on her marble-topped counter. If she continued to work, then along with Con's income, they might be able to afford a flat with a separate bedroom . . . and maybe even their own bathroom. She was all too aware of something suitable that would be available in their building in a few weeks' time.

She watched the security guard unlock the main entrance to the store. The noise of the traffic roaring around Piccadilly Circus echoed across to her.

'Here we go, another eight hours of flogging that fragrance,' moaned Gladys, the girl who worked with her behind the counter. 'And me with an almighty hangover. Just the smell is making me want to puke.'

'Breathe through your mouth then,' Sorcha smiled. She was used to Gladys's constant complaining.

'I suppose I could put a peg on me conk,' chuckled Gladys. 'Might not be the best advertisement Elizabeth Arden's ever had, though.'

'Excuse me for interrupting your little joke, but I want a two-ounce bottle of Blue Grass.'

'Of course, madam.' Sorcha glanced at her customer and realised she'd seen her before, in the store canteen. She took a bottle of Blue Grass off the shelf. 'Would you like it wrapped?'

'No thank you. Just put it in a bag. I'm in a hurry.'

'Of course, madam.'

As Sorcha took a bag and popped the perfume inside, she felt the woman's eyes boring into her.

'How tall are you, young lady?'

Sorcha looked around to see if the woman could be talking to someone else. But no, the question was definitely directed at her. 'Me?'

'Yes, of course you,' said the woman impatiently.

'Um, about five feet and seven inches, I think.'

'Mmm. And what do you weigh?'

Sorcha shook her head. 'I'm afraid I don't know.'

'Waist? Bust?'

Sorcha began to blush. She shrugged. 'No, I've no idea. That'll be two pounds and six shillings.'

'Thank you.' The woman handed over the money. 'What time is your lunch break?'

'Twelve o'clock, madam.'

'Good. Then come and see me on the third floor at five past twelve prompt. I want to take some measurements. But you might do, you might just do. Five past twelve sharp, mind. Good morning.'

Sorcha stared open-mouthed as the woman strode off. She turned and saw that Gladys was watching her too.

'Coo-ee! You know who that was, don't you?'

Sorcha shook her head.

'That is the manager, or chief *vendeuse* as she prefers to be known, of the designer clothes department upstairs. If she wants to take your measurements, she might be interested in you being one of the house models.'

'And what is a house model?'

'It means you wear the gowns that a customer wants to see. It's not really like being a proper model like Twiggy or nothing, but it's more glam than standing here squirting the air all day.'

'I see. Why would she be wanting me, though?'

'Well, you don't scrub up bad, do you, Sorcha? You know you're pretty so I'm not gonna tell you. Oh well, looks like I'll be heading for a new partner in crime behind here. You'll still speak to me when you're all grand on the third floor?'

Sorcha chuckled. 'Of course I will.'

That evening, she sat in the Queen Victoria telling Lulu all about her meeting with Marie Elaine, chief *vendeuse* at Swan and Edgar's.

Since the two girls were so often thrown together because of their partners, they'd struck up a strange friendship. Sorcha had learnt to ignore Lulu's tactless comments. She knew it was just her way.

'It sounds a bit dull, standing around until there's a customer wants to see a dress. But the money is much better than I'm earning in perfumery.'

'Darling, you've gone from shopgirl to model all in one day. Of course you must take it.'

'I don't think Con will approve.'

She looked puzzled. 'Why ever not?'

'Oh, he's never been keen on me working.'

Lulu rolled her eyes. 'Then your Con has to come out of whichever Irish bog he's stuck in and realise that women today have minds of their own. I should hope he'd be proud of the fact his girlfriend is pretty enough to be a model.'

Sorcha put a finger to her lips as Con and Todd approached their table.

Freddy Martin sat and watched his latest signing. The band knew he was there and were on their best behaviour. The usual relaxed banter between numbers had gone, and there was a tension about their playing. Con Daly had been relegated to his position on bass and backing vocals. Freddy wondered whether, if he'd wandered in tonight rather than a few days ago, he would have been as eager to sign them up.

The group needed a considerable amount of work. Freddy closed his eyes as he tried to assemble an image in his mind. These lads were not cut out to be aggressive, badly dressed and loud-mouthed. They were all handsome young men, definitely more Beatles than Stones. They should be clean-cut in a sharp suit, the kind of man you'd be proud to take home to your mother.

Freddy watched each band member, one at a time. Ian was the wild card, obviously a user. His eyes closed as he thumped his drums, mouthing the words of the song. He'd appeal to the more adventurous teenager, although his habit would have to be controlled.

Derek was the angel-faced blond. He was very short – Freddy had spotted his lifts – and looked no older than fifteen. Girls would want to mother him. That would work.

Todd was the arrogant intellectual. Freddy bet that his aquiline features would turn on the middle-class female.

And lastly there was Con, who was undoubtedly the star of the four. His dark, Irish looks and strong physique would surely make any woman swoon. The guy oozed sex appeal. Plus, as a bonus, he also had a great voice.

Freddy knew that bringing Con forward and having him share the limelight would not please the group's present lead singer, but it had to be done. If Todd didn't like it, he knew where the door was. Making sure the boys pulled together was as important as anything else.

A surge of applause came from the audience as they finished a number. The band didn't know it yet, but this was the last time they'd be performing in a dump like this. Next week, the work would begin.

When Derek had climbed onto the dais to begin the first set, his stomach had been in his four-inch-high boots. He'd told Todd, Con and Ian that a girl was coming to watch him tonight. But she hadn't turned up yet. Derek had such a large lump in his throat that it was hard for him to open his mouth for the harmonies. In fact, he was terrified that he was going to burst into tears in front of everyone.

And then, just before the last song of the set, in she had walked, her lovely blonde hair shining around her face. She looked absolutely beautiful, with most of her slim, shapely legs visible below her mini-skirt. She'd come to see *him*. She did love him after all.

Peggy stood nervously at the back, hands planted firmly in the pockets of her jacket. He caught her eye and smiled. She smiled back. Willing the song to end as quickly as possible so he could go to her, Derek lifted his guitar over his head the minute he'd played the last chord and practically leapt off the dais.

'Hello, Peggy!' He almost knocked her backwards as he bounded towards her and threw his arms around her.

'Gosh, hi, Derek . . .' She did her best to extricate herself from his grasp.

'I thought you weren't coming.' His breath was coming in short, sharp bursts and he was sweating profusely.

She stepped back from him. 'I only popped in for a little while. I—'

'Come on, let me introduce you to the other band members.' Derek curled an arm round her back protectively and marched her over to the band's enclave in the corner.

Freddy was there, the other three huddled around him as he talked.

'There you are, Derek. I'm just arranging a meeting next week at my solicitor's to sign the contracts. Can you manage Tuesday morning at ten?' asked Freddy.

'Sure, that'll be fine.' He nodded. 'Listen, guys, can I introduce Peggy? This is Freddy Martin, our manager. Con Daly, Todd, who you know, and Ian Hancock, our drummer.'

'Pleased to meet you, lovely. Can I borrow Derek for a few minutes? You go and sit over there with the other girls,' suggested Freddy, shooting her a smile.

'Of course.' Looking uncomfortable, she turned and made her way round the table to where two young women were sitting.

'Hello, darling. So you're Derek's girl, are you? I'm Lulu and this is Sorcha. Want a Babycham?'

'Thanks.' She sat down. 'I'm not Derek's girl, more of a friend really.'

'Well, you could do a lot worse than Derek. He's a good guy. And soon he'll have girls crawling all over him. Want another drink, Sorcha?' Lulu stood up.

'Yes please.'

'*Scusa me un momento*,' Lulu said in exaggerated Italian before making her way towards the bar.

'Who are you with?' Peggy asked Sorcha.

'Con, the tall, dark one. We live together. Have you known Derek long?'

Peggy nodded. 'Yes, actually, for years. We were in the same class at school. I hadn't seen him for ages . . . and then I bumped into him in a chippy of all places.' She smiled. 'He asked me to come along, so I did. The band seem very good.'

'They are.' Sorcha nodded. 'Freddy Martin is signing them up. They might be headed for the big time.'

'Really?' Peggy seemed a little surprised. Her eyes crossed over to Derek. He looked good tonight. 'Gosh. I can't believe it.'

Lulu was back with three Babychams.

'Here we go, girls. Sustenance for the weary groupies. So, what do you do?'

'I'm at college doing a business course.'

'How interesting. Sorcha here is a house model in Swan and Edgar's and I'm an actress.'

'Really? In films?' Derek certainly seemed to be keeping good company these days.

'Yes. I've done a Hammer Horror and I have a screen test tomorrow for a major role in a new film they're doing at Elstree.'

'Peggy, are you okay?' Derek's hand rested on her shoulder. She nodded, blushing slightly.

'Good, good. We're back up there now. I'll see you afterwards and maybe we'll go for a bite to eat. Catch you later.' Derek bounded away, an enormous spring in his step.

Sorcha and Con arrived home just after midnight.

'Ah, 'tis knackering, all this preparation for fame and fortune.' Con threw himself down on the bed, still wearing his coat.

Sorcha busied herself making a cup of tea.

'That girl of Derek's seemed a bit unsure of herself.'

'Did she? I didn't notice. He goes on and on about his Peggy. He's been in love with her for years, Todd was telling me.'

'I think it might be a bit one-sided, Con. Poor Derek, I hope he doesn't get hurt.'

'He'll cope, I'm sure. Come here.' Con opened his arms and Sorcha climbed on top of him. 'Ah, that feels good.' He held her close to him, then rolled her over so he was looking down at her. 'You know, Sorcha, all that we dreamt about is starting to happen. Next week we sign the contract with Freddy and he begins to put his own money into making us rich and famous. I'll have a weekly wage, which means you can stop working at that department store.'

Sorcha steeled herself. 'But I like working at the department store. And as it happens, I've been promoted.'

'Really? Doing what?'

'I've been offered a job as a house model. I show clothes to customers. The money is two pounds more a week than I'm after getting at the moment. It's a grand opportunity, Con, and I'd really like to take it.'

'But there's no need for you to take it. I just told you. Freddy will be paying us a good wage every week. Now I can keep you. You can leave when you want.'

Sorcha pulled away from him and sat upright. 'You sound like my father. Lots of girls work these days, even if they don't have to.'

'You're not lots of girls.'

'And what am I to do with myself all day while you're off becoming a superstar?'

Con shrugged. 'What do women do while their men work?'

Sorcha hit her fists down on the bed in frustration.

'So, it was grand for me to work while it suited you. Now it doesn't and you're telling me to stop? What right have you to tell me to do anything?'

He stared at her. 'What do you mean by that?'

'I mean that we're not married and—'

'Ah, so this is what it's all about. Fine. I'll marry you.'

'Con Daly, I wouldn't marry you if you were the last man

on earth! I thought you were different from the other men in Ballymore, but you're not. You're just as narrow-minded as any of them. I'm taking the job as a house model and I couldn't care less about what the hell you think!'

Sorcha went towards the front door, opened it and slammed it behind her for maximum effect. She stood outside in the cold corridor for a while, shaking with rage and frustration. There was only one place to go. Sorcha trudged down the corridor, locked herself in the freezing communal bathroom and burst into tears.

15

'Okay, lads, let's go, give them some grief!'

Freddy slapped Con on the back, smiled and gave him a gentle push up the stairs. All the boys looked pale and the nervous energy was crackling around them.

'And now, ladies and gents, introducing the hottest new group to hit Soho for hours: The Leopards!'

A loud cheer went up from the audience in the small, smoky club. Freddy made his way to his table at the back. There was no fear that the audience would disapprove of his protégés: eighty per cent of them had been offered free drinks all night to cheer the boys on.

The band name still wasn't right. It was too aggressive. They'd all struggled to come up with something and had taken Todd's suggestion as the best of a bad bunch.

'Hi, you guys. Welcome to the Basement. I'm Todd, this is Con, Ian on drums and Derek on rhythm guitar. I hope you enjoy your evening with us. Okay, take it away, boys.'

Freddy took a hefty swig of whiskey as the boys began to play. The song was a light frothy number, chosen especially to warm up the audience. He smiled. The boys looked so different to a few weeks ago. Their hair had been cut into short, shiny moptops (much to Con and Ian's disgust), and they were dressed in identical, button-up green suits with black lapels. Freddy closed his eyes and listened to the harmonies. The sound was also much improved. All the boys had been taking singing lessons. Although there was a way to go yet, the voices were beginning to mellow into the all-important 'brand sound' – the quality that would mark them out from the rest.

The first song finished. There was a loud surge of applause. Todd thanked the audience and the band began to play the opening bars of a slow ballad, composed by himself and Con a couple of weeks back.

'Can Someone Tell Me Where She's Gone?' had sent a tingle of excitement up Freddy's spine when they had played it for him in the studio. The song was special. Freddy was going to place it as the first track on the demo the boys were due to record next week. The underlying rivalry between the two frontmen was working in their favour. Each wanted to better the other.

Freddy signalled to the waitress for another whiskey. In a few weeks, the demo would be completed and it would be time to show his product to those who mattered.

Lulu sat in a darkened corner of the club and watched Con Daly intensely. God, he was good-looking.

She glanced to her left. Sorcha was sitting staring nervously into the bottom of her empty Babycham glass. What did Con see in her? 'Anything the matter?' Lulu asked.

Sorcha shrugged. 'No, not really.'

'Come on, you can tell me. Maybe I can help.'

'I don't think so.'

'It's Con, isn't it? Is he playing around?'

'Oh no, nothing like that,' Sorcha sighed. 'He's still sulking about me taking the job as a house model.'

'He'll get over it.'

'Maybe, but there's more.'

'What?' asked Lulu, raising her hands to clap as the number finished.

'Yesterday a woman came into the salon. I modelled two dresses and a coat for her. She came up to me afterwards and told me she was an agent. She wants me to go and see her. She thinks my look is in and I could be getting lots of work in magazines and maybe on the telly.'

'But that's fantastic!' Lulu raised her voice as the group began to play a particularly noisy number. 'What a great opportunity.'

'Maybe, but Con would be having none of it.'

'Have you told him?'

'No. He was in late last night, and besides, I know what he'd say. What do you think I should do, Lulu?'

Lulu looked at Sorcha sternly. 'Go and see this woman. What's the harm in that? I know you love Con, but it's just not acceptable for a woman to have her decisions made by a man.' She took a sip of her White Russian. 'I mean, he's not even your husband.'

Sorcha blushed. 'I know. I'm finding it hard to understand him, Lulu. I'd not have called him a chauvinist before now, but maybe I don't know him as well as I first thought. He's out so much with the band. It's only work that stops me from going mad. What would I do all the day alone?'

'If he was wealthy, you'd spend all his money,' said Lulu, grinning. 'I hardly see Todd either, you know. It's an important time for them, Sorcha. And if I were you, I'd get on with your own life, like I am.' Lulu stretched her arms out on the banquette.

'You're right, of course. It's just that we never get a chance to talk like we used to. I suppose I don't feel as close to him any more.'

'The boys are under a lot of pressure, you know. Freddy expects a lot of them.'

Sorcha nodded. 'You're right. I'm sure once they have a record deal, Con will calm down. And until then I'll have to make my own decisions.'

'Good girl, that's the spirit. Lulu watched with a subtle glint of triumph in her eyes as Sorcha turned her attention back to the band.

'So, Sorcha, we'll be needing some photos – head shots and full-length. Then we can set about getting you some assignments. I suggest you go to see John O'Hara. He's photographed Jean and Twiggy and he'd suit you. I think you're going to do well.' Audrey Bennington nodded her head approvingly. 'Yes, very well indeed. I presume that red hair is natural?'

'Yes.'

'Do you diet to keep that thin?'

'Never.'

'Good, good. Any questions, dear?'

'Um.' Sorcha felt tongue-tied. 'Would I have to leave Swan and Edgar's?'

'Not just yet. Let's see how we go. Most of the magazines are based near you in Soho. Initially I'll try and make your appointments for midday so you can slip off in your lunch hour. Now, let me give John a call and see when he could fit you in.'

As Audrey dialled a number, Sorcha gazed at the walls of her swanky West End office. They were covered in photos of extremely pretty girls, many of whose faces she recognised from magazine covers and advertisements. It was hard to believe this woman thought her attractive enough to join them.

'Right, John. Six o'clock on Thursday. I'll tell her. Yes – see you at the show tomorrow night. Bye, darling.' Audrey put the telephone down and scribbled something on a piece of paper. 'There's John's address. Take a couple of changes of clothes –

one mini-skirt and one trouser suit would be appropriate. He'll send the photos to me and we'll take it from there. Ring me at ten every morning, will you, dear? I can tell you if anything's in for you.'

Sorcha stood up. 'I will. Thank you, Mrs Bennington.'

'Call me Audrey – everyone does, dear. Goodbye.'

On her way back to Swan and Edgar's, Sorcha stopped at Berwick Street market to buy some cabbage and potatoes, then collected a succulent piece of bacon from the butcher's. Tonight, she would cook Con's favourite supper, and tell him about the chance Audrey Bennington had offered her. If he loved her, she reasoned as she walked past Eros, glowing in the bright June sunshine, then he would be pleased for her. And if he wasn't . . . well, that was his problem, not hers.

Sorcha laid the table with a freshly laundered cloth, and decorated it with a bright bunch of peonies and freesias. He'd said he'd be in by eight, and everything was prepared, down to the smell of the bacon she wanted him to walk in to. Sorcha uncorked the bottle of wine she'd bought – an extravagance, but this was an important night.

At half past eight, the telephone rang.

'I'm delayed, Sorcha. Me and Todd have had an idea for a song. I have to stay with it.'

'Oh. I'd cooked,' she replied, deflated.

'Yeah, sorry about that. Don't wait up. I'll be late.'

'Con, I . . .' Sorcha sighed.

'What?'

'Oh, 'tis nothing. Goodbye.'

Sorcha put the telephone down. Her mind was made up. She'd tried to tell him, but it was obvious what came first in Con's life. It wasn't her any more.

Lulu was right. She had to make her own future.

16

'So, lads, the contracts are signed and the studio is booked for next week. There's only one last thing I'm not happy with. We haven't hit on the right name for the group.'

The four band members were lounging in Freddy's sitting room. He was in the process of tearing the gold foil from the top of a bottle of champagne.

'I rather liked The Leopards,' sniffed Todd.

'Sorry, Todd, it just doesn't sit right. The only bit that we should keep is "the". "The" something works well. Any ideas, anyone?'

'How about The Flies? Insect names seem to be the thing at the moment,' quipped Derek.

'Nope, it's too clichéd. Next!' smiled Freddy.

'Blue Heaven? Yeah, I like that,' Ian offered, to no reaction at all.

Freddy stared blankly back at him. 'Yeah. Anything else?'

The boys shook their heads, before Con eventually spoke up.

'How about The Fishermen? I've always thought it was a grand name for a band,' said Con.

'You would: you're an Irish Catholic,' Todd said cynically.

'The Fishermen.' Freddy mulled it over in his mouth. 'The . . . Fishermen . . .' Yeah, I quite like that,' he nodded.

'Me too,' said Ian.

'It's good,' said Derek.

Todd rolled his eyes heavenwards.

'Well, if anyone comes up with something better,' Freddy said, 'let me know. For now, time for champagne. Here's to the hottest group to hit the music business in years!'

'We hope,' said Todd, taking a glass from Freddy.

'No more of that talk. You all have to believe it's going to happen. Otherwise no one else will. Cheers. To The Fishermen.'

'To The Fishermen,' they chorused.

'So, next Thursday, it's back into the studio. We'll trot out a mix of your own stuff, Con and Todd, and some tried-and-tested hits. I've already been in touch with a couple of record companies, warning them that a demo will soon be on its way.'

'I have a few songs as well, actually, Freddy,' said Derek.

'Then bring them along.'

'I will.' Derek's face lit up.

Freddy took Ian into a corner to look through a drum magazine. Todd moved over to Con.

'Want to get together this weekend to do some writing?'

'Sure.' Con nodded.

'Come to mine. Lulu's flat is bigger. How about eleven on Saturday morning?'

'I'll be there.' Con nodded again.

Todd noted that his co-frontman appeared to be a little downhearted. 'Everything okay, Con?'

He shrugged. 'Yeah, fine.'

'You seem a little subdued, that's all.'

'I'm grand altogether, Todd, really,' said Con.

'I've got to go, chaps,' said Derek. 'I'm seeing Peggy tonight.'

'I thought we were on for a celebratory pub crawl?' said Todd.

Derek swigged back his glass of champagne. 'Sorry, other plans. Thanks, Freddy. See you next week.'

Derek left the flat and headed for the nearby tube station.

Sitting on the train on the way into the West End, he surreptitiously took out the brown envelope Freddy had handed to each of the boys after the contracts had been signed. He felt the pound notes crinkle beneath his touch. Freddy had paid them all a month in advance. Derek knew exactly what he wanted to do with the money.

Peggy's front door was wedged between the chip shop and the newsagent's. The paint was peeling off, and the bell hung lopsided on its nail. Heart banging against his chest, Derek rang it. There was no response.

'Darn it,' he cursed under his breath as he tried the bell a second time.

Just as he was about to turn and go, the door opened a couple of inches.

'Is that you, Peggy?'

The door opened a little wider. 'Er, yes.'

Derek could see she was in her dressing gown. Her normally immaculate hair was tangled and there was a smudge of mascara under one eye.

'Peggy, are you ill?'

'That's it. I've got the flu.'

'You poor thing. Is there anything I can do for you?'

'No, no, I just need to stay in bed and sleep it off.'

'What a pity,' sighed Derek. 'I'd booked a table at the Indian in the high street for half past seven. I was going to take you out to celebrate.'

'Celebrate what?'

'The group's new deal!' Derek beamed. 'We signed the contracts this morning.'

'Gosh. Congratulations.'

'Thanks. I . . . I bought you this.' Derek proffered a small, gift-wrapped box.

'Oh, Derek, why? You mustn't waste your money on me.' She felt a pull on her heart at the sight of Derek – who still had the slight appearance of a schoolboy – thrusting the present in her direction. She couldn't take it. She mustn't.

'Because I wanted to buy you a present. Please, have it. I shall be terribly upset if you don't.'

Peggy's face portrayed a half-smile, half-grimace. 'All right.' She held out a hand. Derek put the parcel into its palm. 'Thank you,' she said.

'Any time. Now, shall I call round tomorrow and see how you are?'

Peggy's eyes darted about the street. 'Er, no, don't bother. I'll probably go back to Mum and Dad's if I'm still feeling like this. And it's probably best if you steer clear of Dad.'

Derek ran a hand through his hair and forced a chuckle. 'Yeah, you're probably right about that one. Well, I'll pop round sometime next week and maybe take you out for that Indian.'

'Sure, Derek. Thanks for the present. I really must be going now. I feel awfully shaky. Bye-bye.' She began to push the door closed but Derek stopped her with his hand.

'I've missed you, Peggy, you know that, don't you? I've never stopped after all these years.' His puppy dog eyes implored her to respond positively.

'I . . .' Uncertainty crossed her face. 'I have to go. Bye, Derek.'

She shut the door, secured it with the chain, and made her way upstairs. In the kitchen of her grubby, run-down flat, she went to the front window and tweaked the net curtain back. There, sitting on the bench below, was Derek. She sighed and let the curtain fall back into position. She really shouldn't have taken the present.

Sitting at her fold-out table, she unwrapped the small parcel. Inside the paper was a velvet-covered box, with the name of a Hatton Garden jeweller. Nestling inside was a beautifully engraved heart-shaped golden locket. She removed it and opened the small clasp.

Peggy,
In my heart, always.
Derek

She put her head in her hands and chastised herself. *What have you done?!* Why, after all the unfortunate trouble she'd experienced with Derek years ago, had she ever gone to the pub to see him?

She tried to analyse her decision.

He had always been kind to her, no doubt about it. The thing that had marked Derek out from the countless other men in her life was the respect he'd shown her. Dozens of teenage boys spent their time trying to get into her underwear, but she'd always sensed that Derek genuinely loved her company. The way he used to 'bump into her' on their walks to school had been sweet, and to be adored so completely was unquestionably very flattering.

But the problem was that she had never really fancied him.

Had she led him on all those years ago? Maybe. Either way, it certainly didn't excuse bricks being thrown through windows.

When she had seen him in the chip shop, she had been impressed by his remarkable career development. That, coupled with his beaming smile and swoosh of thick hair, had piqued her interest. However, this locket all but confirmed he was still infatuated with her. And, if she was honest, she would never feel the same. And why on earth did he still insist on calling her by that silly school nickname?

She knew she had to cut him out, again. This time for good.

She replaced the locket, then opened a kitchen drawer and

hid the box at the back of it. She returned to the window. The bench was empty.

She breathed a sigh of relief.

'Darling, where are you?'

She left the kitchen and made her way to the small bedroom. The curtains were drawn.

'You were ages.'

'Sorry.'

'Who was it?'

She slipped off her robe.

'Oh, no one. An old friend,' she said as she sank into the warm bed and his embrace.

17

Helen stepped off the bus and walked along Baker Street. It was the last day of the summer term and a beautiful bright morning. As she went to cross the road, the sound of two young lads wolf-whistling caught her attention. She looked up at the scaffolding, and the men's eyes seemed to be fixed on her. Scanning the area, she confirmed that there were no other young females in sight. The 'compliment', as offensive as some others found it, must have been meant for her. She smiled in secret delight and thought how much she'd accomplished since she'd first taken this short walk from the bus stop to college. No longer was she the plain, gawky girl from Ballymore. Feeling a surge of confidence, Helen blew the men a kiss, to rapturous cheering. She giggled.

Of course, it was both sad and ridiculous that people took you on face value. Helen's startling change of image some months back had opened the door to friendship and acceptance from other girls in her class that had previously been closed. That, coupled with the fact that her reading and writing abilities were improving by the day, meant her self-belief was growing.

The transformation had taken the most enormous amount of discipline. Helen was not blessed with a fast metabolism, plus most fatty foods brought her face out in spots and meant her skin swam in a sea of grease. She had shown herself no mercy. It had worked. She was fiercely proud. Helen chuckled as she thought of going back to Ireland in two weeks' time. In truth, she wondered how many locals would recognise her.

Helen sprang up the steps and into the college. Nodding a hello to her fellow students, she made her way to the classroom at the very top of the building – the room she would always remember as the starting point of her metamorphosis.

'Hi, Helen. Looking forward to the holidays?' Samantha White, a blonde girl whom she sat next to in class, smiled at her.

'Yes.' Helen put her bag down and removed her jacket.

'What a lovely suit. That colour really looks good with your skin tone. Another new one, is it?'

'I got it from Biba last Saturday. Do you really think it suits me?' Helen blushed with pleasure.

'Yes, it's fab.'

'Thanks. Hi, Mags.'

'Morning all.' Mags sat down at the desk on the other side of Helen. She yawned loudly.

'Heavy night, was it?' Samantha raised her eyebrows.

'Yep,' nodded Mags.

'Ah, well, you can lie in from tomorrow,' said Helen by way of comfort.

'Huh, I only wish I could. I have to be up to go to Devon at six o'clock in the morning with my parents. It's the annual summer holiday. A month of wet weather in a damp house by a windswept beach, surrounded by cousins I can't stand.' Mags shook her head morosely. 'This is the last time I go. I made a deal with Dad. I turn eighteen in November and I'm past family holidays.'

Helen looked at Mags, her lovely face a mask of displeasure, and thought how she'd love to be going on a holiday with her own family.

'You're going to miss my end-of-term party then,' said Samantha. 'That's a shame. It's going to be a blinder. My brother's inviting loads of his dishy friends and even our beloved tutor said he'll make an appearance. Talk of the devil – here he comes,' she whispered. 'Mr Sexy himself. Blimey, he looks worse than you do, Mags,' she giggled.

Tony Bryant walked to the front of the class. As usual in his presence, Helen felt her heart rate increase and the palms of her hands become sweaty.

'Morning, all.' Tony slapped his battered brown briefcase onto the table, then leant on the edge of it himself. 'Well, well.' His eyes surveyed the class. 'I've not seen you all looking so bright-eyed and bushy-tailed at any point over the past year.' He opened up his briefcase and took out a sheaf of papers. 'Sam, love, would you save my weary legs and hand these out, please? The names are on the top left-hand side.'

'Of course, Mr Bryant.'

Samantha stood up, took the papers and began to place one on each desk.

'These, my dear scholastic ones, are your marked and corrected first-year exam papers. And if I were most of you, I would not be smiling this morning. This time next year, the marks will be for real. Based on what you have just produced, eighty per cent of you would fail miserably. I know it's the last day of term and I don't want to be a killjoy, but I think a good few of you should take a serious look at whether you're prepared to come back in September and work doubly hard to make up for lost time. Anyway' – Tony shrugged – 'it's your money you're wasting, not mine.' He slapped his thighs. 'Okay, lecture over. Now I'm going to tell you who has scored the overall best marks for the year. This is the only person that I feel is entitled to a good eight-week holiday, and a serious celebration of her achievements over the past nine months.'

Tony pointed. 'Helen, come and collect this amazing prize of a box of Milk Tray to mark your victory.'

Helen knew she was the only student with that name in the class, but she was so staggered, she found she couldn't move.

'Come on, Helen.' Tony was smiling at her, proffering the box of chocolates.

She stood up and the class broke into spontaneous applause.

Blushing madly and hardly able to look Tony in the eye, she took the box of chocolates.

'Well done,' he smiled at her warmly.

'Thanks,' she muttered and went back to her seat.

The rest of the day passed in a blur for Helen. That night she went home and put the Milk Tray on the table by the window, sat in her chair and stared at the box. She wondered how long chocolates lasted, because she would never eat them. She wanted to frame them instead.

The next morning, Helen went to Mary Quant and bought herself a bright lemon mini-dress to wear to Samantha's party. After, she went to her usual salon to have her hair trimmed and blow-dried, then spent the afternoon painting her nails, bathing in scented water, and trying out different make-up looks to see which went best with her new dress.

By seven o'clock she was ready. Helen hailed a taxi so as not to have the wind spoil her hair.

'Where to, love?'

'Er, Sydney Street. It's just off the King's Road.'

'Righto.'

Helen enjoyed the ride across London. The evening was sunny and warm and the world was fast becoming a very nice place to be.

She slipped out of the taxi in front of a tall, white, terraced house. There was music blaring from an open window on one of the upper floors. The front door was ajar, and Helen made her way up the stairs, clutching her four bottles of Babycham.

'You made it! You look great.' Sam was at the door, shouting above the music. 'If you can get in, come in,' she giggled. 'I'm afraid it's a bit of a scrum.'

The small entrance lobby was overflowing with guests, and the cramped interior of the flat was no better. Helen pushed her way through the sea of bodies, not quite sure where she was heading. Eventually, she found herself in the kitchen, having lost Sam altogether. After she had put her alcoholic offerings down on the sticky, beer-stained worktop, Helen was unsure of what to do next.

'Hi, gorgeous, who are you?'

Helen turned around to see an extremely tall young man leering over her, his breath fetid from beer.

'Helen,' she said quietly.

'Who?' he boomed.

'Helen!'

'Oh.' The young man burped. 'Hi, Helen. Wanna drink?'

'Er, I was just getting myself one.'

Helen turned her back on him purposefully, and opened one of the Babychams. At the moment the bottle reached her mouth, she felt a rogue hand pinch her bottom. Helen gasped in horror, and the Babycham went down the wrong way. She coughed helplessly. The tall man placed a large hairy hand on her back and began to thump it, causing the Babycham to spill out of the bottle and down the front of her new dress.

'Stop it, stop it!' she shouted. 'Now look what you've done!' She turned to him, her face a mask of red-hot anger.

The man held his hands up in a drunken apology. 'Okay, I'm sorry, I'm sorry.'

'Excuse me.' She glared as she moved past him.

'I get you.' The man burped again. 'You've got a flabby bum anyway, love,' he mumbled as she pushed her way out of the kitchen.

When she finally found the bathroom, Helen opened the door and locked it behind her. She sat on the edge of the bath, trying to control her breathing. Her cheeks were burning with embarrassment and anger. It didn't take long for her to conclude that she would go home. That awful man had completely ruined her confidence. She was furious at him. She was furious at herself, too – no matter the transformation she had undergone, underneath the expensive clothes and the make-up she was still stupid, plain Helen.

She unlocked the door and headed for the exit, hoping she could sneak out unnoticed. Helen reached the landing outside without being stopped and had begun to walk downstairs when she felt a sudden tap on her shoulder.

'And where do you think you're going?' a familiar voice asked. She stopped, then turned around to see Tony Bryant grinning down at her.

Helen did her best to compose herself. 'I . . . I need a breath of fresh air. It was stuffy in there,' she mumbled.

Tony nodded. 'Me too. Lead the way then.'

Helen turned and resumed walking down the stairs.

'Blimey, it really *was* hot up there.' Tony took out a handkerchief and mopped his brow. 'I think I must be getting too old for that kind of bash.' Outside he sat down on the front step and patted the space next to him.

Helen sat down, her thigh lightly touching his. For a while, neither of them spoke. Eventually, Tony broke the tension.

'You're looking good enough to eat tonight, Miss McCarthy, if I may say so.'

Helen didn't reply.

'Why so down? I'd have thought after coming top of the

class you'd still be on a high. You really should be proud of yourself, Helen. I alone know how hard you've worked. Every essay must take you three times as long as everybody else and you still managed to beat 'em all hands down.'

Helen nodded silently. She was on the verge of tears and did not trust herself to speak.

'Are you going back up there?' Tony indicated the open door. Helen shook her head.

'Right, well, nor am I. Funnily enough I'm not in a party mood either, but I had to show my face. How about finding a pub or a bar somewhere and having a drink to cool down?'

'I . . .' Helen looked at him, a little surprised. 'Okay then.'

'Good.' Tony stood up and offered his hand to Helen. She took it. He pulled her upright, then tucked her hand into his elbow and patted it. 'Let's go.'

They found a pub a few hundred feet away, up the King's Road. Tony went to get the drinks while Helen secured a seat.

'There.' Tony put down the pint and Babycham on the table. 'Here's hoping you get this in your mouth rather than on your shoes.' He smiled. 'I don't know how long everybody had been drinking in there, but I should think most of the afternoon. Anyway, cheers, here's to the summer holidays.' Tony's voice was full of false cheeriness. 'You look as pleased to see them arrive as I am,' he smirked, taking a sip of his pint.

'Don't you like holidays?' ventured Helen, still feeling ridiculously tongue-tied.

'Yes, I do. But it just so happens that the lady of my dreams will be spending a large percentage of them miles away.'

'I see.' Helen's misery accelerated. 'Can't you go with her?'

'Oh, Helen, if only, if only,' Tony sighed. 'Unfortunately, it's not as simple as that. My life never seems to be.'

'Nor does mine,' she agreed, sipping her drink.

'Well, we are a pair, aren't we?' he smiled, before slapping his hands on his thighs. 'Now, I've told you what's wrong with me. So . . . what's wrong with you?'

'Oh, nothing really, just a boy at the party making a hurtful comment, that's all.'

'Really? My, my, what are lads looking for these days? I would have thought you'd pretty much be their ideal woman. Beauty and brains all rolled into one.'

Helen blushed. 'It's kind of you to say so, Tony, but—'

'I'm not just saying it, Helen.' She confirmed that his eyes were earnest and sincere. 'Learn to take a compliment when it's given. To be truthful, I've always been fascinated by you. It's not often one gets to meet a person such as yourself.'

'Don't I know it.' Helen raised her eyebrows.

Tony sighed. 'Honestly, Helen, where did you get your enormous inferiority complex from? You take everything anybody says as a criticism.'

'Well, you are criticising me, aren't you?'

Tony laughed. 'Lord, no. I'm saying you're unique. I'd venture that was a compliment. Put it this way: if someone told me I was ordinary, I'd be devastated.'

'As a matter of fact, that's all I've ever wanted to be.' Helen drained her glass.

He stood up. 'I'll get another round in and then you can tell Uncle Tony what on earth made you have such a nonsensical ambition. Don't go away now.'

Helen watched him as he made his way across the pub. Whoever the girl was who had stolen Tony Bryant's heart, she was the luckiest person in the world.

Six Babychams later, Helen had done an awful lot of talking. Tony now knew more about her than any other human being she had ever encountered.

'Well, well, well,' said Tony. 'You poor old thing you. And here I was feeling sorry for myself.'

'I don't want sympathy,' said Helen abruptly.

'Nor am I going to give it. Listen, Helen.' Tony took her hands in his. 'I want to say something to you now and I want you to think about what I've said to you later. You are nineteen years old. Yes, you've had a rotten deal through life, but now things are starting to work in your favour. You have a large inheritance to make the most of, and you are better placed to do that than many others because you have a gift.'

Helen gave a small hiccup. 'What "gift"?'

'In all my years of teaching, I've never come across a better mathematical brain. When it comes to figures, you leave the rest of us standing. Plus, you've shown in your business management modules how analytical you can be. Put simply, you're good at making logical decisions.'

'In the classroom,' nodded Helen. 'I don't know how I'd cope in the real business world.'

'Brilliantly, I'd say. Find the idea, Helen, and start your own business. Something small to begin with – don't gamble with every penny – and trust your instincts. I think you'll do extremely well.'

'You seriously think I could run my own business?'

Tony nodded. 'Absolutely, no question about it. And you have the liquid funds to put into it. If I had your kind of money, I certainly wouldn't be teaching in a business school, I'd be out there practising what I preach.' He drained his glass.

'What kind of business appeals to you?' Helen asked.

Tony chuckled. 'Oh, I've always had this dream of running a record company and discovering the Next Big Thing. Who hasn't?' He shrugged. 'Or maybe I'd start a travel agency. Overseas holidays are going to become a huge market in the next few years – you wait and see.'

'Last orders at the bar, folks!' called the landlord.

'Want one for the road, Helen?'

'No thanks. I've had too much already.'

'Righto. Maybe you need something to eat?'

Helen shook her head. She was feeling decidedly sick and the thought of food made her feel worse.

'Excuse me, I . . .'

Ten minutes later Helen returned from the ladies', looking pale and withered.

'Oh dear, Helen, I'm sorry. I've encouraged you to drink too much.'

'It's okay. Could you . . . could you call me a taxi? I think I'd better go home. I really don't feel very well.'

'Of course. I'll take you home myself.'

'Sorry, I . . .' Helen sprinted to the ladies' again. When she came back she saw Tony waiting for her by the door.

'There's a cab for us outside.'

'Thanks. I only hope I can make it.'

Tony thought for a moment. 'Look, my place is five minutes from here in a taxi. I'll take you there and you can go home when you feel better.'

Helen nodded, too weak to argue.

Ten minutes later, she was studying the bowl of Tony's lavatory. She couldn't believe there was anything left inside her to throw up. She staggered out into the living room where Tony was pacing the floor anxiously.

'How are you?'

'Okay. Maybe if I lay down for a while, I might feel better.'

'Sure. Here, let me help you.'

Tony led Helen through to a small bedroom.

She lay down on the bed thankfully, and tried to keep her head from spinning. 'I'm sorry, Tony, I'm really sorry.' She promptly fell asleep.

* * *

Helen woke up feeling disorientated. She looked around the room, the gloomy light of early morning seeping in from behind orange seersucker curtains.

Helen felt her brain playing a tom-tom against the back of her temples. She stood up from the bed cautiously and then walked slowly into the sitting room. Tony was lying full-length on the sofa, snoring softly. In a daze, she tried the broom cupboard and the kitchen before finally locating the bathroom. She splashed water on her face and used Tony's toothbrush to freshen her mouth. Feeling a little better, Helen crept back to the bedroom. She was just about to drop off when she felt the bed sink down to her right.

'How are you?'

She opened her eyes and saw Tony staring down at her.

'Better, I think. Although I've got a terrible headache.'

'Can I get you a Disprin?'

'No, it's probably best I rest my tummy for a while.'

'Okay.' Tony removed a lock of hair from her face and smoothed it back. 'I've been worried about you.'

Helen's bottom lip trembled. 'I'm sorry. I can't get anything right, can I? I can't even drink without being ill and ruining a nice evening.'

'Come on now, Helen. No more of that self-deprecation nonsense.' He playfully pressed her nose like a button. 'You're just not used to it, that's all. Besides' – he leant down so his face was no more than an inch or so from hers – 'I happen to think you're lovely.'

He kissed her gently on the lips.

'Sorry. I . . . I just wanted to . . . uh . . .' He seemed shy all of a sudden, and Helen felt her heart expand.

'Do you know, that made me feel a little better.' She gave a half-smile.

'Did it?'

Helen nodded.

'Are you sure?'

'Yes.'

This time Helen lifted her lips to Tony's, encircled his neck with her arms and pulled him down towards her.

Later, as she lay entwined in his arms, watching his hand stroke her naked belly, Helen thought she might have died and gone to heaven. Anything she'd fantasised about during her own furtive attempts at satisfaction had paled into insignificance against the real thing. She had been able to respond naturally to Tony's gentle coaxing and relax enough to enjoy the experience. The fact that her body could provide her with such pleasure was a revelation.

'You're full of surprises, aren't you?' he said with a smile, as his hand moved from her belly to her thigh.

'What do you mean?'

'Well, you're so uncertain of yourself, but just now, my God, Helen, you were wonderful. I can hardly believe it was your first time.'

'It was, really.'

'Then I'm proud it was with me.' He propped himself up on an elbow and stared down at her. 'Helen, you don't regret what just happened, do you?'

'No, not at all.'

'Good. I'd hate it if you thought I'd taken advantage of you.'

'You didn't, or at least, no more than I did of you.'

They both fell silent and lay looking at the rays of sunshine filtering in through the orange curtains.

'Helen?'

'Yes?'

'You know my situation. My lady is away for a while and . . . look, I'd hate to deceive you into thinking this is something it's not. I'll understand if you don't want to see me again, but . . .'

'But what?'

'But I think we could have some fun together for a while, until she comes back, that is. It sounds awful to put it like that, but it's only fair to place my cards on the table so you're not under any illusions. I respect you enormously, and I don't want to hurt your feelings.'

'I understand what you're saying, Tony.'

'If nothing else, I want us to stay friends, though I have to say I'd miss what we just did.'

Helen turned her face away. She was here, and the mystery lady wasn't. That gave her a distinct advantage. He might fall so madly in love with her that he wouldn't want his other lady back. It was a risk she would have to take. The pain would come later, and besides, she was good at pain.

'Tony?'

'Yep?'

She turned back to him and smiled. 'Would you do that to me all over again?'

18

'So, what do you think, Ben?'

Ben shrugged. 'They're . . . okay, man, sort of okay.'

'Just okay?'

''Fraid so.'

'I see. Well, there's no point in my wasting any more of your time. You're the first company I've talked to. Reg over at TCA has already been on the blower. I said I was giving you first refusal.' Freddy Martin stood up.

'And unfortunately, mate, that's what you've got, a refusal.' He walked around the long glass table to shake Freddy's hand.

'I think you're making a big mistake. You should see them live. They're super.'

'Maybe, but it's the little circles of black vinyl we're more interested in. Sorry, Fred, there's just too many bands fighting for a slice of the action right now. Better luck elsewhere, eh?'

'Sure. See you, Ben.'

'See you, Freddy.' He gave a wave before returning to his desk chair.

Freddy walked along the corridor and out of reception before taking the cage lift down to the lobby. He walked towards Golden Square, opened the black wrought-iron gate and found a bench to sit on.

Freddy clenched his fists. 'Fuck!'

The elderly lady at the other end of the bench made a hasty exit.

Freddy was getting worried. He'd approached four of the five major record companies and had so far enjoyed nothing more than lukewarm interest. If RCA said no next week, that left only the smaller independent labels without the big financial clout to give his group the push they needed. Had he got it wrong for the first time? Were The Fishermen nothing special? Should he cut his losses now and forget the whole deal?

Freddy shook his head. An instinct was still burning somewhere inside him. He'd felt it before with The Tin Men. He was sure The Fishermen *had* something. The trick was getting others to recognise it and put their money behind the group, as he himself had done.

Freddy stood up. In a few days, he was seeing RCA. If nothing came of that, then he'd just have to look to the independents.

Derek had returned a dozen times to the blue door sandwiched between the chippy and the newsagent's. After ringing the bell numerous times, he had resorted to loud, intermittent bouts of knocking, all to no avail. He was confused.

It was a Sunday. Ten minutes to nine on Sunday morning, to be precise. After a session of bell ringing and door knocking, the woman who ran the newsagent's came to the door of her shop.

'You're making an awful racket. She's gone away.'

Derek panicked. 'When? Where?'

'Keep your hair on, luvvie. For a holiday, I think. It is that time of year, you know.'

He breathed a literal sigh of relief. 'Of course. Did she say how long for?'

'No, I only knows 'cos she asked me to water the plants while she's gone.'

'So she will be back?'

The woman chuckled. 'Course. Most people come back from their holidays, don't they?'

Derek spun around on his heel and bounded off down the road.

'None so queer as folk,' the woman muttered as she went back inside to sort the Sunday papers.

Sorcha had only just walked through the door when the telephone rang.

'Hello?'

'Hello, Sorcha.' It was her agent Audrey's voice. 'Good news, darling. You've got yourself your first modelling job.'

'I have?'

'Yes. It's a two-page spread modelling knitwear. It's only a morning's work, but it's certainly a start.' Sorcha heard Audrey shuffling through papers. 'Let me see . . . you'll be shooting in St James's Park next Wednesday. You need to be there at eight.'

'Will I need to take the morning off work?'

'Yes. Say you have to go to the dentist or something. We'll see what this job leads to. If the work begins to come in frequently, as I think it will, you can leave. The pay's good. It's twenty pounds.'

'Twenty pounds?' Sorcha repeated excitedly.

'Is that okay?'

'Oh yes, that's grand, just grand.'

'Good. I've given the magazine your home number. They'll call in the next couple of days. Well done, darling. You're on your way now. Bye-bye.'

'Bye, and thank you, Audrey.'

Sorcha put the telephone down and sank into the nearest chair. A triumphant smile crossed her face. In the past four weeks, she had been to two dozen castings and had begun to think that Audrey must have been wrong about her.

The smile left her face as she contemplated telling Con.

A few minutes later, she heard the key in the door. Her fiancé walked into the room, an evening paper tucked under his arm.

'Hello,' he smiled. 'Isn't it a beautiful evening?'

'Yes. Con?' She watched him as he sat down in a chair.

'What?'

'I've just had some news.'

He looked up at her. 'Go on.'

She crossed the room and knelt by his side. 'You have to swear first that you won't be angry.'

He narrowed his eyes as he stroked her hair. 'Now how can I do that without knowing what it is you have to tell me?'

'I tried to tell you before, but there never seemed to be the right moment.'

Con was looking more concerned now. 'I'm all ears and listening to you, Sorcha. Please get on with it.'

'Well, a modelling agent has taken me on her books. Today I got my first job, modelling knitwear for a magazine. And guess how much I'll be paid for a morning's work? Twenty pounds! *Please* say you're happy for me. My agent says this could be the start of lots of work.'

Con folded the paper on his lap and stared down at her for a while before delivering his verdict. 'I can say that if you want me to but it won't be the truth. You know how I feel about you working. That will never change. But it's your decision if you want to go and flaunt your body.'

'Why, Con, don't be so soft! This is a women's magazine.'

'And what happens when it's swimwear they want you to model, or underwear?'

'Then I'll say no.' Sorcha shook her head. 'If nothing else, think of the money, Con. A whole twenty pounds! And more to come after that.'

'You think that makes me feel better? That I can't provide enough to look after my woman like any decent man should?'

'No, Con, you're wrong. Look at Lulu and Todd. Todd doesn't seem to mind that she supports him.'

'Lulu's different.'

'Why is she, Con? Why?'

'Because . . .' He struggled for an answer. 'Because she's . . . English.'

'And what difference does that make?'

Con wrinkled his nose. 'I'd say all the difference.'

'That's a pathetic answer and you know it!' Sorcha forced back the tears. 'I never knew you were like this, Con, really I didn't.'

'Like what?'

'A chauvinist.'

'And who taught you that fancy word? Lulu?'

'No! I may have come from a tiny village in Ireland, but I am literate.' Sorcha shook her head. 'This isn't getting us anywhere, Con.'

'You're right.'

She looked up at him. 'Do you not love me any more?'

Con sighed heavily. 'Of course I love you, Sorcha. That's why I don't want to see you demeaning yourself.'

'But I'm *not*!' She hit the side of the chair in frustration. 'Work isn't demeaning, Con. It gives you self-respect and independence. And until the time comes when your big deal happens, we need the money. And you can't say we don't!'

'Ah, money. It always comes down to that, doesn't it? I'm not going to argue with you any further. I'm late for Todd already.' He stood up.

'Don't walk out, Con. We have to talk about this.' She

watched as he tucked the paper in his jacket pocket and walked towards the door. 'Please, Con, don't—'

The door slammed behind him.

'Hi, Con, Todd's not here.'

'Oh.' Con stood on the doorstep and shuffled uncomfortably at the sight of Lulu in a short bathrobe. 'He said he'd be back at seven.'

'Yeah, that's what he told me. I'm sure he'll be along soon. Come in before half the street sees me *déshabillée*.'

'Thanks.' Con followed Lulu through the door, down the hall and into the sitting room.

'Want a drink?'

'No, thanks.'

'Okay, but I'm going to have one. I just got a call from my agent. I've landed the lead in the next Hammer movie.'

'That's grand news, Lulu. Congratulations to you.'

'Thanks. I must admit I'm pretty chuffed.' Lulu bent down to retrieve a bottle from a cupboard, giving Con a perfect view of two rounded buttocks. 'Sure you won't join me?'

'No, thanks.' Con turned away and went to look out of the window.

'An Irishman refusing a drink.' Lulu poured a healthy amount of whiskey into a glass. 'Whatever next? Cheers.'

'Cheers, yourself.'

'So, no news from Freddy yet?'

'No.' Con sighed. 'He doesn't tell us much but I'm wondering whether he's having problems getting us a deal.'

'Freddy'll get you a deal, Con. I have complete confidence in both him and the group.' Lulu sat down on the sofa and tucked her legs underneath her. She patted the seat beside her. 'Come and sit down.'

Reluctantly, Con did so.

'Excuse me for being personal, Con, but is there something wrong? You look awfully down. Todd was saying you hadn't been yourself for a while, too.'

'I'm grand altogether, really, Lulu.'

'You sure?'

'Yes.'

Lulu stretched out a hand and patted Con's knee. 'Look, Con, I regard you as a friend and I hope you regard me in the same light. If there's ever anything you want to talk about, you know where I am.'

Con studied the hand on his knee.

'That's kind of you, but I'm grand, really.'

Con heard the sound of a key turning in the lock. He jumped, throwing Lulu's hand off his leg and sending her whiskey slopping over the side of the glass onto her bare leg.

'Steady on, Con. You're as jumpy as a kitten.'

'Sorry, sorry.' Con retreated to his spot by the window as Todd walked through the door.

'Evening, all. Sorry I'm late. The tube stopped for ages at Earl's Court.'

'Darling, guess what?' Lulu stood up, put her glass down and threw her arms round Todd's neck, covering his face with kisses.

'What?'

'I got the part of Veronica! I'm going to be a proper film star.'

'Wonderful, darling. I'm thrilled for you.' Todd hugged her, then removed her arms from around his neck. 'Don't you think you should run along and put some clothes on?'

'Sorry. Con caught me while I was in the bath and we've been having such a nice chat, haven't we, Con, darling?'

Con grunted something in reply.

Todd patted Lulu's bottom. 'Go on. Run along now. Con and I have got work to do.'

'You won't be too long, will you?' she pouted. 'I want to go out tonight and celebrate.'

'The sooner you go, the sooner we'll be finished.'

'Okay. Bye, Con.' Lulu blew him a kiss and left the room.

Todd raised his eyebrows. 'Women.'

'I'll drink to that,' sighed Con.

'Want one?'

'Ah, go on then.' Con gave in.

'A problem with Sorcha, methinks?' Todd fixed them both a whiskey from the open bottle.

'She's got herself signed onto a modelling agency without telling me and now it seems she has a job. Thanks.' Con took the glass from Todd's outstretched hand.

'So? Good for her. Where's the problem?'

Con shook his head. 'I wouldn't be expecting you to understand, Todd. We come from different worlds.'

'And you're living in this one, Con. Don't you think you're being a touch old-fashioned about this?'

'In Ireland, women stay at home and look after the children. They cook, they clean, they care for their family.'

'Erm, pardon me, Con, but I can't believe I'm hearing this.' Todd put his spare hand on his hip. 'For a start, you and Sorcha are not married. You live together, which I'd say is a fairly modern thing to do. Secondly, you don't have a family for Sorcha to take care of. And thirdly, this is 1965, not 1865.'

Con shook his head. 'Look, forget I mentioned it, okay? I shouldn't have said anything. I can't be expecting you to understand.'

'Oh, I understand all right. This comes down to a simple case of male ego and nothing else. Have you ever thought about what Sorcha wants?'

'Let's drop it, shall we?' He gave Todd a stern look.

Todd shrugged. 'Fine. We need to get down to some work

anyway. You can put all your angst into your lyrics. But just one word of advice, Con, and I hope you take it as it's meant: Sorcha is a lovely girl. It's pretty obvious she worships you and she's certainly given you as much support as you needed since you came to England. If you carry on like this, you're going to lose her. Then you'd be sorry. Right, lecture over.' Todd made his way over to the piano, lifted the lid and sat down on the stool. 'How did you get on with that middle eight?'

It was past eleven when Con arrived home. He'd left Todd's at nine, then taken a long walk along the Chelsea Embankment. The sight and sound of the water had soothed him and he'd begun to think more clearly.

When he crept into the bedroom, he sensed that Sorcha was not asleep. He removed his clothes and climbed under the sheets, putting a gentle hand on her shoulder.

'Can we talk?'

'Of course.' She rolled over to look at him.

'I want to say I'm sorry, Sorcha. I've been stupid. Will you forgive me?'

'I will.'

'Good. Come here.' He reached for her and she snuggled into his arms. 'Maybe if I try and explain to you, you might understand.'

'Please do.'

'You know where I came from, the kind of childhood I had.'

'Yes.'

'I watched my mammy struggle to feed me and keep a roof over our heads while my daddy got langers every night in the bars. Then when he came home, I saw the way he'd take out his desperation and misery on her. I was there when Mammy went into labour and thirty-six hours later died with the baby, without my daddy ever showing his face.'

Sorcha watched him silently.

'To be sure, I *promised* myself I'd provide for any woman I made mine, give her a grand lifestyle, make sure she never had a day's worry. When we were living in that terrible place in Swiss Cottage all I could see was history repeating itself.'

'Con, that's ridiculous! You're not drunken or violent. And things are getting better. You have a future that you can almost reach out and touch, it's so close. Besides which, I'm *happy* to go out and earn some pennies.'

'I know that now. I took a walk tonight and saw what an eejit I was being. I'm only explaining to you why I've felt like I have. I want to give you the world, Sorcha, that's all.'

He reached out his fingers and entwined them round hers. 'If it makes you happy to go off and do your modelling, then it's fine by me.'

'Thank you. It does, really.'

'There's something else, Sorcha, something that Todd made me think about. I know I've been wanting to give you this grand wedding, but I'd say it's the piece of paper that matters. If you don't mind, then let's marry quietly as soon as possible.'

'Con, I'd marry you in the drain outside if necessary. I've never cared. It's always been you that wanted the big day.'

'You're sure you're not just saying that to make me feel better?'

'No!' she replied emphatically. 'I have a mind of my own. I don't live and breathe completely to please you,' she said, half laughing.

'Then that's settled. We'll organise it as soon as possible.'

'Grand.'

Con reached over and turned out the light.

They slept, their fingers still entwined.

19

Helen signed the letter with a flourish (finishing a letter was still a triumph, after all). She read the page back to herself.

Dear Aunt Betty,
I am so sorry, but I will not be able to come home to Ballymore this summer as I had thought. I have so much coursework to do and just cannot spare the time. I do hope you understand. I will try and get home in October, at the half-term break. Hope this letter finds you as well as it leaves me.
Your niece, Helen

She folded it in three and stuck it in the envelope. It was not the most expansive work of penmanship, but it would suffice. She didn't need to explain her actions to anybody, as Tony had taught her.

Tony . . . Tony . . . Helen stared dreamily out of her window. Since college had broken up ten days ago, they had spent a great deal of time together, mostly in bed. The thought of leaving him in a week's time to visit Aunt Betty in Ballymore was not one she could even contemplate. Besides which, *she* would be back shortly. There was only another two and a half weeks left to make Tony forget the woman completely, if he hadn't already . . .

Helen checked her watch. Tony was due round in an hour. Just enough time to run out to the postbox, then come back and slip into something a little more comfortable. Helen giggled at the thought of the new black silk undies and suspender belt she'd bought that morning.

As she left the flat and walked down the street, she thought how much she had learnt about men in the past ten days. The way to their heart was not through their stomach, as her Aunt Betty had always indicated. Oh no, it was through a very different part of their anatomy. She compared her feelings for Tony Bryant to those she once harboured for Con Daly. Her connection with Tony was deep, meaningful. Perhaps most importantly, her affection was reciprocated. Helen understood now that Con had been no more than a teenage infatuation. How silly she had been.

Helen popped the letter in the box and turned back the way she had come. Surely, *surely*, although Tony had said in the beginning that this was only a bit of fun between two consenting adults, he must have changed his mind by now? Why, only the other night she'd sat astride him, refusing to move until he uttered the three magic words.

'I love you,' he'd said.

Then she'd made him say them louder and louder until he'd screamed in pleasure.

Back at the flat, Helen put the champagne on ice in the freezer box of the Frigidaire. She'd also bought strawberries and cream to eat in bed as a post-coital snack.

Helen studied her figure in the mirror. Love and a considerable amount of physical exercise had meant she'd lost nearly ten pounds in as many days. Although still shapely, for the first time she could actually now see her hip bones. The new black bra supported her breasts so they spilled out over the lace edge. Helen slipped on a black mini-dress, poured herself a glass of champagne and sat down to wait for her lover.

'You really are incredible.'

'Thank you. Want a drink?'

'Yeah. That was thirsty work.'

Helen reached over to the table beside the bed and topped up the two glasses with champagne. She handed one to Tony.

'Cheers.'

'Yes, cheers.' He raised his glass and took a sip. 'Well, who would have thought that you and I would end up spending most of July in bed together.'

'I know. It's amazing.'

'And I think it's made more special because we both know there's a time limit.'

'What do you mean?'

'With my lady coming back soon, that's all.' Tony looked a little sheepish.

'Oh. I see.'

'Don't look like that, Helen. You're making me feel guilty, and you promised you wouldn't.'

'Sorry. Let's talk about something else, shall we?'

'Course. I was thinking the other day that you need to get some work experience in the outside world.'

Helen frowned. 'You mean, a holiday job?'

'I suppose, yes. I've actually got a friend who's looking for a temporary receptionist.'

'A receptionist? What on earth would I learn from answering the telephone?' She was a little offended.

'More about a company than most of the directors probably know.' He smiled.

'I'm enjoying doing nothing. Apart from you.'

'Ah, but this is a fun place to work,' Tony grinned. 'It's a small record company just off Carnaby Street, right where the action is. Plus, it's only for August. Their usual receptionist is going to Australia for a family wedding.'

'You know I don't need the money.'

'No, I know you don't, Helen. I just thought it might give you some experience while you have some fun and widen your circle of friends in London. Look, forget about it now,' he shrugged.

'Okay. Would you like some strawberries?'

Tony put down his empty glass on the bedside table and pulled her roughly towards him. 'Later.'

Three days later, Helen was sitting in the small reception area of Metropolitan Records. She was only here because Tony had seemed so keen on the idea.

She studied the present receptionist, who looked like a Barbie doll, and comforted herself with the fact that if they wanted long blonde hair and needle-thin thighs, she wouldn't get the job anyway.

'Brad'll see you now. Go up the stairs to the first floor. His office is the first on the right.'

'Thanks.' Helen stood up and followed the girl's instructions. She knocked on the door five times before it was opened. Brad was on the telephone. He signalled to her to sit down and indicated two minutes with his fingers.

Helen studied him as he talked. He was short, dark-haired and attractive in a Mediterranean kind of way.

'All right, Freddy, my boy. I'll see you on Friday at one, usual place. Toodle-oo.'

Brad put the receiver down and sat on the edge of the desk, arms folded.

'Helen, nice to meet you, kid. Tony's spoken very highly of you. You shagging him or what?' Brad sniggered, then noticed

Helen had gone bright red. He cleared his throat and went to sit down behind his cluttered desk.

'Tony has probably told you the role's only for a month. Jilly downstairs is off to the land of koalas for her brother's wedding. There's nothing to the job really, just a busy phone line. You pick up the receiver, answer it, press a button to divert it to one of us four that works up here and Bob's your uncle. Dead boring really, except for the fact you get to meet the odd rock star or two.'

Brad spoke at a hundred miles an hour. Helen managed an 'I see' before he was off again.

'Money's a bit crap as well. We're only a small company, been going for a couple of years now and we're just starting to edge in on the big guns. It means we're running on a shoe-string. But you'll get to know a lot of people. We're expanding all the time and if you do a good job, there might be an opening for you in the future.' Brad threw his arms out. 'So what do you think? Want it or not?'

'I—'

'Listen, give me a call tomorrow morning. You're the only girl I've seen so far. You look good and Tony says you're a little brain box underneath that quiet exterior.' The telephone rang. 'Sorry, love, can you see yourself out? This call's from the States. Speak to you tomorrow, okay?' He gestured towards the door.

Helen nodded, stood up and made her way out into the narrow alleyway just off Carnaby Street. The afternoon was hot, the sun still high in a cornflower-blue sky. When she reached the main road itself, the energy was incredible. Everyone around her seemed to be smiling, exuding youth and vibrancy.

Helen suddenly experienced a surge of happiness unlike any she had ever known before. She had just been offered a job in the heart of the most exciting city in the world. New experiences, new friends. She'd be mad to turn it down.

Turning abruptly, Helen retraced her footsteps. She pushed open the door of Metropolitan Records. The Barbie doll looked up at her questioningly.

'Did you forget something?'

'No. I . . . Could you leave a message for Brad? Tell him I will take the job. I'll see him a week on Monday.'

The Barbie doll smiled. 'Right, I'll tell him.'

'Thanks.'

Helen returned the smile and left the building.

20

Con, Sorcha, Lulu and the other three members of The Fishermen sat outside the registrar's office waiting to be called in. Sorcha wore a cream mini-dress from Biba, bought with the twenty pounds she'd received from her modelling assignment. A short veil was secured by a mother-of-pearl crown and her striking red hair was piled up on her head.

Con held Sorcha's hand tightly in his own. As the registrar emerged, the party stood up. Con hung back and let the others go first. Then he turned to Sorcha and kissed her gently on the forehead.

'I'll never forget how beautiful you look today and what a lucky man I am. You are the love of my life. I worship you. I was just wanting you to know.'

Sorcha's eyes filled with tears. 'I love you too.'

'And one day, I swear I'll have the money to give you the best of everything.'

'Con, it doesn't matter. I'm becoming your wife today and that's what is important.'

'Come on then. Let's go, Sorcha O'Donovan. 'Tis the last time I'll call you that.'

They smiled at each other and walked hand in hand into the office.

The ceremony was short and informal. Todd and Lulu were

the witnesses, and as Sorcha and Con came down the steps of the registry office, the others showered them with confetti.

The six of them went to a pub around the corner for a couple of drinks, then back to Todd and Lulu's flat. Lulu produced a lunch of roast beef with all the trimmings and the champagne flowed.

'I had no idea you could cook like this,' said Todd as he placed his knife and fork neatly on his empty plate.

'I can't,' Lulu smirked, 'but the chef at the restaurant round the corner does a mean Yorkshire pudding, and he's a fan of my movies.' She gave Todd a wink. 'More champagne, anyone?'

'Yeah, fill everyone's glasses. It's time the best man made a speech. And as I am the best, I'll make it,' giggled Todd.

Lulu filled everyone's glass and Todd stood up.

'Well, Mr and Mrs Daly. I'm sorry I have no embarrassing stories to tell of Con's youth. All I can say is that since I have known you both, you seem to have brought the luck of the Irish to the rest of us. I'm sure it won't be long until Freddy gets us the deal that we all deserve.'

'Hear, hear,' murmured Lulu.

'Sorcha, you're a brave woman taking on Con. You're beautiful, gentle, sweet-natured and loyal, whereas he's a difficult, strong-willed, determined bastard . . .' Todd paused and stared at Con. 'All the qualities he needs to help The Fishermen make it. And, although I'm loath to admit it, you're bloody talented too. With that and a wife like Sorcha, I should hate you.' He smiled and raised his glass. 'But I'm very glad you found your way into our lives. Congratulations to you both. To the happy couple, Con and Sorcha.'

They all raised their glasses and drank.

'Okay, okay. Now, we have a present for you.' Todd retrieved an envelope from his jacket pocket. 'This is your wedding gift from the band. We all chipped in. You open it, Sorcha.' He handed the envelope to her.

'Thank you.' Sorcha prised it open carefully. Inside, she found train tickets from London to Brighton, plus a letter confirming a room for two nights with full board at the Grand Hotel.

'Your train leaves at six tonight. We all felt you should go somewhere for a honeymoon,' said Lulu.

'I . . .' Sorcha was so choked she could hardly speak. 'Look, Con.' She showed him the contents of the envelope.

'Don't be cross, Con. I know what a proud bugger you are, but you can pay us back in spades when we hit the big time,' put in Todd, glancing at Con's frown.

'Speech, speech!' shouted Lulu. 'Your turn, Con.'

He looked at the gathering round the table. 'Thank you. It's been a grand day.' He raised his glass. 'To our friends, and my beautiful wife.'

'To the success of The Fishermen,' put in Ian.

'Hear, hear,' said Todd.

Derek said nothing. He'd been in an odd mood all day, as if consumed by something. Although physically present, his mind was elsewhere. He downed his glass of champagne, then reached for the bottle to provide himself a hefty refill.

An hour later, Con and Sorcha left to catch the train to Brighton. Lulu started clearing up and Ian went into the kitchen to help her do the washing-up.

'What's up, Del?' asked Todd, as Derek sat morosely in the sitting room drinking his third whiskey.

'Nothing.'

'Women trouble?'

Derek shrugged.

'It's not still Peggy that's troubling you, is it?'

Derek frowned. 'No, course not,' he replied tetchily.

'Good, 'cos you're about to have the ladies falling at your feet.'

'You think so?'

'Of course. We're gonna have fans and groupies screaming outside our hotels, hot sex on tap twenty-four hours a day.'

'Sure, Todd.' Derek looked at his watch. 'Gotta be going, I'm afraid. I promised Mum I'd be back in time for tea.'

'Party pooper. Okay, mate, whatever you want.' Todd slapped him on the back. 'Hopefully we'll have something to celebrate very soon. Freddy told me yesterday that he's got a producer who's interested. I'll see you on Friday at the gig.'

Derek nodded and stood up as Lulu came into the sitting room.

'Thanks, Lulu. It was a good party.'

'That's okay, Derek.'

'I'll see myself out.'

Lulu and Todd watched him as he left the room.

Lulu shook her head. 'Whatever is up with him? He's had a face you could chop firewood on for the last few weeks.'

'Love, Lulu,' Todd sighed. 'Our Derek's in it real bad.'

Derek walked the first three miles, then caught a bus the rest of the way home. Since he'd spent nearly all his money on the necklace for Peggy, he was having to watch every penny until his next advance was due from Freddy.

He left the bus at the stop opposite the chippy. *Surely* she must be back by now? It had been over a month.

He stood on the other side of the road waiting for the traffic to calm so he could cross, when he saw a man press the bell to the left of the blue door. A few seconds later, the door opened and there was Peggy, looking just as beautiful as the picture he carried around in his mind.

Derek's heart filled with relief and happiness at the sight of her, then with horror as he watched Peggy throw her arms around the man on the doorstep.

An old friend, a relative . . . The comforting words ran through Derek's brain.

His thoughts were cut short as Peggy stood on her tiptoes and kissed the man.

Derek watched in pained disgust for a good minute before the stranger put his arm around Peggy's shoulders and the two of them went inside. The blue door shut behind them.

Derek stood there, rooted to the spot, his limbs paralysed with shock. He felt dizzy and faint. His stomach heaved and he threw up, the vomit covering his precious boots.

Helen answered the ringing phone. 'Metropolitan Records, how can I help?'

'Hello, love, you new?'

'Yes. I'm the temporary receptionist,' Helen replied politely.

'Where's the luscious Jilly? Run off with a rock star?'

'No, she's in Australia.'

'I see, I see. Anyway, can I speak to Brad?'

'Of course, Mr . . . ?'

'Just tell him it's Freddy.'

'No problem.' Helen rang through to Brad.

'Yes?'

'I've got Freddy on the line.'

Brad grunted. 'Tell him I'll call him back later. I'm in the middle of something now.'

'Okay.' Helen reconnected with Freddy. 'Brad sends his apologies but he can't talk now. He's been tied up unexpectedly.'

'How uncomfortable for him,' Freddy quipped.

'He says he'll call you back later.'

'Okay, but you can tell him from me, if he doesn't get back to me by half three, he's missed his chance. Ta-ra, love.'

Helen put the telephone down. It rang again. She picked it up, hoping it might be Tony. It wasn't. Her heart sank. If he hadn't called by now, the chances were he wouldn't make it.

Helen had been in her new position for just over a week. It had taken time to master the switchboard and to learn not to panic when all the lines went off at once. But now she was in control and beginning to enjoy herself. The job was fun and all sorts of colourful people passed through her reception area.

It was clear that Brad was completely disorganised, making appointments and then cancelling at the last moment, leaving her to deal with irate managers and temperamental fledgling pop stars. Even in her short time with Metropolitan, Helen could see the company needed to reorganise itself and employ more staff.

She did not, of course, voice her opinion. She was only a lowly temp, but it was interesting to ponder, during quieter moments, what she herself would do if she ran the company.

Tony had been right. The work experience was useful. She could imagine how dull the actual job might become after a few months, but for now it was new and exciting. She'd already had three invitations to see various groups performing at hip venues in Soho. She'd asked Tony if he fancied coming, but he'd been unable to make it last week and she didn't want to turn up by herself.

'Please ring.' Helen stared at the switchboard, willing Tony to call. The magic must have worked. The switchboard lit up.

'Metropolitan Records, how can I help?'

'Hello, sweetheart, it's me.'

'Hello. Can you make it for lunch?'

'Er, no.'

'What about tonight?'

'Yes, I was calling you to suggest we meet tonight. I'll pick you up at work and we'll hit the town, give ourselves a really good evening.'

'Okay.' *The last hoorah*, thought Helen gloomily.

'I've got to run. See you at six.' He hung up.

Helen stared into the distance. Even though Tony hadn't said anything, Helen knew *she* was back. She reckoned she had returned a few days ago, around the time Tony had started to cut her short when Helen rang his flat. It was a blessing she had this job. If she had been at home all day, she'd have gone mad.

Helen sighed. Tonight she would know for certain.

Just after six, Tony came strolling through the front door of Metropolitan.

He leant over the desk and kissed her on the cheek.

'You look wonderful. Work must be suiting you.'

'It is, thanks, Tony.'

'Come on then. Let's move.'

It was a hot, sultry August night and London was buzzing, but Helen could not shake off her gloom. The pair wandered into a nearby bar for a drink and chatted about Metropolitan Records. Or, rather, Tony asked questions and Helen gave monosyllabic answers.

Eventually, the conversation petered into nothingness and they both sat staring into space.

'Oh dear,' said Tony. 'You know, don't you?' She nodded. 'What can I say? If it makes any difference, I had no idea how attached to you I was going to become.'

'It doesn't make any difference.'

'No, I didn't suppose it would.'

'You're back with her then?'

'Yes,' Tony nodded solemnly.

'And we're finished?'

'Please don't say it like that, Helen. Parts of our relationship are, but I'd hate to think that I'd lose you completely.' He reached for her hand, which was surprisingly cold for such a hot evening. 'You're so special, Helen. I mean it.'

'Stop before I throw up,' she groaned.

'I'm sorry, it wasn't meant to sound insincere. I do mean it. You're one of the most amazing women I've ever met.'

She looked up at him. 'Then why, if I'm so special and amazing, are you going back to *her*?'

Tony shrugged. 'Because I love her, I suppose. Plus, she needs me to look after her. She's . . . fragile.'

'And I don't need you?'

'No. You can look after yourself. She's not strong like you.'

There was another long silence. Tony sighed. 'Look, Helen, I really would hate to see us part on bad terms. We both knew from the outset this was a temporary thing. Now we're in danger of losing a friendship and that would be very sad. Don't you agree?'

'Yes, I suppose so,' she replied slowly.

'I'd like to think that if ever you needed advice or help, you'd be able to come to me. I'll understand if you feel you can't see me for a while, but maybe when you've had a chance to think about it, you'll see what I'm saying makes sense.'

'I can cope. And of course I still want to remain friends. We all need friends, don't we, Tony?' She smiled at him with no emotion, then drained her glass. 'I really must be going.'

'So soon? What about dinner?'

'I said I might drop in at a gig I've been invited to.'

'Oh, okay. It sounds as if you're really settling in at Metropolitan.'

'I am.'

'Don't get too settled. I'll be wanting to see your face in my classroom in a month's time.'

'I'll be there.' She kissed him lightly on the cheek. 'Bye-bye, Tony.'

'Bye, Helen.'

She climbed down from her bar stool. Without looking back, she left the bar.

That night, Helen did not sleep. But rather than giving way to the desolation, she tried to analyse the positive aspects of the summer. From a purely objective standpoint, Tony had done a lot for her in the past year. She no longer felt like a plain lump, and thanks to him, Helen knew she had the ability to please men. He'd also given her faith in her own intelligence and she had every reason to believe her future would be bright. Put simply, her short relationship with Tony had given her a confidence she had not known was within her.

Even so, all these brave thoughts did not take away the pain of rejection.

How did someone harden their heart, seal it off so there'd be no more suffering? Helen didn't know yet, but it was a question she was determined to find the answer to.

21

Derek rang the bell at the side of the blue door, his legs shaking. With no response forthcoming, he held the bell down until he finally heard the sound of footsteps on the stairs. He needed to see her. If he could just make Peggy understand that no man could ever love her like he could . . . This gesture was just the thing.

The door opened. She smiled uncertainly at him.

'Hello, Derek, how are you?'

'Fine, fine.'

'Good.' There was an uncomfortable silence. 'I don't—'

'Where've you been?' Derek cut her short.

'Away on holiday.'

He sniffed. 'Well, you might have told me, Peggy. I've been worried sick.'

'I . . . sorry, Derek.' She thought it best to placate him.

'Never mind. You're back now and that's all that matters. These are for you, to say welcome home.' Derek handed her a large bunch of roses.

'Er, thanks. That's very sweet of you.'

'That's okay. Can I come in?'

'Look, Derek, it's not really a good time. I have to go out in half an hour and—'

'Just for a few minutes,' he urged.

She took a moment to consider. 'Okay then.' She opened the door wider so he could walk through, then shut it behind them. They climbed the stairs to the flat and she led the way into the sitting room.

'These are beautiful.' She smelt the flowers and laid them on a side table. 'So how's the band?'

'It looks as though we might have a deal very shortly.'

She gave a warm grin. 'That's brilliant. You must be very pleased.'

'I am.'

She had not suggested that Derek sit down, but he did so anyway. 'I came to ask you something.'

'What is it?'

He took a couple of deep breaths. 'Well, I . . . You know how I've always felt about you. I love you, Peggy. I always have and I always will. There'll never be another girl for me. And now it looks as though I can give you what you deserve. I mean, a nice life, lots of money, a home of your own. So . . .' Derek fumbled in his pocket and brought out a small leather-covered box. He handed it to her. 'I want to ask you to marry me.'

She took the box and opened the lid. There, nestling in the velvet, was a delicate solitaire diamond ring. She stared at it for a moment, then sighed and shook her head slightly.

'Oh, Derek, you really are so sweet.' She reached forward onto the coffee table, put the box down and picked up a packet of Embassy. 'Want one?'

'No, thanks. I don't smoke. It's bad for my voice.'

'Of course.' She took a cigarette out of the packet and lit it, inhaling deeply as she did so. She sat down opposite him and stared at him intently for a few seconds before she spoke again.

'Derek, I can't tell you how flattered I am. Nobody has ever asked me to marry them before.'

Derek's hands twisted round on themselves. 'So?'

'So, I'm almost embarrassed that you've bestowed the honour on me. I really don't feel as though I deserve it.'

'But you do, you do. You're the most wonderful woman in the world, Peggy,' he answered wholeheartedly.

Guilt consumed her. She took another heavy drag of the cigarette. 'Derek, have you at any point felt as though I've led you on? Given you the impression that I might accept a marriage proposal from you?'

'No, you haven't,' he shrugged.

'I'm glad. Because I'm terribly fond of you. I always have been. And who knows? If the situation was different, then . . .' Her voice trailed off and she stared into the distance.

'What "situation" are you talking about, Peggy?' Derek croaked from a dry mouth.

She took a last drag then ground the cigarette into an ashtray. 'The thing is, Derek, and believe me, there is no easy way to say this, I'm afraid I can't accept your proposal because I'm in love with someone else. In a few weeks' time I'm moving in with him. I want to spend the rest of my life with him, Derek.'

Derek did not speak. He couldn't. His heart beat so hard against his chest he could hear it in his ears.

'Are you okay, Derek?'

He didn't reply, just stared at her, horror on his face.

'I'm so sorry. I really don't want to upset you or hurt you. I feel terrible that I might have given you the wrong impression, but really, I don't see how I could have done. After all, I only came to one of your gigs. We haven't even been out on a proper date, have we, Derek?'

He continued to stare at her.

'Derek.' She swept her hair back from her forehead in agitation. 'Say something, please.'

At last he shook his head. 'I can't.' He stood up, his body visibly shaking. 'I must go.'

'Derek, please don't leave like this! Can't we talk about it? Maybe I could make you understand. I still want to be your friend. I . . .'

She followed him as Derek lurched towards the door and almost tumbled down the stairs in his eagerness to leave. 'Derek, the ring! You've forgotten the ring!'

The door slammed shut behind him.

She slowly made her way back to the sitting room, sat down heavily and lit up another cigarette. She pulled the ring out of its velvet nest and tried it on her finger. It fitted perfectly. She sighed and removed it, replacing it back in its box. When she had finished her cigarette, she took the box into the kitchen and placed it at the back of the kitchen drawer, next to the necklace.

22

Brad appeared in front of Helen and dumped his in-tray on her desk. 'Can you hold the fort for half an hour, love? I know it's your lunch break but everyone else is out. You can take a break when I get back. I shouldn't be long.'

'Sure.'

'Good girl. Oh, and can you sort out my in-tray if you get a chance? There's stuff from months ago I haven't got around to reading. Keep what should be actioned and bin the rest.'

'But I—'

'Use your common sense. You seem to have lots of it. See you later.' Brad jogged towards the door.

The hour between one and two was always quiet. Helen had been looking forward to her daily salad sandwich at the cafe round the corner. Sighing, she pulled the in-tray in front of her and began to sort through its contents.

Thirty minutes later, her reception desk was covered with paper. Helen was horrified at what she'd found. Twelve unpaid bills stretching back over four months, and seven follow-up demands only now opened by her own fingers. Several threatened legal action. But the worst, from the Inland Revenue, named a court date in two weeks' time. The amount the Revenue alone were demanding ran into thousands of pounds.

Helen couldn't understand how Brad could have ignored

such aggressive, threatening letters. If he didn't respond soon, surely Metropolitan would find itself in serious trouble. Helen shook her head and began to sort the letters into three piles: urgent, very urgent and incredibly urgent. She'd have to give Brad the bad news when he returned from lunch.

'I like their sound, I like their look and I definitely think they've got something.' Brad took a sip of his pint.

'Good. So are you going to make us an offer or what?'

Brad shrugged. 'I dunno. We're a small company, Freddy. We have four quite successful groups and one mega-seller on our label. You're asking for serious time and money to be spent on your lot. Our resources are stretched as they are. If this had been a year ago, I'd probably be snapping them up, but as it is, we're at full stretch with the bands we do have.'

'Come and see them, Brad. They really are great live. Trust me on this,' Freddy implored his old friend.

'Sure, I'm willing to do that. The problem is, I know the kind of deal you'll want financially, and I just don't think Metropolitan Records can provide it at the moment.'

'Look, you know how I admire you as a producer, Brad. You're one of the best, and I really think Metropolitan is going to take off in the next couple of years. Therefore, if you're willing to give my boys a shot, we in turn might be prepared to come to some kind of a compromise on the financial side of things. We could, for example, take less upfront for a larger royalty.'

Brad drained his pint glass and smiled at Freddy. It was a decent compromise. 'Okay, you win. I'll come and see them at their next gig.'

'Thursday night at the Civic. Should be a good crowd. They've gathered quite a following.'

'Fine. I've got to run, mate, sorry. I'm late for my next appointment as it is.'

'No problem. I'll meet you at the Civic on Thursday at seven thirty. Try to make it as near to the start as you can.'

'Sure. Cheers, Freddy.'

Freddy watched Brad leave the pub. He signalled to George the barman to pour him another pint. He hoped he hadn't sounded too desperate, but Metropolitan Records really were his last port of call before he had to admit defeat.

It was 6.30 p.m. and there was still no sign of Brad. Everyone else had gone home. Helen prowled round the reception area wondering if she should just leave the bills on her boss's desk with a note attached to them.

Just as she was putting her coat on and switching off the lights, Brad swung open the front door.

'Hi, kid. You still here?'

'Yes.'

'Working overtime even as a temp, eh? Jilly will have to watch out for her job. She always vanished at five thirty on the dot. Go home now, love. See you tomorrow.' He started to walk past her in the direction of the stairs.

'Brad, I was waiting for you actually.'

He spun around. 'Yeah? Why?'

'Because of these.' Helen scooped the pile of bills off her desk and handed them to him.

'What exactly are "these"?'

'The contents of your in-tray. I really think you'd better read them.'

'I will, tomorrow.'

'No, I think you should read them now actually,' Helen urged.

Brad shrugged. 'Okay.' He sat down on the orange sofa and flicked through the pile, his hands slowing down and his brow furrowing as he began to take in the contents of the letters. Helen sank down into the chair behind the desk.

Brad let out a whistle. 'Dearie me.' Helen said nothing. He looked up at her. 'Right old mess this, isn't it?'

'Not if you have the money to pay them immediately, no.'

There was silence as Brad looked past her. 'I don't think we do, love, I don't think we do.' He put the bills down and nodded, seemingly to himself. 'Fancy a drink?'

He looked so desolate Helen felt she couldn't refuse.

Half an hour later, in a bar around the corner, Brad was on his fourth whiskey.

'The problem is, Helen, that I'm a record producer, not an accountant. I used to work for one of the big guns. My job there was spotting talent and producing their LPs. I was good!' He took a swig of his drink. 'I set up on my own a couple of years back because it all seemed so easy. I took out a bank loan, put all my savings into starting Metropolitan and things really have gone very well. I mean, The Trojans stand to make us hundreds of thousands if they conquer America, as it looks like they will.'

'If that's the case, why, if you don't mind me asking, have you got a problem paying these bills?'

Brad sighed heavily and drained his glass. 'Cash flow, love, cash flow. We're owed thousands of pounds from record shops. Being a small outfit, we have to sell on a sale-or-return basis. Obviously, we want to get as many LPs as possible into the shops. So we have to absorb the upfront costs ourselves until we're paid.' Brad put his head in his hands and rubbed his temples. 'Also, the record business is all about speculating to accumulate. We give our groups advances, then pay for the recording, manufacturing, marketing and distribution of their records. All we can do is sit and wait until we start seeing the return. It's just whether it'll be soon enough to stop us going down the tubes.'

Helen nodded.

Brad was staring at her. 'Any ideas? You're the one doing a business course. Are we doomed?'

'I'm no expert and I'd have to look at your bank statements to see what comes in and what goes out before I could give an opinion. To be honest, I think you should contact an accountant, someone qualified to make a real judgement.'

'Yeah, but what do I pay him with? Buttons?'

Helen scratched her head. 'Have you really got no money in the company account?'

Brad leant back on the shabby banquette and folded his arms. 'Maybe a few hundred quid.'

'Oh dear.' Helen liked Brad and wanted to help. 'Why don't you pop across the road and get the cash books and I'll get you another drink.'

'It comes to something when your temp receptionist is having to sort out your finances and pay your bar bills. Yes please.' He smiled gratefully.

Forty-five minutes later, the two of them were poring over the books.

Helen shook her head. 'Oh, Brad, things really are dire. It seems the letters I uncovered today are just the tip of the iceberg.'

'I know. We did have a part-time bookkeeper, but six months ago he left and I just haven't replaced him. I thought I could do it myself, but I'm up to my eyes with other things and, to be honest, I was hoping that maybe if I didn't face it, it would go away. It won't, will it?'

'No, Brad, it won't.' On home territory, her quick brain cleaving through the columns of figures, Helen was feeling more confident of her opinions. 'It's difficult to study these here with all this noise. I could take the books home with me tonight and try and go through them properly. I'm not saying I'll have any answers for you, but I can at least give you a clearer indication of exactly where you stand.'

The Last Love Song

'Helen, you're a gem.' Brad was looking at her as if she alone could save him. 'You know I can't pay you.'

'Yes, Brad,' she smiled, 'I've just about gathered that much. Call it work experience. It'll be good for me.' Helen closed the two books and tucked them under her arm. 'I'd better be going. Are you in first thing tomorrow morning?'

'I think I'd better be.'

They stood up and walked towards the door of the pub.

'Try not to worry. I'm sure there'll be a way out.'

'Do they have escape tunnels in debtors' jail? Night, Helen.'

'Night, Brad.'

The following morning, Helen entered Brad's office. He was still in last night's clothes, and hadn't shaved.

She put the books on his desk and sat down.

'Do you want the bad news or the bad news?' Brad let his head drop onto his desk. 'The company is over twenty thousand pounds in debt. Even if you collected every single penny that's outstanding from your creditors next week, there would still be a five-thousand-pound shortfall.'

Brad nodded silently.

'However, I did do a medium-term forecast for you last night, looking at a growth of sales of fifteen per cent a year, not even considering the large amounts The Trojans may well earn for Metropolitan if they take off in the States as you believe they will. As long as the company is run on a more prudent and sensible basis, the figures in the next couple of years start to look much healthier.'

'That's all well and good, but how do I get from here to there?' sighed Brad.

'Well, it's only my opinion, and as I've said, you should seek the advice of a professional . . . but I think you have three alternatives.'

'I'm all ears, Helen. Hit me with it.'

'Number one, you petition for bankruptcy immediately and wash your hands of the company. That'll get everyone off your back. Number two, you try and find a buyer for Metropolitan Records who will look at the medium-term forecast and at least cover your debts if not actually paying you much for the company. Or number three, you find a private investor to inject a considerable amount of cash into the business immediately.'

'I see.' Brad shook his head. 'None of them sound very palatable. Any way you look at it, I lose control of my little empire. That's why I left the big guys, to have some autonomy.'

Helen shrugged. 'But you said last night you weren't an accountant, Brad. If you're going to run a company, at the very least you should have someone who is competent to look after the financial side of things.'

'I know, I know. I've got it all wrong, Helen. Well, there's no point in dragging it out any longer. I'll have to declare myself bankrupt. After all, it's unlikely anyone will want to buy a pile of debts.'

Helen took a deep breath.

'Actually, Brad . . . I might.'

The idea had come to Helen in the early hours of the morning. Her brain was still working overtime, even though she'd closed the books, got into bed and switched off the light in a vain attempt to get some sleep.

If an injection of cash could be made, and as long as the company was run sensibly, Helen sensed there was a possibility of serious success. Metropolitan's major attribute was Brad himself. In a very short time he'd sniffed out several bands who were headed for success and signed them up. The music business certainly respected him. All he needed was to make one successful discovery every couple of years and the potential payoff was huge.

But how did one set about convincing a bank that this was the case? No reputable financial institution would take the chance. It had to be a private investor, someone who saw the potential and was prepared to take a risk.

Helen had sat bolt upright. The answer was staring her in the face.

She had switched on the light, retrieved the books and a large pad of paper, and begun to sketch out what kind of level of finance she'd be prepared to offer and, equally, what she'd expect from Metropolitan in return.

Helen knew Brad was desperate and also that he was hopeless with money. This put her in a strong position, but she didn't want to abuse that. If she was to invest in Metropolitan Records and become a partner in the company, then things had to be fair from the start.

She'd be risking almost twenty-five thousand pounds just to keep the company afloat. Then she'd have to provide some liquidity to see the company through the next twelve months, until the cash started to flow in.

'You?' asked Brad, astonished.

'Yes, me.'

'Not being rude, Helen, but where would you get hold of the kind of money Metropolitan needs?'

'My parents died when I was young and their money was invested for me. It's grown into a very substantial amount. I inherited it all on my eighteenth birthday.'

'Blimey, love, you're full of surprises, aren't you?' said Brad. 'And exactly why would you want to help?'

'Because I want to do something with my money and I can see Metropolitan's potential.'

The telephone rang on Brad's desk. Helen answered it and passed it to Brad.

'It's Billy Friar, the manager of The Trojans, from the States.'

'This'll be a long one. They've been trashing hotel rooms again. Look, let's meet up at one for lunch to discuss things further.'

'Okay.'

Helen went downstairs and sat behind the reception desk. Her adrenalin was pumping, her concentration wandering as she answered the telephone.

'Hello, Metropolitan Records. Can I help you?'

'Yeah, Brad, please. It's Freddy Martin.'

'I'm afraid he's in a meeting. Can I take a message?'

'Tell him not to forget about the gig at the Civic tonight. I'll see him there around half seven.'

'I'll tell him, Freddy.'

'Good girl. Wanna come along to the gig tonight and see the hottest band around?'

'I'm afraid I'm busy. Another time maybe.'

'Sure. Mind you tell him to be there tonight.'

'I will. Goodbye, Freddy.'

'Bye, love.'

An hour later, Helen and Brad were eating sandwiches in the pub.

'So, what you're saying, simplified, is that you'd be prepared to pay off Metropolitan's debts, and also inject enough money to keep us going for the next twelve months?'

'Yes.'

'And what you want for that in return is fifty per cent of the company?'

'That's correct.'

Brad sighed and shook his head. 'I dunno, love. I'm so used

to being autonomous. Would I have to run to you every time I had to make a decision?'

'A financial decision, yes. As far as the music side of the business goes, I'll be completely guided by you. I'm well aware I know nothing about bands and what sells. If you spot a group with potential, as long as the figures work, then that's fine by me.'

'Okay, okay, so, let's put a test case.' Brad took a bite out of his sandwich and chewed thoughtfully. 'I'm going to see a group tonight. I've heard their demo and if they're as good live, I'd be keen to sign them. Would I have the autonomy to do that?'

'Well, I presume what would happen is that we'd sit down and work out a suitable and sensible financial package. But yes, if you thought they had what it takes, I'd be happy to go along with you.'

'So you really would leave that side of things to me?'

'Absolutely.'

Brad nodded. 'Okay. Now, I have to say this, love, you are only a temporary assistant with an inheritance and a year's business course behind you. Do you think you could cope with running the financial side of Metropolitan?'

'No, not immediately. I thought maybe we could employ an accountant for a while, someone who has had experience in the music business. They could put some order into the company and at the same time train me to keep the financial side of things on track. Only when I'm completely confident I can do the job myself would I look to take over the reins. Remember, it'll be my money keeping the company going and I don't want to jeopardise things by running before I can walk.'

'That sounds sensible. I know a good accountant chap who left Parlophone a while back. He won't be cheap, though.'

'Then I'll have to learn quickly, won't I?' she smiled.

Brad rubbed his face with the palms of his hands, then yawned. 'I'm wrecked, Helen, absolutely wrecked.'

'I'm sure you are. Look, Brad, why don't you sleep on it? But make a decision by the end of the week. The sooner you make your mind up, the sooner we can deal with the Inland Revenue and start clearing some of these debts. Otherwise there might be no Metropolitan Records at all.'

'Yeah, you're right. Blimey, Helen, it must have been fate you coming to work for us. At least now I've got an option. And whatever I decide, I'm grateful for all your help.' Brad stood up. 'I'm going home for the afternoon. I've got to get my head straight about all this and I can't do that until I've had some sleep.'

'Okay, Brad. If anyone calls, I'll tell them you're in a meeting.'

She watched him as he sauntered out of the pub, his hands deep in his pockets.

She knew he'd agree. What choice did he have?

She smiled, thinking what a pleasant alternative to pain a smidge of power was.

Brad woke at six o'clock, feeling disorientated and hungover. He showered, made a strong cup of coffee, then picked up the telephone and dialled Tony Bryant's number.

'Yep, everything she told you is true. She's a very wealthy young lady with a hell of a head for figures. But she's still naive emotionally. Don't you dare manipulate her, Brad.'

'Huh? I think it's her who's manipulating me. She holds all the cards and is asking for half of the company.'

Tony chuckled. 'That's my girl. She's had a bloody good teacher, don't forget, Brad,' he quipped.

'So you think she's kosher?'

'Oh yeah, totally. Helen's as straight as a die. If I were you, I'd snap her and her money up before someone else does.'

'You think I should give her half the company?'

'Well, from what you've said, there isn't a company for much longer. Remember, half of something is better than all of nothing.'

'Yeah, I suppose you're right. Anyway, thanks for the advice.'

'Any time. Let me know what happens.'

'I will. Bye, Tony.'

Brad swung out of his flat at ten to eight and headed for the Civic, a trendy club just off Brewer Street. Watching a potential signing was the last thing he wanted to do when he wasn't sure whether he'd got a record company or not, but the earache he'd receive from Freddy if he didn't turn up just wasn't worth it.

Brad pushed his way through the crowd at the bar and ordered a beer, then tried to find a dark corner so Freddy wouldn't spot him.

The group came on stage to decent applause and a lot of wolf-whistling. There was no doubt they were an attractive bunch of lads.

The group started with one of the songs on the demo tape. They played it well and the audience's reaction was positive. Then the bass guitarist came forward and took the microphone.

'I've got a new one for you all. It's called "Can Someone Tell Me Where She's Gone?" Okay, let's go.'

The bass guitarist sang the first verse alone, accompanied only by the lead guitar. He had a great voice, deep and melodious. At the chorus, the band backed him with tuneful harmonies and a well-constructed arrangement. The middle eight needed some work, but the tune was undoubtedly catchy. Brad felt the hairs prickle on the back of his neck. The audience had fallen silent, but after the last note a huge surge of applause rang round the club.

The song was something special. Brad could still hear the

haunting melody line in his head. It was a perfect Christmas debut single. It was August now . . . under four months to record the single, organise the PR and launch the group onto the scene. If they could compose songs like that on a regular basis, he was on to a winner.

Brad stopped himself. It was pointless getting excited until he knew what was happening with Metropolitan. On the other hand, if he did bite the bullet and sell Helen McCarthy half the company, this band could be his.

Brad had heard enough. He left the Civic and walked back to the office. He unlocked the front door, ran up the stairs and searched his cluttered desk for his address book. Having found Helen's details, he locked up the office and hailed a taxi.

'Hello.' She was wearing a dressing gown and her face was shiny with some kind of cream that she'd hastily tried to remove before answering the door.

'Sorry it's so late, Helen, love. Can I come in?'

'Of course.' She let him pass.

'Nice place you've got here,' he commented as he stood uncomfortably in the middle of the room.

'Thanks. Please sit down, Brad.'

He did so. Helen took the armchair opposite and waited expectantly.

'Look, Helen, I just came to say that if your offer's still on the table, I'll take it. I've put so much work into Metropolitan that I couldn't bear to lose it. This way, at least, I'm only losing half.'

Helen nodded, pleased. 'Wonderful news! We need to finalise some details then and obviously get some documents drawn up by a solicitor.'

'As soon as possible,' Brad agreed. 'I presume you'll be cutting short your business studies course?'

'Well, it does seem rather pointless now I have the real thing to keep me busy.' She smiled.

'I'm not casting aspersions on your obvious head for figures, but you will have an awful lot to learn.'

'I know. And that's why we'll employ an accountant as soon as possible.'

'Fine. As long as you are happy to do that, and you really will be prepared to let me get on with the creative side of the business without interfering, then let's run with it.' Brad smiled at her and held out his hand. 'Shake on it.' Helen grasped it firmly. 'Howdee, partner,' he laughed. 'Welcome to Metropolitan Records.'

'Thank you, partner.'

'Look, I'll leave you to get your beauty sleep now. We can talk tomorrow morning.'

'Sure.'

'Oh, just one more thing.'

'Yes?'

'I've seen a band who I really think might have something. I know the timing isn't good but if I don't snatch them up, then someone else is bound to. I want to call their manager and make them an offer tomorrow. It would mean putting up some kind of initial advance, but I really think they're worth it.'

Helen wondered if Brad was testing her. She shrugged casually.

'If you think Metropolitan Records needs this group, then I won't argue against it. I've no idea how much a band is worth.'

'Depends how desperate they are,' he laughed. 'I reckon we can get this particular group for a relatively small amount of money.'

'That sounds like a good start.'

'Yes, well. Anyway, I'll leave you be.' Brad stood up and headed for the door. 'Night, Helen, and thanks for saving my bacon.'

'That's okay. There's just one other thing that needs addressing.'

'What's that?' Brad turned.

Helen's eyes twinkled. 'I think we should find ourselves a new temporary receptionist, don't you?'

23

'Well, did he turn up?'

Six pairs of expectant eyes gazed at Freddy.

Freddy shrugged. 'I don't know, Todd, I really don't. If he did, he didn't make himself known to me, but they do that sometimes. I'll give him a ring tomorrow morning.'

A chorus of cursing rang out from the band members.

Lulu and Sorcha squeezed their respective men's hands in a show of support.

'Don't get downhearted, lads. Even if he didn't show, there's no reason why he wouldn't turn up at a gig next week. Come on, what can I get you to drink?'

'Beers all round, I think,' Todd answered.

'And gins for the girls, Freddy,' said Lulu.

Freddy stood up and made his way to the bar.

'I dunno.' Todd lit up a cigarette. 'I always said I wasn't sure about Freddy. Maybe we should be looking for another manager. He keeps saying he'll get us a deal, but most of the big boys have turned us down.'

'Give your man a break, Todd,' said Con. 'He's doing his best. Besides, maybe it's us, our music. Maybe we're not after being as great as we think we are.'

'Bollocks, Con! We may have been a bit rough around the edges a few weeks ago, but now we're shit-hot!'

'And who has helped us tighten up? Why, your man Freddy, that's who,' murmured Con.

'Boys, boys, come on now. There's no point in fighting amongst yourselves,' said Lulu.

'Yeah, peace, man. It's all cool. Anyone want a drag?' Ian smiled beatifically and waved his joint in the air.

'No thanks. Where's Derek?' asked Todd.

'Last time I saw him he was heading for the bogs. Right miserable so-and-so he's been tonight,' said Ian.

It was true. Derek had been nothing short of morose all evening.

'Woman trouble, no doubt,' said Todd as Freddy arrived back with a tray of drinks. 'He's always been a bit . . . sensitive in that department. Anyway.'

'Cheers,' said Freddy brightly, raising his glass to his lips. No one else responded. 'Come on, lads. No one said the path to fame and fortune was going to be easy. I told you it might take some time.'

'Freddy's right,' said Lulu. 'You've got to keep believing in yourselves. Otherwise, why should anyone else?'

Derek slunk back to the table. He had large grey rings under his eyes, which themselves were bloodshot and angry. When he sat down, the mood at the table, already low, plummeted through the floor. Lulu made a face at Todd, and gestured to Derek with her eyes. Todd nodded.

'Come on, Derek, let's go and get some fresh air.'

Derek failed to respond. Todd put an arm around him and practically had to lift him from the bar stool.

Outside, Todd lit up a cigarette. 'So,' he muttered, taking a puff, 'what's up with you?'

Derek didn't respond.

'It's not to do with that Peggy, is it?'

Derek's pale cheeks filled with colour.

'It is, isn't it? Did she tell you where to get off?'

Derek remained silent.

'Honestly, Derek, you're an idiot! You've had a thing about her since you were thirteen. Haven't you got the message yet? I mean, she's an attractive girl, sure, but nothing spectacular. Believe me, there are plenty more where she came from.'

'What would you know about her? She's the most beautiful, kind, gentle girl in the world. There'll never be another like her, never!' Todd had always thought his cousin a sweet little fellow, but tonight, Derek was manic. 'We had our problems in the past, but she came to see the band play. Why would she do that unless she loved me?' Derek hit the brick wall of the pub with an open palm. 'She took the necklace I bought her. She wouldn't have done that unless she wanted me. It just doesn't make sense!'

'Perhaps she was being polite?' Todd offered.

'Shut up, Todd. I know her!' Derek looked up at his cousin's bemused face, teeth gritted.

'Okay, okay, I'm sorry. Calm down.' Todd took a large drag on his cigarette. 'Even if she is some sort of goddess, Derek, surely she can't be worth this awful state you're in?'

'I wouldn't expect you to understand. Just leave it, will you?'

'All right, I'm sorry.'

They stood silently for a while, taking in the night air.

'It's not her, you know.'

Todd looked round at Derek. 'What do you mean?'

'It's him.'

'Who's "him"?'

'This man she's seeing. She'd have said yes to me if it wasn't for him. He's turned her head. He's bad for her.'

'Are you trying to say that you asked Peggy to marry you and she refused?'

Derek nodded.

'Aha, now it all becomes clear. She turned you down because she has another boyfriend?'

'Yes, but she doesn't love him, I know she doesn't.' Derek shook his head adamantly.

Todd was beginning to feel out of his depth. 'I've said it before, mate, when we make it – which we will – women will be queuing up to date you. You'll forget all about Peggy!'

'You don't get it. Nobody gets it. The whole point of the band is to impress *her*.' Derek stared at Todd intensely. 'Without her, I'm nothing.'

Todd shifted about uncomfortably. 'Well, I wouldn't say that, Del. You're a bloody good guitarist for one thing!' He laughed heartily, but Derek remained stony-faced, his mind a million miles away. 'Anyway, let's drop it now. Coming back in for a beer?'

Derek shook his head. 'No. I'm going home.'

He spun on his heel and sunk his hands into his pockets. As he walked away, Todd could hear him mumbling to himself. 'It makes no sense. No sense . . .'

Todd watched his cousin march off into the distance, stubbed out his cigarette on the wall, and went back inside.

Brad picked up the telephone on his desk and dialled Freddy Martin's number. This was a call he'd enjoy making. The line rang twice before it was answered.

'Freddy, Brad here.'

'And where did you get to last night?'

'As a matter of fact I was there. Apologies for not making contact but I had to rush off early.'

'No worries. What did you think?'

'Of The Fishermen?'

'Yeah.'

'I thought they have definite potential. Which is why I want to offer them a deal.'

'I see.' Even though he was trying to play it cool, Brad detected both relief and joy in Freddy's voice.

'They need work, Fred, and time. And a lot of money.' Brad rocked on his desk chair as he recalled the performance. 'The thing that sold them to me was that second number, "Can Someone Tell Me Where She's Gone?"'

'It's good, isn't it?' Freddy replied.

'It's got Christmas Number One written all over it, Fred.'

'I'm glad you think so.'

Freddy wasn't giving anything away, as Brad expected. 'Tell you what, that bass player is something special. What a voice.'

'Con Daly. He wrote that song with Todd Bradley.'

'Yeah, well, that's another reason why I'm interested. Metropolitan would want all publishing rights to their songs.'

'Hold on a minute, Brad. If you're saying you want to offer my boys some kind of a deal, why don't we get together next week sometime? Thrash things out over lunch?'

'Okay. Name the day.'

'Would Wednesday suit?'

'Fine by me. Drop by the office at one. I'll book a table somewhere close by.'

'Great. See you then.'

'Sure. Cheers, Freddy.' Brad put the telephone down as Helen appeared in the doorway. He beckoned her in.

'I've called a solicitor and made an appointment for next Tuesday,' she said. 'I gave him an idea of what we had in mind and he's going to have some sort of basic contract drawn up that we can fiddle around with.'

'Good.' Brad tapped his biro on the top of the desk.

'The sooner we sort out the legal details, the sooner we can start paying those outstanding bills.' Helen looked down at the mess on Brad's desk. 'And start implementing some organisation around here.' She picked up a black-and-white photograph lying on the top of a precarious pile. 'Who is this?'

'The group I want to sign. They're called The Fishermen. What do you think of them?'

Helen studied the photograph. 'They look fine.' She was just about to put the photo down when, from under one of the gleaming pageboy haircuts, a familiar face caught her eye. Glancing at the bottom of the photo, she read, 'Todd, Con, Ian and Derek are The Fishermen.'

Brad watched her as she swayed slightly.

'You okay, Helen?'

'I'm fine, just fine.' She placed the photo back on the desk. 'Have . . . have you called their manager yet?'

'Yes. We're meeting next Wednesday. As long as you're happy with the figures I'm working on, then I'll put the offer to him over lunch.'

Helen had regained her composure. 'I'm sure we'll be able to come up with something. As we know, you're the one with the nose for talent. I'll see you later.' She offered him a strange little smile and left the room.

The following Wednesday, Helen waited in an agony of tension for Brad to return from his lunch with Freddy Martin, The Fishermen's manager. She hardly dared look too eager, after all she'd said about keeping costs low for the time being, but, truth be known, if The Fishermen had wanted four times what she and Brad had agreed to offer them, Helen would have capitulated.

And all for the look on Con Daly's face when Brad introduced her as a director of Metropolitan Records . . . He had held all the power in their former lives. She would have done anything for him. But now, the tables had turned. Her value was not determined by the gaze of Con Daly. That pleased her, perhaps more than she had anticipated.

To stop herself from thinking on what Brad and Freddy were talking about, Helen picked up the telephone and dialled Tony's number. She'd been unable to get hold of him for the past few days and he still didn't know her news.

'Hello?'

'Tony, it's me, Helen.'

'Helen, hello.' He sounded harassed.

'How are you?'

'Okay, okay. You?'

'Very well. I have news, Tony. You are speaking to the almost-fifty-per-cent-partner of Metropolitan Records.'

'What?'

Helen quickly ran through the events of the past week.

'Wow, Helen, that's amazing! Congratulations.'

'Thank you. It's not going to be a signed-and-sealed deal until next week, though, but I don't think anything will go wrong.'

'I think you've made a very shrewd investment. Brad knows what he's talking about when it comes to music. Blimey, Helen, at this rate you'll be a tycoon before you're twenty-one!'

'I do hope so, Tony,' she said seriously.

'I presume this means we won't be seeing you back in my classroom when the new term begins?'

'It does.'

'I'll miss you. I've lost my best pupil.'

'Well, it's thanks to you that this opportunity has presented itself. So, I was going to suggest that next week, after I've signed the contracts, I take you out to dinner to celebrate. I owe you a lot, Tony, really.'

'You owe me nothing, sweetheart. All I did was give you a little bit of confidence.'

'Whatever, I'd still like to treat you. Why don't we meet at Kettner's at eight on Thursday?'

'I see you're getting to know all the "in" places to eat already,' he teased. 'Next Thursday would be perfect as my lady's going away for a few days.'

'Then I look forward to it.'

'So do I. Bye, sweetheart.'

'Bye, Tony.'

24

Freddy rang around the four members of The Fishermen and asked them to meet at his flat at six thirty that evening. He then went down to his local off-licence and bought four bottles of the best champagne they had in stock.

Walking home along Belsize Park Road, Freddy acknowledged his relief. After weeks of wondering whether he'd put his reputation on the line for nothing, his persistence had paid off. Okay, so it wasn't RCA or EMI, but after an intense negotiation with Brad, Freddy reckoned he'd got himself and his lads a good deal.

At six twenty-five, Todd arrived with a sullen-looking Derek.

'Come in, come in,' said Freddy jovially. He led them into the sitting room. 'How are you, Derek?'

'Fine, thanks.' Derek nodded and sat down, his hands in his jacket pockets.

Freddy glanced at Todd, who shrugged.

'Well, Derek, I just might have some news to pull you out of your blues.'

'Really?' said Derek unenthusiastically.

The doorbell rang again.

'Todd, let the others in whilst I organise the drinks.'

Waiting in the sitting room, the four band members heard the pop of champagne corks.

'Do you think . . . ?' began Todd.

'If there's champagne, I presume . . .'

'Now wouldn't news of a deal be grand, Derek?' said Con.

'Yeah, it would,' Derek replied morosely.

'Right, here we are.' Freddy brought two open bottles and five glasses through on a tray. He placed it on the coffee table in the centre of the sitting room.

'Now, before I start pouring, I want to tell you the news and give you a brief outline of what has been agreed between myself and Brad Owen of Metropolitan Records.'

'Metropolitan? They have The Trojans, don't they?' murmured Todd.

'Sure do, and Brad wants to add The Fishermen to the label. We've got a deal from Metropolitan on the table, lads.'

Freddy studied each of their faces in turn. Todd was grinning from ear to ear, Con looked stunned, Derek managed a raised eyebrow and Ian wore the same serene expression he always did.

'Metropolitan, eh?'

'Well, feck me, it looks like we've done it after all, lads!'

'Hey, just think of the groupies, man.'

'We're gonna be rich.'

Freddy let the boys chat amongst themselves for a few minutes as he poured the champagne.

'Now,' he said, handing them each a glass, 'there is, of course, lots to go through with you, but I'll give you the bare bones now. Metropolitan want to sign you for two albums and five singles, the first single being released this Christmas. Brad Owen thinks "Can Someone Tell Me Where She's Gone?" is a potential seasonal hit.'

Freddy paused to let this news sink in. 'As far as the money is concerned, the advance isn't going to make you millionaires overnight, but the royalty rates are one per cent above the norm to make up for the smaller upfront advance. This really starts to work in your favour if The Fishermen begin to have major success. With me so far?'

There was a general nodding of heads.

'Good. As far as Metropolitan are concerned, I'm impressed with their track record. They've only been going a short time and as you mentioned earlier, Todd, they've had a big success with The Trojans. It shows they can cut it amongst the big guns. They're not RCA, but there's no reason why in a few years' time they shouldn't be joining the top five record companies. And the advantage to signing with a smaller label is that you will be a big fish in a small pond. Metropolitan *have* to make you work if they themselves want success. That means they'll be putting in a huge amount of effort.' Freddy ran through the order of business in his head. 'And of course, last but by no means least, you'll have a producer who I think is one of the best in the business. Brad Owen worked with a lot of the top groups when he was with RCA. Having him on the recording side is a huge bonus. So, there's the nub of it! I highly recommend you accept the offer.'

The boys looked at each other uncertainly, overwhelmed by the reality before them.

'I can't take it in,' said Todd. 'I'd convinced myself it wasn't going to happen and now we're sitting here talking about albums and singles and . . .' He shrugged. 'It's amazing.'

The others nodded their heads in agreement.

'So, would you say there's a chance that you might consider accepting Metropolitan's offer?' Freddy smiled.

'What do we think, boys?' asked Todd.

'What kind of dosh can we expect to begin with?' asked Derek, who had perked up a little.

'Approximately double what I'm now giving you each week.'

'Wow,' commented Ian.

'And of course, once the records start selling, we could be looking at ten, twenty times that and upwards.'

'What about the publishing rights to any songs we compose?' asked Con.

'Metropolitan have them, I'm afraid. Pretty standard practice unfortunately. But the composer will obviously get an extra royalty payment on sales of any of his own songs.'

Con nodded.

'Any other questions, or can we drink this champagne before it goes flat?'

'I think we'd be idiots to turn this down,' said Todd.

'Me too,' said Derek. 'Just think of the money. We'd be able to buy whatever we wanted . . . I could . . . well, we could achieve . . . anything. Nobody could touch us.' He stared into the distance.

Con cut short the awkward silence. 'If the producer's as good as you say he is, then I'm for it,' he beamed.

'Man, I'm game,' smiled Ian.

'Then we're agreed.'

The four boys nodded.

'Great. To The Fishermen,' Freddy said, raising his glass.

Todd, Con, Ian and Derek raised their glasses too.

'To The Fishermen.'

25

Helen signed the final paper with a flourish. She looked up at Brad and the young solicitor, her cheeks glowing with excitement.

'Well, there we are, Miss McCarthy. Just the money transfer from your bank to complete, which I can arrange this afternoon, and fifty per cent of the issued share capital of Metropolitan Records is yours. Congratulations.'

Helen smiled at the solicitor. 'Thank you, Mr Brierley.'

'Yes, congratulations, Helen.' Brad added his felicitations in a perfunctory manner. Helen understood how he must feel. She stood up and held out her hand to Richard Brierley. 'Thanks for all your help.'

'Any time, Miss McCarthy.'

'Goodbye.' Brad stood up and followed Helen out of the office, down the stairs and out into the bright sunshine of Holborn.

'Drink to celebrate?' she suggested.

'Er, would you mind if I didn't? I'm meeting Freddy at five to run through the new contract. It's four now and I have some calls to make back at the office.'

'I understand. Then I think I'll make my first executive decision and take the rest of the afternoon off.'

'You deserve it, Helen.' Brad hailed a taxi. It stopped and

he opened the door. As he was about to climb in, he turned back. 'Thanks – for everything.'

Helen nodded. Brad gave a tight smile and the taxi set off along Holborn.

Just before eight that evening, Helen walked into Kettner's. Her hair was freshly washed and styled, and she was wearing a new green mini-dress from Biba. While she waited for Tony to arrive, she ordered some champagne, then took a notepad out of her new briefcase and began to write herself a task list for tomorrow. Nick Rogers, the accountant whom Brad had recommended, was starting at Metropolitan. At eleven, the two of them had an appointment with the Inland Revenue to discuss the outstanding tax bill. Afterwards, they were meeting Brad for lunch to go through the cash-flow situation for the next six months. Now she was responsible for the business, she would run a tight ship.

'Thank you.' She smiled up at the waiter as he placed the champagne in an ice bucket by her table.

'You're welcome, madam. Shall I pour?'

Helen looked at her watch. Tony was fifteen minutes late.

'Why not?'

When the waiter had left her table, Helen lifted the glass of sparkling liquid to her lips. 'Here's to you, Helen, and your future,' she whispered to herself. She put the glass down and began to write further notes to herself.

BETTER UNDERSTAND MUSIC SCENE. This heading was vitally important. Until she knew more about the industry and its ways, Helen knew she was working at a disadvantage. It was impossible for her to have an informed financial opinion if she didn't know the first thing about what sold and what didn't. Brad would always have the upper hand.

Check out up-and-coming bands. Buy top twenty

singles and record player, she scribbled underneath the main heading.

Read twelve months' back issues of Melody Maker . . .

Forty-five minutes, six sheets of paper and half a bottle of champagne later, there was still no sign of Tony.

Helen stood up and asked to be directed to a public telephone. She dialled Tony's number. The telephone rang but there was no reply. Maybe he'd just been delayed and was on his way.

Half an hour later it was obvious Tony wasn't coming. Helen ordered herself a large salad and munched her way through it, unsure of what to do. She tried ringing his flat another four times, but there was still no answer.

Finally, Helen paid the bill and walked outside. She wondered if he'd forgotten, but thought it unlikely. Feeling deflated, cross, and more than a little worried, Helen hailed a taxi. The black cab took her down The Mall and through Chelsea on its way to Wimbledon.

'Can you stop here for a moment?' The car drew to a halt. 'Wait here, will you? I'll only be a moment.'

'Righto, miss,' the cabbie replied.

Helen climbed out onto the pavement and walked back three houses to Tony's basement flat. Nervously, she tiptoed down the steps, dreading the thought that his 'other woman' might be there and that was why she'd been stood up.

She knocked three times. At the third knock, there was a light click, and the door opened of its own accord. There was no one behind it. Clearly, it had not been shut properly.

Gingerly, she pushed it open. The flat was in darkness.

'Hello? Tony, it's me, Helen.'

There was no reply.

'Tony?'

She searched along the corridor wall for a light switch and pressed it.

'Damn.' The bulb had gone.

Helen felt her way along the wall until she arrived at the sitting room door.

'Tony? Are you here?'

Thankfully the light was functioning, and the sitting room was illuminated brightly when she pressed the switch.

It was also empty.

Helen walked through the room to the kitchen. The tiny room was in a horrible mess, and there was a funny smell coming from the cooker. She peered into the saucepan on top of the hob and jumped back in disgust, putting her hand over her mouth as she gagged. Whatever meat had been in the pan had turned to a squirming mass of maggots. She stood panting in the sitting room.

'Tony?'

She shivered. He obviously wasn't at home. From the state of the kitchen, she suspected he hadn't been around for the past few days. Quickly, she checked the bedroom. The bed was made and the room neat. She returned to the sitting room and searched for a pen and paper in Tony's bureau drawer.

Thurs night.
Tony,
  Where did you get to? Came looking for you.
Give the new director of Metropolitan Records a call.
  Love,
  Helen

She left the note on the coffee table, and leaving the front door exactly as she found it, ran up the steps to her waiting taxi.

* * *

216

The flat was in silence again, apart from the drip of the tap in the bathroom. The water in the bath, once a bright red pool, had turned a deep copper colour. In the midst of the water, his hand still clutching a bar of soap, lay Tony Bryant. He stared, unseeing, up at the ceiling.

26

'Hello, Sorcha. Come in and sit down. You look wonderful. Have you had your hair restyled?'

Sorcha picked her way through the piles of photos, envelopes and general mess that lay strewn on Audrey's office carpet. She removed a pile of magazines from the chair in front of the desk and sat down.

'Yes. They cut it for the baked beans shoot last week.'

'Did they really? And did you ask for a fee?'

'No. I didn't know I should.'

'Don't worry. I'll ring them. They know they have to agree a change of hairstyle beforehand, and pay you for it. However, it looks so nice that I think they've done you a favour.'

'Thank you. Con liked it too.'

'Good, good.' Audrey removed her reading glasses, giving a clearer view of the huge brown eyes that had once made her the highest paid model of the forties. She placed her long, elegant fingers in a steeple and stared across the table at Sorcha. 'Did you see the *Woman's Own* spread last week?'

'Yes.'

'It looked very, very good. In fact, I've had five calls since yesterday asking about your availability.' Audrey smiled widely. 'I think the time has come to give up the day job, as it were.'

'You mean leave Swan and Edgar's?'

'I think it would be safe to do so. There you go.' Audrey handed Sorcha an envelope. 'That might make you feel a little more comfortable. The cheque's for quite a lot of money.'

'Thank you.' Sorcha took the envelope and put it in her handbag.

'The sooner you leave, the better. How much notice do you have to give?'

'A week.'

'That's perfect. I have two upcoming bookings confirmed in ten days, and three provisionals for the week after. All good jobs. I've also had a telephone call from an advertising agency who saw your spread in *Woman's Own*. They're looking for a girl to promote a new night-time drink. It'll be competing in the Horlicks, Ovaltine market. They want a girl-next-door type rather than an out-and-out glamour puss.'

Sorcha was in a daze. 'I see.'

'If you got the contract, it would make you famous, Sorcha. The company want to run a series of television advertisements along with billboard posters and pages in magazines. It would be a year's exclusive work. You'd be under contract to them and wouldn't be able to take anything else. We haven't discussed money yet, but we'd be talking a big deal. The gentleman I spoke to was extremely keen to see you for it. What do you think?'

Sorcha ran her hands through her hair. 'It sounds grand, Audrey. But I suppose every model in London will be seen.'

'They're certainly casting around, yes. Shall I fix up a time for the end of this week? There'll be a preliminary meeting with the advertising agency, and then, if they approve, a follow-up with the big guns from the company itself.'

'Fine, but this week will have to be during my lunch hour or after work. I can't let my boss down again, even if I am handing in my notice. She's been very good to me.'

'I understand. I'll let you know when and where.' Audrey gave a warm chuckle as Sorcha stood up. 'I should go and spend some of that cheque on a special present for yourself. You're doing awfully well, dear.'

'Thank you.'

The telephone on Audrey's desk rang.

'Can you see yourself out?'

'Of course.'

Audrey waved as she picked up the receiver.

Outside the office, Sorcha reached into her bag and pulled out the envelope she had been given. Tearing it open, she read the amount on the cheque. It would take her four months to earn the same at Swan and Edgar's. A feeling of disbelief washed over her as she carefully returned the cheque to its envelope and stowed it away in an interior pocket of her bag.

A strong breeze was blowing, which brought Sorcha out of her daydream. She glanced at her watch. It was ten past six, and she was meeting Con at seven in their favourite bar. She shivered and pulled her cardigan closer around her shoulders before hurrying down the street.

The shops were still open on Carnaby Street. Sorcha made for the warmth of a boutique. She leafed through the racks of dresses and pulled out a couple that appealed. Five minutes later, after slipping off her clothes in the curtained changing room, she pulled on a dress which was short and woollen. Drawing back the curtain so she could survey herself in the big communal mirror, Sorcha stopped in her tracks.

Standing by the till talking to the shopgirl was someone so familiar that Sorcha's initial reaction was to step back and hide before she was spotted.

Surely it couldn't be?

Gingerly, Sorcha pulled the curtain back a couple of inches and peered through the gap. The young woman had her back to Sorcha. Her hair was different and she was much slimmer . . . Until she saw her face again, she couldn't be sure.

Sorcha watched as the woman took her change and her plastic bag and walked out of the boutique.

'Okay, lads, take a listen.' Brad pressed the button on the panel and the studio was filled with music.

The four group members listened silently until the song was finished.

'So, what do you think?'

Brad stared at them.

'It's feckin' grand, Brad, that's what it is,' said Con.

The others shared their agreement.

'You're happy with the new instrumentations in the middle eight?'

'Very happy.' Con nodded. 'It's improved it no end.'

'Great. We'll cut the single. In a couple of weeks' time, I'll be able to show you your first piece of vinyl. I think we're on to a winner, boys!' Brad spun boyishly on his swivel chair. 'I'm going to discuss it with Freddy but I think we might put the single forward to be played on *Juke Box Jury* at the end of November. The television show is great publicity.'

Todd looked nervous. 'Even if the jury trash the song?'

Brad shrugged. 'We have to cross our fingers they won't. Anyway, I gotta dash back to the office. Please can everyone be here at ten tomorrow so we can have a good couple of hours working on track seven? I'd like to lay it down in the afternoon. We've only got six weeks until the launch.' He jumped to his feet.

'Sure. Bye, Brad.'

'Cheers, boys. You did good today, really good.' With a wave, he disappeared out of the control box.

*   *   *

Con spotted Sorcha sitting on a stool amongst the noisy throng of Hades bar.

'Hello, my love.' He threw his arms around her shoulders and kissed her.

'Hello, darling. I got you a beer.' Sorcha pointed to the glass on the counter, then took a sip of her gin. Con squeezed in beside her.

'Is that a new dress?'

'Yes. Audrey gave me a large cheque and I decided to treat myself.'

'I'd say you were right to do so.' Con took a sip of his beer. 'We've finally finished "Can Someone Tell Me Where She's Gone?"'

'And?'

'It sounds brilliant. Just grand,' he grinned.

'I'm so pleased.'

Con studied Sorcha. Although she looked as pretty as always, and the soft green of the new woollen dress matched her eyes, her face was pale and she seemed distracted.

'Are you okay, sweetheart?'

'Yes, yes, I'm fine, why?'

'You look . . . strange, that's all.'

'Do I? It's just that . . . no . . .' Sorcha shook her head. 'I'm being an eejit, really.'

'Come on now, you can tell me. What is it?' He reached across the table and took her hand.

Sorcha sighed. 'You'll tell me I'm being stupid, but I was in a boutique down the street trying on this dress and I thought I saw Helen.'

Con frowned. 'Helen who?'

'Helen McCarthy, from Ballymore.'

Sorcha watched Con's face shift from puzzlement to unease. 'Right. Well. Was it her?'

'I don't know. By the time I'd looked again she'd turned around and I couldn't catch a glimpse of her face.' Sorcha shrugged and shook her head. 'It probably wasn't her. I mean, this woman was much thinner and smarter and her hair was different, but—'

'Now what would Helen McCarthy be doing in a boutique in Carnaby Street? You obviously just saw someone that looked like her.'

'She really did, Con, I swear.'

Con let go of Sorcha's hand, seemingly a little agitated. 'Well, even if it was her, what's the harm? She and Ballymore are long in our past.'

'I know.' Sorcha sighed. 'It was so odd. When I saw her, I felt like a ghost was walking over my grave. I don't know why it's unsettled me so much.'

Con softened again, putting his arms tightly around Sorcha's shoulders. She snuggled into him. 'There, there, Sorcha.' He stroked her hair lovingly. 'You worrying that you might have seen Helen McCarthy when we have so much to look forward to. Everything is starting to go right for us now. I think you look for things to worry over.'

'You're right.' Sorcha straightened herself up and shook her head in a visible attempt to remove the tension hanging over her. 'And Audrey had some good news for me. She wants me to leave Swan and Edgar's. I have five bookings in the next three weeks and a very big interview for a grand job later this week. It's to promote a new malt drink. Audrey says it will make me famous if I get it.'

'Quite the career woman, aren't you now?' Con teased.

She looked at him anxiously. 'You are happy for me, aren't you?'

'Of course I am, Sorcha. I can't say I'm finding it easy that you're so much your own woman, but I am learning to live with it, even if I might prefer you barefoot, pregnant and in the kitchen . . .'

'Are you serious?'

'Do I look it?' Con chuckled and planted a kiss on her forehead. 'I'm starving. What about treating your man to a dinner at that restaurant around the corner? We can sit and dream about number-one singles and fame and fortune.'

Sorcha picked up her gin and swallowed what remained in the glass in one go. As she put it down, Con saw the colour had returned to her cheeks and her eyes were sparkling. He felt he had navigated that well, despite the fear in his own belly. If Helen *was* in London, and she and Sorcha were to meet without his presence to control the situation . . . the consequences didn't bear thinking about.

'Con Daly, you got yourself a deal.'

27

'Helen speaking.'

'Hi, Helen. I have a Detective Inspector Garratt in reception for you.'

Helen frowned. 'You do?'

'Yes. He's asking to see you urgently.'

'Right. You'd better send him up.'

Helen put the receiver down, and, straightening the papers on her desk, wondered why on earth a policeman wanted to speak to her.

Three minutes later, there was a peremptory knock on her office door.

'Come in.' Helen watched the door open. An extremely tall, thin man with a shock of greying hair entered her office.

'Helen McCarthy?'

'Yes.'

'Detective Inspector Garratt, Scotland Yard.' The man held out his hand across her desk.

Helen offered hers and felt the strength of the man as he shook it.

'Sorry to disturb you, but I'm conducting an investigation and I think you might be able to help me with my enquiries.'

Helen was confused and uneasy. 'I don't know how but . . . please take a seat.'

Detective Garratt sat down on the chair, which was hardly adequate for his long legs.

'Miss McCarthy, I believe you know a man by the name of Tony Bryant.'

'Yes, yes, I do.'

'Good, good.' Garratt's eyes slowly moved about the room, taking in the surroundings, before they fixed on Helen's gaze. 'Mr Bryant was found dead in the bath at his flat a week ago. He'd been stabbed several times. It was a vicious attack.'

Helen stared at the detective, too shocked to react.

Garratt studied her for a while before he spoke again.

'I am sorry to be the bearer of such bad tidings. Was Mr Bryant a good friend of yours?'

Helen felt tears pricking the back of her eyes. She nodded.

The detective took a notepad from his pocket and began to flick through its contents. 'Were you at his flat last Thursday?'

Helen nodded again.

'Good. We found the note you'd written. May I ask how you gained entry? Did you have a key?'

Helen shook her head. 'No . . . no . . . the door was open. Excuse me, I—' Her breath was coming in short sharp bursts and she rested her head in her hands in order to control the dizziness.

'I understand, Miss McCarthy. Take your time.' Garratt didn't adjust his posture. He was still leaning in towards Helen, expecting an answer.

'The door was open.'

'Open, you say? Was there any sign of forced entry?'

'I . . . no,' Helen sobbed.

'Sorry to give you such a shock. I presume you and Mr Bryant were close?'

'Yes. I mean, no . . . we . . . we were very good friends. He'd been my tutor at college and . . . and . . .' Helen reached down and rifled through her handbag for a handkerchief. She blew her nose hard. 'I'm sorry. I . . . I just can't believe what you're telling me. Are you sure it's Tony?'

'Unfortunately, yes. His father has given a positive identification.'

Detective Inspector Garratt watched and waited as Helen wiped her eyes, blew her nose again and swept a hand through her hair in an attempt to regain her equilibrium.

'When you went to Mr Bryant's flat last Thursday, did you enter the bathroom?'

'No. I called out to him a few times. If he had been in the bath, I thought he would have heard me.'

'Of course, Miss McCarthy. Do you know of anybody who had a grudge against Mr Bryant? Any secrets he may have confided to you about any trouble he was in?'

Helen was resolute. 'No, absolutely not. Tony was always so . . . *happy*. As I said, he was very good to me. He helped me a lot.'

DI Garratt cleared his throat. 'You understand that I have to ask the nature of your relationship with Mr Bryant?'

'What do you mean?'

'What I mean, put bluntly, is whether you and Mr Bryant were lovers?'

Helen did not hesitate in her answer. 'We were for a while, in the summer, but that had finished.'

Garratt nodded slowly. 'I see. May I ask why the affair ended?'

'Because Tony's girlfriend came back. It was what we'd agreed – that we'd stop when she returned.'

'And do you have any idea who this girlfriend was?'

'No. I never met her. Obviously,' she added.

'But you think they were seeing each other again recently?'

'Oh yes, I'm sure of it.'

'I'm surprised, then, that we haven't heard from her. Mind you, we've only just released the story to the media. Perhaps we'll hear something soon.'

'If it's any help, Tony did mention something about her going away for a few days. Maybe she's not back yet.'

'Maybe.' DI Garratt's piercing gaze rested on Helen once more. 'So, there was no animosity between you and Mr Bryant at the end of the affair?'

'No. I knew how things were from the beginning. I accepted the situation. I had no choice.'

Garratt ran his tongue around his mouth in contemplation. 'Miss McCarthy, were you in love with Mr Bryant?'

Helen looked down at her hands resting on the table. 'Yes. I suppose I was. He was so very kind to me when I needed a friend.' She looked up directly at Garratt. 'He was the first person who had made me feel special.'

'Hmm. So, on the Thursday night of your visit to his flat, he was meant to be meeting you somewhere?'

'Yes. We'd arranged a dinner – a celebration at Kettner's. Tony didn't arrive so I went to look for him. I still can't believe it. Who on earth would want to murder him?'

'That's what I intend to find out.' Garratt slapped his thighs. 'Well, thank you for answering my questions. I'll leave you my telephone number, and if you think of anything that might be relevant, please contact me immediately.'

Helen swallowed hard. 'Of course.'

Garratt stood up, his head almost touching the low ceiling. Helen tried to stand but her legs had turned to jelly.

'Don't get up. Goodbye, Miss McCarthy.'

'Goodbye, Detective Inspector Garratt.'

He nodded and left her office. Helen sat staring into space, her whole body numb.

'Tony, Tony, why?' she questioned to the empty air.

Eventually, Helen reached for her handbag and staggered to her feet. She walked slowly across the carpet to her office door, then made her way down the stairs to reception.

'I . . . I'm going out for the afternoon,' Helen told the receptionist. 'I won't be back.'

'Okay, Helen. Are you all right? You look ever such a funny colour.'

'No, I'm fine, thanks, Jilly.'

Helen opened the door and walked along the street. She turned into the nearest bar and ordered a double whiskey. Once she had downed that and her head had cleared a little, Helen left the bar and walked swiftly to the nearest off-licence. Five minutes later, hugging a full bottle of scotch to her breast, she hailed a taxi and headed for home.

28

'So, Jukebox Jurors, take a listen to this. It's the debut single by The Fishermen. It's called "Can Someone Tell Me Where She's Gone?" and it's out for Christmas. Let's hear it.'

Seven pairs of eyes stared nervously at the television screen as the sound of the new single came flooding through the small speaker.

'Remember, lads, if they trash it, it doesn't matter. There've been several huge number-one hits that have been voted a miss by the panel.'

Freddy's words comforted no one in the room. Con held tightly to Sorcha's hand. Lulu sat on Todd's knee, her arms wound round his neck. Derek's hand shook as he reached for his beer and there was even a trace of tension apparent on Ian's face. They sat in silence as the record played.

'No doubt about it, lads, whatever they say, it's a bloody good song,' murmured Freddy as the last strains disappeared and the camera swung back to David Jacobs.

'Okay. There we are, panel. "Can Someone Tell Me Where She's Gone?", the debut single by The Fishermen. So, Jody, let's hear what you have to say.'

'Well . . .' The established pop star twiddled with her pen on the table.

'Get on with it,' muttered Todd.

'I loved it.'

'*Yes!*'

'Wow, man!'

'Shh, you lot, let's hear what she has to say.' Freddy waved an arm to silence the room.

'I liked the melody line, the lyrics, and from their photo, I think I might like the look of them as well,' giggled the pop star.

'Right then, on to you, Jimmy.'

'Here goes,' muttered Freddy. The record producer had a reputation for trashing seventy per cent of what was played.

'Not bad, I suppose, if you like that sort of thing. A bit run-of-the-mill. It might make the top thirty, as everyone likes a soppy record at Christmas, but' – Jimmy shook his head – 'if they do make it with this one, I reckon they'll be a one-hit wonder. Nothing special.'

The air in the sitting room turned blue. Cushions were hurled at the screen.

'And now you, John. What did you think of the song?'

The disc jockey nodded. 'As usual, whatever Jimmy dislikes, I like. It's a smashing record. I'll certainly be giving it airtime over the next few weeks. I reckon The Fishermen will go far. They're my tip for the top this week.'

Screams of delight resounded around the sitting room.

'And Paul? What about you?'

'Loved 'em.'

'Way to go, boys,' murmured Freddy.

'So, let's vote. A hit or a miss?'

The panel held up their cards. David Jacobs rang the bell to signal a hit.

'Three hits and one miss for The Fishermen. Now then, we'll move on to the new single by . . .'

Freddy stood up, switched the television off and turned to

face the others. 'Well, lads, Brad and I were in two minds as to whether we should release it to *Juke Box Jury*. It's always a gamble, but if it pays off, it can give you a hell of a start.' He smiled at them benevolently. 'You're on your way, boys.'

The telephone rang just as Sorcha had dribbled shampoo onto her hair.

'Oh, for goodness' sake,' she murmured, taking her head out of the kitchen sink and searching for the towel she thought she'd put on the drainer. It had fallen onto the floor. Bending down, she picked it up, wound it round her head turban-style and padded across the room to the telephone.

'Yes?' she said sharply.

'Hello, darling, what's wrong?'

'Hello, Audrey. I'm sorry. It's just that our phone never stops ringing these days.'

'What it is to be popular, my dear.'

'Well, it's not me they want to speak to. It's Con. I've no idea how half the journalists get this number.'

'That's the price of fame, my darling. Talking of which, I have some very good news for you. Can you stop by my office this afternoon for a chat?'

'It would have to be quick, Audrey. Con's record company are throwing a big party for the boys for getting to number two in the hit parade. We'll know later today whether they've climbed to number one.'

'Your chap *is* doing well, isn't he? Even as a devotee of Beethoven, The Fishermen have managed to enter my consciousness. Married to your very own pop star, no less.'

'If I ever see him again,' murmured Sorcha. 'He's out from morning till night being famous.'

'Well, I wouldn't worry about that. I have plenty to keep you busy, dear. See you later.'

'Yes, bye-bye, Audrey.'

'Bye, darling.'

Sorcha put the telephone down and went back to the kitchen sink. The December day was freezing and her skin had turned goose-pimply in her bra and knickers. Hurriedly she washed her hair, pulled on Con's thick terry-towelling robe and put the kettle on to boil. She made herself a cup of coffee, then settled in an armchair by the gas fire to warm herself up.

The past two months had flown. Sorcha could hardly believe it was Christmas in three days' time. Since the start of Brad's marketing campaign and the release of 'Can Someone Tell Me Where She's Gone?', Sorcha had hardly seen Con. The band had spent three weeks on the road doing a whistle-stop tour of the country, performing their new single in as many clubs as Freddy could book them into. Once back in London, and with the track rising up the charts, it seemed every music publication, radio station and TV chat show host wanted to interview The Fishermen.

Even though Con was exhausted, he looked happier than Sorcha had ever seen him. She was thrilled for him and the rest of the band, although she'd be glad when tonight was over and they could settle down to the quiet Christmas they'd planned.

'No parties, no people, just you and me, my darling,' Con had whispered to her last night after they'd made love.

'I can't wait. I miss you,' she'd whispered.

If Audrey had good news for her, then they might have a lot to celebrate.

Sorcha turned around and saw the condensation dripping down the window. She stuck her finger in it and drew a small heart with her initial on one end of an arrow and Con's on the other.

'How far we've come, Con, how far we've come.'

* * *

Helen arrived home at half past four. Tonight was very important and she wanted plenty of time to get ready.

She ran a bath and put her plastic cap on to protect her freshly styled hair. Submersed in the hot water, Helen lay staring at the ceiling, trying to relax. Just the thought of tonight sent her pulse racing.

She had made sure that her presence at the party would come as a total surprise to Con. On the couple of occasions he and The Fishermen had been in Metropolitan's offices, she had made herself scarce. It was only last week that she'd ordered the new headed business stationery with her name in print in the bottom right-hand corner: 'Helen McCarthy, Director.'

She yawned as the water began to calm her. Beneath the nervous energy, Helen knew she was physically and mentally drained. For the past twelve weeks she'd been putting in sixteen-hour days. Work was a balm. It stopped her from dwelling on Tony and the terrible thing that had happened to him.

The story of his murder had been in all the newspapers. Detective Inspector Garratt had appeared on television appealing for anyone to come forward with information about the killing. She'd called Samantha, her friend from college, to find out when the funeral was taking place. Samantha had told her that it was to be a quiet, family-only affair. Nevertheless, she'd sent flowers to the church and later visited his grave to say her own private goodbye.

As far as Helen knew, the crime was as yet unsolved. She'd spent night after night lying awake pondering on who could have done such a thing. She wondered how the other lady in Tony's life was feeling and was almost comforted by the thought that there was someone else who was probably missing Tony as much as she was.

'Oh, Tony, Tony,' she murmured as she began to soap herself.

If she hadn't been so busy at Metropolitan, Helen honestly thought she may have gone mad.

During the day, she'd worked away quietly in the small upstairs cubbyhole that she proudly called her office. Nick Rogers, Brad's accountant friend, had been a great help in showing her the financial ropes. Together, they had paid off the outstanding bills, brought the accounts up to date and put the company back on track.

In the evenings, Helen had concentrated on getting to know the music business. When she was not attending gigs, she was at home listening to records and reading every publication she could get her hands on.

Helen towelled herself dry. Still in her plastic cap, she sat down in front of the dressing-table mirror and began to apply her make-up. She had put a lot of thought into what she should wear for The Fishermen's party. In the end, she had found a wonderful trouser suit in blue lurex that suited her colouring and showed off her cleavage.

Forty-five minutes later, she was ready to leave. She checked her reflection in the mirror and gave a satisfied smile.

A power in the music business, someone to be reckoned with. That was what she wanted. If she couldn't have love, power made a suitable substitute.

29

Sorcha left Audrey's office and hailed a taxi.

'The Waldorf Hotel, please.'

'Right you are, miss.'

The taxi drove off and Sorcha sat in the back, her head spinning. Audrey had just told her that she'd been offered a year's contract as the 'Mighty Malt' girl. They were going to pay her a fortune and Audrey had said it was likely that her face would soon be as famous as Con's.

She'd already decided to save her news for Christmas Day. It was Con's night tonight, and they could celebrate her success later.

The taxi pulled up at the Waldorf. Sorcha paid the driver and entered the hotel.

'Sorcha Daly, you look radiant!' Con put his arms round her shoulders and guided her into the banqueting suite hired for the party.

'Thank you. You look . . . well, you look exhausted, Con.'

'Yep, I'm jiggered, but as happy as a sandboy. Everyone else is here. We have a table in the corner.'

Flashbulbs popped in their faces as they made their way across to join the rest of the group, already on their fourth bottle of champagne.

Ian had a girl on either side of him and the three of them

were sharing a joint. Derek looked uncomfortable with a large woman on his knee, who was almost smothering his face with her ample bosom. Todd was deep in conversation with an attractive woman, while Lulu sat silently on the other side of him, looking morose. Her face lit up when she saw Sorcha and Con.

'Come and join the happy band. Sit by me and talk to me.' She patted the seat next to her. 'He's so engrossed with his new friend from *Melody Maker* that he's not even said hello yet.' Lulu rolled her eyes. 'Champagne for you both?'

'Thanks, Lulu.'

She shared out the remainder of a bottle between three glasses and handed one to each of them. 'Cheers.'

'Cheers. Have you seen Freddy yet?' asked Con.

'No. He and Brad don't seem to have arrived. Do you know half these people, Con?'

'Some of them.' Con stared at the crush in the room. 'It's queer the way you suddenly have so many friends when you become famous.'

'Sure is,' drawled Lulu.

'Hi, folks. Everyone present and correct?' Freddy appeared behind Con and Sorcha with Brad at his elbow.

'We thought you might have forgotten tonight's little low-key celebration, Freddy.'

'Hardly, Lulu. Something important came up and Brad and I had to discuss it. Is Derek alive under that pile of femininity?' Freddy frowned at the sight of the large woman who'd submerged Derek completely and appeared to be giving him mouth-to-mouth resuscitation. 'Listen, lads. I need a word. Could you remove your appendages for five minutes? We'll talk before everyone's too far gone to hear.'

Reluctantly, Ian's two ladies left the table, followed by the big-breasted woman and lastly the *Melody Maker* journalist.

'Done it again, Freddy,' said the journalist as she went past. 'Great bunch of lads.' She trailed her finger along Brad's collar. 'We must get together sometime. Renew our acquaintance.' She blew Todd a kiss. 'See you later, sweetie.'

Lulu growled under her breath.

Freddy took two chairs from the neighbouring table and he and Brad sat down. 'Right, attention, please. I have news,' said Freddy. 'The Trojans are going back to the States after Christmas and we've just agreed a deal with their record company over there to sign The Fishermen.'

The boys stared at Freddy silently.

'Not only that, but they want you to join The Trojans on tour as their support act. You'll leave for New York at the end of January and be back end of April for the launch of the album. Well?' Freddy stared at the four blank faces. 'Someone say something, please.'

'It's great news, Freddy, really, isn't it, boys?' said Con.

'Yeah. The good old USA, millions of people panting to buy our records,' smiled Todd dreamily.

'And get into our trousers,' added Ian coarsely.

'So you're all happy then?' asked Brad. 'I think it's a wonderful opportunity. If you can crack it in the States, then you really have made it big.'

'It's all too much to take in,' muttered Derek.

'I know. Well, after tonight, you've got a week off for Christmas. You all look knackered. I suggest you disappear off somewhere and have a break. Take time to enjoy the success. Trust me, the first taste is always the sweetest.' Freddy looked at the empty bottles of champagne on the table. 'We seem to have run out.'

'I'll go in search of some.' Brad left the table.

A painfully thin man, his face ravaged by years of substance abuse, slapped Freddy on the shoulder.

'Hello, Freddy, long time no see. Another success under your belt then.'

'Mick, what the hell are you doing here?' Freddy turned around and was soon deep in conversation.

'Hey, Sorcha, great news about the States. I might get my theatrical agent to line me up some meetings in LA while we're there. And the shopping in New York is meant to be fantastic. While the boys work, we can spend all their hard-earned money in Bloomingdale's and Macy's. I can't wait,' giggled Lulu.

'Excuse me.' Sorcha stood up. 'I need to go powder my nose.'

'Are you okay?' Con saw that Sorcha had gone pale.

'Yes, I'll be fine, really.'

As she left the table, the journalist from *Melody Maker* appeared again and sat herself down next to Todd.

'I'm going to personally throttle that little tart in a minute,' Lulu whispered to Con under her breath.

Con was still gazing across the room in the direction Sorcha had taken.

Lulu put her hand on Con's knee. 'I'll bet you can hardly believe this is happening.'

'You're right, I can't.'

'You deserve it, Con. You have such talent. You gave the band what they were missing.'

'All four of us contribute to the success, Lulu,' Con answered abruptly.

'Champagne, everyone.'

Brad was back with a tray, glasses and two bottles of bubbly. Lulu quickly removed her hand from Con's leg.

Sorcha touched up her lipstick and smiled falsely into the mirror.

Tonight was not the night to think about either three months away from Con, or turning down the Mighty Malt contract. There was bound to be a way around it. She mustn't spoil the evening for either of them.

As she brushed her hair, she heard the cistern flush and was just about to head for the door when she heard a familiar voice.

'My, my, what a small world.'

Sorcha's heart nearly missed a beat.

Helen McCarthy stood behind her, smiling. Sorcha stared at her reflection in the mirror.

'Helen . . . What are you doing here?'

'Oh, a work thing, you know.'

'Really? You work in London, do you?'

'Yes, yes, I do.'

Sorcha nodded, trying to match Helen's calm demeanour. She was so very different, so . . . confident.

'How long have you been in England?'

'Oh, almost as long as you. I left Ballymore a couple of months later.'

'I see.'

Silence hung between them, broken by a sudden roar and surge of applause from the room outside. Finally, Sorcha made a move towards the door. 'Well, I must go back.'

'Of course. Well now, it's nice to see you again.'

'Yes. You look good, Helen,' Sorcha said, trying to avoid gritting her teeth.

'Thank you. You do too. I think we've all changed a lot since Ballymore.'

'Yes. Con and I are married.'

'I heard. Congratulations to you both.'

'You heard?' Sorcha could not hide her surprise.

'It's amazing what a small town London can be. And life is full of coincidences, isn't it?'

240

'Yes. Well, goodbye, Helen.'

'Goodbye, Sorcha. I'm sure I'll be seeing you again.' Helen offered her a smile that seemed to exude genuine warmth. Given the last time the women had seen each other Sorcha had been ready to strangle Helen, she was somewhat taken aback.

Offering Helen a stilted smile in return, Sorcha hurriedly left the ladies'.

She arrived back at the table desperate to speak to Con, but he'd been surrounded by a television crew.

'Great news, Sorcha.' Freddy caught her by the arm. 'We've just heard on the grapevine that the single's gone to number one, although it won't be confirmed till tomorrow.'

Sorcha tried to collect herself. 'That's wonderful, Freddy.'

'It is, isn't it?' he said smugly. 'Con and Todd can take most of the credit for penning such a great ballad. In a few moments I'm going to get the boys to sing. Then the night is yours.'

'Sorcha, Sorcha, isn't it grand?!'

Con was by her side. The television crew had moved on to Todd.

'Yes, it is, Con. Grand.' Sorcha's attention had been caught by the sight of Helen McCarthy being guided through the crowd by Brad towards their table. 'Con, look. Look who it is! I just met her in the loo. I told you I thought I'd seen her in Carnaby Street.'

Con followed Sorcha's gaze. His elation was replaced by nerves.

'Jesus, Mary and Joseph,' he whispered.

They watched transfixed as Brad and Helen arrived by their side.

'Con, Sorcha, can I introduce you to Helen McCarthy?'

'As a matter of fact, Brad, the three of us have met before. Nice to see you again, Con, and congratulations,' Helen interjected.

'Thanks, Helen,' Con managed. 'And, er, how exactly do you fit into this scene?'

'Oh, didn't you know? Helen's the other director of Metropolitan,' said Brad. Con's eyes nearly extricated themselves from their sockets. 'She looks after the financial side. We don't let her out of her cubbyhole upstairs very often, so that's probably why you've never met! I suppose you could say she's the power behind the throne. Be nice to her,' Brad warned, half jokingly. 'She's the one that holds the purse strings.'

'Yes. Be nice to me, Con.' The words were said with a smile, but Helen's eyes were fixed on him.

'Have you met the rest of the band?' Brad asked.

Helen shook her head. 'No, I don't believe I have.'

'Come on then, let's remedy that.'

Helen held out her hand to Con. 'It looks like we'll be having quite a bit to do with each other in the future, Con. I look forward to it.'

Helen's hand hung in the air. Con was embarrassed into taking it.

'Yes.'

'Goodbye, and a merry Christmas.'

'Sorcha, my girl,' Con said as he watched Helen being introduced to the rest of the band, 'yer man needs a drink.'

Helen watched the trees outside her window, illuminated by the glow of the street lights. She was too worked up to sleep. Tonight had been, without a doubt, the best evening of her life. The shock on Con and Sorcha Daly's faces when they'd heard of her position at Metropolitan had put her on a high. Of course, they had never expected her to amount to anything. Little could they ever have fathomed that, one day, Helen would hold the key to the palace. It had been particularly edifying for her after the way it all ended in Ballymore. That whole situation was embarrassing to think about now. The *new* Helen would never have let it happen.

Sorcha laid her head on Con's shoulder as the taxi drove them home to Hampstead.

'Did you enjoy tonight, Sorcha?'

'Oh yes. Did you?'

'I thought it was wonderful. But you weren't your normal self. Is anything wrong?'

'I . . .' Sorcha stared out of the window. 'No.'

'Are you sure?'

'Yes.'

Con made love to her when they arrived home. Afterwards, she lay in his arms, his hands stroking her hair.

'It's all starting to come true.'

'Your dream?' He nodded. 'You deserve it, Con.'

'And you deserve the life that fame brings with it. I can give you everything now, Sorcha. There'll be no more struggle, no more having to demean yourself for a few pennies.'

Sorcha swallowed hard. 'Yes.'

'And imagine us going to the United States of America! I can hardly wait.'

Sorcha was silent. Con shifted positions so he could see her face. 'Are you not excited about the trip? Freddy said it will be first class all the way. Luxury cars, hotels – all expenses paid.'

'It'll be wonderful, Con. It's just . . .'

'What?'

She'd intended to save her good news for Christmas Day. But somehow, it didn't feel like good news any longer.

'I was offered a job today. It would be a year's contract with very, very good money. Audrey says it would make me famous.

The problem is, I'd be starting work just as you flew to the States.' Con studied her face silently. 'I don't know what to do,' she sighed. 'I'd love to take the job, but we'd be apart for over three months.'

'So that's why you were looking so down tonight.'

'Yes. Oh, Con, what do you think?'

'I'm thinking it's sad that anything should spoil our happiness. It's silly asking me, Sorcha. You know what I want.' Con let go of her and lay back on his pillow. 'It's a disaster for a marriage to spend a long time apart.'

'So I couldn't trust you on your own then?'

Con waved her away. 'I'm not saying that. You know I'm not. It's your choice, Sorcha. I can't stop you.' He sighed. 'I suppose it's a question of priorities.'

'Of course you're my priority, Con. But it seems a shame to have to turn such a big opportunity down.'

Con turned to her. 'What about the opportunity of seeing America?'

'I know, I know. And I can hardly bear the thought of being parted from you for three months. But I've worked hard for my success. I know it's not as grand or important as yours, but it's mine.'

'Okay, but where will it lead? I mean, I was only thinking tonight that now we're on our way to being financially secure we could maybe start a family. Will you be leaving our babies with a stranger to go off modelling?'

'Of course not! But that's in the future, not now.'

He shook his head. 'Ah, Sorcha, there was me thinking I'd managed to provide you with the dream and it seems you have a different dream altogether.'

'No, I don't at all, Con.'

'Look, let's drop it. I'll not stop you, Sorcha. All I can say is that I love you and I'll always want you by my side.'

He rolled away from her and shut his eyes. Con hoped that his guilt trip had worked. He needed to be sure that Sorcha stayed as far away from Helen McCarthy as possible.

After a while, Sorcha climbed out of bed and went to sit in the chair by the window. Dawn was starting to break. She watched her husband sleeping for a long time.

It was daylight before she slipped back in beside him, her decision made.

Part Two

Separation

30

London, July 1969

It was announced yesterday afternoon that Metropolitan Records have been successful in their bid to acquire the Evergreen label. The deal covers all Evergreen artists signed to the firm at present. Evergreen have been struggling for some time, and the bid from Metropolitan comes not a moment too soon for the ailing company, established earlier in the decade and responsible for launching such names as Simon Morrison, Peggy Valance and Richie Davis.

Only four years ago, Metropolitan were a small independent company, struggling for a slice of the market share. Since then, they have gone from strength to strength, with bands such as The Trojans and The Rattlers.

But it is, of course, the phenomenal success of The Fishermen that has shot the company finances into orbit. With eight number-one hits in fifteen countries over the past three years, plus three albums turning platinum both here and in the United States, Metropolitan have established themselves as a major player in the music industry. The acquisition of Evergreen should give them the push they need to join the top five British record labels.

Helen McCarthy, Metropolitan's young financial director (and at present one of few senior women in a male-dominated industry), was unavailable for comment yesterday. The mysterious Miss McCarthy, who rarely gives interviews, but has

done so much to steer Metropolitan into its strong financial
position, was said to be out of the country on a short holiday.
Brad Owen, Metropolitan's creative director, commented that
Evergreen's acquisition could only improve and enhance the
label's current artist list.

'I look forward to working with the artists involved,' he told
reporters during a short statement.

With debts running into hundreds of thousands, it remains
to be seen whether Miss McCarthy can wave her financial
wand and turn Evergreen's fortunes around.

Metropolitan are at present refurbishing a building in
Bedford Square to house both themselves and their new acqui-
sition.

Helen folded the two-day-old copy of *The Times* neatly on her
knee and pushed it into a pocket of her briefcase.

'Ladies and gentlemen, please return to your seats, extinguish
all cigarettes and fasten your seat belts. We will be landing at
Heathrow in approximately ten minutes.'

Helen gazed out of the window as the plane banked over
London and prepared to land. She allowed herself a small
smile. The five days in Nice had been just what she needed. It
was the first holiday she'd taken in three years. The tough
negotiations with Evergreen had taken up much of the past
two months. It had been a hard battle which had left even her
titan resources drained and in need of a break.

Her trip had not been all pleasure. Yesterday she'd had a
meeting with John Hale, a young American producer, currently
with EMI in the States. In a couple of months' time, John
would be joining Metropolitan to take charge of Evergreen
and its rebuilding process. If he was a success there, then Helen
hoped it might be possible to have him fill Brad's shoes.

He was fast becoming a liability, morphing over the last

few years into an overweight, bleary-eyed alcoholic. Nonetheless, as a producer he could not be bettered when on-song. The Fishermen loved him. Helen knew she'd find it hard to persuade them to give another producer a try on their next album.

Brad had one last chance. She'd send him back to the clinic in a few weeks, dry him out and put him into the studio with The Fishermen in September. If he didn't hold off the alcohol this time, then it really was time to oust him. Brad thought he was untouchable, but Helen knew of ways and means, foul though they might be, to get rid of him once and for all.

Brad may have begun Metropolitan, but it was her baby now. She was the one who had steered its rise from nowhere into a company with a turnover approaching fifteen million pounds per annum.

And she would have no one, *no one*, spoil her hard work.

The plane touched down on the runway. Helen decided she'd go home to her Holland Park mews house for a shower and a change of clothes, then she'd pop in and check how the work was going at the new offices. She'd pored over the plans with the architect, and after six months of gutting, rewiring, replumbing and replastering, Metropolitan was set to have a very impressive headquarters. Her pride and joy were the three recording suites in the basement. They were state-of-the-art and had cost more than the refurbishment of the rest of the building put together. In the long run, it was a shrewd investment.

In a few weeks' time, Metropolitan would be totally self-contained. All their artists could record under one roof, which would save on the high cost of renting studios elsewhere.

As she walked down the ramp from first class and into the terminal building, Helen felt a spring in her step. Things were going better than she ever dreamt. She was a rich, successful young woman.

Work was more than enough to compensate for the loneliness of her personal life.

Still no love, but enough power now to make up for it.

31

Sorcha nibbled at a piece of toast and reread the article dominating the front page of *The Daily Telegraph*.

AMERICANS WALK ON THE MOON

She looked up and out of the window at the burning blue sky. Neil Armstrong and *Apollo 11* were somewhere up there, a tiny craft amongst the vastness of space. Sorcha shook her head. It was impossible to comprehend. Her newspaper predicted that the recorded pictures of the first walk on the moon would be broadcast at around lunchtime. She would watch them on the new colour TV they had just had installed in the sitting room.

Sorcha stood up and placed her plate, cup and knife in the sink. She looked out of the kitchen window across the immaculately manicured lawns and sighed.

A beautiful house in Hampstead, overlooking the heath, a rich, successful husband that thousands of women the world over dreamt about at night, and more money than she could ever imagine spending.

Yet she felt miserable and unfulfilled.

Why, oh WHY did I turn down that contract?

She sighed.

Con had been thrilled when she had told him of her decision to go to the States with him. As the adulation for The Fishermen grew, and Con found himself mobbed by screaming girls everywhere he went, Sorcha was sure she'd made the right choice. She knew she could trust Con – it was the women she was not so sure of.

One night, the two of them had arrived home at their flat in Hampstead in the early hours to find a young girl in their bed. Stark naked. Con had managed to get her to leave with an autographed photo and one of his old unwashed T-shirts.

This had prompted them to move to somewhere more secure. After they returned from the States, they'd rented a flat in Chelsea with twenty-four-hour porterage, very near to Todd and Lulu.

The Fishermen had gone from strength to strength. Another two number-one hits had followed in that first year. The time seemed to fly as she and Con were wined, dined and fêted by all that met them. It had been huge fun in the beginning: jetting off all over the world, staying in the best hotels, meeting the kind of people that Sorcha had only read about in magazines or seen on the television.

And Con was always attentive and loving, apologising if he had to leave her in the hotel room to go off for an interview or a rehearsal. He'd furnish her with money to go shopping. Sorcha had a wardrobe filled with expensive clothes bought from all over the world.

Then, slowly, the constant travel and screaming fans had started to take their toll. Sorcha would never have believed that she could grow tired of shopping, but that was the truth. Lulu had been there to keep her company at first, but as her career as an actress had taken off, she'd spent less and less time on the road with Todd. Sorcha had begun to yearn for some stability and a break from the endless rounds of packing and unpacking suitcases. So, two years ago, they'd found a lovely Victorian house on the edge of Hampstead Heath. It needed major renovations, and Sorcha had elected to stay at home more often to oversee them. Refurbishing the house had been a challenge she had relished. She only wished Con was home more to enjoy it.

His absences, however, did not deter his fans. There were always three or four young girls on vigil outside the front gate, desperate for a glimpse of their hero. The high wall surrounding the house now boasted an ugly necklace of barbed wire to keep out Con's unwanted admirers. On more than one occasion, girls had spat at Sorcha when she drove out of the gates in the little Austin that Con had bought her for her birthday.

She hated the animosity, the uncomfortableness of being disliked not because of who she was but because of whom she was married to. Running the gauntlet of the fans outside caused Sorcha to think twice before she went out anywhere. Consequently, she spent more time than was good for her closeted inside the house.

Lately, she'd begun to feel a little like a prisoner.

She'd talked to Con about it, and all he could suggest was that she start to travel with him more often. However, the thought of hanging around in endless hotel rooms was even less appealing than staying at home, where she at least had her comforts.

Subsequently, she'd seen less and less of Con in the past few months.

Is he happy? she wondered to herself, then felt horrified that she didn't know the answer. Con was her husband. They lived in the same house, shared the same bed, and yet she had felt lately that they were somehow drifting apart.

'If only, if only the baby would happen,' she whispered.

Despite two years of letting nothing stand in their way, Sorcha had not yet fallen pregnant. She thought how ironic it was that when Con and she had first met, she'd been completely terrified of conceiving a child. And now, when it was so very much what she wanted, God would not oblige.

Maybe this was her punishment.

For some reason, lately she'd been thinking a lot about the past, and Ballymore. Her mother still wrote monthly, enclosing press cuttings of Con that she thought her daughter might have missed. Sorcha thanked her profusely each time she wrote back, not having the heart to tell her that The Fishermen had their own press department which collated news about the super-group from the four corners of the earth.

Her mother included news of her father in her letters – of how his business was thriving, of the fact that he was now head of the Ballymore Board of Trade and Commerce. It was obvious from her mother's letters that Seamus had still not softened in his attitude towards his daughter. She had accepted the fact that she'd probably never see her father again.

Sorcha busied herself around the kitchen even though she knew Miriam the cleaner would be in tomorrow, which made her own domestic energies pointless.

Sorcha sat down abruptly at the table, polish in one hand, duster in the other. That was exactly it.

She was totally surplus to requirements.

If she decided to go to bed today and stay there for a week, the only person who might notice, or indeed care, was Con. And she wasn't even sure that was guaranteed.

Abandoning her own fledgling career, Sorcha had known she was dedicating her life to her marriage. She had decided to be positive about it, embracing the lifestyle and wanting to support him in any way she could.

But Con now had a team of staff that looked after his every

need. The only territory that was hers alone was in the bedroom. And she wasn't providing what they wanted in there.

But if she was honest, it wasn't really any of those things that was the nub of the problem. They were surmountable. But Con had begun to change.

She could hardly bear to admit it to herself.

At first, she'd blamed it on the pressure he was under. There were no courses or books to tell you how to deal with the whole world wanting a slice of you. He'd seemed to cope very well to begin with; they'd laughed together about the underwear and the photographs of naked women offering their bodies, and the interest the media had in the minutiae of his life.

And then, a few months ago, as his fame reached seismic proportions, it had started to get to him. When he was home, he was morose and short-tempered. He'd sit in front of the TV news, swearing about the situation in Northern Ireland, or becoming steamed up by the war in Vietnam. He'd started to air his views in public, even attending peace rallies and marches.

Sorcha hadn't minded initially. If these causes gave him an outlet for his frustration, she'd accept it. But lately, it had begun to take over. Sorcha had recently voiced the opinion that it was all very well to sit in his big Hampstead house with his nice cars and more money than he knew what to do with and air his left-wing views, but wasn't he being a touch hypocritical?

Con hadn't spoken to her for three days.

She checked her watch. Almost eleven. Time to wake him up. She'd heard him arrive home in the small hours last night, from some anti-war protest in central London.

Sorcha stood up and put on the kettle. This weekend there was nothing on. She brightened considerably at the thought. A small oasis of time for the two of them to be together.

Ten minutes later, she entered the bedroom, still swathed in

257

darkness against the bright sun. She looked at Con, an arm thrown above his head, his expression, for once, peaceful. She set the tray down on the table at the end of the bed and kissed Con on the lips.

'Morning, darling.'

Con stirred, then smiled, his eyes still closed. His arms wound around her and he pulled her onto the bed to kiss her.

'Morning, Sorcha-porcha. This is a nice way to wake up.' His hand snaked under her blouse.

She looked down at him. 'I love you.'

'I love you too.' He tried to pull her back towards him but she resisted.

'Con, I was thinking I'd come to New York with you when you fly out for your next concert. I could do with a break from this house.'

'That's a grand idea, Sorcha. New York will cheer you up.'

'And, Con, you have nothing on this weekend, do you?'

'Er, well . . .'

'I know you don't. I looked in your diary. I was thinking maybe we could go away for the night somewhere. It seems ages since it was just the two of us.'

'Maybe. I'm sure you could persuade me.'

'I will certainly try,' she smiled.

Con pulled her down towards him.

'Morning, all! Thought I heard stirrings.'

Sorcha sat bolt upright as Lulu, her eyes heavy with sleep and wearing a T-shirt that only just covered her modesty, entered the room and bounced onto the bed beside them.

Sorcha could have wept.

'I didn't know you were here,' she said quietly.

'It was so late when we arrived back from the protest that I crashed in the spare room. Went well last night, didn't it, Con? Should make the front pages today.'

258

'You should, anyway,' quipped Con. '"Well-known actress attacks policeman at rally." Do you know how lucky you were to avoid being arrested?'

'I wish I had been. The only reason I wasn't was because the little shit was kicking the crap out of a poor defenceless student at the same time as I was jumping on his back to stop him. That would go down really well on the front page of the *Express*. Got any cigarettes?'

'Try my pocket.' Con pointed to the heap of clothes on the floor by the window.

Lulu jumped off the bed, rifled through Con's pockets and pulled out a packet of Embassy. She lit one up and climbed back on the bed.

'Does Todd know you're here?' asked Sorcha.

'No. And I have no intention of telling him. We had a bit of a barney before I left for the protest. He doesn't think it's good for his image to have his wife portrayed as a militant.'

'Even if you are,' smiled Con.

'It's not my fault that I care what happens to this stinky old world. Read the papers this morning, Sorcha?'

'Yes.'

'Anything in there about last night?'

'Not that I saw. I think the fact Neil Armstrong made it to the moon took precedence.'

'Damn! Why did it have to be last night? The papers'll be full of nothing else for days now. We might as well have not bothered.'

Sorcha climbed off the bed. 'Well, I'm interested in it if no one else is. I'm going down to the see the pictures on television. Are you coming, Con?'

'Let me wake up a while, Sorcha, will you?'

'Okay. Shall I go and see if I could book somewhere for tonight?'

'Tonight? You're not thinking of going away, are you?' said Lulu.

'We were, yes.' Anger burned in Sorcha's eyes.

'But, Con, they're holding a candlelight vigil outside the American embassy. It would really help if you turned up and—'

Sorcha walked out of the room and slammed the door shut behind her.

32

'Con, what exactly is this shit?'

Con looked up from his sheet music to see Todd glaring at him from the piano stool.

'That "shit", as you put it, is a song I wrote last week in support of the American vets.'

Todd stared at him. 'And you seriously want The Fishermen to record it and put it on our new album?'

'Yes. Why not? It has meaning, a message. I'd say it might make people stop and take notice of just exactly what is going on in this world.'

'Jesus fucking Christ!' Todd swept a hand through his hair. 'Between you and Lulu, I'm getting no respite!' Todd played the opening bars of the song, before crashing his hands down on the piano to release a cacophony of discordant sounds. 'I give up. Apart from the fact that the lyrics include four swear words, which means the song will be banned by every radio station and mainstream record shop the world over, there's no frigging melody line, mate. We're a pop group, Con!' Todd stood up. 'We release records that kids like to dance to. I hardly think the line "the young ones die in their thousands, their red blood turning the fields to rust, the insects swarming in the dust" is going to light up a disco.'

Con reached for his packet of Embassy and lit a cigarette.

'Todd, how many times have we had this conversation? What's the point of our music and fame if we're not using it to do some good? These soppy, meaningless love songs feather our own nest. But they don't give anything back. We have the power to change the world for the better.'

Todd sighed and shook his head slowly. 'Boy, have you changed. There's me, happy to trot out pleasant ballads, grateful for my nice house and bulging bank balance . . . and there's you, sticking two fingers up at all that.'

Con continued to smoke his cigarette silently.

Todd sighed. 'I dunno, Con. I just think it's a shame you seem to glean so little pleasure from your achievements. Just occasionally think back and remember how badly you wanted fame and fortune.'

Con still did not respond.

'And there's such a thing as abusing your position. Okay, so you're a famous pop star, but you're not a politician. You're going to put a lot of noses out of joint, especially if you carry on so noisily about Ulster.'

'I—'

Todd stretched his hands out. 'Please, Con, spare me the political diatribe. I've heard it all before.' He crossed the room and took a seat on the green velvet sofa next to his writing partner. 'Listen, I can understand your vehemence over the situation in Ireland. At least it's part of who you are. But it's all these other causes that you seem to throw yourself into. For example, the Vietnam War. I mean . . . you're not even American. Or Vietnamese! The whole thing's happening thousands of miles away and—'

'Yes, and isn't that just the attitude that stops anything changing? The "well, it's not affecting me so I'll ignore it" philosophy?' Con stood up. 'I'd say I've had enough for today. I'm going home.'

'That's right, Con. Walk out again. Jesus! Just for once in your life try and remember your priorities. We're recording an album in a couple of months' time. At the moment we have two and a half songs. Three and a half if you include the pile of shit you brought in this morning. At this rate we won't be bringing out an album at all, because frankly, I've just about had enough! I'm trying to hold this band together while you run around playing Bolshie, *and* egging on my wife into the bargain. In case you've forgotten, we've the concert in Central Park in a few weeks. A quarter of a million people are going to turn up to see us and we haven't even worked out a playing order. Now that's what *I* call letting people down, you—'

The door of the rehearsal room slammed behind Con.

'—son of a bitch,' murmured Todd to thin air. 'Bugger it.' Todd slid back down onto his piano stool and shook his head.

God, he was pissed off. Con was behaving like a complete arsehole, and had been for months now. He couldn't remember the last time they'd sat down and really sparked off each other, as had been the case in the beginning.

Con and he had been labelled as the songwriting partnership of the decade. In the early days of their success, they'd flown along. Todd, with his eye for the commercial catchy melody, had been toned down by Con's more serious lyrical approach. They'd written some wonderful songs – songs that Con now trashed as 'meaningless crap'. They'd worked late into the night, stimulated and excited by the words and music they seemed capable of producing so easily.

But now the two of them were lucky if they could stick at it for more than a couple of hours. The rapport seemed to have disappeared. The pair were sailing off in opposite directions. Todd wondered if they would ever meet in the middle again.

Had the rot set in, as it had in so many other groups over the years? Everyone knew that the Con Daly and Todd Bradley partnership was the lifeblood of the band. If that continued to disintegrate at its present rate, then what future did The Fishermen have?

And then there was the Lulu problem.

Lulu and he had married four years ago, just before they'd flown to the States to support The Trojans. The two of them had had a great party of a wedding, inviting friends new and old and being mobbed as they emerged from Chelsea registry office.

Over the next couple of years, Lulu's career as an actress had really started to flourish. She'd done a new play in the West End for which she'd received an award and serious critical acclaim. It had felt then that the couple were unstoppable. What had happened since?

Lulu had followed Con's lead and embraced the political scene, becoming more and more involved in what Todd saw as hopeless, pointless causes. Instead of enjoying their dual success, she was always rushing around trying to save the world and sometimes bringing her smelly, unkempt fellow activists into their lovely Chelsea home.

In the past few months, Todd had seen less and less of her. She seemed to spend more time with Con and Sorcha in Hampstead than she did at home.

They'd not had sex for over a month.

Yesterday, he'd tried and she'd refused him. They'd had a huge argument and she'd stormed off. He didn't know where she was now, but that wasn't unusual these days.

Was she having an affair with Con?

It was a thought that had to be contemplated, considering the amount of time they spent together and their shared interests.

God, he loved her. Difficult, spoilt and selfish as she was, he worshipped the ground she walked on.

Todd wondered what Sorcha thought of her husband's close

relationship with his wife. The last couple of times he'd seen her, Sorcha had looked completely miserable.

Maybe he should give her a ring and suggest they meet up to discuss their respective partners. At any rate, the situation could not be allowed to continue. Todd was watching his marriage disintegrate. Something had to be done and fast.

The door of the recording studio opened silently. Todd turned around at the sound of footsteps behind him.

'Hello, Derek, what brings you here?'

Derek still looked like a teenager pretending to be a grown man, even in his smart designer suit.

'Hi, I was just passing on my way to lunch. I thought I'd drop in. Where's Con? I thought the two of you were working together today.'

'We were, but . . .' Todd shrugged. 'We took an early lunch.'

'Oh.' Derek fidgeted nervously.

'What?'

'It's just that . . . I've written a song. I want you to listen to it. I . . . I'd like it to go on the new album. I think it's about time one of my compositions made it to vinyl.'

'Have you got the music with you? At the moment, Noddy could write for the album and I'd be grateful,' Todd quipped. Then, seeing the look on Derek's face, he checked himself. 'Sorry, mate, only teasing. Let's have a look.'

Derek pulled out some sheets of music from his jacket pocket and handed them to Todd. He unfolded them and placed them on the piano.

'I know you think I can't write songs for toffee, but I showed some of my stuff to a producer last week and he said he liked it. I'm fed up with you and Con taking the piss and if you don't want this song, then I'll give it to someone who does.'

Derek stood there like a petulant little boy, his bottom lip quivering.

Todd was in no mood for another set-to. He held up his hands. 'Okay, okay. I'm sorry, Derek. Let's see what we've got. I'll play, you sing.'

The song was a gentle ballad, nothing special, but a definite improvement on anything Derek had composed before.

'Well,' Todd said, handing the music back to Derek, 'I think it's got possibilities.'

'I think it's pretty good as it is,' Derek said stubbornly. 'What needs changing?'

'Well, nothing major. We need to perk up the chorus, write some orchestrations for it, et cetera.'

'I think it's just as good as "Can Someone Tell Me Where She's Gone?". It's only because it's my song that you're being so snotty about it.'

'Look, mate, I'm not being snotty at all. I really do think the song has potential. Let me show it to Con and see what he thinks.'

'I don't care what Con thinks. I want the song on the album.'

'Okay, okay. What's it called by the way?'

'"Peggy". It's just called "Peggy".'

Todd raised an eyebrow and smiled. 'Of course.' This was the icing on the cake. 'Well, that's me for the day. Are you rushing straight off or can you join me for some liquid refreshment at the Dog and Gun round the corner?'

Derek checked his Rolex. 'I've got twenty minutes before I meet her.'

'Good man.' Todd stood up. 'Who's "her"?' he asked as he flicked off the light switch. The two of them left the studio and walked up the steps into the heart of Soho.

'Oh, some model I met at a club the other day.' They walked companionably along the busy street.

'Do you think you'll ever fall in love and settle down, Derek?

All these gorgeous women that seem to pass through your bed. Have you never thought of marriage?'

Derek turned to look at Todd.

'Yes,' he said, 'once. But never again.'

33

The telephone rang. Sorcha opened her eyes and absorbed the greyness of the early morning. The telephone lived on Con's bedside cabinet. She lay there for a few moments more, hoping he'd wake up and answer it. He didn't, so she threw off the covers and padded round the bed to pick up the receiver.

'Hello?'

'Can I speak to Sorcha Daly?'

'Mammy? It's me.'

'Sorcha, how are ye?'

'I'm okay. And you, Mammy? How are you?'

'Well now, Sorcha. I have some bad news for you.'

'What, Mammy?'

'Your daddy passed away yesterday. He had a heart attack. I was wondering whether you might come home for the funeral. It's tomorrow.'

'Oh, Mammy, are you okay?'

'I'm coping. The neighbours have been fierce kind. It was the shock more than anything. He was walking home from a meeting in the community hall and dropped dead there and then, in the middle of Connolly Street.'

'I'm so sorry, Mammy, I really am.' Although Sorcha struggled to feel sorrow in her heart for her dead father, there was plenty of compassion for her mother. 'You say the funeral's tomorrow?'

'Yes.'

'Then I'd have to fly over today.'

'Would you, Sorcha? Oh, would you?' There was desperation in her mother's voice.

'Of course.'

'Thank you. Apart from anything, it would be grand to see you. And Con, if he's of a mind to come. I . . .' The catch in Mary's voice betrayed her bravery. 'There's a lot to organise.'

'Mammy, I can't promise but I'll do my best. I'll call you back as soon as I've news.'

'Do you have the office telephone number?'

'Somewhere, but give it to me again.' Sorcha searched in Con's bedside drawer, finding a felt-tip pen and an empty cigarette packet. 'Okay.' Sorcha scribbled the number down. 'I'll ring you back as soon as I can.'

'Bye, Sorcha.'

She put down the receiver and sat staring into space. A hand on her naked back made her jump out of her skin.

'Steady on, it's only me. Who was that?'

'My mother.'

'Your mother? What did she want?'

'She called to tell me that my daddy died yesterday.'

'Ah.' Con lapsed into silence, trying to gauge his wife's reaction. 'Do you want sympathy, Sorcha?'

She turned around slowly and looked at him. 'No. But he was my father. I'm sorry he's dead. He was only in his fifties.'

'How's your mammy?'

'She sounds as though she's not really taken it in. Con, the funeral's tomorrow. I must go home for it and I should probably stay a few days afterwards.'

'Of course you must go. Jenny's in at nine. We'll get her to organise the flights.'

Jenny was Con's part-time secretary who came in to deal

with the sacks of fan mail and any general administration required.

'And what about you?' she asked quietly.

'What about me?'

'Would you not think it appropriate to come with me, at least for the funeral?'

Con looked at her in surprise. 'Me? Go back to Ballymore for the funeral of the man who wanted to throw me in jail?' Con shook his head. 'No, Sorcha, I don't think so.'

She bit her lip. 'But, Con, remember how we said that one day we'd go back and everyone would want to know us in Ballymore? Surely this is the moment?'

'I'm not a hypocrite, Sorcha. It would be wrong of me to attend the funeral of a man I disliked and who disliked me.'

'And what about me? Maybe *I* need you by my side.'

'Be honest, Sorcha, you can't be sorry he's dead. You hated him.'

There was a pang in Sorcha's heart. 'That isn't the point.'

Con was reaching for his cigarettes. 'Isn't it?'

'No! If you can't understand why I'd like you to be by my side when I return home after all these years, then forget it, just forget it.' She shuddered, stood up and reached for her dressing gown. 'I have a lot to do if I'm to leave this afternoon.'

'Ah, Sorcha, please. Let's not have another argument. If you're sorry, then I'm sorry your daddy's dead. But even if I wanted to, I couldn't come to Ballymore today. You know the band's deep in rehearsal for the Central Park gig next week.'

'Rehearsals haven't mattered a damn when you've had a sit-in or a protest to go to, have they? But then I suppose I have to accept that me and my feelings come bottom of your list of priorities. After all, I'm just your wife! You couldn't give a damn how I feel, could you?'

'Sorcha! Sorcha, please!'

She'd already left the room, slamming the door behind her. With a sigh, Con sank back onto the pillows.

Sorcha heard Con's car screech out of the drive on his way into the studio in central London. Then she went to Jenny's office to organise her flights.

'Con was looking for you.'

'I popped out for some fresh air.'

'Oh. Well, he said to say that he'd try and get home before you left, but if he didn't, you're to leave a number where you can be contacted. I've already called Aer Lingus. The direct flight to Cork is full. You'll have to change at Dublin. The plane leaves Heathrow at two thirty, arriving in Dublin at half past four. There's a ten-to-six flight down to Cork, which arrives in at ten to seven. I've held this afternoon's travel, but the airline needs to know when you're returning.'

Maybe never, Sorcha thought as she stared at the corkboard behind Jenny's desk. She had stuck particularly funny fan letters onto it, along with promotional shots of Con and the band. She shrugged. 'I've really no idea.'

'Then I'll organise an open return.'

'Yes. Thanks, Jenny. I must go up and pack.'

'Of course. I'll order a car for you for half past twelve. That should give you plenty of time. And, Sorcha?'

'Yes?'

'I'm really sorry about your dad.'

'Thank you. I'll see you later.'

Sorcha's taxi arrived in Ballymore at just after half past eight that evening. She felt exhausted from the long day of travelling.

She hadn't wanted to brood on either the situation she'd left behind or the one in front of her, so she'd spent the journey

271

with her head buried in the pile of glossy magazines that she'd bought herself at the airport.

Darkness had only just fallen in the village. She remembered going to bed as a child at nine o'clock with the sun just setting. There were only six hours of darkness in high summer.

Sorcha looked out of the taxi window at the familiar landmarks. Little seemed to have changed, apart from the odd shop closed up because its owner had presumably died, and a new tea room on the corner.

When she'd lived here, she'd hardly been able to wait to leave for her new, exciting life with Con in London. She'd thought Ballymore dull, the people insular. Back then, Sorcha could not understand why anyone would want to live out their life here.

But now, there was something comforting and secure about its unchanging, quaint nature.

'That'll be five pounds, thank you now, Sorcha.' The taxi stopped in the square in front of her parents' house.

The familiarity of a stranger using her first name was strikingly different from the impersonal attitude of London.

The taxi driver got out, opened the boot and placed her suitcase on the pavement.

'There you go, and a pound for your trouble.'

'That's grand altogether. Thank you. Have yourself a good stay.'

Sorcha smiled ironically. 'Thanks. Goodnight.'

As the taxi drove off, Sorcha picked up her suitcase and walked to the front door of her house. She rang the big brass bell.

A few seconds later the door opened.

'Sorcha! Sorcha! Oh, I can hardly believe it's really you.'

Her mother pulled her into her arms. Sorcha dropped her suitcase and returned the hug. When they pulled apart, their eyes were full of tears.

'Come in, come in.' Mary picked up the suitcase and walked up the stairs.

The smell was so familiar – brass polish and disinfectant, liberally applied in the hall every other day on the doorknob and tiled floor. For a moment, everything spun around her and Sorcha caught the banister to steady herself.

Mary stopped and turned around.

'Are you all right?'

Sorcha nodded. 'Fine, Mammy.'

'Your daddy's in there, but we'll share a tot of whiskey before we go in to see him.' Mary had reached the top of the staircase and was indicating the dining room.

Mary left Sorcha's case outside the kitchen, ushered her inside and closed the door firmly behind her.

'Now, let me look at you.' She smiled as her eyes ran over her daughter. 'I think, Sorcha O'Donovan, that you have grown into a real beauty.'

'And you don't look a day older yourself,' lied Sorcha.

'Do I not? Well, it's kind of you to say, but I know the years have not treated me kindly.' Mary smoothed down her dress over her bulging hips. 'Sit down, sit down. I'll pour us both a drink.'

The bottle was on the table, a third empty. Mary filled up two glasses and passed one to Sorcha.

'Well, 'tis an ill wind, as they say. I lose a husband but my precious daughter returns. *Slainte.*' Mary raised her glass and took a large gulp. 'Ah, there's no doubt it helps calm the nerves, but I'll be langers if I have much more.'

'And you have every right to get a little tipsy, Mammy. The shock must have been terrible.'

'It was, it was. Sean Moloney, the young guard, arrived at my door last night to tell me what had happened. The doctor had been called, but there was nothing he could do.' Mary gave a little hiccup and blushed. 'Excuse me. I'm not used to the hard stuff. So, they brought him back here and John the undertaker arrived first thing to measure up. I put him in his best Sunday pinstripe suit and chose a cedarwood coffin. I've spent the day opening and closing the door. You know how it is here. The whole village arrived to pay their respects. I ran out of sherry at lunchtime and had to run to Nora Connolly's to get some more.'

'You seem to be coping very well, Mammy.'

'Thanks be to God, it was quick. That's what people have said to me. I don't think he would have known what was happening.'

'I'm sure you're right.'

Mary took another gulp of whiskey, which left her with an empty glass. 'Want a top-up?'

Sorcha shook her head.

'The last one, to give me Dutch courage to face your father. Thinking of it, I always needed Dutch courage to face your father,' she smiled weakly.

'What time is the funeral?'

'Two o'clock, but they're coming to take him away at nine in the morning. There's a mass at eleven just for the family. Father Moynihan wanted to take him this evening to have him lie in overnight, but I thought you might like to say a private goodbye.'

Sorcha grimaced then drained her glass. 'Come on, Mammy, let's go and get it over with.'

'Yes, I suppose we'd better.'

The two of them stood up. Sorcha led the way out of the kitchen and across the landing to the closed dining-room door. She swallowed hard, then turned the handle and opened the door.

The coffin was lying on the highly polished dining-room

table. Sorcha blessed herself, as did her mother. Then she reached for her mother's hand and, together, they shuffled forward and peered inside the coffin.

Apart from the fact that he'd lost a considerable amount of his hair in the past five years, her father looked exactly the same. Clearly, he'd worn better than his wife. In death, his lips were tinged with grey and his skin looked like alabaster.

'Shall I leave you for a few minutes?'

'No, stay, Mammy, please.' Sorcha gripped Mary's hand, finding her father's presence in death as intimidating as it had been in life. Both women stared at the body in silence.

'Done a grand job, though, hasn't he?'

'Who?'

'John the undertaker,' Mary whispered, as though she might disturb Seamus from his eternal sleep if she ever raised her voice.

'Yes.'

'And you think the suit was right?'

'Perfect.'

'Well now, do you want to stay any longer?'

Sorcha shook her head and they both filed out of the dining room.

'There, you've seen him and I don't think we need to bother again.' The relief on Mary's face was evident as they made their way back to the kitchen. 'Can I get you anything to eat, Sorcha? You must be hungry from your journey?'

'No thanks, Mammy. I'm past eating.'

'Well, what about a big Irish breakfast tomorrow morning?'

'That would be lovely, but we might not have time.'

'Ah, 'twill take me no time at all. Now, would you like a bath? I've heard it's fierce filthy up in those aeroplanes.'

'No,' Sorcha smiled, 'but I'd love a cup of tea.'

Mary crossed to the range and stood the large stainless-steel kettle on a hotplate. The visit to the dining room seemed to have sobered her up somewhat.

'It's a shame Con wasn't able to make it.'

'Yes. Unfortunately he's off to the States next week. The band are giving a huge concert in New York and they're rehearsing at the moment.'

'How famous he's become, Sorcha! Who'd have thought it? And him living like a knacker in a hut on the beach. Those I told will be disappointed he's not with you.'

'Really?' Sorcha watched her mother pour the boiling water into the blue enamel teapot, still doing sterling service after all these years. 'I would have thought Con was the last person people around here wanted to see. They couldn't wait to rid the town of him.'

'But now everyone is his best friend.' Mary stirred the teapot. 'Last year we had a journalist asking questions about Con around the town. You'd not believe the number of people who swore they were like a brother to him and the amount of women who had once been his sweetheart. He came here too.'

'Did he? And what did you tell him?'

'I didn't get a chance. Your daddy slammed the door in his face.'

It was one of the only things Seamus had ever done for which his daughter was grateful.

'There you go, a nice hot drop.' Mary put the cup down in front of her.

'Thanks.' Sorcha sipped the tea. 'Ah, there's no one in the world that can make a cup of tea like you, Mammy.'

'Thank you, I'm sure.' Mary smiled and sat down at the table. 'Sorcha, there are so many things I want to ask you about the last few years. It's hard to know where to start.'

'I know.'

'Maybe after tomorrow we can sit down and catch up properly. Or are you rushing back?'

'I . . . I haven't thought about it yet, Mammy. Let's take one day at a time, shall we?'

'Of course.'

Sorcha stifled a yawn.

'You poor thing. You're exhausted and here's me chattering away like an old fishwife. Let's get you to your bed. You'll need your sleep before tomorrow. You'll be on parade, Sorcha, there's no doubting that. I reckon it'll be one of the best-attended funerals ever in Ballymore, with all the folks rubber-necking to catch a glimpse of Seamus O'Donovan's famous son-in-law.'

'Well, I'll be sorry to disappoint them,' Sorcha said bitterly.

'I'm glad he's not here. It'll give us a chance to get to know each other properly again. Come on now, to bed with you. It's almost midnight.'

Sorcha followed her mother up the stairs to her bedroom. She drew in her breath when she saw the way that it had lain undisturbed since the day she'd left it almost six years ago.

'Everything's as it was. I vacuumed and dusted every week, to keep it nice.'

Sorcha fingered the china animal collection on her dressing table. She'd treasured it as a child.

'I'm amazed Daddy didn't have the room fumigated and stripped,' she laughed.

'He was after suggesting we redecorated and got rid of your things, but I stood up to him on that one. This room was all I had of you and I wasn't going to let it go.'

'He really hated me, didn't he?' Sorcha sat down on the bed and clasped a teddy to her breast.

Mary looked to the floor and shook her head. 'No, Sorcha. You've got it very wrong there. He loved you so much. Worshipped you, in fact. You took ten years to arrive, a gift from God. When you fell in love with Con, he just couldn't cope. So, he did the only thing he could do and cut you out of his life altogether. He had such grand plans for you, Sorcha.' Mary sighed. 'It's partly my fault. If I'd have given him more children like the rest of the women round here were able to give their husbands, then maybe the load on your shoulders would not have been so great. Talking of which, I'm fairly surprised that you and Con haven't a little one yet.'

'Ah, Mammy, it's not for lack of wanting,' sighed Sorcha.

'It'll happen, I'm sure. The trick is not to worry about it. Now, have you your night things in here?' Mary lifted her suitcase onto the end of the bed and opened it. Sorcha lolled on her mattress and watched as Mary busied herself hanging up her clothes and arranging the contents of her washbag on the dressing table.

'There now, your things are sorted. I'll leave you to get undressed.' Mary hovered in the doorway, unwilling to leave.

Sorcha understood. She stood up, walked across to her mother and put her arms round her shoulders. 'If you get lonely in the night, come and wake me.'

'Oh, I'll be fine, don't worry your head about me.'

'And, Mammy, it's grand to be home.'

'Really?'

'Really.'

'Goodnight, Sorcha.'

'Night, Mammy.'

Sorcha sank into bed, every bone in her body aching for the peace and sleep. But every time she began to doze off, she thought of the stiff, grey-lipped corpse dressed in its Sunday church suit lying on the dining-room table. In the end she turned on the light, pulled down an old children's book from her shelf and started to read.

After a few minutes, she became aware of the sound of sobbing.

She climbed out of bed and padded across to her mother's room. As a child she'd been forbidden entry without knocking. Tonight, she opened the door and walked into the darkness.

'Mammy? Mammy?' Sorcha searched for the bed and climbed in under the sheets.

'I'm sorry, Sorcha, really I am. I didn't mean to disturb you. And you so tired.'

'I couldn't sleep either. Maybe we'll both feel better when Daddy has gone out of the house.'

'Yes, yes, I'm sure we will. Oh, Sorcha, I . . . I'm trying to be brave, but I can't believe he's gone. And you know the worst thing?'

'What, Mammy?'

'I don't know whether I ever loved him. Sometimes I could swear I even hated him. But he was all I had. And in his way he was a good husband. He looked after me.'

Sorcha snuggled in closer. 'Budge up and let me get comfortable. I'm staying here tonight.' She rearranged herself on the pillows that had only two days ago supported Seamus's head. Then she reached for her mother's hand under the covers.

'I missed you, Mammy, something fierce.'

'You did?' Mary sounded calmer.

'Oh yes. Now, before the birds start their dawn chorus, let's both of us try and get some sleep. Night, Mammy.'

'Goodnight, sweetheart.'

34

Con, unusually, woke early. He lay with his eyes closed, willing sleep to return. He had a busy day rehearsing in the studio, then he was speaking at a rally of the Campaigners for Peace in Trafalgar Square in the evening.

After half an hour of trying, Con gave up and reached for his packet of cigarettes. He lit one up, then lay back on the pillows and took a deep drag.

He felt, as he had for some time, unsettled and unhappy.

'Why?' he whispered to the empty room.

Con Daly, the boy from nowhere, with statistically little chance of making anything of his life, had risen to achieve fame and fortune beyond his wildest dreams.

So why did nothing give him pleasure any more? He knew how difficult he was being with Sorcha, Todd and the rest of the band, yet it seemed he couldn't help himself.

He was still in his twenties. He was too young for a mid-life crisis, surely?

Even music, always the great passion in his life, no longer gave him the buzz it once had. He thought of next week and the huge open-air concert in Central Park. Con no longer felt anticipation or excitement. All he could think of was the crush of bodies that would await his limousine – the pushing and shoving that saw him protected by minders as he made his way backstage.

To top everything off, rehearsals had not been going well. Todd and he had done little more than argue about what they would play. Con wanted to try some of the new stuff he'd written, but Todd argued that with almost a quarter of a million people in attendance, they should stick to the tried and trusted numbers that had made them such a huge success. 'That's what the fans will be coming for,' he had said. And he was probably right.

Con felt the claustrophobia weigh in on him. It was as if his fame, which should give him so much power, had taken away his freedom both personally and professionally.

He could no longer go where he wanted or write what he felt he should. Creatively, he felt stifled. He knew Todd disapproved of his political anthems, but then his bandmate was a middle-class boy who'd never known what it was like to go to bed so hungry your stomach ached.

Con ground out his cigarette into the pot plant that stood on the floor near the bed.

He had too much success to be so bitter. What the hell was he becoming?

Moodily, Con lit up again. He'd even started to drink to the point of oblivion, after all those years living with his father and swearing he'd never do the same.

Sometimes he caught Sorcha looking at him, her face a picture of sadness.

He'd shut her out, he knew he had. And yesterday, when she'd been so desperate for his love and support, and he'd been unable to give it to her. There was a definite chance he could lose her . . . but the numbness in his heart seemed to prevent him doing anything about it.

Con got out of bed and showered, before heading downstairs to brew himself a large pot of coffee. He piled it on a tray with a mug and a packet of biscuits, then picked up his guitar and began to tinker with a tune that had been going around in his head for the past few days.

'Shit!'

It just wouldn't come any more.

'Jesus, Mary and Joseph! What's happening to me?'

Con picked up his coffee cup, stood up and looked out of the window. It was a lovely August morning. He watched his electric security gates slide open, and Jenny's car pull into the drive. As the gates closed, he saw one of his most loyal fans attempt to squeeze between them. As was most often the case, the extra strong gates – bespoke built – won.

Con shook his head in despair. Would she one day look back and wonder why she wasted some of the best years of her life sitting outside the gates of a rock star's house?

Con sipped his coffee and listened as Jenny opened the front door. He'd go and make chit-chat – anything to take him away from the maudlin thoughts swimming about his head. He mused at the hours he'd spent alone in his hut on the beach, sometimes not seeing another person for a week. These days, he dreaded his own company.

At least tonight he'd be out with Lulu. She was the one person who brought him out of himself. Con admired her focus and determination. She didn't give a damn what others thought of her, and was prepared to go to any lengths to publicise her cause.

He opened the door to his study and walked across the hall. Jenny's voice carried out of her office. He stopped to listen.

'He's had another one, Inspector . . . Yes, it's the sixth . . . Oh, pretty much the same . . . the letters cut out of a news-paper, the usual murder threat. Yes, this time the postmark's Southampton. The weirdo certainly gets around! No, I haven't yet, but I think the time has probably come. Will you? Okay then, I'll call you back when I've spoken to Metropolitan. Goodbye, Inspector.'

Con heard the click of the receiver. He opened the door. 'Morning, Jenny.'

She turned round. 'Hello, Con, you're up early.'

'Yeah.' Con was staring at the paper in her hand. He snatched it from her.

GONNA GET YOU COMING SOON YOU BASTARD IRISH FILTH.

Con shuddered involuntarily and dropped the letter onto Jenny's desk.

'Did I hear you say that was the sixth such epistle I've received?'

'Yes. Look, Con, don't panic or anything. It's all under control. We didn't want to worry you unduly.'

'Someone's sending me murder threats and no one bothers to tell me.' Con forced a chuckle. 'How old do you think I am, Jenny? Ten?'

'I'm sorry, Con, really. You've been perfectly safe, though. There's an unmarked police car that sits outside the house every day. It's followed you everywhere for the past month.'

Con was startled. 'Has it now? Jesus, the police must be short of something to do if they can spare someone to babysit me. I've had these sorts of letters before. It's just cranks with nothing better to do than to scare me.'

'Well, I spoke to Helen McCarthy when these things first started arriving and she decided it was a matter for the police because of all the Troubles in Ulster and your, er, well-publicised attitude towards them. The previous letters never made a point of highlighting your nationality. Anyway, I've spoken to the inspector and he wants to drop in and have a word with you.'

'We're in the studio rehearsing all day but . . . tell him he can see me there at lunchtime. I'll buy him a beer and a sandwich for his trouble.'

'Okay, will do.'

Con stood up. 'I'd say I need some air. I'm going for a walk on the heath before I leave for the studio.'

'Fine. Try not to worry, Con. You really are being well looked after.'

Con smiled thinly and left the room. He opened the front door and stepped out into the fresh, warm air, heading for the concealed gate at the bottom of the garden which led directly onto the heath. His heart was beating fast as he undid the padlock. Con felt stiflingly hot all of a sudden, and there was a tight band around his chest. After relocking the gate, he set off at speed onto the heath, his breath coming in short, sharp bursts.

It wasn't long before he came to a halt, his breath too short to allow him to go any further. He crouched down under a tree, his head in his hands.

'Oh, Jesus,' he panted as he rested on his haunches.

Sorcha . . . New York . . . the new album . . . and now these threats. The pressure was intolerable. Con had a burning urge to disappear to where no one would find him.

He wiped his forehead and stood up, taking some deep breaths.

The option was always there if he wanted to take it. He was amazed at how much the thought comforted him. Maybe he was just tired and worn out from the punishing schedule of the past four years.

Con looked at his watch. He was already late for rehearsals.

Feeling calmer, he walked slowly back home across the heath.

35

Sorcha stood next to her mother at the graveside as they watched Seamus's coffin being lowered into the earth. She glanced at Mary's face. Her mother was pale, but dry-eyed. Seamus's sister was sobbing, but then Sorcha remembered that Orla cried buckets at weddings and christenings too.

'All right, Mary.' Father Moynihan spoke softly. 'You can go forward now.'

Mary took a couple of steps, knelt down, and picked up some earth from the pile that would eventually cover her husband for ever. She threw her handful into the hole and it splattered on top of the highly polished cedarwood coffin. Sorcha found herself thinking what a waste of a hundred pounds it had been, and that a shroud really was much more practical.

Stop it, stop it! A voice in her head told her she should feel remorse – *something* – but in truth, she was empty. She squeezed her eyes closed.

Forgive me, God. I can't pretend I loved him when I didn't.

She opened her eyes and watched as the rest of Seamus's relations filed by the grave, each throwing in a handful of earth.

'Will you?' Mary whispered.

Sorcha acquiesced to please her mother.

'Right. That's all over now, Mary,' said Father Moynihan. 'I'll escort you and Sorcha back to your car.'

'Thank you, Father. You'll be coming back to the house for a glass of sherry, I hope?'

''Twould be grand, Mary.'

Sorcha followed her mother and Father Moynihan through the crowd of mourners. There were certainly many familiar faces. She kept her head down, not wishing to make contact just yet. After all, most of them would be coming to the house for the wake.

A photographer from the local paper stood by the entrance to the graveyard. He'd been hovering when the cortège had pulled up in front of the church and had watched hopefully as Sorcha and Mary climbed out.

'Is your husband not here with you, Mrs Daly?' he'd asked Sorcha as the driver had closed the door of the car behind her.

'No.'

Sorcha had hurried past into the church.

Now he came forward, aimed his camera and took a photograph of the three of them walking towards the car.

Sorcha turned in anger. 'Have you no scruples?'

'Pardon, Mrs Daly, but we don't get many wives of world-famous pop singers in the vicinity.'

Sorcha did not reply as she followed Mary and Father Moynihan into the back of the funeral car, which pulled off on the start of its short drive to the square. Mary reached for Sorcha's hand and squeezed it.

'Okay?'

'Yes. You?'

'Yes. It's nearly over, Sorcha.'

She could hear the relief in her mother's voice.

Once they arrived home, Sorcha installed Mary and Father Moynihan in the sitting room with a restorative glass of sherry, while she went into the kitchen to oversee the food preparation. Two of Mary's friends had been working away since the early morning to provide a feast for the mourners.

Mrs Hurley, whom Sorcha had known since she was a baby, spoke shyly to her. 'Sorcha, could you possibly pour the sherry? Then Eileen and I can hand it around as people start to arrive.'

'Of course I can. And as you're doing such a grand job in here, why don't I hand it around as well?'

'Of course, Sorcha. Whatever you want.'

For the next hour, Sorcha did her duty and furnished the assembled company with a glass of sherry or orange squash if they preferred. People she had known since childhood – who had chastised her for almost knocking them over in the street or making too much noise as she played with her friends – now talked to her shyly, as though she was some strange alien being. Their attitude upset her more than her father's death. It under-lined her complete lack of identity and the fact that she didn't seem to fit in anywhere.

As the sun beat down relentlessly, windows were opened, sandwiches consumed and more sherry sent for from Mrs Connolly's store. With Seamus properly laid to rest, the men removed their jackets and black ties, the ladies their hats, and everyone began to relax. Sorcha wished they would all go home, but she knew that it was unlikely the last person would leave until late in the evening – and the chances were that they'd be carried out.

The sitting room was stifling. Sorcha's head began to spin. She needed some fresh air. Her mother was deep in conversation with Georgie O'Hea, one of the town's shopkeepers, her face flushed from the heat and the sherry. Sorcha determined it was safe to leave for a while. She hurried down the staircase to the front door.

The air outside was cooler, and Sorcha gulped some into her

lungs before walking across the road towards the square. She hadn't even reached the gate when she heard her name being called.

'Sorcha Mary O'Donovan! It *is* you!'

Sorcha turned around. There, running across the street towards her, was Maureen.

'Sorcha!' As she reached her, Maureen opened her now plump arms and threw them around her shoulders. 'Ah, Sorcha! I was so afraid I might have missed you. I couldn't get here any earlier 'cos I had no one to mind the kids but . . .' Maureen tried to catch her breath. 'Ah, Sorcha, 'tis grand to see you again.'

'And you, Maureen. You look wonderful!'

'Do I? Three little ones and as many stones, but I was never built to be Twiggy, was I now?' She smiled. 'Where are you going?'

'To sit in the square and get some fresh air.' Sorcha indicated the open first-floor window of her home. 'It's hot and squashed in there.'

'Grand. It'll give us a chance to have a chat.' Maureen tucked her arm into Sorcha's and they walked towards a bench in the middle of the deserted square.

'So,' Maureen said as she sat down heavily and patted the seat next to her, 'tell me everything, right from the beginning. I'm desperate to know how one minute you were with me at the convent and the next you'd run off to England with Con Daly!' Maureen dug Sorcha hard in the ribs. 'I was fierce hurt you didn't confide your secret in me. I was supposed to be your best friend.'

'I'm sorry, Maureen, really. Things happened so quickly. The only reason I didn't write was that Con thought it best to make a complete break.'

'Well, I can't say I wasn't tempted to steam open the letters you sent to our house to pass on to your mammy. To find out what really happened, like, but I managed to control myself. She never said anything to me when I'd drop the letters round, mainly because your daddy was always lurking in the background.' Maureen gave a gentle shrug. 'I suppose I can forgive you. At least it gave us girls something to gossip about. We spent months speculating,' she giggled. 'The story went that you were pregnant by Con. Was that the truth?'

'No,' smiled Sorcha wistfully. 'It wasn't. All that happened was that my daddy found out Con and I were seeing each other. He forbade me to see him again and so we decided to run away.'

'And you get married and he becomes rich and famous and . . . oh,' sighed Maureen dreamily, 'it's like something out of a romance story. Is Con with you, Sorcha? The whole village is hopping with excitement. The rumour was that the whole band might come. I'd hoped so. I think that Todd Bradley is fierce gorgeous.'

'No, he's not. The band are very busy in London. They fly to the States in a few days' time.'

'For the concert in Central Park. I know. I'm a member of their fan club,' Maureen chuckled.

'So,' said Sorcha, desperate to move away from the subject of her errant husband, 'tell me about you.'

'Oh, there's nothing very exciting or unusual to tell. Not like your life, Sorcha. Perhaps your mammy told you I married Tommy Dalton a few months after you left?'

Sorcha smiled. 'Yes, she did.'

'We live in the flat over the shop with our three babies: Tommy Junior, Sean and Teresa, my dote of a little girl. Tommy works downstairs all the hours God sends and I work some he doesn't,' sighed Maureen. 'It's been a struggle to compete, what with the big new supermarket opening up at the end of the village, but things are fine now. We've saved enough money to buy a plot of land. We'll start building our bungalow there next spring. It'll have a kitchen with a separate dining room, a sitting room and three bedrooms, can you believe? At the moment we're only having one – bedroom that is. The kids have that and Tommy and I sleep on a put-you-up in the sitting room. Ah, Sorcha, I can't wait to move in. Think of all that space! It'll be just grand.'

'It sounds it, Maureen. So, you're happy?'

'Whatever happy is.' She shrugged. 'I mean, we all had so many dreams about the glamorous lives we'd lead when we were grown, how different they'd be to our mammies' and daddies', but they were dreams. I've stayed in Ballymore, I'm the wife of a grocer and I have three kids. Almost identical to my mammy's life . . . Except I think I'll stop at four or five little ones and get Tommy to tie a knot in it.' Maureen smiled. 'I understand now why Mammy always looked so tired. There were ten of us!' Maureen raised an eyebrow at her old friend. 'I read in my fan magazine that you and Con don't have any little ones yet.'

'No, but we hope one day we will have.'

'Ah, you simply must have some. They're the lifeblood of a marriage. Sometimes, if I'm feeling a bit low in the evenings, I go into their bedroom to see their angelic faces and it somehow makes things worthwhile.'

The two girls sat in silence for a few seconds.

'And what of Katherine? And Mairead?'

'Mairead married that awful John Donohue. You remember, the one who smelt of manure and had the terrible acne?'

Sorcha giggled. 'I remember. How could Mairead fall for *him*?'

'Because he started taking a bath once in a while and the spots disappeared almost overnight. He's grand and handsome now so, Sorcha. They live on his parents' farm outside the town. We meet up from time to time but she has two under three and no car of her own so it's hard. And as for the beauteous Katherine . . .' Maureen lowered her voice. 'Well now, there is an interesting one.'

'What happened?'

'Well, Katherine got into Trinity College, as everyone expected she would. She was all set to go up there in the autumn when she turned round and announced she was marrying Angus Hurley.'

'Angus Hurley? We once went to the cinema together. I never knew Katherine liked him!'

'Well now, nor did my brother. She was walking out with him at the same time she announced her engagement to Angus.'

'Oh dear. What did your brother say?'

'He was in a desperate state. Mammy packed him off to stay with my auntie and uncle in Dublin. He never came back. Got himself a job as a salesman and has his own flat in Ballsbridge alongside a brand-new car. He's a partner in the company now. It's an ill wind, as they say. He's never married, mind. I think Katherine broke his heart.'

'And you've never asked her why she married Angus?'

'I only see her at mass. You know what the Hurleys are like – above themselves, thinking they're grand because Daddy Hurley owns the factory and they're rolling in it. Katherine's become one of them. They live in the old rectory overlooking the sea.' Maureen tutted. 'She always looks like a fashion plate but her face is as long as Father Moynihan's sermon. So, that's the three of us up to date for you. How long are you staying in Ballymore, Sorcha?'

Sorcha had begun to daydream about the past. 'What was that?'

'I asked how long you were staying.'

'Oh, I really don't know. I have to be back in London for the weekend. Con and I fly off to New York on Tuesday.'

'All that jet setting. And I suppose you live in a wonderful big house?'

'Yes, our house is big.'

'And have money to buy anything you want?'

'I suppose.'

'Then why aren't you radiant with happiness, Sorcha?' Maureen studied her.

'I—'

''Tis your daddy's death, I suppose,' she mused. 'Ah well, it comes to us all. Listen, if you're free tomorrow, why don't you come for tea with us? You can meet the babies, and Tommy, if I can drag him out of the shop.'

'I'd love to, Maureen, really, as long as my mother will be all right on her own. I was thinking I'd stay at least tomorrow.'

'Of course. Well, I have to be off now to see to the babies. I promised Deirdre I'd only be a few minutes but I did *so* want to see you. If there's a problem, drop into the shop. If not, I'll see you at half past six tomorrow.' Maureen stood up. 'I really am sorry altogether about your daddy, but at least it means I got to see you again, Sorcha. Goodbye.'

'Bye, Maureen.'

Sorcha watched as her former schoolfriend hurried across the square in the direction of the high street. From behind, she looked the image of her mother.

Sorcha sat for a few minutes longer, listening to the poignant strains of a mourner singing an old Irish ballad. Standing up, she walked back to the house and opened the front door.

She passed by her father's office and paused, wondering if she should go inside and telephone Con. She was torn. A part of her was desperate to speak to him, but her pride was preventing her. After a while, she carried on up the stairs.

36

Lulu's heart sank as she heard the key in the lock. She had hoped to have left the house by the time Todd returned from rehearsals. Unfortunately, he was early, and she, as usual, was running late.

'You're back early.'

'Yeah, well, we've just had a piss-awful rehearsal. Con and I had another major argument over the running order in Central Park.'

'Oh dear,' she said insincerely as she walked past him and reached into the coat cupboard for her trusty combat jacket.

'Then Ian turned up two hours late, stoned out of his mind. He had some hippy woman in tow, who he insisted should sit in for the session.'

'Mmm.' Lulu searched for her car keys in her numerous pockets.

'And Derek . . . Derek just whinged on and on about his precious song. He not only thinks we should include it on the album, but now he's saying he wants us to play it in front of a quarter of a million people in Central Park!'

'I see.'

'Con steamed into Derek and told him his song is, as he puts it, "feckin' desperate" and there was no way it was ever seeing the light of day. Derek stormed out and didn't reappear, so we were sat there twiddling our thumbs while Ian and this stranger crouched on the floor and recited a mantra.'

'Really? How nice. If you're not taking your car out again today, can I borrow it? I can't find my keys anywhere.'

Todd looked at her. 'You've not heard a word I've just said, have you?'

'Pardon?'

'I rest my case.'

'Sorry. Well, can I?'

'Can you what?'

'Borrow the car?'

'Of course.' Todd handed her the keys. 'Where are you off to?'

'I have to see Gus at his office to discuss this part I've been offered with him.'

Todd watched as she shrugged on her combat jacket.

'And which part is this?'

'The one I told you about.'

'The one where you have to bare all for that avant-garde plonker that likes to call himself a serious director when his films are nothing more than pornographic filth?' Todd sneered.

'Todd, sometimes you sound like a middle-class, strait-laced moralist from the suburbs.'

He placed his hands on his hips. 'That's probably because I am.'

'But you're meant to be a hip rock star, sweetie.'

'Okay, fine. I'll go and snort a couple of lines, then jump into bed with some groupies.'

'It would probably do you good,' muttered Lulu under her breath.

'What did you say?'

'Oh, nothing,' sighed Lulu. 'It's just that at times you can be so dull.'

'Thanks a bunch. Okay . . .' Todd grabbed her, pinned her against the wall and put his lips harshly to hers. A hand snaked up under her top.

'Stop it, stop it!' Lulu wrenched herself out of his grasp.

Todd watched as she wiped her lips with the back of her hand.

'Christ, you should see the look on your face. Do I disgust you that much?'

'No. Sorry, time of the month and all that.'

Todd sank into the chair by the telephone table in the hall. He sighed. 'What is going on, Lulu? We haven't made love for weeks now. You seem to be deliberately avoiding me. You're out most nights when I get home. I can't remember the last time we spent an evening together.'

'Sorry. It's just the way things are.' She shrugged.

'Too busy with your career, your causes and Con Daly to have time for me?'

'You have loads of places and parties you could go to, Todd.'

'Yes, I do. But it just so happens that the time I do have off I would prefer to spend at home with my wife.'

'God, you *are* getting boring.'

Todd shook his head. 'I give up. Go on, Lulu, go and get your tits out for your director friend. You're probably getting them out for Con too, for all I know.'

'Don't be juvenile, Todd. Look, I'll be late tonight.'

'What a surprise.'

'Bye.'

The door slammed and Todd gave a little wave in its direction.

'Bye-bye, Lulu.'

*　*　*

Con stared at the telephone. He knew he should call Sorcha, but the sound of her hurt, strained voice was not something he was able to deal with tonight. He left his study and went into the kitchen to grab a beer from the fridge.

A terrible rehearsal, a row with Derek and then that Detective Inspector Cross had stuck his beak-like nose through the glass of the studio.

They'd gone to the pub, where Cross had laid down the law. Apparently, a Loyalist hit list had been discovered, on which, along with leading Republican politicians and activists, Con's name had been included. He'd suggested that Con keep a low profile and curtail his political activities if he valued his safety. He'd also suggested that Helen McCarthy hire a couple of bodyguards to supplement the police cover. The inspector thought it doubtful there'd be a problem in New York, but he was recommending some protection from the NYPD to be on the safe side.

'You really think the poison-pen letter may have come from a Loyalist group?'

'The possibility has to be considered. It may only be a co-incidence that we discovered the hit list in the same week as you got the letter, but it's better to be safe than sorry. Just mind your backside, Mr Daly, until this situation calms down.'

The detective had left the pub and Con ordered himself two double whiskeys. Then he had driven home to his empty house, whereupon he'd tried to take his mind off his problems by concentrating on a new song. At half past four he'd given up and found solace in the fridge.

Con took a slug from the beer bottle. Lulu would be here soon. That would take his mind off things. She was coming over to discuss an idea she had about Con meeting up with John Lennon in New York and maybe joining his 'bed-ins' for peace for a few hours in front of the camera.

The telephone rang. Con walked across the hall to the study and picked it up.

'Yeah?'

'Con, it's Helen.'

'Oh, hi.'

'How are you?'

'I'd say today has not been the best, Helen.'

'No. I'm sure it hasn't. Can I drop by tomorrow morning at about nine? I realise it's early, but as you know, Metropolitan are moving offices at present and everything is totally chaotic. And I'd really like to speak to you before you fly to New York.'

'I suppose.'

'Sorry, but we do need to talk. About all sorts of things. Okay?'

'Okay. Bye, Helen.'

He put the telephone down. He and Helen had maintained a distant but professional relationship over the years. Of course, that first night he'd seen her in London, he had been filled with dread. The last thing he needed was his past catching up with him. But, as days had turned into weeks, and weeks into months, Helen had remained tight-lipped and out of the way.

But now, she wanted to talk.

Con sighed. If Helen's manner was less than warm, she made up for it with her cool efficiency. And with Brad hitting the bottle so regularly, he was glad there was someone at the helm of Metropolitan who knew what day it was – because Brad certainly didn't. That was a further problem. The man simply wasn't up to producing their new album – if one actually ever got written.

'Shit!' Con's frustration at the complications of his existence prompted him to chuck his beer bottle across the room. It hit the door but did not break, bouncing noisily and then rolling to and fro across the tiled floor.

The door opened.

'Okay, I surrender, please lay down your arms.'

Lulu appeared in the kitchen, her hands up, a look of mock fear on her face.

'It wasn't meant for you, Lulu. I've just had a rough old day and Heil Helen phoned to cap it all and . . .' Con shrugged sheepishly. 'Yeah. Sorry.'

'Oh dear, oh dear.' Lulu leant against the door. 'I saw Todd before I left. He looked as happy as you do. What is going on at the moment?'

'Got all night?'

'I might have.' Lulu's eyes twinkled.

'Then I'll tell you. But before I do, I have to get some food inside me. I haven't eaten since breakfast.'

'Really? Where's Sorcha? I thought she'd be serving one of her stomach-bloating casseroles on the dot of seven as she usually does.'

'Now now, Lulu. As a matter of fact, she's in Ireland. Her father died and she's gone home for the funeral.'

'I see. When's she back?'

'Dunno.' He shrugged.

'Like that, is it?'

'Possibly.'

'I also need to eat. The trouble is, unlike your lovely wife, I can't even boil an egg. We'll have to go out.'

'There's the French place in the village. Let's go there.'

'Fine. Do you think escargots are counted as meat? I adore snails soaked in butter and garlic.' Lulu followed Con towards the door.

'You'd be doing the local gardeners a favour. There's been a plague of the buggers this year.' Con smiled as they strolled towards his car.

They drove out of the gates, Con unusually failing to wave

to his loyal groupies sitting on the pavement outside. He checked his rear mirror and saw a Rover move from its parking space opposite his home. It followed them down the hill towards Hampstead Village.

'See that car?' Con nodded to the mirror.

'Yes?'

'I bet you a fiver it parks behind us.' Con slid the car to a halt in front of the restaurant.

Lulu looked at him in astonishment as the Rover drew up a few yards behind him. 'How did you know?'

Con swung his long legs out of the car. 'I'll tell you over dinner.'

The maître d' found them a table in an alcove. Con sat with his back to the window and his fellow diners in the hope he wouldn't be recognised.

Over an excellent supper of escargots, a huge steak for Con and a cheese soufflé for Lulu, they drank a few of bottles of good red wine. Lulu chattered on about an audition she'd attended yesterday for a film.

'They want me to appear topless. Of course, Todd doesn't approve. But what's wrong with nudity, for Christ's sake? If they offer me the part, I'll take it. The director's wonderful, very young, very open-minded and bloody gorgeous actually. We got on like a house on fire.'

Con drained his wine glass and the waiter immediately refilled it. He stared at Lulu across the table as she talked about the Victorian novel that the film was based on.

'Coffee for *monsieur* and *madame*?'

'Yes please,' said Lulu. 'So when is Sorcha back?'

'As I said, I can't say I know. Sometime over the weekend.' Con reached for his cigarettes.

'But she's flying to New York with us on Tuesday, isn't she?'

'She's meant to be. Anyway, let's talk about something else.'

'Okay. Tell me about that car sitting outside the restaurant. Are you being followed?'

'As a matter of fact I am. I'm under the protection of your men at Scotland Yard. I've had several murder threats sent through the post. The police don't know whether they're from a crazed fan or a militant Loyalist group. Either way, it's made me uncomfortable.'

'Oh, Con, I'm sorry. How awful.'

'I've been told to keep my head down and to behave myself. No more peace protests or rallies or marches for a bit. Sorry to let you down, Lulu, but there it is.'

'It's a shame, but you mustn't put your life in danger.'

Con took a swig of wine. 'So you don't think I should say feck it and continue just the way I was? I thought you might.'

'No, absolutely not. You being dead isn't going to further any cause. And besides, I couldn't bear the thought of losing you.'

'Grand, because I have no intention of disappearing just yet.'

She stared at him. 'Life without you would be awful.'

Con stubbed out his cigarette and looked into Lulu's clear green eyes.

'Shall we go home?'

She smiled at him. 'Yes please.'

Con woke the following morning to the insistent buzzing of the front doorbell. Leaning across Lulu, he looked at the time. Five to nine.

'Shit! Shit! Feck it!'

Lulu rolled over and opened her eyes. 'What is it? What's wrong?'

'It's Helen McCarthy. She called yesterday and said she wanted to see me this morning. I'd forgotten altogether.'

Con leapt out of bed and pulled on his jeans and a T-shirt. 'Jesus, I feel rough. I was langers last night, wasn't I?'

'We both were.' Lulu rubbed her temples.

An awkward silence hung in the air. 'We were . . . well behaved, weren't we?' Con asked.

Lulu raised an eyebrow. 'Why, don't you remember?'

Con shook his head. 'Nothing beyond the restaurant.'

Lulu gave Con a fox-like grin. 'Well, Con Daly. I am offended.'

Con put his head in his hands. 'Jesus, please tell me we didn't . . .' Lulu shrugged and gave a giggle.

The doorbell buzzed again. 'Shit. Please, *please* stay up here. I'll come and fetch you when Helen's gone.'

Lulu nodded, turned over and closed her eyes. Con opened the bedroom door and hurried downstairs to open the front door.

'Morning, Helen.'

She was as immaculate as always in a cream cotton midi-dress and matching jacket, her make-up impeccable. She scanned him from head to toe.

'Heavy night, was it? You look dreadful.'

'I feel it. Come in.'

'Thanks. Did I wake you?'

'You did. My alarm clock's in Ballymore.'

'You mean Sorcha?' Helen's brow furrowed as she followed Con through to the kitchen. 'Why has she gone?'

'Her daddy died a couple of days ago. She went home for the funeral.'

Helen paused for a moment. 'I see. That's a shame.'

'Is it?' Con opened the fridge and took out a bottle of milk.

'Yes. Seamus O'Donovan handled my estate in Ballymore. He did a good job with it too. It means I'll have to get someone else to look after it now. Or maybe the time has come to sell it,' she mused. 'Anyway, can we make some coffee?'

'To be sure.' Con swigged milk from the bottle, padded over

to the kettle and switched it on. Helen put her briefcase down on the table and pulled out a chair.

'Where's Todd?'

'How do you mean? At home, I'd say.'

'Well, his car's parked in your drive. I presume the reason you're looking so rough is that the two of you had a session last night.'

Con continued to spoon coffee and sugar into two mugs. 'We did,' Con lied. 'He was too drunk to drive so he took a taxi home.'

'Oh.' Helen stared at the jacket hanging over the back of the chair next to her. 'That's Lulu's combat jacket, isn't it?'

'She was around with Todd yesterday and she forgot to take it. It was warm last night.' Con brought the two cups of coffee to the table and sat down opposite Helen. 'So what is it that has brought you out here so early on a Friday morning?'

'Well.' Helen took a sip of her coffee. 'I wanted to tell you that Metropolitan are going to employ a couple of bodyguards as from tomorrow. DI Cross suggested we should. They'll be with you twenty-four hours a day.'

'Will they be sleeping on a mat outside my bedroom door?'

'Con, this is no laughing matter. Scotland Yard are taking it very seriously. Although I hate to say it, you've probably brought this on yourself. All the gabbing to the press about your views on certain political situations definitely won't have helped you. I suggest you button up that mouth of yours from now on.'

'Christ, I feel like a feckin' schoolboy! Yours is the third lecture I've received in the past twenty-four hours.' Con took a slug of his coffee. 'Not on a hangover, please, Helen.'

'I'm sorry, Con. It's only because we care about you.'

'Sure it is. If I was dead, it wouldn't be good news for the future of The Fishermen, would it?'

'If you were dead, the publicity would be phenomenal and we'd sell millions of copies of the band's greatest hits,' replied Helen coolly. 'Don't be silly and self-indulgent, Con.'

'Yeah.' Con reached across the table to retrieve his cigarettes. He took one out of the packet and lit up. 'It's not been a good week.'

'So I hear. Derek marched into my office yesterday lunchtime saying you'd insulted him and won't even consider putting his song on the new album.'

'He's right. I won't.'

'Why not?'

Con glanced at Helen as he exhaled. 'Have you heard it?'

'No.'

'Well now, I'd say if you did, you'd understand why I've said no.'

'Okay, Con. You know I would never interfere with your creative opinion, but in light of the fact that Freddy is in the States, Brad is away—'

'Is he? Where?'

'He's taking a . . . short break in the country.'

'You mean he's drying out. Yet again.'

'People in glass houses shouldn't throw stones, Con. From the state of you this morning, I'd be inclined not to pass judgement. Anyway, as I was saying, due to the fact that Brad won't be around for another month or so, someone has to discuss these things.'

'Fair enough.'

'Derek also told me that the rehearsals for next week have been a shambles. You and Todd are apparently spending most of your time arguing.'

'Derek has been running to teacher and telling tales, hasn't he now?'

'No. Apart from his gripe about your refusal to countenance

his song, Derek is concerned, as he might well be, that things in the band are falling apart.'

'Listen, Helen, everything is grand, just grand. Every group has their ups and downs. We've been together a few years now and this kind of disagreement is bound to occur from time to time. Don't interfere, please. Todd and I will work it out.'

A door slammed upstairs.

'What was that?'

'I left the window open in the bedroom. The door is always catching the wind.'

Helen looked outside at the perfectly still, humid day. 'Oh.'

'We're in the studio together today and we'll have a good session. It always comes together on the night, although . . .'

'What?'

'Well, there is one serious problem the band have at the moment. Todd and I were going to wait until we saw Freddy in New York, but . . .'

'Go on?'

'Ian. He's becoming a liability. He turns up late and stoned out of his head and insists on bringing his harem into the studio. His drumming is deteriorating to the point of incompetence. He'll lose track halfway through a song and start to play something different.'

Helen nodded. 'Okay, as you said, there's not much I can do until Freddy's back, but then we'll have a meeting.'

'I'd be sorry to see the fella go, but if he's not improved by the time we record in September, we'll have to think about replacing him.'

Helen looked at Con. 'Maybe you should be more worried about *having* something *to* record. How many tracks have you got?'

'Three, maybe four.' Con shrugged.

'There's another six at least to go then. What about Todd?'

'I'd say he has a few as well. Look, Helen, I've told you, it'll all be grand.'

'Good. I'd hate to see The Fishermen start to disintegrate. So many groups do and I want it nipped in the bud before things deteriorate any further. I really think you and Todd should sort out your differences, come to some musical compromise and get on with it. For what amounts to some petty squabbling, there's too much to lose.' Helen glanced at her watch. 'Look, I'd better go.' She stood up. 'Oh yes, I nearly forgot. We're sending you to New York two days ahead of schedule, just to be on the safe side. Your ticket's booked under the name of Dylan Moore, but British Airways know all about it. Your new minders will accompany you.'

'You mean, I fly out Sunday?'

'Yes.'

Con shrugged. 'If it keeps you happy, Helen.'

'If it keeps you alive, Con.' Helen sucked her teeth. 'Do you own a gun by any chance?'

'No, I'm hoping I never have to either.'

She nodded slowly. 'Hmm. I have one. Just a small handgun that I keep in the locked drawer in my office. You can never be too careful these days.'

'Jesus, Helen.'

'It's just I had a . . . friend who was murdered. Seemingly out of nowhere. One has to protect oneself. Why don't you think about getting one, just in case?'

'Ah, Helen, I'll let the police worry about any shootings.'

'As you wish.' She composed herself. 'I really want you to pull your socks up, Con. I need The Fishermen to stay together. I think you owe me that.'

'Oh, do I now?'

'Frankly speaking, yes.' She winced a little. 'In truth, I feel absolutely awful about what I did for you all those years ago.'

Helen's gaze wandered to the window. 'I was a different woman back then.'

Con nodded. 'I'd probably agree with you on that front.'

'So we have an understanding then? You'll sort everything out with the band?'

Con narrowed his eyes. 'You're so sure that I owe you a favour, Helen.'

Helen crossed her arms. 'Do I really need to remind you?'

37

West Cork, Ireland, July 1964

Helen woke to a beautiful sunny morning. Knowing how quickly the weather could change and not wanting to waste a minute of it, she threw on some clothes, said a quick good morning to her aunt as she passed through the kitchen and went to saddle Davy. She loved riding on summery Sunday mornings: the beaches were deserted as the rest of the town was at mass.

A good canter along the shore left Helen feeling exhilarated and ready for breakfast. As she trotted homeward, she saw a distant figure running away from the beach. She watched as the figure retrieved a bicycle from a hollow in the dune and dragged it onto the road.

'Sorcha O'Donovan,' she breathed, wondering what she was doing out here when every other God-fearing Ballymore citizen was in church.

Sorcha waved at someone behind Helen, then pedalled off at high speed towards the village.

Helen turned and saw Con Daly perched on top of a sand dune. He was only a few feet away from her.

'Morning to you, Helen. And isn't it a beauty?' He smiled at her.

A sob choking her throat, she could only nod in his direction. With a click of her heels, she rode off along the beach.

After a good burst over several hundred feet, Helen felt

greatly improved. She tried to reason why seeing Con and Sorcha together had upset her so much. She had accepted that, although she was a little in love with Con, there was no chance he would ever give her a second look. Perhaps, she reasoned, it was that Sorcha O'Donovan had everything she didn't: a loving family, popularity, and effortless good looks. Well, now she had Con Daly too.

Helen pulled Davy's reins and brought him to a stop, before taking a moment to enjoy the vastness of the Atlantic Ocean. The expanse of grey-green water stretched as far as the eye could see. Some days, it was as still and glassy as a millpond. On others, the waves thrashed and roared like a vicious mythical creature. Today, the water lapped gently against the sand, and the vista would not have looked out of place on a postcard sent from a Mediterranean shore. Helen stared at the ocean for a long time. It was beckoning, alluring . . . She shook her head. Helen turned Davy around on himself, before taking a leisurely trot towards home.

As she approached the dunes, she saw a figure giving her a wave. Was it . . . ? Yes. Con Daly.

When Helen waved back, Con began to coax her over.

'Helen McCarthy!' he called. 'I want to talk to you.'

A small surge of adrenalin washed over her, and she steered Davy towards Con's dune. He made his way down onto the beach and gave the horse's nose a scratch.

'Ah, you've got yerself a fine fella here, Helen.'

'Thank you, Con.'

'How is he at being tied up?'

'He's good.'

'Well then, why don't you hop on down? We can leash him to my hut. I was thinking we could share a hot drop?'

Tea with Con? This was not an opportunity Helen was going to turn down. 'Okay.' She dismounted her stallion and led him by the reins through the dunes to the shack Con called home.

'Ah, 'tis a far cry from your own palace, Helen, but it's mine. Here.' He took Davy's reins and attached him to a stretch of nylon rope, which in turn was connected to a timber post emerging from the sand.

'Will he be all right here, Helen?' She nodded. 'Grand. Come on in.'

Helen followed Con into the small, dank abode. There wasn't much within its four walls, save for a battered old sofa, with an indentation where Con clearly slept. She also noted a stove with a small fire burning.

'Have a seat, Helen. I won't be a minute with your tea.'

'Thank you.'

Con produced a pair of grimy-looking mugs from a battered cupboard and placed the kettle on top of the stove.

'I often look up at the hall and think of you, Helen McCarthy.'

Helen's cheeks were immediately red-hot. 'Oh, do you?'

Con nodded. 'You must get lonely up there, all by yerself.'

'You must get lonely too.'

He shrugged. 'Ah, it's not so bad down here. I've only the one room! But if I were rattling around that grand house all day, I know I'd end up driving myself mad.'

Helen tried to force a giggle, but some spittle caught in the back of her throat, and she ended up coughing loudly. 'I have an aunt,' she managed, recovering herself.

'Ah, so you do.' Con poured the boiled water into the mugs, before steeping some pre-used leaves.

'Here we are.' Con handed Helen her tea and sat close to her on the sofa, so that his leg was lightly touching hers. Butterflies began to flap in her stomach. 'We're cut from the same cloth, aren't we, Helen?'

'What do you mean, Con?'

'We're both different. Not afraid to follow our own path.'

Following the same path as everyone else was pretty much all Helen had wanted to do for her entire life, but she understood where Con was coming from. 'I suppose so.'

'Don't you just want to spread your wings and get away?'

'Out of Ballymore?'

'Further. Out of Ireland.'

'Oh. Maybe. I remember you saying that you want to go to London.'

Con took a moment to look deeply into Helen's eyes. 'Oh yes. I'd say I want that just about more than anything.'

A pregnant pause hung in the air, as if Con was expecting Helen to talk. She obliged. 'Well . . . why don't you?'

'Why don't I what?'

'Go to London.'

Con sighed and stood, slowly crossing the hut to stare out of the solitary window. 'I would if I could, Helen.' He shook his head sadly. 'But it's impossible.'

'Why?'

'My heart would break if I left.'

Helen was unsure of what to say and took a moment to formulate her response. 'Well . . .' she offered, 'Ballymore certainly is a beautiful place.'

Con chuckled. 'Ah, 'tis not Ballymore I'd be missing.'

She understood. 'Oh. You mean Sorcha O'Donovan.'

Con nodded morosely. 'Yes. I'm in love with her. But she won't come with me.'

Helen was hardly thrilled to be counselling Con on the subject. 'I'm sure you could convince her,' she managed.

He shook his head. 'I wish I could, Helen. But she spoke to her daddy the other night and sounded him out. She says he wouldn't accept it. So she's going to stay put.' Con took a gulp from his mug. 'Don't you have some business with Seamus?'

Helen nodded. 'Yes, he manages my estate for me.'

'What's he like?'

She inhaled deeply as she considered her response. 'Efficient.'

'No, I mean as a man, like. Is he a fierce old dragon like Sorcha tells me?'

'I . . . don't really know. He's my solicitor, so I pay him. He has to be nice to me.' Con looked a little disappointed at the answer. 'But I can see how it wouldn't be good to get on the wrong side of him.'

Con swallowed the remainder of his tea and returned to the sofa. He sat cross-legged and faced Helen, his face a little more intense now. 'Sorcha said that if she told her daddy about me and London, he'd throw her out of the family. Do you think that sounds about right?'

Helen considered it. Whenever she had called around for dinner, it was true to say that Sorcha and Mary appeared apprehensive around the family patriarch. 'Yes, I reckon so.'

Con bowed his head. ''Tis a terrible thing, that. Sorcha's only crime is falling in love with me.' Even though Con was openly discussing his feelings for Sorcha, Helen's heart still panged at the sadness she perceived in his eyes. 'Ah, Helen. We've been alone our whole lives, haven't we?'

'Yes,' she muttered.

'And now, I discover the one person who made me feel better about everything can't come with me when I leave Ballymore. Only you can know how sad that makes me. Imagine having someone in your life who took the pain away, and you had to consider losing them . . .'

Helen did not have to imagine. 'Have you thought about staying?'

Con slapped the side of the sofa. 'I can't. Sorcha doesn't realise it, but we could never be together here. Not properly.

Her daddy wouldn't let us. You know the whole town is after thinking I'm a tinker.'

'Yes. And they think I'm strange.'

Con jumped to his feet. 'That's exactly what I'm talking about! No one understands us like we understand each other.'

'I suppose that's true, yes.'

'We're clever. But no one sees our cleverness, because they have ideas about us in their heads before they've even met us.' He began to pace around the room. Helen was a little unsure of the direction the conversation was taking. 'Sorcha O'Donovan just needs to be brave and trust me. You trust me, don't you, Helen?'

Helen swallowed hard. 'Yes.'

'You and I have to look out for each other. We need to be our own little team and watch each other's backs. You know that I'll always be here for you?' Helen remained silent. 'I will, Helen McCarthy.' Con stopped pacing and took her hand. 'Would you be there for me, Helen?' he asked, his eyes wide and pleading. 'I'd never forget it.'

She was assured in her answer. 'I will, Con, of course.'

He broke into his trademark beaming grin. 'I knew you'd help.'

Helen had begun to understand what was being asked of her. It would be painful, yes, but it would please him. There was no debate. 'I'll be sure to put in a good word for you when I'm next with Seamus.'

Con dropped her hand. 'If only it were that simple.' Helen was deflated that her suggestion hadn't pleased him. 'Seamus is a smart man. If you suddenly start speaking well of me out of the blue, he'll work it all out, and stop Sorcha from seeing me.'

'Oh. What do you want me to do?'

Con took a pause. 'I want Sorcha to be free.'

'I'm not sure that answers my question,' Helen replied.

'Seamus needs a shock. If he sees Sorcha and me together, then he'll disown her, and we'll be able to go to London.'

Helen was taken aback. 'Goodness, Con. Do you really think that would be—'

He cut her off. 'You and I both know that Sorcha O'Donovan would be better off without her daddy ruling her life. Remember, we're more observant than anyone else. We both *know* that this is the best thing for her.'

'And you,' Helen reminded him.

Con shrugged off her comment. 'Maybe so.'

Helen steeled herself. 'What are you asking of me?'

'I want you to send Seamus to the beach when Sorcha and I are together.'

Helen's heart skipped a beat. 'Oh, Con, I . . .' She shook her head. 'He'll be fierce angry.'

'I know.' Con folded his arms. 'That's the whole point. If I have to take a slap or two, then I will.'

Helen rubbed her hands together, agonising over Con's request. 'I really don't know if I could do that, Con. It seems a little unfair on everyone. Myself included.'

Con looked hurt and took a while to reply. 'Okay, Helen. I understand. I just thought . . .' He waved his hand. 'It sounds silly.'

'What?'

'I really thought we understood each other. That we were the same. I guess I was wrong. Sorry to have interrupted your ride home.'

Helen stood up, embarrassed, placed her half-full mug on the stove, and began to make her way to the door. Before she could reach out for the handle, Con grabbed her hand and drew her close to him.

'You'd be setting me free, Helen.' With his spare hand, he gently turned her face towards his and placed a light kiss on her cheek.

Helen melted. 'You'd do the same for me?'

Con nodded slowly. 'Of course I would.'

Helen gulped. Con Daly had her in the palm of his hand. 'All right. I'll help you,' she whispered.

Con removed a strand of hair from Helen's face. 'I knew I could rely on you.'

38

'In truth, I've never forgiven myself.' Helen shook her head. 'I broke up a family for you. Sorcha didn't deserve that.'

Con rubbed his unshaven chin. 'Why have you never said anything to her all these years? I've been waiting for that moment ever since seeing you again.'

Helen shrugged. 'What would that achieve? It would only hurt your wife.' She folded her arms. 'Plus, if I'm honest, I'm ashamed that I was so easily manipulated by you. I was a little girl, lost and unsure of herself.' Helen met Con's gaze. 'And you knew that.' He lowered his eyes. 'Anyway,' Helen continued, 'I suggest you sort out the band. Otherwise I may well change my mind about telling Sorcha.'

Con held his hands up. 'Fine.'

'Right.' Helen walked to the kitchen door, opened it and stepped into the hall. Both she and Con looked up as the stairs creaked. Lulu stood halfway up, hovering uncertainly.

'Oh, er, hi, Helen, how are you?'

'Fine, Lulu. And you?' she asked coldly.

'Fine. I was just leaving. You haven't seen my car keys, have you, Con?'

Con swept a hand through his thick dark hair and sighed deeply. 'They're most likely in your jacket pocket, Lulu. It's hanging on the kitchen chair.'

'Thanks. I have to run. I've got to see my agent at half past ten.' She tripped down the stairs and went into the kitchen.

Helen headed for the front door. 'Goodbye, Con.'

'Bye, Helen.'

She stepped outside then turned to him. 'Screwing his wife is not the way to sort out your problems with Todd.' Helen's eyes were cold. 'You're treading on thin ice. I'd take care if I were you.'

Con watched as Helen walked to her Porsche and climbed in. He slammed the front door and banged his fist against it as he heard her car roar out of the drive.

'I'm sorry, Con, really I am. I was trying to sneak out but I couldn't find my keys.'

Lulu stood behind him, her face contrite. 'She won't say anything, will she?'

Con said nothing, just shrugged.

'I . . .' Lulu placed a hand on Con's shoulder. 'That sounds like a really difficult situation with Sorcha.'

Con slowly turned his head to look Lulu dead in the eye. 'Yeah. It was.'

She gave a small shrug. 'Well. Your secret's safe with me.'

Con raised an eyebrow. 'Is it?'

'Of course, silly.' Lulu grabbed her jacket, blew Con a kiss, and headed for the door.

Con leant against the wall, sank down to the floor, and placed his head in his hands.

39

Sorcha was passing her father's closed office when she heard the telephone ringing inside. She entered and went to the desk to pick up the receiver.

'Hello?'

'Sorcha? It's Con. How are you?'

'Hello, Con. I'm . . . okay.'

'Is the funeral over?'

'Yes.'

'And is your mother all right?'

'All things considered, she's doing exceptionally well. And you? Are you okay?'

'I'm grand, Sorcha, just grand. Are you flying home tomorrow?'

'I was planning to fly home on Sunday, but when I called the airline they said the plane was full. So I'm on the Monday flight, which means I'll be home in time to travel to New York with you on Tuesday.'

'Ah, now, that's why I'm calling. There's been a change of plan. I'm flying out on Sunday.'

Sorcha bit her lip. 'Why?'

'I promise there's a very good reason, Sorcha. But there's no problem. You come home and fly over as you would have done on Tuesday and I'll see you in New York. Is that okay?'

'Fine.'

'Grand. Well, see you next week in the Big Apple then.'

'Yes. Goodbye, Con.'

Sorcha put the telephone down. She was on the verge of tears. Con had been civil, but there'd been no warmth in his voice, no hint of the closeness they'd once shared.

Had he stopped loving her? She just didn't know.

Sorcha sighed, left the office and walked across the hall. As she opened the front door she heard the rumble of thunder. She shivered, wondering whether to go back upstairs and retrieve her raincoat, but she was late already. She could always borrow something from Maureen to get her home.

Sorcha decided to put all thoughts of Con out of her head, desperate to enjoy the evening with her oldest friend. She headed across the square and down the high street towards Maureen and Tommy's shop. After the ten-minute walk, her arms were covered in goose pimples. Sorcha pushed the door open. Tommy stood behind the counter grinning at her, his face still a childish mass of ginger freckles.

'Ah, Sorcha! 'Tis grand to see you. You're looking so well.'

'You do too, Tommy.'

'Maureen's upstairs. She's been slaving in the kitchen as if the Blessed Virgin herself was coming to tea. Here, I'll show you up.'

Tommy beckoned her round the counter and pushed open the door at the back of the shop. In the narrow corridor, all manner of boxes were stacked haphazardly. Sorcha edged past them and followed Tommy up the wooden stairs.

'We had a delivery this afternoon. I'll maybe join you later but I'll have to sort it all out. Anyway, I think Maureen wants you to herself for a while. In here.' Tommy pushed open a door which led to a small, steamy kitchen. 'Your guest has arrived, sweetheart.'

Maureen, red-faced from her exertions, wiped her hands on her apron and came to kiss Sorcha.

'How are you?'

'I'm well, very well.'

Before Sorcha had time to move, three small heads with ginger hair appeared from the room next door and clung on to the back of Maureen's legs, their impish eyes peeping at Sorcha from behind their mother's skirt.

'Is this her, Mammy? The one who's married to the famous singer?' asked the tallest boy.

'Aye, she is,' smiled Maureen.

'I'll be downstairs a while, sweetheart. Call me when it's ready.'

Maureen nodded as Tommy closed the door.

'Come on now, you three, let your mammy go so I can show Sorcha into the sitting room.' Maureen rolled her eyes as she turned and headed across the kitchen, three little pairs of hands still clinging to her legs. 'Come in here and sit down, if you can find the space.'

Sorcha followed Maureen into a tiny room, furnished with a battered sofa, a coffee table and an old black-and-white television perched precariously on a small shelf. The floor was awash with children's books and toys.

'Ah, you three! Look what you've done. You promised you'd keep it tidy for me,' Maureen chastised them as she bent down to pick up a rag doll and a car. She went over to the window and sighed. 'I'd send them out into the yard to play, but the heavens have opened. Sit yourself down, Sorcha. There's a little whiskey to drink if you like.'

'No, just a glass of orange squash would be lovely.' Sorcha sat down. As she did so, the smallest child, her face covered in freckles, her hair a mass of thick, curly red, came shyly towards her, climbed on her knee and stuck her thumb in her mouth.

'Honest, Teresa, you are an incorrigible child. She'll take a lap from anyone,' Maureen said proudly. 'Fierce outgoing she is. How she'll be at sixteen with the lads I dread to think.'

'Introduce me to your two boys,' encouraged Sorcha.

'This is Tommy Junior.'

'Hello, Tommy. And how old are you?'

'Four, missus.'

'Well now, you are a big boy. And your brother, how old is he?'

'Sean's three. Still a baby.' Both boys moved slowly towards Sorcha.

'I'll be getting your drink,' said Maureen. 'You look after your Auntie Sorcha now.' And she went into the kitchen.

An hour later, after Sorcha had read several picture books, played with toy cars and admired drawings scribbled in her honour, Maureen called them in for tea. She picked up Teresa and went into the kitchen. The round table in the corner had been covered with a lace cloth and Maureen had put a pretty floral decoration in an old vase in its centre.

'The table looks lovely,' Sorcha enthused.

'Thank you. Sit where you're comfortable. I'll call Tommy.'

The two boys were already sat up, so Sorcha squeezed by them and perched with Teresa still in her arms.

'There now. Tommy's coming. I'll serve up. I've cooked bacon and cabbage to remind you of your old life,' smiled Maureen.

Tommy entered the kitchen with a bottle tucked under his arm.

'Wine, no less, Tommy? Jesus, Sorcha, you are honoured,' teased Maureen as Tommy searched in the drawer for a corkscrew.

Eventually, they were all sitting down and Teresa was torn off Sorcha's knee and placed in her wooden high chair. Sorcha looked down at the mountain of bacon, cabbage and potato in front of her.

'This smells delicious, Maureen.'

'And I want to see that plate clean. You're a little too skinny for my liking.'

'Take no notice. She's just jealous because of her generous curves,' smiled Tommy.

'And who was it that gave them to me, Tommy Dalton? Three babies in four years?'

'And I love every ounce of them, as you well know. Sean, take your hands out of your potato and eat with your spoon!'

As she ate, Sorcha listened to the playful banter between husband and wife and the affectionate way they chastised their offspring. She found herself envying the warmth in the tiny, cluttered home.

Later, with the three children tucked up in their broom cupboard of a bedroom, Tommy laid out the plans for the new bungalow on the kitchen table. Maureen took Sorcha through every detail.

'Of course, Tommy and I will do most of the work ourselves to save money. It'll take that bit longer but it'll be worth it when it's done, especially with another on the way.'

Sorcha looked at Maureen in surprise. Maureen rolled her eyes and nodded. 'I suspected but it wasn't confirmed until I visited the doctor's this morning. At least it gives us a goal. And we wanted another, didn't we, Tommy?'

'So you tell me, sweetheart.' He put his arms round her waist and kissed her on the cheek.

Sorcha joined Tommy for a tot of whiskey in celebration.

'Goodness, it's past ten. I ought to be leaving. Mammy's fine in the day, but then it gets to this point at night and she starts to become maudlin.'

Maureen tweaked back the curtain and looked out. 'Fair drowned you'll be, Sorcha. I'll get you an umbrella and a jacket.'

'Thank you. And bless you for such a grand dinner. I feel completely stuffed.'

'Not as stuffed as I'll be in a few months' time,' laughed Maureen, disappearing off to retrieve a brolly and a jacket.

'Bye, Tommy. Maybe next time I'm here I'll be coming to visit the bungalow.'

'With God's help, let's hope so.'

'Come down and I'll see you out,' called Maureen from the bottom of the stairs.

Sorcha walked down and followed Maureen through the shop to the front door. She opened it and Sorcha saw the high street was awash with puddles.

'Just to remind you you're back in the Emerald Isle,' laughed Maureen. She put both of her arms around her friend and hugged her tightly. 'Don't be a stranger, Sorcha. Write to me, won't you?'

'I will, I promise. I can't tell you how lovely it's been to see you. And I'm so glad you're happy, Maureen. I think your family are gorgeous.'

'Aye, I've no complaints. It's not a bad little life I have for myself.' She nodded. 'You take care, Sorcha.' Maureen looked deeply into her old friend's eyes. 'You know, it strikes me that there's something worrying you at the moment. Am I right?'

'I . . .' Sorcha wavered for a few seconds, then shook her head, pride preventing her from pouring out her marital problems to Maureen. 'I'm concerned about my mother. I hope she'll be all right when I have to leave her to go home.'

'You know how it is in Ballymore. The village will rally round. She'll not be short of company, that's for sure.'

'Yes. Of course. She has plenty of friends. I just feel guilty for going.'

'I'm sure your mammy understands you must be with your

husband. If my better half was a handsome, famous pop star, I'd not be torn from his side for more than a few seconds.'

Sorcha opened the umbrella. 'Here I go. Bye, Maureen.'

'Bye, Sorcha.'

She stepped out into the downpour. The rain drove into her back as she hurried up the high street, and she arrived home a dripping, sodden mass.

'Jesus, Mary and Joseph! You're like a drowned rat! Here, let me take your wet things and I'll run a bath before you catch your death!' Mary fussed around her as Sorcha peeled off her soaking clothes.

In the bath, Sorcha pondered her evening at Maureen and Tommy's. She wondered how the couple survived in that cramped little flat with those three beautiful but exhausting children.

'Love,' Sorcha said as she draped a flannel over her face. That's what it was. Tommy and Maureen adored each other and their children. It didn't matter that they had very little and had worked all hours for everything they did have.

Maybe Con and she had too much.

But did they have enough love?

They used to, that was for sure.

Sorcha refused to believe it had gone. Granted, things had not been right for some time, but surely it was solvable?

She knew her marriage was at a crossroads. If she left things as they were, there was no hope. But if she was prepared to try to make a new start, wash the slate clean and forget all the niggling problems that had forced the two of them apart; *plus* – and this was the most important thing of all – if she could persuade Con to do the same, then maybe they had a chance.

She *could* do it.

Sorcha removed the flannel from her face.

'I love you, Con Daly,' she informed the ceiling.

And for that love, she was prepared to fight.

'Now, are you sure you don't want to come back with me?'

'No. I want to stay here and get on with my life. There's so many things I want to sort out. Your daddy left me well provided for and I've already had someone mention they're interested in taking over the practice. I think I'm best to sell the house lock, stock and barrel. I'll find a smaller place in town somewhere.'

'I was only thinking of a break, Mammy. A few days. I'd love you to see our house in London.'

'And I will come, Sorcha, maybe in the autumn. But just leave me be for now.'

Sorcha studied Mary for signs of impending depression, and decided that her mother was looking much better.

'If you get lonely, call me, any time of the day or night.'

'I will of course, but I have a lot of friends here who have already given me invitations. In fact, I've never been so popular,' Mary smiled. 'Now put your coat on and be off with you. The taxi'll be here at any moment.'

Ten minutes later, Mary embraced Sorcha as the driver put her suitcase in the boot. It was still pouring with rain and Sorcha shivered involuntarily.

'I hope you're not on for a cold. Keep yourself wrapped up.'

'I will.' Sorcha gave her mother one last hug. 'I know I shouldn't say this, because it was such a dreadful few days for you, but I have enjoyed it.'

Her mother gave her the warmest of smiles. 'Me too. And now there's no reason why you shouldn't come home whenever you want. Bring that husband of yours next time.'

'I will, I promise.' She ran to the car and hopped inside, Mary following her under the umbrella.

'May God go with you, Sorcha.' She swallowed back tears. 'See you very soon, Mammy.'

The driver started the engine. 'I'll call you to let you know I'm home safe. Goodbye.'

Sorcha's mother stood on the pavement, watching the taxi until it disappeared around the corner of the square.

For some awful reason, Mary O'Donovan had the strangest feeling that she wouldn't be seeing her daughter again.

Sorcha said a silent goodbye to Ballymore. She swallowed hard and noticed the roughness in her throat. Her mother was right: she was on for a cold.

The rain-washed streets glistened as the taxi sloshed through the puddles. This was where it had all begun for her and Con.

She was determined she would not let it end.

40

'Morning, Katie.'

'Morning, Miss McCarthy.'

'As it's such a beautiful day, I think I'll take my breakfast outside.'

'Of course, Miss McCarthy. The usual?'

'Yes. Thank you.'

Helen picked up her post and sauntered through the French doors onto the small patio. She placed the letters on the table and sat on a wrought-iron garden chair. She closed her eyes and put her face up to the sun.

Thank God it was Saturday. And thank God that, at ten o'clock last night, the last box had been moved from Metropolitan's old premises to its new home.

The building was going to be fantastic when everything was organised. Helen thought of her big office on the top floor. It had been decorated to her explicit taste with antique furniture, a thick green carpet, and heavy damask curtains draping the large window. She'd even had a small en-suite bathroom installed for those times when it was impossible to get home before going out in the evening.

She reached forward and tore open the thick brown envelope on top of the pile of post. Enclosed were details of a large country house near Cobham in Surrey, complete with gym in the basement and indoor swimming pool. She read through the details.

It sounded promising, and somehow familiar. Helen looked at the address again and realised it was the home of a well-known singer who'd fallen on hard times due to his continued drug abuse. She'd attended a party there a couple of years ago. The house was magnificent, and going cheap for what it was. The poor chap must be desperate.

Helen shook her head. She just could not understand the singular need for nefarious substances that seemed to hold the music business in its grip. She rarely drank, and if she did, she usually limited it to a couple of glasses of champagne. In truth, she despised the feeling of not being completely in control of her actions.

'Here's your breakfast, Miss McCarthy.'

Katie, the daily maid, put the tray of juice, tea and warm croissants on the table in front of her.

'Thank you, Katie.'

Helen sipped the juice and decided the house in Cobham was probably worth seeing. She folded the details neatly back into their envelope and cut open a croissant.

Having eaten it, Helen sat back in the chair to enjoy another few minutes in the sun. She'd not slept at all well last night, her brain buzzing with thoughts of the new building, but also the revelation that Con was having an affair with Lulu Bradley.

She'd spent the night thinking how she could stop things before either Sorcha or Todd found out about it. With the problems the band had been having so far in the studio, this would be the final straw. It could signal the demise of The Fishermen altogether. That meant she'd be losing her most valuable business asset at a time when the company's worth was of utmost importance.

Helen had decided to float Metropolitan on the stock

exchange as soon as possible. It would bring in a lot of money which could help expand the empire. With this plan in the pipeline, it was not the time for any rumours in the City of problems with the label's biggest money-spinner.

Helen sighed. She could control things financially, but the private lives of her stars was something over which she had no power.

Helen thought how ironic it was that she'd once wished every bad thing on Con and Sorcha's marriage and would have enjoyed watching it fail.

And now, here she was, praying they'd stay together.

Sorcha arrived home at ten o'clock on Monday evening feeling wretched. She'd shivered during the flight to Dublin, then discovered there was to be a two-hour delay caused by the terrible weather. Wearily, she unlocked the front door, dropped her suitcase in the hall and climbed the stairs to the bedroom. Without removing her clothes, she fell onto the bed and closed her eyes.

Dawn broke and light streamed into the un-curtained bedroom. Sorcha moaned but did not stir. Sweat dripped off her, staining the pillows.

The telephone rang, but the sound did not wake her.

The day passed, and dusk began to fall. Rumblings of thunder could be heard in the sky and bright flashes of lightning lit up the heath. Then the rain began, breaking the humidity.

Sorcha started to shiver uncontrollably. Her dreams were confused. She was in her bedroom at Ballymore. The door was opening, and in walked her father, his lips tinged with grey, wearing his best Sunday suit. *He's dead, he's dead*, a voice told her.

An ear-splitting scream scorched the air in the bedroom.

'Sorcha, Sorcha! Whatever is it?'

Hands were gently shaking her . . . It was her father, trying to take her with him . . .

'Sorcha, it's Helen, wake up. You're having a dream. It's okay, really, it's okay.'

She opened her eyes. The room was full of evening shadows. Helen McCarthy was standing over her. She tried to pull herself up onto her elbows, but failed and sank back onto the pillows with a groan.

Helen put a hand on her forehead. 'Sorcha, you have a very bad fever. I think you've been delirious. I'm going to call the doctor, okay?'

Sorcha nodded. Her eyes hurt if she held them open, so she closed them and promptly fell asleep.

She was awoken by a hand on her forehead.

'It's only Doctor Deane, Sorcha. I'm just going to check you over.'

'Ow, my eyes sting,' she remarked feebly.

'Can you open your mouth wide?'

Sorcha did so, then lay there as the doctor inspected her throat, checked her neck, listened to her heartbeat and finally stuck a thermometer under her tongue.

'Well now.' Doctor Deane packed his instruments away in his medical bag. 'You seem to have a nasty case of the flu. Aspirin and bed rest are my prescription.'

Sorcha was beginning to come to. There was something nagging at the back of her mind, something important. She suddenly remembered what it was.

'What time is it?' Her throat was so sore it hurt to talk.

'Half past seven in the evening.'

'What . . . day is it?'

'Tuesday, the nineteenth of August. You're at home, in your bed in Hampstead,' said the doctor.

'Oh no, oh no!' Sorcha wailed, struggling to sit up. 'I was

meant to be on a plane this morning, flying to New York! Con! I—'

'Don't panic,' said Helen, appearing behind Doctor Deane. 'Con called Metropolitan when he couldn't contact you last night. He'd rung your mother in Ballymore and she'd said you'd caught the plane back to London as arranged. When you didn't check in at Heathrow this morning, I came round to find out if you were okay. It's a good job I did by the looks of things. What did you do to yourself while you were away?'

'It rained a lot. I must have got a chill. Helen, can you book me on a flight tomorrow morning? I must get to New York. I—'

'Don't be absurd, my dear,' said Doctor Deane. 'You are no more capable of getting on a plane tomorrow than you are of sprouting wings and flying there yourself. You are sick, Sorcha, and have to stay put until you're better. Doctor's orders. Now, have you a friend or a relative that could come and stay for a few days, fetch and carry and keep an eye on you?'

'I . . .' Sorcha bit her lip as tears appeared in her eyes.

'Don't worry, Doctor, I'll sort something out,' said Helen.

'All right, but I'm imploring you, no silly antics unless you want to end up in hospital with pneumonia.' The doctor stood up.

'I'll see you out,' Helen said.

'Thank you. Cheerio, Sorcha. Behave yourself.'

Sorcha lay feeling horribly sorry for herself. She was stuck in bed, with Con in New York, and, to top it all off . . . *Helen McCarthy* for a nurse.

Helen came back up the stairs, a fizzing glass of aspirin in her hand.

'Right, drink this.'

She helped Sorcha upright and sat on the end of the bed, watching as she grimaced upon reaching the bottom of the glass.

'Good. Now, I'm going to stay with you until you're better. Tomorrow I can use Jenny's office and have urgent calls rerouted here from Metropolitan. Talking of telephones, I must call your mum. She was imagining all sorts of terrible things, apparently. Then I can phone Con. He won't be in the hotel at the moment, but I can at least leave him a message to let him know you're okay.'

'Use that phone.' Sorcha pointed weakly to the instrument by the bed.

'Will do.'

Helen picked up the receiver. 'Maybe you could have a word with your mum as she probably won't believe you're okay until she speaks to you herself. Right, give me the number.'

Once Sorcha had uttered a few reassuring words to Mary, and Con's hotel in New York had been called, Helen stood up. 'I'm going to make myself some soup. I saw some tins in the cupboard. Do you think you could manage some yourself?'

Sorcha shook her head.

'All right, but tomorrow you have to start eating.'

'I will, I promise.'

'Can I get you anything else?'

'No. Thanks, Helen.'

'Okay.'

Helen left the room and made her way downstairs to the kitchen. She opened a can of soup, poured the contents into a saucepan and placed it on the hob to warm. When she'd finished her dinner, she went into the sitting room to watch the news. A little later, she climbed the stairs to the bedroom and pushed open the door. Sorcha was asleep. Helen checked her forehead and found she was much cooler.

She took a shower, and after looking in on Sorcha one last time, Helen climbed into bed in the guest room, propped herself up on her pillows and opened her briefcase. The documents prepared by the City accountants handling the share flotation had arrived this morning.

Columns of figures lay unread on her lap as she stared into space, her usual flawless concentration deserting her.

When Helen had heard that Sorcha had not boarded her plane to New York, she'd immediately assumed Sorcha had discovered Lulu's affair with Con. The notion had sent her racing over to Hampstead. Helen had hoped to smooth things over (after all, she knew what it was like to be played by Con).

But now, Helen was sure Sorcha didn't know. She'd been quite happy to let her telephone Con's hotel. It was just a coincidence that she'd been too sick to make the flight to New York.

Nonetheless, Helen felt unsettled. Columns of figures were controllable. People's emotions, however, were totally unpredictable.

Con's suite at the Sherry Netherland was full of people he hardly knew. Representatives from the American record company, PR bods, journalists and photographers lounged around smoking, drinking and talking. It was an impromptu party with Con the forgotten host.

This was the usual scene when the band hit town, but tonight, Con was not interested. He wanted to have a relatively early night and try to get his head together for the concert tomorrow. The band had done a tech run that afternoon in Central Park. Considering the lack of preparation, it had not gone badly. But there was no doubting the tension between the four of them: Derek was hardly acknowledging him, still sulking because of the rejection of his song; Ian was on Planet Gaga as per, but it seemed at least that Todd had enough professionalism to put aside their differences and get on with the job in hand.

Con felt a hand sweep across his back.

'Hello, Con.'

'Lulu.'

He turned around and forced a smile. Con hadn't felt comfortable in her presence since he had woken with her in his bed the other morning. He still had no memory of the occasion, and whenever he tried to establish the facts from Lulu, she simply giggled.

'Where's Todd?' he enquired.

'Gone to our suite.' The hand snaked under his shirt. 'Get rid of everybody.'

'Lulu, Jesus Christ! We've got a room full of journos and paparazzi.'

'As I said, get rid of them. You look tense. I'll help relax you.'

'Shh, please!'

'As long as you promise.'

'Okay, okay.' He cleared his throat. 'Ladies and gents, the party's over. I want some peace.'

There was a disappointed silence for a few seconds, then the conversation resumed its former volume.

'They're leeches, these people,' sighed Con. 'They grab hold, then hang on for dear life.'

'Get your heavies to start removing people. That's what they're paid for,' said Lulu, glancing across to the two muscular men who stood by the door.

'Ivan!' Con shouted over the top of a couple of heads.

Ivan acknowledged Con's call and pushed his way through the crowd. 'Yes, Mr Daly, what can I do for you?'

'Empty this room, will you? I want to hit the sack.'

He nodded. 'Leave it with me.'

Ten minutes later, the last straggler had been evicted, leaving only Lulu, Con and Freddy in the sitting room.

'Bit early for you, isn't it?' Freddy remarked.

333

'I'm fair exhausted.'

'Well, go and get your beauty sleep. I'll leave you in peace. Come on, Lulu, I'll escort you back to your suite.'

'I think I can manage to find it all by myself, thanks, Freddy,' she replied tartly.

'Okay,' he shrugged. 'I'll see you tomorrow, Con.'

The door closed behind him. Lulu wasted no time in winding her arms around Con and kissing him full on the lips. He quickly extricated himself from her grasp.

'Come on, Lulu. We're both married, for God's sake.'

'Don't be silly. No one ever needs to know . . .'

'That's not the point, Lulu.'

She frowned at him. 'Come on, Con. We both know how unhappy you are. You hardly spend any time with Sorcha. Every free moment you get, you're out with me.'

'No, I'm out at rallies, which you happen to like attending. And I might be unhappy, but it's not Sorcha's fault. She's done nothing apart from try to love me well.' Con ran his hands through his hair as he crossed the room to plant himself on the edge of the king-size bed. 'It's the fact that The Fishermen have the power to do some good in this shit-show of a world, but instead we just pump out soppy ballads for teenagers to snog along to.'

Lulu skipped over and sat next to him on the bed. 'Oh, don't be so down on yourself. It's not *just* teenagers . . .' She grabbed Con's face and planted another deep kiss on him. He pushed her away with a little force.

'No, Lulu. I'm serious.' He stood up and crossed the room to the minibar, where he fixed himself a whiskey.

Now she was perturbed. 'I don't understand you, Con Daly. You've got just about everything that a human being could wish for, but you're so bloody grumpy. *Of course* it's your marriage that's getting you so down.'

Con downed his drink. 'You're wrong. It's nothing to do with my marriage.' He shook his head. 'Actually, no. It's *all* to do with my marriage. I've been so caught up in trying to fix the world's problems that I haven't spent enough time on Sorcha.' He refilled his glass. 'I've had my priorities all wrong.'

Lulu parted her legs. 'You can say that again. Come here. I'll make you feel better.'

Con sighed. 'Please leave me alone, Lulu. Being here without Sorcha has made me see things clearly. Jesus,' he continued. 'I should have been there for her this weekend.'

Lulu straightened up from her insouciant position. 'Sorcha's boring. She doesn't understand your world. Unlike me.'

'She might not understand my world, but she understands me,' Con snapped. 'I love her more than anything. I've got a lot of work to do to fix things.'

Lulu narrowed her eyes. 'You love her more than anything, do you?'

'Yes.'

'Then why, all those years ago, did you steal her away from her family?'

Con hung his head in shame. 'I couldn't stand to be without her,' he whispered.

'But you didn't respect her enough to stay, and you weren't brave enough to sort things out yourself. You used Helen McCarthy to do your dirty work.'

'Don't remind me.'

'Oh, I will remind you,' she said. 'You were very selfish, Con.' She stood up and began to walk slowly over to him, like a lion approaching a wounded gazelle. 'But now you have a chance to do something unselfish. We're meant for one another, Con. Don't fight it.'

Con stood still as Lulu placed her hands on his chest and looked up into his eyes. He chose his words carefully.

'Lulu. I am very sorry if I've given you the wrong idea. Yes, we've spent a lot of time together. But we were using our joint fame to promote peace in the world. And that's it.' He removed Lulu's hands from his chest. 'As for the other night . . .' He shook his head. 'I can only put it down to getting langers. It won't be happening again.'

Lulu's face twisted into a sneer. 'It didn't happen in the first place.'

Con furrowed his brow. 'What?'

'We got back to yours, and after about two minutes of kissing – which was feeble, by the way – you just kept mumbling about Sorcha. So I left you to pass out on your bed.'

Con was filled with rage. 'You let me think we slept together!'

Lulu shrugged. 'You missed out. I'm very good.'

Con grabbed her arm. 'Get out.'

'Ouch! Let me get my bag at least.' Con led her towards the door, before throwing her out into the corridor. A few seconds later, Lulu's pink Chanel clutch was launched at her, and the door slammed in her face.

Just what the hell did he see in his wife anyway? She was a simple girl from an Irish backwater. And she was *the* Lulu Bradley – a movie star who would have men queuing around the block for hours just to spend five minutes alone with her. Con could have had it all. Who did he think he was to treat her like that?

Lulu resolved that if she couldn't have Con Daly, then Sorcha couldn't either.

If she did this in the right way, she'd get some decent press too.

Even though it grated on her to admit it, Sorcha had to concede that Helen had been very good to her over the past forty-eight hours. Without her help, she dreaded to think what she would have done.

By the end of the week, Sorcha was sitting up and feeling like she might just live to see her twenty-second birthday after all.

There was a brief knock and Helen appeared with a breakfast tray. As always, she was perfectly made up and dressed in an expensive trouser suit.

'How are we this morning?' Helen studied her as she placed the tray on Sorcha's lap. 'Looking better. Good.' She walked to the window and drew back the curtains. 'Another beautiful day. Eat up your breakfast and I'll run you a bath. A soak in the tub'll make you feel a hundred per cent better.'

Sorcha nodded and Helen left the room. She wondered if the director of Metropolitan Records had missed her true calling – she'd have made the most wonderful matron. Sorcha drank her orange juice, then pushed the cornflakes round the bowl. Her appetite had not really returned – in fact, the sight of food still made her feel queasy.

'Well, that was a pathetic effort, Sorcha.' Helen declared as she re-entered. 'How are you ever going to regain your strength if you don't eat?'

'I'm sorry, I just can't, Helen. I feel sick.'

'Go on wid ya,' she smiled. 'I'll let you off. Have your bath and maybe afterwards you could come downstairs and sit in the sunshine.'

Sorcha slowly padded into the bathroom, where Helen had filled up the tub with sweet-smelling bubbles. She gazed at her face in the mirror and sighed. Sorcha was pale and haggard, with big dark rings under her eyes. It was hardly the way she wanted to look as she attempted to patch up her marriage.

She stepped into the water and slid down, her entire body submerged under foam.

In a few hours' time, Con would be getting up and going through his usual pre-concert routine, something she had once been a part of. She fondly recalled the times she'd stood on the side of the stage as he played to his thousands of fans, then smiled as he dashed off to towel down, give her a hug and tell her how much he loved her . . .

Half an hour later, Sorcha sat on the terrace, the hot sun calming her nerves. Helen had gone to Hampstead Village for supplies, insisting she tuck a rug over Sorcha's knees before she left. She closed her eyes and dozed.

Sorcha was woken by sounds from the kitchen. She stood up and walked inside. Helen was unpacking the shopping.

'Have a nice rest?'

'Yes, thank you.'

'Good. You look much better today. I don't know what you like to eat, so I bought lots to tempt your appetite.'

'Helen, I just wanted to thank you for looking after me. You've been very kind and I don't know what I'd have done without you.'

'Oh, it was nothing,' she replied brusquely, stowing cans of soup away in the larder. 'I'm sure you'd have done the same for me.'

'Actually, Helen, I don't know that I would have. Look, what I'm trying to say is that of all people, I didn't expect you to care what happened to me. Can we put the past behind us and start again?'

Helen stopped with a tin of baked beans in her hand. She turned and looked at Sorcha, an expression of mild surprise on her face.

'Oh, Sorcha, the thing I did to you . . . I . . .' Sorcha was surprised to see Helen looking a little emotional. 'That was a long time ago. What happened before . . . well, we were kids. It was another life. I can't even reconcile who I am now with the girl I was then.'

'Agreed, you have changed a fair bit.' Sorcha grinned, relaxing a little.

'I'm quite upset to think that you felt I was harbouring some kind of childish grudge against you. We're adults now, it was in the past and very much forgotten.'

'I'm glad. And I really am sorry for the way I behaved towards you.'

'Sorcha – I mean this when I say it – there really is no need for you to apologise.' Helen gave her a curt nod. 'Well, that's that then.' She continued to stow away food.

'I'll be fine by myself now, you know. I'm feeling lots better. Why don't you go home? You must have lots of things to do.'

'Are you sure, Sorcha?'

'Absolutely.'

'Okay. I might just pop into the office for a few hours this afternoon. I hate to think Metropolitan might have got on fine without me. I can come back and make you some supper.'

'There's really no need.'

'Well, I'll ring you before I leave the office and we can decide then.'

Helen insisted she make Sorcha some beans on toast before she left. Sorcha dutifully swallowed them down, thinking Helen would never go if she didn't. Helen went to fetch her things from the spare room and Sorcha saw her to the front door.

'You know where I am if you need me.'

'Yes, but I'm sure I won't.'

'Okay then. Bye, Sorcha.'

'Bye, Helen.' Sorcha reached forward and pecked her on the cheek.

A blush spread across Helen's face. She picked up her briefcase and walked to her Porsche. She dumped her things on the passenger seat and started the engine, and with a toot of her horn she was off.

Sorcha spent the afternoon on the terrace reading a book. Later, she left a message at Con's hotel asking him to ring her, then spoke to her mother just to reassure her she was on the mend. At five, Helen called to check in on her.

The moment she put the telephone down, it rang once more. She picked it up, hoping it was Con.

'Hello?'

'Mrs Daly?'

'Yes?' The voice sounded muffled.

'I thought you'd want to know that your husband has been lying to you for many years.'

'What? I . . . Who is this?'

'Let's just say that Helen McCarthy isn't the reason that you had to leave Ireland.'

'What are you talking about?'

'Ask him, ask her. Goodbye.'

The telephone clicked down. Sorcha stared at the receiver in disbelief. She grabbed the back of the chair. Could it have been a crank call? Possibly. But what crazed fan could have known about her reason for following Con to London? And Helen McCarthy's connection to it all? To stop her mind racing, she went into the living room and switched on the six o'clock news. She *would* not, *could* not think about it, or the fact that her husband was thousands of miles away and hadn't, so far, bothered to return her call.

In a couple of days' time, he'd be home. Then they could sit down and sort things out.

Whatever her good intentions, Sorcha lay wide awake till the early hours, the voice and its poisonous tidings ringing in her head.

41

The welcoming committee that greeted The Fishermen at Heathrow on their return from New York was, as always, raucous. The viewing galleries were packed with screaming fans. Airport security had the group, plus Freddy, bundled into a car by a back door, but the crowd were like bloodhounds. Once one was on their scent, the rest would follow.

'Jesus, I hate this,' moaned Con as faces pressed against the windows and hands tried unsuccessfully to open the locked back door.

'You'd hate it more if they weren't there to greet us,' commented Todd.

At last, the limousine freed itself of the mass of fans and the driver headed for central London.

Con looked behind him and saw the police car tailing them.

'Home sweet home,' he murmured under his breath.

'Well, that was another unqualified success, boys,' smiled Freddy from the front seat. 'You looked and sounded great.'

'I don't know how you heard us, Freddy. With two hundred and fifty thousand screaming fans, we could have played nursery rhymes and no one would have known the difference,' murmured Derek.

'Yeah, well, that's as may be, but I reckon the gig will go down in rock history. You attracted a crowd almost as big as the Beatles when they played the Hollywood Bowl. You can still cut it, there's no doubt about that.'

'Did you ever question it, Freddy?' asked Todd quietly.

'Well, I did get the impression that rehearsals hadn't exactly gone smoothly.'

'You know what they say: terrible dress rehearsal, great show,' Todd mused.

'Freddy, something has to be done fast about your man there.' Con indicated Ian, who had fallen asleep with his mouth open. 'He managed to fluke it on Saturday. But I'm not risking another live gig until he's clean.'

Freddy nodded. 'Okay, I'll sort it. I think we need to meet up at the end of the week, have a chat about the new album and make plans for the next few months. I'm seeing Helen on Wednesday for lunch. She says she has something she wants to talk to me about. Anyone got any ideas?'

Those who were awake shook their heads.

'Stop here and Con and I will catch a cab up north. It'll be faster. The driver can take the rest of you home,' said Freddy.

The driver pulled over on Hammersmith Broadway.

'Con, shall we get together?' Todd asked. 'With Lulu in LA for a couple of days, I've got the house to myself. Come over.'

Freddy was signalling for a cab.

'Sure, Todd. Give me a bell.'

Freddy and Con got into the taxi and it headed towards Belsize Park.

'You will do something about Ian, won't you, Freddy? If we're ever to get this album completed, he's got to shape up. To be honest, if he doesn't, we'll have to think about replacing him.'

'I've said I'll have a word and I will. You seem very tense, Con. Have done all week. Is something wrong?'

'No, I'm grand altogether.'

'Is it these murder threats?'

'Well, it's not ideal to find yourself on some nutter's hit list, but I'm coping.'

'They'll track him down soon, no doubt. Is anything else troubling you?'

'No.' Con stared out of the window.

'Okay,' Freddy sighed. 'Look, any problems, give me a shout. I'm only down the road.' Freddy tapped on the glass. 'Just here'll be fine.' The taxi pulled to a halt. He climbed out, his holdall slung over his shoulder. 'As I said, call any time. Send my love to Sorcha. Helen says she's been really poorly.'

Con nodded. 'Bye, Freddy.'

'Where to now, mate?' asked the taxi driver.

'Hampstead.'

'Righto.'

The taxi continued the few miles to the Daly household, where the gates slid open to welcome Con home. He handed the driver the fare, and let himself inside.

'Sorcha? Sorcha?'

He walked through the quiet house and found his wife sunning herself on the terrace at the back. She turned when she heard him and stood up.

'Con, I didn't hear you.' She walked over and put an arm around his shoulders, then kissed him.

'How are you? Freddy says you were very rough.'

'I was, but I feel so much better seeing you.'

'Me too, Sorcha-porcha.'

There was an awkward distance between the pair. Neither knew exactly what to say, until they both talked at once.

'Would you like a drink?'

'Think I'll have a shower.'

'Why don't you go upstairs and take a shower and I'll bring you a drink?' she suggested.

'Sounds like a grand idea.' Con nodded and headed for the stairs.

'You could have rung, Con.'

'Yeah, sorry.' He swept a hand through his hair and shrugged. 'Things were a bit hectic.'

He continued climbing the stairs. Sorcha stood and watched him disappear, a lump coming to her throat.

Come on, come on, you have to try, otherwise things will never improve.

She went into the kitchen to make herself some tea and get Con a beer.

When she went upstairs, the bathroom was empty but still steaming from Con's recent shower. She found him lying naked on their bed, smoking a cigarette.

'I brought you a beer, cool from the fridge.'

'Thanks.'

She sat down on the bed and handed him the beer, which he rested on his flat stomach. A shiver of wanting ran through her. It had been over a month since they'd made love.

'We need to talk.'

Con, suddenly drained from the hectic schedule of the last week, sighed heavily. 'I know.' He pulled himself into a sitting position and took a swig of beer. 'What would you like to talk about?'

'Us.'

Con nodded. 'Go on.'

'Well, for starters, there's been an awful tension around us for weeks now. We don't seem to communicate any more. You're always out at rehearsals or on some cause with Lulu. And when you *are* home, we never seem to talk. You knew how sick I was and you didn't even bother to call me while you were in New York. I'm starting to wonder . . .'

'What?' Con looked at her wearily.

'Whether you love me any more.'

He sighed and closed his eyes. 'Oh, God. You're right, Sorcha. I've been getting things very wrong.' He put his beer down on the side table and opened his arms. 'Would you come here?'

Sorcha climbed into his embrace.

'I missed you,' Con whispered. 'I'm sorry for putting everything else before you. That's all going to change.'

'You've been so cold, so distant. It's been like living with a stranger. Not the old Con who was funny and relaxed and never let things get on top of him.'

He gazed up the ceiling. 'You're right. Perhaps I've forgotten who the old Con was.'

Sorcha took a deep breath. 'And is the new Con still in love with his wife?'

Con shifted his gaze and looked into his wife's eyes. 'Sorcha. I love you more than anything. I'm just so sorry that it's taken me this long to get out of my own head. I promise that I'm coming back to the real world.'

Sorcha was momentarily overcome with happiness. She wanted to kiss him, but she needed to understand the mysterious phone call.

'Con,' she said after a pause, 'is there anything about our past that I don't know?' She studied his face carefully.

It took him a while to reply. 'What exactly do you mean?'

Sorcha immediately knew that he was hiding something. 'When we left Ballymore.' She recalled the mystery caller's ominous words. 'Was Helen McCarthy the real reason my daddy found out about us?'

The colour drained from Con's face. 'I . . .' There was nothing more he could say.

Sorcha steeled herself. 'Tell me everything. Now.'

Con sat up straight. 'Did Helen say something? That bitch. She really can't be trusted.'

'As a matter of fact, I don't know what I'd have done without her last week. She was kindness itself.' Sorcha stood up, her legs feeling shaky, her mouth dry. 'So, out with it.'

Con sunk his head into his hands and told his wife the truth.

Sorcha's face hardly moved, but tears streamed from her eyes and down her cheeks. When she went to leave the room, Con tried to follow her.

'No! No.' She held up her hand, which was physically trembling. Con slunk guiltily back onto the bed, like an admonished dog.

It was more than an hour before Sorcha returned. When she opened the bedroom door, Con had not moved a muscle, but wore a harrowed, drained expression. He had clearly been crying.

'I think it's best if I go away for a while. I can't bear to stay here any longer.' Sorcha stood for a few seconds looking down at him. 'I'm going to pack my things.'

As she filled a suitcase with clothes, Con lay on the bed silently, his eyes closed. When she was confident she had enough to last her a good week, Sorcha shut the case and picked it up, swallowing back tears. She walked to the bedroom door.

'Goodbye, Con.'

He didn't reply. Or couldn't.

Sorcha shut the bedroom door, walked down the stairs and into the kitchen. In the drawer of the dresser was a chequebook. She'd need it to pay for a hotel, or maybe she should fly straight home to Ballymore . . .

All she knew for now was that she needed to get out of the house and away from Con. She could hardly believe their parting had been so calm, so cold.

Sorcha closed the front door behind her, threw her case into the back of her car and drove out of the gates.

A groupie stood up as she drove by. Braking hard, Sorcha wound down the window and stared into the dope-filled eyes of the young woman.

'I'm going. He's all yours.'

She wound up the window as the girl looked at her in confusion. Tooting her horn, she zoomed off down Heath Road.

42

On Thursday afternoon, the band was scheduled to have a think-tank session regarding the album in one of the new recording studios at Metropolitan. Later, Freddy was joining them and they were all going out to supper.

Derek arrived to find Con already in situ, strumming away at his guitar.

'Hi, Con.' Con did not acknowledge him. 'I hoped I might find you here. I want a word.'

'Fire away.' Con did not stop softly strumming his guitar.

'I know I've gone on about it but I need my song on the new album. Otherwise I'm going to have to reconsider my position with the band.'

'Really?'

'I don't know whether I want to continue being part of The Fishermen.'

'Have you told Freddy this?'

'No, but I have told Helen. She's in full agreement. She thinks I should get my shot.'

'Does she now? That's interesting, considering your woman hasn't heard the song.'

'She has. I sent her a tape and she says she thinks it could be very good with a bit of work,' Derek said petulantly.

Con stopped strumming and looked up at Derek.

'I'm only saying this one more time, and then the subject is closed. Your song stinks, Derek. It's desperate altogether. We are not some little amateur band that can put any old crap on our new album. And that's what your song is: crap. If you don't like it, then do as you say and leave the band. I really couldn't give a shit. Now if you'll excuse me, I have work to do.' Con resumed his strumming.

Derek glared at Con for a while before he spoke.

'I don't know what's happened to you recently. You used to be such a decent guy. It must be the fame that's turned you into a miserable shit. If that's the way you feel, then fine. Find another rhythm guitar player.'

Con shrugged but didn't reply.

'I'm warning you, Con Daly. You're an arrogant Irish bastard who's putting an awful lot of noses out of joint. You're going to get your comeuppance soon.'

Derek left the studio. Con sighed and continued to play. The tune he was working on was starting to take shape.

At ten past three, the studio door opened. Todd headed straight for Con and slammed his fist into Con's face. The blow sent Con tumbling backwards onto the floor.

'You *bastard*! You *bastard*!' Todd climbed astride Con and proceeded to use his face as a punchball. From his prone position all Con could do was raise his arms to try to protect himself.

'Who the *fuck* do you think you are? You bastard, you bastard!' Todd continued to pound his fists into Con's now bloody face.

'Jaysus, you're killing me, Todd! Stop it!'

'Give me one good reason why I shouldn't kill you? Coming on to Lulu behind my back. *My* wife! Your mate's wife!' Todd landed a punch in Con's stomach.

'What?!' Con screeched.

'You of all people know how much I love her. Last night she tells me that you've been all over her for weeks.' He whacked Con again. 'She said she was lucky to get out of that hotel room in New York after you grabbed her and kissed her.'

'Todd, that's not—'

'Well, you've really done it now. It's over. It's all over. You've ruined everything.' Todd choked back tears. He looked at Con below him. His nose was bleeding profusely.

'You've destroyed the band, Con. I never want to see your bastard face again.'

'What the hell is going on?'

Todd turned round and saw Freddy standing in the doorway.

'You can ask Con what the hell is going on. Excuse me.' Todd pushed past Freddy, walked through the control room and left the suite.

'Bloody hell, Con. What did you do to ask for this?' Freddy knelt down and offered an arm to help Con upright. He staggered a little as Freddy placed him in a chair. 'Stay here. I'll get something to help clean you up.'

Freddy walked through the control room to the kitchenette at the end of the corridor. There was a pile of serviettes by the coffee machine. He wet a few and returned to Con.

'You really do look like you've gone the distance with Muhammad Ali,' he quipped as he dabbed at the blood on Con's face. 'I think your nose could be broken, old son. We'd better get you to hospital and get it checked.'

'No thanks, Freddy. I'll be fine, really.' Con winced as he touched it. 'I'm sure it looks worse than it is.'

'I'll call you a car then. Go home and let Sorcha nurse you. Maybe now isn't the time to go into detail about what just took place.'

Con nodded as Freddy went back to the control room and dialled reception.

'Car's ordered. Where are the others?'

'Derek left and Ian's yet to arrive,' murmured Con.

'Typical. So, I suppose supper's off then?'

'Could be looking that way.'

'Okay. Come on, I've asked the car to meet us right outside the door. Don't think it would do for Con Daly's screaming fans to see him like this. Can you stand?'

Con heaved himself out of the chair. 'Yeah.' He followed Freddy out of the recording suite and up the stairs into reception. A car pulled up outside and beeped its horn.

'There you go.' Freddy ran to open the door. 'Hop in. Listen, I'll give you a bell tomorrow to see how you are. You'd better fill me in then as to exactly what's going on.'

'Sure. Thanks, Freddy.'

Freddy closed the door and the car sped off along the road. Sighing heavily, he made his way back inside and down to the recording suite.

Ian was floating down the corridor towards him, wearing a long, garish kaftan. He made the peace sign to Freddy. 'Hi, man, what's occurring? Where are the others?'

For some reason the bizarre sight of Ian – at least two hours late and in a complete world of his own – caused Freddy to burst into laughter.

'Gone, Ian. You missed 'em, mate. Hold on two ticks while I turn the lights off in the recording suite, and you and I will go for a beer.'

'Not beer, man. I don't like beer.'

'Well, whatever tickles your fancy. I need a drink.'

The two of them walked back upstairs to reception.

Freddy leant over the desk and smiled at the young receptionist. 'Could you send someone down to recording suite number three? There's a bit of a mess that needs clearing up.' Freddy tapped his nose. 'Keep it between you and me, can you?'

'Of course, sir.'

'Thanks, Melody. See you soon.'

Freddy put an arm round Ian and steered him to the front door.

'Let's find a boozer, old son.'

Con studied his nose in the mirror. It was numb and did seem wonkier than usual. He'd broken it once before in a punch-up when he was a kid. He'd see how it looked tomorrow and maybe visit the Royal Free if it still didn't feel quite right. The rest of the cuts and bruises seemed pretty superficial. Con dabbed at them clumsily with TCP.

'Jesus, what a day . . . what a week,' he sighed to his reflection.

That bitch, Lulu . . . Not only had she given Todd that nonsense story, but she'd obviously been the one who'd spilled the beans to Sorcha.

'Hell hath no fury . . .' he mumbled.

Con decided the best thing to do was to take a couple of aspirin for his throbbing head and have an early night. He was starving, but since Sorcha had left, the supplies had run low. If she were here now, she'd tend to him. He missed her . . . he really missed her . . .

Opening the medicine cabinet, Con pulled out the aspirin, filled up a toothmug with water and swallowed them down.

He stripped off his bloody T-shirt and jeans, feeling too exhausted even to take a shower, and went to the bedroom.

43

CON DALY IN SPLIT WITH WIFE

Steeling herself, Sorcha read the story underneath the page-two headline.

In a sensational split, Con Daly's wife Sorcha has left the family home in Hampstead. Our inside source says Sorcha Daly stormed out over Con's growing relationship with Lulu Bradley – actress, peace campaigner and wife of Todd Bradley. The pair have regularly been seen together at marches over the past few months.

Neither Con Daly nor Todd Bradley were available for comment, but their manager, Freddy Martin, said that the situation was dealt with amicably by both sides and won't affect the future of The Fishermen.

However, an insider at Metropolitan Records said there were fisticuffs in a recording suite recently. A glance at the admissions records in accident and emergency at the Royal Free Hospital, Hampstead, tells us that a Mr C. Daly was admitted with a broken nose and cuts to his face in the early hours of last Friday morning. He was later released and has been lying low in his sumptuous mansion on the edge of Hampstead Heath.

It remains to be seen whether this delicate situation will affect one of the most successful songwriting partnerships of the decade; both Mr and Mrs Daly and Mr and Mrs Bradley have enjoyed a close friendship over the years.

Sorcha Daly's whereabouts are unknown. A record company spokesman refused to comment other than to suggest that Mrs Daly might have gone to stay with relations abroad.

Sorcha reread the article and wondered who had leaked their split to the press. She suspected that it was someone at Metropolitan – news of discord within the band might drive sales. Was there anything going on between Con and Lulu? Who knew. She hoped that whoever had wanted their payday from the tabloids had provided it as a convenient reason for the split. She hoped the fight with Todd had truth in it, though. A broken nose was little less than Con deserved.

The telephone rang. Without thinking, Sorcha picked it up. 'Hello?'

'Reception here. We have a call for you, Mrs Daly.'

'Okay.' She waited.

'Mrs Daly?'

'Yes?'

'Mrs Sorcha Daly?'

'Yes?'

'Glad we've found you, Mrs Daly. The *Mirror* newspaper here. We'd like to ask you for an exclusive interview on the situation with your husband and Lulu Bradley. We'd be prepared to pay you a lot of money, or donate the same amount to a charity of your choice. Obviously, the interview would be extremely sympathetic towards yourself. How do you feel about—'

Sorcha slammed the telephone down. Why, oh *why* had she not thought to book in under an assumed name? Fingers trembling, she dialled reception. 'Please, no more calls are to be put through to my room. If anyone else rings for me, can you tell them I've checked out?'

'We'll do our best, Mrs Daly, of course.'

'Thank you.' Sorcha put the telephone down. The Hampstead Post House had hardly been the most discreet or distant place to go to, but she'd felt so incapable of driving when she'd left Con. It had seemed a comfortingly anonymous place to stay for a few days while she decided on a course of action.

Sorcha sat down on the edge of the unmade bed and tried to think. The media were on to her. In a matter of an hour she knew there would be a pack of reporters waiting for her outside. She had to move fast, but where should she go?

Home, to Ireland? With the media brouhaha that was about to take place, she thought it unfair to put that burden on her newly bereaved mother, in addition to the prying eyes and wagging tongues of Ballymore.

'Help,' she murmured. She'd never felt so totally alone.

Should she move to another hotel? Sorcha shook her head. She'd feel so vulnerable. It only took one receptionist or porter to tip off the press.

There was only one person she could think of that might be able to help.

She reached for the receiver and dialled the number she knew by heart.

'Metropolitan Records.'

'Helen McCarthy, please.'

'I'm sorry, but Miss McCarthy is in a meeting and cannot be disturbed.'

'This is urgent. Tell her it's Sorcha Daly. I have to speak to her *now*.'

'Okay, Mrs Daly, hold on and I'll see what I can do.'

Sorcha waited in an agony of frustration.

'Sorcha, it's Helen. Where are you?'

'I'm at the Post House in Hampstead. Oh, Helen . . .' Sorcha swallowed a sob. 'Did you see the *Daily Express*?'

'Yes, I saw it.'

'I'm sorry to call you, but the *Daily Mirror* have just phoned me. The press know where I am and they'll be swarming all over the place soon. I . . . I don't know what to do.'

'Okay. First, stop panicking. We'll get you out of there. Pack your things and I'll send a car to you now. You can go to my house in Holland Park. No one will find you there. Katie, the maid, will let you in. Stay there until I get home, then we can discuss it further. There must be a back door you can use at the hotel?'

'I don't know, I really don't.'

'Come on, Sorcha, hold it together. I'm going to put the telephone down now and call the hotel manager. I'll have him escort you to a rendezvous with the car. Okay?'

'Yes. Thanks, Helen. Sorry. It's just all so . . . sordid.'

'I know. I'll call you in an hour. You should have arrived in Holland Park by then. Bye, Sorcha.'

Sorcha put the telephone down and reached for her case, flinging the bits and pieces she'd brought with her back inside. Then she dressed and searched for her sunglasses to hide her pale, drawn face from the possible intrusion of a camera lens.

'Dammit!' They were in her car, parked outside. They might as well have been on Mars.

Sorcha closed her case and sat on the bed to wait. A few minutes later, there was a knock on the door.

'Who is it?'

'Mr Adams, the hotel manager. I've just talked to Miss McCarthy.'

'Okay.' Sorcha unlocked the door.

The manager smiled at her. 'She's asked me to escort you to your car. I sent it round the back.'

'Thank you.'

'If you'd like to follow me.' He picked up her case and set off down the corridor towards the lift. 'I'm afraid there's a pack of newshounds and photographers at the front waiting for you to emerge. There's only one exit for cars from the back, so the cab will have to run the gauntlet. It's the best we can do.'

They took the lift to the ground floor and Sorcha followed him through a maze of corridors.

'Here we are.' The manager stopped in front of an emergency exit and pushed the mechanism. A car was waiting by the pavement. Sorcha hurried over to it, pulled open the back door and got inside as the manager placed her case in the boot. He tapped on the window and motioned for Sorcha to wind it down.

'It's been a pleasure having you, Mrs Daly. I hope you'll recommend us to your friends. Here's our bill.' He handed her a white envelope.

'Thank you. I'm very grateful for your hel—'

'Hey! There she is! Sorcha's round here!' a voice screamed.

Sorcha wound up the window and the driver pulled forward. As the car turned the corner, an onrush of reporters and photographers came running towards the car.

'Don't worry, love. We'll get through. Won't take a minute. I'll run the buggers over if needs be.' The elderly driver pressed on his horn and continued to drive forward determinedly into the mass of people.

Flashbulbs popped and reporters knocked on the window, mouthing words Sorcha couldn't hear. She looked straight ahead and willed herself not to cry. Eventually, they reached the car-park exit and Sorcha watched the reporters scatter and head for their vehicles.

'Now, miss, hold on to your hat and we'll lose the little rats.'

The car suddenly lurched forward into the traffic, eliciting a cacophony of horns. Ten minutes later, after driving down backstreets that even Sorcha had no idea existed in Hampstead, the car joined the main flow of vehicles around Swiss Cottage. Swerving in and out of lanes, the driver headed for St John's Wood and central London. He looked in his mirror and smiled at her.

'We've lost 'em, love. You're okay now.'

'There's your case, Mrs Daly.' The taxi driver put Sorcha's belongings in the hall of Helen's mews house.

Sorcha smiled gratefully. 'Thank you so much.'

'Any time. Adds a bit of variety to my day. You take care now. Goodbye.'

'I'll show you to your room, Mrs Daly.'

Sorcha followed Katie, Helen's maid, up the narrow stairs.

'I have some bread and pâté downstairs when you're ready.'

'Thank you. I'll be down shortly.'

She sat down on the bed and wept with relief.

After lunch, Katie announced that she had to go and do a little shopping and pick up Helen's dry cleaning.

Just as Katie left, the telephone rang. Uncertainly, Sorcha walked towards the receiver and tentatively picked it up.

'Hello?' she whispered.

'Helen here. In future, we'll have a code. I'll ring three times, hang up and then call straight back. Are you okay?'

'Fine now I'm here. The driver was brilliant.'

'I've used Dan for years. He's completely trustworthy. Anyway, I just wanted to make sure you were okay. I've got a meeting now but I should be home by six. Make yourself comfortable. Watch an old film on TV or something.'

'Thanks, Helen. I'll see you later.'

'Bye, Sorcha.'

She put the telephone down and, for the first time, took proper notice of her surroundings.

The house was so tidy as to be almost unlived in. Other than two immaculate cream sofas and a long smoked-glass coffee table with a pile of seemingly untouched glossy magazines in one corner, there was no other furniture. The white walls were mostly bare, the odd framed print here and there. A superb Bang & Olufsen sound system with three-foot speakers took up most of one wall, and a small television sat in the corner. Sorcha made her way back upstairs and opened the first door she came to. It was a little larger than a broom cupboard, furnished with an antique writing desk and leather chair. There were shelves lining two of the walls with rows of large books stacked neatly on them. Sorcha pulled one out.

Copyright Laws in the Music Industry – New updated edition.

Leaving the room, Sorcha tried the next door along the corridor and found the bathroom – small but serviceable. The third door along led to her own neat guest room.

The last room had to be Helen's bedroom. Sorcha pushed open the door and stood on the threshold in surprise. Compared with the uncluttered elegance of the rest of the house, this room was completely different. The double bed was covered in a colourful patchwork quilt, and resting against the wrought-iron headboard were numerous cuddly toys. An old-fashioned dressing table was jammed with lotions and potions and down one wall ran a full-length mirrored wardrobe. On the other walls hung what could only be described as nursery prints, depicting teddy bears and children playing oranges and lemons.

'A child's room,' murmured Sorcha. It reminded her very much of her bedroom in her parents' house in Ballymore.

She pulled open the top drawer of a large oak chest. There

she found black silk stockings, soft to the touch beneath her fingers, camisoles, bustiers, suspender belts and knickers, all in black too.

Sorcha closed the drawer and smiled. 'Maybe not such a child's room.'

She shut the door and walked downstairs.

The only sound that broke the silence was the tick of the kitchen clock. Sorcha picked up a magazine and, settling down on the sofa, immersed herself in an article on the elegant garden of an eminent actress.

At almost seven o'clock, a key turned in the lock and Helen appeared in the sitting room.

'Hi, how've you been?' She put her briefcase down.

'Fine, thank you.'

'Good. Did Katie make you welcome?'

'Very. Your dry cleaning's hanging in the wardrobe and there's lobster and salad in the fridge for supper.'

'That woman is a gem,' smiled Helen. 'Listen, I'll just pop upstairs and take a shower. It's really sticky out there. I think it might thunder tonight. Why don't you set the table on the patio and we can eat the lobster outside? It might be the last chance we get this summer. And don't worry, it's totally private. There's a bottle of wine in the fridge. Open that and have a glass. I sure need one and I should think you do too.'

Sorcha went into the kitchen, opened the wine and collected two glasses, cutlery and plates. She unlocked the patio doors, relieved to see that there was a high brick wall surrounding the flagstones.

Helen was back downstairs within fifteen minutes, looking cool in a blouse and a pair of linen slacks. Sorcha studied her as she placed dinner on the table and sat down. She certainly knew how to make the best of herself.

'Cheers.' Helen raised her wine glass. 'You probably don't

feel like you've got much to celebrate at the moment. To be honest, nor do I. So let's drink to things getting better.'

Sorcha raised her glass and took a sip of wine. 'It really is very kind of you to let me come here, Helen. It was my own stupid fault. I should have thought that word would leak out.'

'Well, next time you leave your husband, can you hole up somewhere a bit more glamorous than the Hampstead Post House?' Helen smiled as she picked up her cutlery.

'It was the first place I came to, that's all.' Sorcha attempted to spear a piece of lobster with her fork.

'Listen, nobody's looking. Let's use our fingers.' Helen tore apart a claw. 'So, any thoughts on the future, Sorcha? Is this separation permanent?'

'No, none at all. To be honest, I've been a bit of a coward. I haven't wanted to think. I'm not sure whether it's the remnants of that awful flu I had last week, but I'm still feeling pretty rough. When I was at the Post House I slept for hours.'

'It's shock, I'm sure.' Helen wiped her hands and dabbed at her mouth with a napkin. 'Look, Sorcha, it's no good me treading on eggshells. Do you want to talk about what's happened with you and Con or not?'

'I . . .' Sorcha shrugged and shook her head. 'I don't know. I mean, even if I'm not talking about it, in my head I'm thinking about it all the time so, yes, maybe it's better I do. He told me about what he asked you to do.' Sorcha cast her eyes to the floor. 'Back in Ballymore.'

Helen looked a little shocked. 'God, Sorcha – I can't apologise enough. I was a different person back then, I . . .'

Sorcha held her hands up. 'Really, Helen, you don't have to apologise. I don't blame you for anything.'

Helen swallowed hard. 'That's very generous.'

'Con has always been very good at getting what he wants. Do you know if anything's been going on with Lulu?'

Helen shrugged. 'No. But for what it's worth, I wouldn't believe a word the papers say. Knowing that woman, I wouldn't be surprised if Lulu leaked the story herself. Apparently she's told Todd that Con's been trying it on with her for weeks.' Helen sniffed. 'But I don't buy it. She's seen an opportunity to place herself as the woman that came between the songwriting partnership of the decade. She wants her star to rise, no matter the cost to anyone else.'

Sorcha managed a sad chuckle. 'Maybe so. Lulu did seem to permanently be at our house, but I really thought it was because of their shared interests. I believed Con loved me.' Sorcha tried to hold back her tears. 'He's changed so much in the past few months, Helen. I feel like I hardly know him any more.'

'Yes, he has changed.' Helen sighed. 'And this situation really is causing me almighty problems.' Helen caught herself. 'Nothing compared to how you're feeling, of course.'

Sorcha waved her hand. 'It's all right, Helen. I know how badly this affects your business.' She shook her head. 'In some ways I wish The Fishermen hadn't become so successful so quickly. It would have given us more time to adjust. I might not be Con's biggest fan at the moment, but I do realise that pressure was . . . and still is enormous.'

Helen placed her fork neatly by the side of her plate.

'Do you want to know what I think, Sorcha?'

'What?'

'I think Con's heading for some kind of breakdown. He's lost it, feels that he can't cope any more. What I'm trying to say is that I don't think you should completely give up on him. The man totally screwed up all those years ago, yes. But then so did I.' Helen gave Sorcha her warmest smile. 'I suppose you have to remember that it was all because he couldn't bear the thought of a life without you.'

Sorcha rubbed her eyes. 'That's one way of looking at it. Another is that he stopped me from having a relationship with my father, and consequently the rest of my family. Not to mention my friends. Seamus O'Donovan was hardly Santa Claus, but the choice to cut him out of my life should have been mine alone. What a selfish thing to have done.'

Helen took a sip of her wine. 'I should have never agreed to any of it. I'm as much to blame.' She chose her next words carefully. 'Con needs you, Sorcha. He always has. You're the one link he has to his past.'

Sorcha picked at her cuticles. 'In between sleeping, I've had some time to think about myself for once. I've given up everything for him, Helen. Right since the beginning, what he wanted came first. I left Ballymore, I supported him when he came to London . . . I even gave up my career just as I was offered a major modelling contract. I did it because I loved him, and because I really believed he loved me. Now I feel like everything's built on a foundation of dishonesty. He's trodden all over me and as good as thrown me away when he thought he didn't need me any more. I may still love Con, but I don't think I like him.'

Sorcha reached for her wine and took a big gulp. 'The Lulu thing hurts, too. I thought we were friends. Clearly she was using me as a way to get closer to Con.' She massaged her temples. 'And this media interest is awful, like rubbing salt into the wound. How long do you reckon I have to hide myself away?'

Helen shrugged. 'Who knows? Depends what else happens in the next few days. The minute something more interesting comes along, they'll be off your back. Let's both pray that happens,' she said gently. 'I'll be able to report back to you tomorrow. I've got a meeting with Freddy in the morning to establish if there's a way forward for The Fishermen after all this. Whether we can get Todd and Con in the same room, let alone *leave* them together to write this album that's looming ever closer is another matter.'

'I'd imagine you might struggle at the moment.'

'Well, it's not just Todd that hates Con. Your dear husband has managed to completely alienate Derek by telling him his precious song is a pile of rubbish. Very subtle of him. Derek called Freddy and told him he refused to work with Con again and was leaving the band. It's probably hot air, but who knows with Derek? He's an unusual character to say the least.'

Sorcha drained her wine glass and stared into space.

'It's all so sad.'

'What is?' asked Helen.

'Well, they were all such good friends and now . . . well . . . It's just a desperate mess.'

'It is. And unfortunately, I have to try to sort it out. The Fishermen are an industry, Sorcha. And whatever their personal problems, they have a contract with Metropolitan.' Helen looked up as a streak of lightning illuminated the darkening sky. She wiped her forehead. 'There is going to be a storm, thank God. I despise the humidity. Shall we clear up?'

Later, Sorcha went upstairs to take a shower. The thunder rumbled directly overhead and while she dried herself she heard the first drops of rain on the windowpane. By the time she was back downstairs there was a torrential downpour outside. Helen was sitting at the dining table, a pile of papers in front of her, but her attention was focused on the storm outside too.

'Isn't it magnificent?' she murmured. 'Puts everything into perspective. I loved watching them come in from the sea in Ballymore.'

'So did I,' smiled Sorcha.

'Anyway, I think it's time to hit the sack. I'll probably be gone by the time you wake up. I like to get to the office by eight.'

'No problem.'

Helen packed her papers into her briefcase, locked it and stood up.

'Okay. I'm going up. Turn the lights off when you follow, will you?'

'Yes, goodnight, Helen.'

'Night.'

Sorcha sat down in Helen's place and watched the storm raging outside.

Twenty minutes later, she made her way up the stairs to bed, musing how much she'd once disliked Helen McCarthy and how, after the past few days, she'd come to respect her more than anyone else.

44

Helen was up at a quarter to six. She hung out her suit, used the bathroom and was just crossing the landing when Sorcha bolted out of the bedroom and headed for the loo, slamming the door hastily behind her. Helen listened as Sorcha retched violently, then continued on her journey to her bedroom.

Once ready to face the day, Helen came out of her room and knocked on Sorcha's closed door.

'Come in.'

Helen entered. Sorcha was lying on her bed, her eyes closed.

'Are you okay? You look awfully pale.'

'Yes, I'll be fine in a minute. I think I must have had too much wine last night.'

'You only drank a couple of glasses, Sorcha.'

'Then maybe it's tension. It's happened a couple of times since I left Con.'

'Always in the morning?'

'Yes.'

Helen sat down on the end of Sorcha's bed. She picked a piece of lint off the bedspread. 'I don't suppose you could be pregnant, could you?' A look of sheer panic appeared on Sorcha's face.

'I . . . no, of course I'm not.'

'So you're not late or anything?'

'I don't think so. I haven't thought about it with everything else going on . . .' Sorcha racked her brains. 'Maybe I'm a little late, but it's most likely stress. Con and I . . . we've been trying for ages and nothing's happened so, no, I'm sure it's other things.'

Sorcha's confusion gave Helen no further information. 'Well, whatever it is, it's not exactly healthy for you to be ill like that every morning. Why don't I get my doctor to pop round and check you out?'

'There's really no need, Helen.'

'I think there is.'

'Give me another day. If I don't feel any better tomorrow, I promise I'll see a doctor.'

'Okay.' Helen stood up from the bed. 'I've got to go. Katie'll be here in an hour. Any problems, call Maggie, my secretary. She'll know where I am.'

'Will do.'

'Bye then.'

'Bye.' Sorcha's head dropped back onto the pillow.

'Oh, Jesus, Mary and Joseph,' she murmured. 'Not now. Oh, please, God, not now.'

'So, what is the score, Freddy? Have we a band or haven't we?'

Helen tapped her gold pencil on her desk, waiting for the soft soap, the procrastination.

'It's not looking good, Helen, not good at all. Todd refuses to speak to me. I've been round to see him but he won't answer the door. I know he's there because his cleaning lady told me. And as for Con, well, he's lolling around in bed looking mean and moody with stitches in his face. Derek seems to be under the illusion that he's resigned from the band and has stormed off abroad somewhere. And Ian, well, I'd say if we do manage to get some kind of order in the ranks, we should think about replacing him anyway.'

'What about the album?'

'To put it bluntly, I'd forget it. There's no way it's happening at the moment.'

'So, where do we go from here? I mean, I could sue you. We have a deal. The Fishermen have to produce.'

'I am aware of that, Helen, but I don't know what more I can do. I think maybe the best thing is to give everybody a bit of space and let things calm down a bit.'

'There isn't time. I want the album in the shops for Christmas.'

'Then you *will* have to sue. I'm no miracle worker and besides, what kind of music are those boys going to make in the state they're in?'

'I take your point, Freddy, but The Fishermen's personal lives are no problem of mine.'

'Oh, come on, Helen. That's a bit harsh.'

'Yes, but it's the truth. If The Fishermen split up, the hole in Metropolitan's profit forecast is deeper than the Pacific. It's vital that for the next few months the company remains stable. I will *not* tolerate their bad behaviour affecting my company. So, you can tell your boys that unless they kiss and make up and are in the studio first thing on Monday morning, I will begin legal proceedings for breach of contract against them immediately.'

Freddy shrugged. 'Okay, okay, I'll have a word with them and tell them what you've said. I'll get back to you as soon as I've rounded up the prima donnas. Who'd be a manager, eh?'

'Lots of people, considering the screw you get out of them,' Helen replied calmly.

'You're a hard woman, Miss McCarthy.' Freddy stood up,

hesitated, then leant over the desk. 'As a matter of fact, I wanted to see you about something else. I've found a duo, girl and boy. They're American actually, but he writes the songs and she sings them beautifully. I reckon they're the sound of the seventies. They look good too. Shall I send you a demo?'

'By all means. You know we're always on the lookout for new talent.'

'These two might just plug your Pacific hole. Cheers, Helen. I'll be in touch when I have news.'

Helen watched him leave the office, then sat back and took a couple of deep breaths.

She held out little hope for Freddy's powers of persuasion. 'Dammit, dammit!'

Sorcha put on her jacket and walked downstairs.

She *had* to know. That meant braving Kensington High Street, the nearest place she was sure would have a chemist.

She tucked the glass jar containing her sample in the front pocket of her handbag, buckled the bag and then set off along the mews and out onto Holland Park Avenue. The storm last night had broken the humidity and today there was a cooling breeze and a touch of autumn in the air.

She was back forty-five minutes later, feeling pleased she'd managed to accomplish her mission without being spotted, but disappointed she wouldn't know the results of her test until Monday. An entire weekend to agonise. Naturally, she'd given a false name to the pharmacist. She could only imagine the headlines if the media got wind of her possible pregnancy.

Katie had left her some sandwiches. Sorcha nibbled them disconsolately, then, feeling exhausted, went upstairs to her bedroom to lie down.

Of course, now she thought about it, it all made perfect sense. The exhaustion, the nausea – classic symptoms of pregnancy.

All those months of wanting a baby.

What would she do?

Would she tell Con?

These were questions she could not answer.

At half past six, the bell rang. Nervously, Sorcha peeped through the spy-hole.

'Hello? Sorcha, are you there? I work at Metropolitan Records. Helen asked me to drop by with an urgent envelope for her on my way home. She told me not to disturb you, but the envelope won't fit through the letter box. Would you open the door?'

Sorcha stood in an agony of indecision.

'I know you had lobster and salad for supper last night, if it helps,' said the voice.

'Okay.' Sorcha ran back the bolt and turned the lock. She peered round the door to find an extremely pretty girl with big blue eyes and long blonde hair standing on the doorstep. The girl looked somewhat familiar, but Sorcha couldn't quite place her face.

'Hi. Thanks for trusting me.' The girl proffered a large brown envelope. 'Can you make sure Helen gets this?'

'Of course. Have we met before? You look ever so familiar.'

'I've been at Metropolitan for a while. Maybe you've seen me there.'

'Yes, maybe.'

'Oh well, I must go. Bye.'

'Yes. Bye.'

Helen was late home that night. She flopped onto the sofa, accepting the glass of wine Sorcha handed to her.

'God, what a day.' She took a sip. 'Have you plans for the weekend?'

Sorcha shook her head.

'Then you can come down to Surrey with me and see my new house. I'm meeting the interior designer there to discuss wallpaper and curtains. If you want, that is.'

Sorcha nodded. 'Anything to take my mind off the situation.'

Helen took another sip of her wine and eyed Sorcha. 'So. Do you think you *are* pregnant?'

Sorcha took a deep breath. 'There's a good chance I am, yes.'

'What will you do?'

'I have absolutely no idea.'

'Well, we can worry about that when Monday comes. We've both had a stressful week. Let's give ourselves a couple of days off, shall we?'

'We can try. Oh, by the way, someone dropped in an envelope for you. It's there on the table.'

'Thanks.'

'She's a very pretty girl.'

'Isn't she? I was at business college with Mags when I first came to London. She turned up for an interview at Metropolitan a week ago. Her CV was a bit patchy, but I gave her the benefit of the doubt and she's doing a great job. She's only filling in for my usual secretary, who's just gone on maternity leave. But if she continues like this, I might offer her the job permanently.' Helen sighed. 'All the men love her, of course. To be born beautiful like you and Mags . . . what an advantage it is.'

'Oh, Helen, these days you put us all in the shade.'

'I have to work very hard to look how I do. The right clothes and make-up help, but I watch what I eat every day of my life to keep the pounds off. It's a continual struggle.'

'But worth it, Helen. You always look great.'

'Thanks. Now, talking of food, what's for supper?'

*   *   *

371

A little later, the women went to their respective bedrooms.

They both lay sleepless, Sorcha praying that the result of the test would be negative, Helen hoping against hope it would be positive.

She knew the tiny thing inside Sorcha Daly's womb might be the only thing that could save The Fishermen. And, she hoped, Sorcha too.

45

Sorcha watched the dawn rise on Monday morning, thankful that the weekend was finally over. At nine o'clock, she could ring the chemist.

'Up early?'

Sorcha was forcing down a piece of plain toast when Helen arrived downstairs.

'Yes. I didn't sleep too well last night.'

'I can imagine. Look, I have a meeting this morning but I should be back in the office by lunchtime. Give me a call and let me know the news.'

'I will.'

Helen glanced at her watch. 'I'd better go.' She placed a hand on Sorcha's shoulder. 'Try not to worry. It'll sort itself out. See you later.'

At seven minutes past nine, Sorcha put down the receiver. Her whole body was trembling. Even though the news was no surprise, there had still been a chance that she'd been wrong.

'Miss McCarthy, come in.'

Helen followed Jeremy Swain into his large office overlooking Old Street.

'Coffee?' he asked as she settled herself in the leather chair in front of his desk.

'Thank you.'

Jeremy sat down, rang through to his secretary and asked her to bring a pot of coffee and two cups. He opened the file lying in front of him.

'Well, things are looking good for the share issue. There's a buzz about it in the City.'

'Good.'

'The valuation is looking healthy. My analysts have predicted a thirty-per-cent growth in the next two years.' Jeremy looked up as his secretary brought in a tray. 'Thanks. Leave it there and we'll pour.'

Helen watched Jeremy fill two cups with strong coffee before offering milk and sugar.

'I was thinking of setting the flotation for around the middle of November. What do you think?'

'I'm happy to go with you on dates.'

'Okay, fine.'

Helen took a sip of her coffee. 'Jeremy, can I just check the projection figures for The Fishermen?'

'Sure. They're your largest asset at present, responsible for about twenty-five per cent of Metropolitan's turnover.'

'What would happen if the band announced that they were splitting up?'

Jeremy stared at her across the table. 'It would be extremely bad news for the flotation. Is it likely?'

'Put it this way, they're having a few personal problems. I'm hoping they'll be sorted out, but I can't guarantee it.'

'I see. Well now, this does rather throw the cat amongst the pigeons. I had read something about one of them in the papers last week but I don't take much notice of the scandal rags. Unfortunately, other people do. Apart from anything else, when you're going public, any media coverage you receive needs to be positive. And of course, without The Fishermen, there'd be approximately twenty-five per cent wiped off your turnover and probably more off the profit forecast.'

Helen drained her coffee cup. 'Everything you're telling me I already knew,' she sighed.

'Could the band delay their split for, say, six months? That would allow the flotation to take place at the company's present value. Your investors will realise that the world of popular music is unstable, and if The Fishermen are to split, so be it. Of course, there is every chance that in six months' time, Metropolitan may have discovered a new group that will make it big. And you'll still retain the rights to The Fishermen's songs.'

'So the timing of the split is crucial.' Helen drummed her fingers on the desk. 'The trouble is that you're dealing with people here, rather than an inanimate commodity. I can put pressure on them to stay together for another six months or so. They *are* still under contract to us. They have an album to record, plus a single. If they don't produce, I could threaten to sue them.'

'Another step you obviously don't want to take at present. There's nothing like a court case for putting investors off. Metropolitan needs to be whiter than white for the next few weeks, Helen.'

'Of course.' She glanced at her watch. 'I'm seeing their manager in forty-five minutes. I'll have a clearer indication of the position after that.'

'The only other thing you could do is delay the flotation. It would be a shame, what with the company riding so high at present. And any sudden change of plans makes the City jittery and therefore harder next time round.'

Helen stood up. 'We'll just have to wait and see. If you have any other thoughts, please do let me know.'

'Other than one of The Fishermen being shot dead, becoming a legend and massively boosting sales of their former albums, I don't think I have much to offer you,' smiled Jeremy. 'Keep me informed, Helen.'

'I will.' Helen held out her hand. 'Goodbye, Jeremy.'

Helen arrived back at the office and slid the flotation details into her locked drawer. As she did so, she realised something was missing. She felt around at the back. She was sure the gun had been there last time she'd looked.

Her intercom beeped. 'Freddy Martin for you.'

'Send him in.'

Helen closed the drawer, making a mental note to have a thorough search of her office for the gun. If she couldn't find it, she'd need to inform the police as soon as possible.

Freddy strolled through the door.

'So, Freddy, what news?'

'Do you want the bad news or the bad news?'

'Go on.'

'I managed, after several attempts, to gain an audience with Todd. God, he looks rough. He has all the curtains drawn in his house and he's playing the Grateful Dead over and over. It turns out Lulu's gone and left him.'

'Okay, get to the point, will you?'

'He's talking about The Fishermen in the past tense. As far as he's concerned, it's over, for good. He told me he was considering moving abroad, that he couldn't stand being on the same land mass with that "wanker", as he affectionately calls Con.'

'Okay, what about Con?'

'Same story. Doesn't want to know.'

'Derek?'

'Naffed off abroad. Don't know where. Can't get hold of him. Sorry, Helen.'

'Ian?'

'Oh, I saw him all right, for the difference it made. He's happy to do *whatever anybody wants, man,*' mimicked Freddy.

'It's no laughing matter, Freddy. Metropolitan's flotation is coming up in a couple of months' time. If The Fishermen split, their in-fighting could wipe millions off the value of the company.'

Freddy sighed. 'What can I do?'

Helen's eyes were hard and cold. 'I've no idea, Freddy, but you'd better come up with something, otherwise I'll sue the band to high heaven.'

Freddy stood up. 'I'm sorry. I'm just as pissed off about this as you, you know. They're my livelihood too. Maybe you'd have more influence. I still believe in time this will blow over.'

'We don't *have* time, Freddy. See yourself out, will you?' she said abruptly, before picking up the receiver on the desk and beginning to dial.

Freddy shrugged and left the room.

'Yeah?'

'Con, it's Helen McCarthy.'

'What do you want?'

'To talk to you. Urgently. Shall I come to you or do you want to meet somewhere for lunch?'

'I'm busy today, sorry.'

'Make yourself un-busy. I'll be with you in an hour.'

Helen slammed the telephone down, wondering why she had invested so much effort in arrogant, childish pop stars when she could have had a nice easy life dealing with bloodstock or raw sewage. She dialled her home number, let it ring three times then put the receiver down and rang again.

'Hello?'

'It's me. Have you rung?'

'Yes.'

'And?'

'It was positive.'

Helen attempted to strike the right tone between compassion and practicality. 'Well, it wasn't a surprise.'

'No, but I'm pretty shaken up.'

'I can imagine, Sorcha. Keep your chin up, I'm here for you. Try not to brood.'

'It's a bit difficult when I'm a prisoner in your house with nothing to do but think.'

'I know, I know. There are many options we can talk about. Just keep going until tonight. We can discuss everything over a glass of wine. Well, perhaps an orange juice!' She forced a chuckle, but Sorcha did not respond in kind. 'Sorry.'

'That's all right. I'll do my best.'

'Good girl. See you later.'

'Thanks for ringing, Helen.'

'That's okay. Courage, Sorcha. Bye for now.'

Helen made a couple more telephone calls, then picked up her briefcase and left her office.

'I'll be out until after lunch,' she said to Mags.

'Okay. Have a nice time.'

Helen raised her eyebrows and took the lift downstairs.

'Come in, why don't you?' Con looked as if he had the weight of the world on his shoulders.

Helen followed him across the hall and into his study. 'I don't want to see you, you know.'

'Tough shit.' Helen watched as Con slumped onto his sofa and picked up his guitar. She slung her briefcase into a chair.

'What do you want, Helen?' he asked, strumming aimlessly.

'To talk.'

He turned to look at her. There was a week's growth of

beard on his chin and purple bruises under his eyes from his broken nose.

'You look dreadful.'

'Thanks.' Con looked away again. 'I don't want you in my house for any longer than necessary, so get on with it.'

'I will. You're intent on leaving The Fishermen, I presume?'

'I've an idea there's no band left to leave, but yes, I'm out.'

'You haven't announced this yet to the media?'

'No.'

'Don't. If you're prepared to hang on for six months without breathing a word of the split, I'm prepared not to sue you for the uncompleted album.'

'That's very kind of you, Helen, but don't you think the media might have guessed something is up already?'

'Yes, but all the gossip can be nipped in the bud by a press release. All you'd have to do is to lie low for a while.'

'And what about Todd? Do you think he'll be keeping his mouth shut too? Will he be prepared to pretend everything's okay?'

'We'll see. If he's sensible and doesn't want a lengthy court battle which Metropolitan are sure to win, then he'll play ball.'

'Helen, can I ask why it's so important to you that we wait to announce our split?'

'Metropolitan's going public in November. The value of the company will plummet if The Fishermen announce a split now.'

Con smiled. 'It always comes down to money with you, doesn't it, Helen McCarthy?'

'Yes, I suppose it does. I've worked very hard to build my company—'

'Brad's company.'

'Our company – and I don't want to see my work go to waste.'

Con nodded. 'I understand that. The trouble is, I really couldn't give a bugger about money. So you suing doesn't bother me. You can have it, have the lot. I was thinking I was better off without it anyway.'

'It's so easy to say that when you *have* got it. Just remember those days when you were first in London, struggling to keep a roof over your head.'

'At least I was happy. Sorcha and I were happy.' Con's eyes hardened. 'I don't feel I owe you any favours any more. You go ahead and sue if you like. I'll do whatever I wish. And I want out. Now.'

'All right, Con. And this is the last time I'll offer. If you keep your mouth shut for the next few months, in the spring Metropolitan will offer you a solo contract with the kind of money you could not refuse.'

'Did you not hear what I was just saying, Helen?' He stared at her in amazement. 'I've just told you that I'm not interested in money. And if you were the last record company on earth, I wouldn't sign a new deal with you. Do you hear?'

'Perfectly.'

Helen picked up her briefcase. She had one last trick up her sleeve.

'But there is the question of the single. We must release a new track before Christmas. If I can't persuade you and Todd to write and record a song, then I shall release the song that Derek's written. "Peggy" will go out under The Fishermen's name.' She looked at him for a while. 'You'd better let me know what you want to do about that.'

Con gazed at her in horror as she walked to the door.

'You wouldn't do it, Helen.'

She turned and shrugged. 'It seems you've left me with no alternative. Goodbye, Con.'

He sat still and silent as he heard the front door shut behind her, then the sound of her car starting.

* * *

Con strode across the heath, his head down. His throat felt constricted, his breath coming in short, sharp bursts. He realised he wanted to cry, something he'd rarely felt since he was a small boy.

Con sat on a bench, leant forward and put his head in his hands. After a few minutes, he began to feel calmer. The peace and space of the heath was soothing.

He looked up. The sky was blue with small powder-puff clouds drifting across the horizon.

'Jesus, it's all such a mess,' he sighed.

He loved Sorcha, but he'd screwed up his marriage well and truly. His glittering career was running off the rails. To top it all off, some lunatic was sending him death threats and he felt as though he didn't have a friend in the world.

Not that he deserved friends. He'd behaved like a complete arsehole these past few months, alienating almost everyone around him.

Con stared into space. He didn't know what the answers were. Maybe he should meet with Sorcha, apologise, and see if she would forgive him and come home.

As for the band – he couldn't see a way back from where they were. He didn't give a damn that Helen might sue him, but he did care that The Fishermen's last single would go down in history as an insipid, badly written love song.

Helen McCarthy was clever, he'd give her that. The one thing that would get him into the studio for the last time was his artistic pride.

Con thought of the tune that had been buzzing in the back of his mind for the past few days. '*Losing you, after all these years of loving you . . .*' he sang. It was a long time since he'd felt the need to write a romantic ballad.

Con stood up. He wanted to write it for Sorcha. He'd go home and work on the song while he had the urge. If it turned out to be as strong as he felt, then he might call Helen and suggest he record it as their Christmas single.

After that . . . he didn't know. Maybe he should get the hell out of England, go away for a while.

Con stood up and walked towards his house.

He didn't know who the hell he was any more.

46

Helen was feeling calmer as she drove home that evening. She'd received a call from Freddy to say Con had been in touch with him. Apparently Con had a song he was working on which he was prepared to record as The Fishermen's final single. Freddy wasn't sure what Todd would have to say as there was no answer from his house, but he suggested they go ahead and have Con do a rough cut in the studio. They also agreed they'd let Derek, who'd returned from Spain that afternoon, lay down his track too, just as a precaution.

As Helen negotiated Hyde Park Corner and headed for Holland Park, she considered the implications. Was it possible that she could manoeuvre Con's estranged, frightened and pregnant wife back into her husband's arms? If he was reunited with Sorcha, there was a possibility that Lulu would return to Todd, apologies would be made, Con and Todd would be reconciled and the whole thing would blow over as Freddy had suggested. Not only that, but with a baby on the way and a grateful Con by her side once more, she thought that Sorcha had a chance at true happiness. Helen *owed* her that.

All she had to do now was engineer a meeting.

Sorcha was sitting out on the terrace nursing a glass of wine that contained no more than a sip.

'Hello. How are you?'

'Okay, I think. I hope you don't mind but I opened a bottle. I probably shouldn't drink, what with the baby, but . . . I thought I'd have one final glass.' Sorcha shrugged.

'I don't think that amount will hurt. I'll join you. You look very pale, Sorcha.'

'Wouldn't you, in my shoes?'

'Yes, yes, of course. I'll just get myself a glass.' Helen went to the kitchen, returned and poured herself some wine. She sat down and studied Sorcha's wretched expression.

'Any idea what you're going to do?'

'Have a baby in seven months' time.' Sorcha gave a shrug and a half-smile.

'You won't tell Con?'

'No.'

'Do you not think he has the right to know?'

'I don't know.'

'You'll bring the baby up alone then?'

'Maybe I'll have to.'

'Well, you could always—'

'No.' Sorcha shook her head. 'I couldn't. Even if I don't go to mass any more, I still believe. I could never bring myself to terminate the pregnancy. What Con has done is hardly the baby's fault, is it?'

'Can you really say you don't love him?'

'No. Of course I still love him, Helen. I'll always love the rat.'

'Well, if you're totally set on not telling Con, you have to think about the future. You'll have to consider where you're going to live.'

'I know. I've been thinking about that today. I was wondering if I should go home to Ballymore. But can you imagine the town gossips? I couldn't take it. I don't want to overstay my welcome with you. I'll start looking for a flat tomorrow.'

'Don't be silly, Sorcha. You can stay here as long as you want.'

Sorcha felt her eyes filling with tears. 'Oh, Helen, you've been kinder to me than I deserve.'

'Nonsense,' said Helen brusquely. 'As a matter of fact, I've really enjoyed the company.'

'I think I might have gone mad if I hadn't had you to talk to.'

'Well then, that's settled. You'll stay with me for the time being, okay?'

Sorcha smiled gratefully. 'Okay.'

Two days later, Sorcha was awoken from an afternoon nap by the telephone. It rang three times then stopped – Helen's code. Sorcha waited for it to ring again.

She picked it up after the first ring.

'Hello?'

'It's me. Listen, would you do me a favour, Sorcha? The car's gone in for a service and the garage has just rung to say they need to fit some new brake pads. I can't collect it until tomorrow morning. Would you come to Metropolitan and pick me up? I thought we could go for a bite of supper. It might do you good to get out.'

'Okay.' Sorcha was reluctant to go near Metropolitan, but after Helen's kindness, she could hardly refuse such a small favour.

'Good. I'll tell the receptionist to expect you. She'll know where to find me. See you around six.'

'Yes, bye, Helen.'

Sorcha put down the receiver and locked the front door behind her.

Con entered the glass doors of Metropolitan Records and strolled up to the reception desk.

'Hello, Mr Daly,' the receptionist smiled. 'Suite two is all ready for you. I'm Miranda, by the way. I started here last week.'

'Oh.' Con frowned. 'Is suite one not available? That's where I usually work. I much prefer it.'

'Er . . .' Miranda scanned the booking list. 'No, I'm sorry. Mr Longthorne is working in it.'

'No, Derek left half an hour ago while you were at lunch,' said Melody, the other receptionist. 'He said he wouldn't be back, so you can go in there.' She leant over and smiled at Con, dangling the key on her fingers.

'Thanks, Melody.' Con took the key and walked off through the lobby to the stairs leading down to the basement.

'Mr Daly, you haven't signed in,' Miranda called after him.

'Leave him be, Miranda.'

'But Miss McCarthy said we *always* had to get everybody to sign in no matter who they were,' persisted Miranda.

'In this building, Con Daly is above God and Helen said nothing about immortals. Now answer that switchboard, for goodness' sake.'

Con unlocked the door to recording suite one. As he entered, he could smell Derek's pungent aftershave still lingering in the air. His mohair cardigan was neatly folded on the sofa and a pile of notes in his small rounded handwriting were taped to the desk. It was obvious he had not yet finished.

Con hoped the receptionist was right and he wouldn't be back today. The last thing he needed was a showdown with his former bandmate.

He sat down on the swivel stool and switched on the console. The song inside him was ringing round his head, asking to be laid down. He'd record the melody line first. The song should be as simple as possible, just him and his old acoustic guitar. The chorus was where he could turn up the volume and arrange some nice harmonies and instrumentation for Todd, Ian and Derek, *if* they agreed to play on the last track.

Con took his guitar out of its case and disappeared into a world of his own.

Sorcha pulled up in front of Metropolitan Records at five to six.

As she'd driven across London, she had begun to think about the child growing inside her. It was what she'd wanted all those years. Whatever the problems she faced, she would not think of the baby as something negative.

Sorcha touched her stomach timidly. 'We'll be fine, baby,' she murmured. Then she reached for her handbag, got out of the car and walked through the entrance.

'Hello.' Sorcha felt uncomfortable and nervous being inside the building so closely associated with Con.

'Hello, Mrs Daly. Miss McCarthy's just called me to say she's downstairs in recording suite two. She asked for you to go straight down and join her as she might be a while yet.'

'I . . . okay,' Sorcha acquiesced, praying she wouldn't have to hang around long. She took the steps down to the basement and headed along the dimly lit corridor to recording suite number two. The room was in darkness and the door was locked. The receptionist must have got the suite number wrong. She walked further along and peered into suite one. The lights were on, but it too looked deserted. Sorcha pushed the door open and stepped inside. The control room and the recording studio beyond the glass were empty. Turning, Sorcha went to leave, but before she could grab the handle, the door was opened for her.

Con stood there, a plastic cup of coffee in his hand.

They stared at each other. Sorcha noticed Con had visibly paled.

'Hello, Sorcha.'

'Hello.'

'Were you looking for me?'

She thought she saw hope in his eyes.

'No. Helen, actually. The receptionist said she would be down here.'

Con shook his head. 'No. I've not seen hide nor hair of her all afternoon. Why would you be looking for Helen?'

'Because she asked me to meet her here. We're going out to supper.'

'I didn't know you and Helen were so friendly.'

'We are. I'm staying with her, actually.'

'You and Helen McCarthy are housemates?'

'I had nowhere else to go. Helen's been very kind.'

Sorcha felt dreadfully dizzy. She took a step towards the door.

'The receptionist must have got it wrong. I'll go back upstairs.' She began to sway.

'Are you okay?'

'Yes, I . . .' She was seeing stars. *Not now, please,* she begged her body as her legs threatened to give way completely.

Con caught her as she fell, the cup of coffee he'd been holding splashing to the ground. He half dragged, half carried her to the couch in the corner and laid her on it. Her eyes were closed and her complexion grey.

'Sorcha, Sorcha.' He patted her cheeks as her breathing came in short, sharp bursts. He watched helplessly as she gave a low moan and struggled to open her eyes.

'I'll ring for a doctor. You're a terrible colour altogether.' He stood up.

'No, it's passing, don't. I'll be fine in a minute. Could you get me some water?'

'Don't move. I'll be seconds.'

Con left the studio, filled a glass with water from the kitchenette tap and ran quickly back along the corridor.

'There.' He proffered the water and Sorcha raised her head to take a sip.

'I'm sorry, Con. I feel a complete eejit.'

'Don't be silly. The smell of Derek's aftershave is enough to make anyone feel faint,' he smiled.

'Was he here?'

'Earlier. And it still lingers.'

Sorcha sat up. Con watched the colour slowly return to her cheeks.

'Are you ill?'

'No. I'm fine.' She was willing herself to find the strength to stand up and leave. 'I must find Helen.'

'Reception will know you're down here. Rest a while. You look a sight still.'

'Thanks. As a matter of fact, so do you.'

'Todd broke my nose.'

'No less than you deserved.'

'I don't know about that. Nothing ever happened between me and Lulu, you know.'

'If you say so.'

'I'm sorry, Sorcha.'

'So am I.' She was feeling better and wanted to leave. She swung her legs off the sofa.

'Do you have to go?'

'I . . . oh, Con.' Tears filled her eyes.

'Don't cry, Sorcha, please. I can't bear it when you cry and I know it's me who's responsible.'

He sat down next to her and rested a hand on hers.

'I . . . I've written a song. For you. I've been down here messing around with it before it's recorded properly next week. Would you listen to it for me?'

Sorcha sniffed. 'If you really want me to.'

'I do.'

'Okay. Let me go to the ladies' to tidy myself up a bit.'

'Sure.'

Con gave her a weak smile as she left the room. He shivered, then grabbed Derek's cardigan and put it on. He sat down in front of the console to rewind the tape.

Sorcha splashed her face with cold water and replenished her lipstick. Seeing him again was so painful. She'd listen to his song, then find Helen and leave.

'It's called "Losing You". Ready?'

'Sure.'

She went to sit down on the sofa as he pressed the play button, his back towards her on the stool in front of the recording console. She heard the strains of a soft guitar through the speakers.

'Losing you, after all these years of loving you,
Is the hardest thing I've ever been through.
And it's true, after all the things I've said to you,
And the way that I've been cruel to you,
What else could I expect you to do?
Losing you, losing you.'

Sorcha's eyes began to fill with tears as Con started to sing along to his own voice.

'So I'll try, for as long as it might take me,
And if you don't return, it'll break me.
I love you.
Please come home, for the home is where the heart is.
And all this being apart is killing me.
Losing you, losing you.'

Sorcha stood up, her eyes blinded by tears.

'I love you, Con,' she murmured, unheard over the music. She walked slowly towards him.

Suddenly she was aware of a figure standing just inside the door.

'Hello, I . . .'

For an instant there was confusion in the figure's eyes. Sorcha watched the figure raise both hands and point a gun at Con's back.

'What are you—?'

The figure pulled the trigger.

'*No!*' Sorcha dived for Con. A bullet whistled through the air, shattering the glass panel, followed by another and another.

Sorcha fell against Con, knocking him off the stool to the ground, her body shielding him from the hail of bullets.

The figure left the room.

The music still played.

Part Three

Reunion

47

London, 1986

'There you go, Helen. Check it if you want. We didn't nick your change, or those nice gold earrings. You could sell those for a few bob now, I'd bet.'

Helen nodded as she surveyed the contents of the brown bag. She had last seen it and its contents on 21 December 1969.

'Anybody coming to meet you?'

Helen shook her head.

'Will you be okay by yourself? It's a different world out there nowadays.'

'I'll be fine.'

'Well then, good luck to you. Behave yourself. I wouldn't like to see you back here again.'

'No.' Helen took the small bag from the counter, turned and followed the screw to the governor's office. She knew it was normal to receive a pep talk before being released.

'Come in, Helen, and sit down.' The governor, a small, thin woman in her sixties, put down the papers she was studying and removed her glasses.

Helen sat.

'Well, as you're aware, you're being released under licence. I wanted a quick word before you left. How do you feel about stepping back into society again?'

'Fine.'

'Good. You've been a model inmate and we've had little cause to be sitting here opposite each other, which is more than I can say for ninety per cent of our other guests. I hope the BA you've gained in law will stand you in good stead in the future.'

'It kept boredom at bay.'

'I'm sure.'

The governor studied Helen McCarthy. The young woman who had arrived in her office seventeen years ago, vehemently protesting her innocence, had changed beyond recognition. The inactivity and diet of starchy food had contributed a good three stone to Helen's frame. Her hair hung long and lank to her shoulders. In the charity-shop Crimplene dress that had been found to discharge her in, she looked a decade older than her forty years.

'Helen, I know how you've always protested your innocence and how much time, money and effort you put into your two failed appeals, but it's over now. No recriminations, no vendettas. That would only lead straight back in here. You're still a young woman. Take what you have of life, use what you've learnt here and go and start afresh. Do you know where you're going?'

Helen nodded. 'Oh yes.'

'Good. And of course, one of the terms of your licence is that you report to your parole officer every two weeks. Don't miss one appointment. As well as keeping an eye on you, they're there if you need a chat or advice.'

'Of course.'

'Well then, I won't waste another second of your time. You're free to go, Helen.'

Helen stood up and reached out her hand. 'Goodbye, Mrs Curtis.'

'Goodbye.'

Vivien Curtis watched Helen leave her office. She sighed. Almost every new prisoner who arrived at her prison protested their innocence. Helen McCarthy had spent thousands on two fruitless appeals. Certainly, there had been a lot of circumstantial evidence . . . Who knew?

She closed Helen's file and stowed it away under 'Past Inmates'.

Helen stared out of the window as the taxi drove her into central London. Everything seemed bigger, brighter. The cars on the busy roads around her looked like something out of the space age, and the shop windows were filled with furniture and fashions that she had only glimpsed on the television and in the papers she had read.

Seventeen years – seventeen years for a crime she had never committed. Seventeen years to ponder *who* the real perpetrator was. Most of her money had gone on lawyers' fees. She still had her mews house in London and the estate in Ballymore which, by the sound of it, was a festering heap of damp, decay and dry rot.

And that was it.

She'd lost her precious company. Metropolitan Records had been floated successfully a year after she'd been incarcerated, with a newly reformed Brad, who had taken great pleasure in writing to her in prison to notify her that she'd been voted off the board of directors.

Several times in the early days she'd contemplated suicide. Her life was over, her plans turned to dust. She'd taken any kind of medication they'd offered her to try to blank out the pain. Only the thought of getting out and clearing her name had kept her going. Her BA in law had given her the knowledge that she would need if she was to succeed.

'Just here, thanks,' she called to the taxi driver as they approached the mews entrance.

'That'll be twelve quid, love.'

Helen gulped. She had twenty pounds in her purse that she'd been issued with when she left the prison. A journey like this would have cost her no more than two pounds seventeen years ago.

She paid the taxi driver, climbed out and walked to the peeling front door. She turned the key in the lock and walked in.

The house smelt musty, but it was tidy and dust-free. Katie had been paid a small retainer to keep an eye on it.

Helen put down her holdall and went into the sitting room. Despite herself, she smiled. The furniture could be sold as a treasure trove of sixties memorabilia, in perfect condition.

She wandered around, knowing she must rid herself of the nightmarish memory of the last time she'd been in here . . .

48

September 1969

Helen had presumed the knock on the door at eleven o'clock that evening was Sorcha, come back from Metropolitan either to cry on Helen's shoulder because it really was over between her and Con, or to pack up her things and move back to Hampstead. The last person she expected to see was a police officer.

'Good evening, are you Helen McCarthy?'

'Yes. Is there a problem?'

'I'm afraid so. Can you confirm that you're a director of Metropolitan Records?'

'Yes.'

'I'm sorry to inform you that there has been a serious incident at your business premises.'

'Oh, God. Who? What? Is anybody hurt?'

'I'm not at liberty to disclose those details at present. Would you accompany me to the station, madam?'

'Of course, but . . .'

Helen had been driven in the back of the car to Paddington police station, her mind spinning. A young constable had taken down her statement, which consisted of a description of her movements between five and seven p.m. That was when the 'incident' was alleged to have taken place.

'Thank you, madam,' said the constable.

'For God's sake, can't someone tell me what the hell has happened?'

'The detective is busy at the moment, but he'll be with you shortly to explain.'

'Can I make a telephone call?'

'Not at present.'

Helen was left stewing for over half an hour before a familiar face came into the room.

He looked weary. He'd aged in the past few years.

'Miss McCarthy, I believe we've met before.'

'Yes – although I'm afraid I can't remember your name.'

'Detective Inspector Garratt. We talked about the murder of your friend Tony Bryant about three or four years ago.'

That was it. 'Yes. Please, Inspector Garratt, can you tell me what is going on?'

The inspector sat down and rubbed the stubble on his chin. He eyed her. 'You really don't know?'

'Of course not! Tell me, please.'

'Oh, Miss McCarthy, it seems you have a propensity for being in the wrong place at the wrong time. At approximately six thirty this evening, an unknown gunman shot at Con Daly and his wife Sorcha in recording suite one in the basement of Metropolitan Records.'

Helen stared at Garratt. 'No, I . . . Are they—'

'Mr Daly was not badly injured, but I'm afraid Mrs Daly's condition is critical. She's in intensive care at Charing Cross Hospital. The prognosis isn't good.'

'I . . . I must go to the hospital now!' Helen made to stand up but the inspector waved her down.

'All in good time.'

'They went after him, tried to kill him like they said they would.' Helen bit her lip.

'Who tried to kill him?'

'Surely you know Con Daly has been receiving death threats for some time? That he has a police protection squad with him night and day?'

'Yes, I do know that, but having had a brief word with Mr Daly earlier, we think it was someone he, and certainly his wife, knew. Apparently, Mr Daly heard his wife say "hello" just before they started firing. That rather rules out a hit man from any political terrorist group, wouldn't you say?'

'Yes . . . I suppose so . . . I . . .' Helen put a hand to her throbbing temple. 'I . . . I'm sorry. This has all been a terrible shock.'

'Of course. Miss McCarthy, the night security guard says he saw you come up from the basement at about ten past six.'

'Yes. I'd been to check that Con and Sorcha were still down in the recording suite.'

'But Mr Daly says he didn't see you or speak to you. Why would that be?'

'Because I didn't want to disturb them, or interrupt their possible reconciliation. Which I'd arranged, by the way.'

'So you'd arranged for Mr and Mrs Daly to be in studio one together?'

'Well, recording suite two as a matter of fact, but yes.' Helen stared at Detective Inspector Garratt. 'That's not a crime, is it? I was only trying to help, to get them back together.'

'And you're saying they were both alive and well at ten past six?'

'Yes, absolutely.'

'I see. Miss McCarthy, are there any other ways out of the building, other than by the front door?'

'Yes. There are three emergency exits, but they're kept locked for obvious reasons. The keys are encased in glass above the door, to be broken in case of fire.'

'Are there duplicates of these keys?'

'Yes. They're kept in a locked drawer in my office.'

'I see. The problem I have, Miss McCarthy, is that the security guard swears that you were the only person he saw leaving the building between six and quarter to seven, the time that Mr Daly alerted him to the situation. None of the emergency exits were tampered with, and the building was searched from top to bottom when the police arrived. It was deserted.'

Helen could feel the sweat starting to drip off her back. Her mouth had gone completely dry.

'Surely you're not trying to say that . . .'

'Say what, Miss McCarthy?'

'That I . . . that I . . . It's ridiculous! Just because a security guard says I'm the only person he saw leave, surely that doesn't mean . . .' Helen could not even bring herself to voice the words. 'He could be lying! There's not a shred of proof. I feel as though you're accusing me!'

'I'm doing nothing of the kind, Miss McCarthy. I'm just trying to establish the facts, put together the pieces of this mysterious jigsaw. Would you happen to own a gun, Miss McCarthy?'

Helen blushed. 'Yes.'

'For any particular purpose?'

'I'm a member of a gun club. I've taught myself to shoot. I'm a wealthy woman who lives alone. After Tony's death I felt I should try to protect myself. There are so many madmen around that I thought it was worth having.'

'And would you be able to show us where the gun is right now?'

'No. My gun was stolen from my locked drawer. I noticed it was missing a couple of days ago. I notified my local police station at the time.' Helen put her hands over her eyes and shook her head. 'I can hardly believe I'm having to answer these idiotic questions. Why on earth would I want to harm Con Daly or his wife? He's Metropolitan's biggest star, and

Sorcha has been living with me for the past two weeks. She's my friend. For Christ's sake, I was only trying to give them an opportunity to be together this evening, not to murder them!'

'Well now, these are all questions that will be answered in due course. That's enough for tonight. Someone will drive you home. I'd prefer it if you didn't leave your house for a while. You won't object to someone coming to search the premises, will you? You obviously have nothing to hide.'

'No, but you can damn well obtain a warrant beforehand. I'll be instructing a lawyer and I might sue for harassment. This whole conversation has been totally preposterous.'

'I'm only doing my job, Miss McCarthy. And I'd certainly suggest you instruct a lawyer.' He stood up. 'Goodnight.'

Con listened to the beeping of the monitors. He tightened his grip on her small white hand.

'Sorcha, Sorcha-porcha, *please* pull through. Come back to me, come back,' he murmured.

'Do you want a coffee, Mr Daly?' The night nurse was behind him, her gentle Irish accent comfortingly familiar.

'No, thanks anyway.'

The nurse checked the labyrinth of tubes that were attached to Sorcha.

'Any change?'

She shook her head. 'No. Keep praying, that's all I can suggest.'

Con nodded. He shifted his sore arm, bandaged to protect the skin graze he'd sustained from a flying bullet.

'Sorcha, Sorcha, open your eyes and talk to me, tell me who did this. You saw, you saw. Those bullets were for me, not for you. You shouldn't have tried to save me. I should be lying there, not you, not you, my love.'

Tears came to his eyes.

He began to hum. Then softly he began to sing the words to 'Losing You'.

Con felt a slight pressure on his hand. Her eyes flickered open and she moved her head a little. He leant over her.

'Sorcha, my angel, it's okay, I'm here, I'm here with you.'

She was trying to speak to him, but he couldn't hear her through the oxygen mask. Tentatively he moved it down to her chin.

Detective Inspector Garratt was watching through the glass. Swiftly he entered the room and went to the other side of the bed, pad and pen in hand.

'Jesus, can't you leave us alone for five minutes?' Con muttered.

'Ask her, Con.'

'Ask her what?'

'Who it was she saw.'

Con nodded. 'Okay, okay. Who was it, Sorcha? Who was it?'

Her eyes filled with tears. 'It was . . . I can't remem— the name.' She shook her head in frustration, as DI Garratt scribbled every word she spoke.

'Sorcha, was it Helen McCarthy you saw?'

Relief came into Sorcha's eyes. 'Yes, Helen . . . ask Helen . . . an old friend . . .'

She began to gasp for breath. 'I . . . love you, Con . . . *we* love you . . . we love you.'

'Come now, enough is enough.' The night nurse was behind him.

Her eyes closed as the nurse returned the oxygen mask to its proper position. Sorcha's breathing became steadier.

Garratt eyed Con across the bed. 'There you have it. I'll leave you to it. I'm sorry to disturb you at such a time, but it's better we knew.' He stood up. 'I'll pray for her, Mr Daly. We'll need to speak tomorrow.'

The detective left the room.

Sorcha died at ten past three that morning without uttering another word.

'Mr Daly, I'm so terribly sorry. There really was nothing we could do.'

Con stared out of the window. He hardly heard the doctor's words. Dawn was breaking over London. A new day beginning. A day that Sorcha wouldn't see.

'If she had been further along in her pregnancy, we could maybe have tried to save the child, but as it was, well . . . she was only just twelve weeks.'

'I . . .' Con turned to look at the doctor. 'What did you say?'

'The baby. It couldn't have survived.'

'What baby?'

'Mr Daly, are you telling me you didn't know your wife was pregnant? I'm afraid I just presumed that—'

'Sorcha was having a baby?' He could hardly voice the words.

'Yes. I'm so sorry, Mr Daly.'

'No, no . . . I . . .'

Con rose from his chair and let out a howl of anguish. He stood up, left the room and began to run blindly down the corridor.

'Con! Con, where are you going?'

Freddy was sat on a chair at the bottom of the corridor. He followed Con as he began to run down the stairs.

'Con, please!'

Con stopped on the stairs and turned to look at Freddy. He saw tears were falling freely down Con's face.

'My wife . . . my baby . . . Oh, sweet Jesus . . . I killed my wife and my child . . . I killed them . . . I killed them.'

49

They came with their search warrant at half past eleven the following morning.

They took her house to bits, emptying drawers, pulling back the carpets, even tearing open the collection of toy animals that lay on the bed and removing their stuffing.

Helen sat out on the patio, unable to witness the destruction, hands clenched in her lap, thinking that perhaps she'd stepped into some horrible nightmare.

DI Garratt arrived after lunch. He joined her on the terrace, pulled out a chair and sat opposite her.

'Sorcha Daly died in the early hours of this morning.'

Helen gripped the sides of her chair. She swallowed hard. 'Then I hope you catch the bastard that killed her.'

'Rest assured, I intend to.' Garratt put a couple of transparent envelopes on the table, and a bulky brown one. 'Helen, where do you usually keep your gun?'

'I told you. In the locked drawer in my office.'

'We found your firearms certificate there, but as you said, the gun was missing.'

'I told you. It disappeared.'

'Until we made a thorough search of Metropolitan's premises.'

Helen raised her eyes and stared at Garratt coldly. 'What on earth are you talking about?'

Garratt pulled out a gun from the interior of the brown envelope. 'Is this yours, Miss McCarthy?'

Helen leant forward to take a closer look. 'It might be. It's certainly the type I have.'

'We've checked the serial number on the gun against your licence. It's your gun. Could you tell me where it was found?'

'I *told* you. Last time I saw it, it was upstairs in the top drawer of my desk.'

'So, can you think of anyone who would have used your gun to kill Sorcha Daly, then hidden it in the cistern of the ladies' toilet in the basement of Metropolitan Records?'

Helen let out a short laugh. 'No, Inspector, I can't.'

'Believe me, it's no laughing matter. Your gun was the murder weapon. The bullets match those found in recording studio one. Your fingerprints were all over it.'

Helen stared at Garratt. 'They would be. It was my gun. It's obvious. Someone is trying to frame me.'

'You think so? Then I'd say they've done a pretty good job, Miss McCarthy.'

'This is like some bad detective story. You have absolutely no proof, no motive, no witnesses . . .'

'I'm afraid that's where you're wrong. Just before she died, Mrs Daly told us it was you she saw at the door, you who shot at her.'

Helen's entire body turned to ice. 'She said *what*?'

'I believe you manoeuvred Mrs Daly downstairs into the basement, into a studio that was soundproofed so no one could hear the shots as you murdered her. Mr Daly told us all how you were jealous of his wife, stemming from years back—'

'Enough! Enough! I'm calling a lawyer!'

Detective Inspector Garratt stood up. 'Do that, Miss McCarthy, right now. You're going to need all the help you can get. Helen McCarthy, I'm arresting you for the murder of Sorcha Daly. You do not have to say anything, but anything you do say will be taken down and could be used as evidence against you . . .'

50

London, 1986

Helen stood atop the exact slab on the terrace where they had handcuffed her wrists. She looked down. The mortar had been replaced with moss and lichen. Her anger and outrage had started here, seventeen years ago, and never for a moment had they left her.

Even at night, her dreams were colourful, filled with the media circus that had followed her arrest, and the trial, where Con Daly had broken down in tears as he told the jury that Sorcha had been three months pregnant, that Helen knew, and had therefore not only murdered his wife, but his child too.

Helen sighed. She'd never stood a chance.

Seventeen years to think and brood over who it was that had set her up so perfectly. Of course, the one person she needed was dead.

At first, she couldn't believe that after all her kindness to Sorcha, she had accused Helen of the shooting before she died. But, as she went through the trial, and witness after witness came up to speak against her, to talk of her obsession with her business, her hard nature, the way she was always alone . . . her faith in human nature had disappeared completely. During her incarceration, Helen had accepted that to the outside world, she appeared callous and unsentimental. Little did everyone know that all she longed for was acceptance. If she was business-minded, it was only because, for her entire life, she felt she had something to prove. How ironic that it had been her undoing.

She hadn't made friends in prison, trusting no one. She'd let her guard slip with Sorcha for a short time and look what had happened.

Helen walked slowly indoors. She made her way upstairs, where the empty carcasses of her furry animals had been re-arranged on the bed.

She sat down and reached for a skinny teddy.

No vendettas, no recriminations . . .

The words of the governor rang in her head.

Should she forget about the past, sell this house and the one in Ireland and go abroad to a place where she could start afresh?

Helen clutched the teddy to her chest.

No. Her anger was all she had to live for.

51

Derek straightened his tie. Looking in the mirror, he studied the beige suit, ten years old but stamped with the mark of expensive tailoring. It was important that appearances be kept up this afternoon.

To all the world he was still Derek Longthorne, ex-member of The Fishermen, now a successful businessman and entrepreneur.

He'd dyed his hair last night and thought it might have been a mistake. Maybe he'd used too much peroxide. His hair shone like a halo of bright yellow sunshine, highlighting his grey eyebrows and the skin that was beginning to sag around his jowls. He sighed. It was too late to do a repair job.

Derek looked around the bedroom to check that everything was neat and orderly, then walked into the sitting room. The sofa, a good fifteen years old, was threadbare. He'd taken a needle and cotton and tried to patch up the bits where the material had given way completely, but there was no denying its tattiness. The room, once so bright and welcoming, needed redecoration.

He hated the place. It was symbolic of the demise of his fortunes.

Derek walked into the kitchen and turned the kettle on.

His hand shook as he reached in the cupboard for the jar of coffee.

The meeting this afternoon might just save him.

It had been only six weeks ago, when he was poring over the heap of accumulating bills and wondering how the hell he was going to pay them, that the telephone had rung.

It was Freddy Martin. He asked how Derek felt about The Fishermen getting together for a big charity concert at Wembley Stadium this coming July. There was no pressure, Freddy had said. The others hadn't decided and, as Derek knew, Con was at present listed as missing. He'd suggested Derek think about it and contact him in a couple of weeks. Derek had put the telephone down and was tempted to get down on his knees and give thanks to the God he didn't believe in.

Album sales for The Fishermen had been huge after the tragedy of Sorcha's death and Con's disappearance. 'Losing You', the song Con had written and recorded for Sorcha, had stayed at number one for twelve consecutive weeks. After all this time, the band's albums still sold steadily across the world.

Derek should still be a wealthy man. And he could have been, if he hadn't decided to sink all his money into Morgan Electronics, a company making computer chips. The company had sucked almost every penny out of him before finally going into receivership a year ago.

Derek was now completely reliant on his twice-yearly royalty cheque, most of which had to go to paying off debts. His Chelsea flat was worth a considerable sum, but as a last-ditch attempt to keep Morgan Electronics afloat he'd had to put it up as collateral. Then when the company went under, he'd needed to remortgage the place to seventy-five per cent of its value to hold on to it.

Derek had thought of approaching a couple of labels with the idea of recording a single then maybe an album, but his one attempt to go solo had flopped so disastrously that it was doubtful he'd find any interest.

He still thought 'Peggy' was a great song.

Derek stared off into space. Rarely a day went by when he didn't think about her and wonder where she was. Her parents had moved away, her flat was occupied by a cheerful West Indian family and it was as if all trace of her had vanished.

Probably holed up with Con in the Bermuda Triangle, he thought as he added a sweetener to his coffee. The diet he'd started a couple of weeks ago was proving unsuccessful. The scales announced gleefully each morning that he'd lost nothing. At this rate he'd have to bite the bullet and go to a gym. He did not fancy a worldwide estimated audience of two billion commenting on his middle-aged spread.

Especially as Todd still looked so young. The years had treated him well. He'd managed a smooth progression from pop star to producer and had recently started his own independent record label. He'd never remarried after divorcing Lulu, but he was rarely without a female companion. They met up occasionally, to chat, but it always ended in painful reminiscences. As much as Todd sneered at Derek's obsession with Peggy, Derek knew Todd was still in love with Lulu.

Lulu: now a huge Hollywood star, all shoulder pads and big lips in her prime-time American soap. Derek smiled when he remembered that smelly combat jacket she'd always worn and the anti-war demonstrations she'd marched on.

They'd all changed in those seventeen years, but perhaps the biggest surprise was Ian. He lived in a rambling house near Windsor with his wife, Virginia, and their three children. He ran a successful garden centre and was the epitome of a happy family man. No drink, no drugs, no smokes . . . Christ, Derek had endured some boring evenings at his house.

This afternoon, the three of them plus Freddy were getting together to discuss the forthcoming concert. The idea had been agreed in principle; after all, as Derek had said to Freddy when he'd called to arrange the meeting, if it was going to help poor starving kids in Africa, what was giving up a few afternoons in his busy schedule?

Derek downed the coffee, then put the cup under the tap, rinsed it and placed it upside down on the draining board.

A single maybe, launched especially for the concert, with some of the proceeds going to the charity, then maybe an album . . . a worldwide comeback tour . . .

Of course, anything beyond the concert was not really viable unless the absent pop star appeared. Con had been an egotistical bastard, but he'd been severely and justifiably punished. Derek was prepared to forgive and forget if *only* he'd come back. *Then* . . .

Derek trembled at the thought of the wealth glittering before his eyes as he locked the door behind him. It would be back to the good old days.

I love you, we love you . . .

The continuous tone sounded in his ear, signalling that her last breath had been taken . . .

I'm so very, very sorry . . . There really was nothing more we could do . . . Are you telling me you didn't know your wife was pregnant, Mr Daly? . . . Yes, ask Helen . . . I sentence you to life imprisonment for the murder of Sorcha Daly . . .

He screamed and sat up, sweat pouring down his face as it had done night after night for seventeen long years.

He lay there, watching the dawn peep through the gaps of the slowly crumbling roof. Already, at six in the morning, he was stiflingly hot despite the wet weather outside. He got out of bed, walked down the grand but very dusty staircase, and pulled open the front door. Beyond the mossy gravelled drive lay a carpet of soft green grass, and further still, undulating fields.

Paradise, for some. Home for him.

Con walked along the pathway and then ran across the unkempt lawn, forcing himself to expel his breath, before collapsing on the damp grass. He turned over and looked up to the sky, wondering if she was watching him, or whether the body that had been laid in the ground – and now had surely turned to dust – was all that remained.

How could there be a God?

There was no God.

The stirring was inside him again.

He'd thought he might finally have found the place in which he could live out his life. He had returned across the Irish Sea to feel close to her. The empty McCarthy mansion proved to be a perfect hideaway from the world. After all, there was no Helen to maintain it, and it had remained totally uncared for ever since the aunt had died. Better still, due to unpaid bills, there was no electricity, no telephones and, what was more, no televisions. Nobody bothered him here. Any time he had to go into town for milk or bog roll, he'd layer himself in hats, sunglasses and enormous jumpers. Even without any of the paraphernalia, Con doubted that he'd be recognised. His prodigious beard and long hair rendered his reflection a stranger.

Yesterday, on such a trip out for sustenance, he'd spotted a newspaper. The front page reported that there was to be an enormous charity concert in aid of the starving children in Africa. It was the first good thing he'd seen the music industry do in a long, long time. The idea was inspired.

Con sat upright. What was he thinking of? Why would he leave his safe, secure corner of earth to go back to civilisation and bad memories? Still, he'd been away long enough to know he'd never find peace. Maybe the only option was to return and face the past.

Two days later, Con left the house and hitchhiked to Cork airport, rucksack over one shoulder, guitar over the other.

Lulu watched the new hairdresser backcomb her hair into the trademark bouffant that millions of women across the world had tried to emulate.

'Ouch, you're scalping me,' she snapped.

'Sorry, Ms Bradley, only trying to do my job.'

Lulu raised an eyebrow. 'When's Trish coming back?'

'When she's had her baby, Ms Bradley.'

'The sooner the better from what I can see.'

The hairdresser said nothing. The door opened and Jeff, the floor manager, came in.

'Ready, Lulu, honey?'

'If I'm not, it ain't my fault.' She indicated the hairdresser still struggling to tease her hair into the right shape.

'Give Marcie a break, Lulu. It is her first day.'

'No room for amateurs on this show, Jeff.'

'There you go, Ms Bradley, all done.'

Marcie showered her in a fug of spray. Lulu got up from the chair and followed Jeff out along the corridor.

'Hey, what's up with you? If you don't watch out, your reputation as "bitch on the screen but an angel off it" will go up in a puff of smoke.'

'Sorry, Jeff.' Lulu sighed. 'I'll apologise to Marcie later. I'm not myself today, that's all.'

'Well, get your teeth into being a grump over there. We're in the kitchen for scene two.' They'd arrived in the studio. Lulu followed Jeff to the sumptuous kitchen set where even a lettuce drier could be found in the fourth drawer of the solid-oak cabinets.

'Hi, Lulu. Looking gorgeous as always.' The director's voice came through the speakers from the gallery above. 'Okay, go over to Paige. We'll take it from the top. It's a Friday afternoon and I know we all want out for the weekend so let's try and catch it in one take.'

Lulu walked over to the willowy blonde who last year had been Miss Wisconsin and was now set for superstardom as the new young beauty of the most successful soap on American television.

Paige smiled at her shyly. 'Hi, Lulu.'

'Yeah, right. Let's get on with it.'

'Okay, studio. We're ready for a take.'

Silence fell.

The clapperboard opened and shut. '*Flamingo Grove*, episode forty-six, scene twelve, take one. And action.'

On the way home in her limousine, Lulu dialled her PR's number.

'Chas, I'm thinking of going to the UK for a couple of weeks during the summer recess. Want to line me up something to convince the studio to fly me over on Concorde? I'm dying to try it. All my friends say it's fabulous.'

'I'll do what I can, honey. You know how huge your UK audience is. The only problem is that most of the chat shows are on summer recess too. But leave it with me and I'll see what I can do.'

'Thanks. Oh, and also, can you organise me two tickets for the Music for Life concert at Wembley. If I'm over there anyway, it seems a shame to miss it.'

'I'll try, but they're like gold dust both in London and New York.'

'Pay what you have to, okay?'

'Okay, honey, will do. Be in touch.'

Lulu put the telephone down.

Her analyst would say she was mad to go back, but there was not a Jungian quote or a Freudian reference that could possibly stop her.

52

'Todd, come in and make yourself comfortable.'

'Thanks, Freddy.' Todd sat down in a large armchair. Freddy had spared no expense for this get-together, hiring a comfortable suite at the Savoy. Todd surveyed the ageing Freddy, in his late fifties and now completely bald, but still a noise in the music business. He'd recently signed a young duo from the East End and secured them a deal with Todd's new record label. He wasn't particularly keen on the idea of the frothy music they played but saw the huge commercial potential, just as Freddy had promised.

'Are the other two coming along?' Todd checked his watch as Freddy opened a bottle of champagne.

'Yes. Are you on or off the booze?'

'One glass of the fizzy stuff shouldn't hurt, but I'm going to have to make it snappy. I've a meeting at half past four.'

Freddy handed Todd a glass. 'Sure. We should be done by then.'

The door opened and in walked Ian. 'Hi, chaps, how are we all?'

'Fine.' Without asking, Freddy handed Ian a glass of mineral water as he sat down opposite Todd.

'If we do play this gig, I hope we can find you something trendier than a cardigan and a pair of cords,' chuckled Freddy, surveying Ian.

'You want me back in my kaftan, do you?' Ian smiled. 'I don't think I'll have time to grow my hair.'

'You're the only one of us who the media are bound to comment looks better than he did seventeen years ago,' replied Todd.

'Well now, that's what the love of a good woman, no meat and a system free from toxins can do for you, Todd.'

'Spare me before I puke, Ian.'

They both looked up as Derek entered the room.

'Hi, Derek.'

All three men resisted the temptation to stare at the glowing yellow halo on top of his head.

'Champagne, Derek?'

'Yeah, sure.' He took the glass from Freddy and sat down in the last spare armchair.

'Right, well, before we start discussing future plans, I'd just like to say what a pleasure it is to see you three together after all this time. I know you've kept in touch during the years but it's nice to see, even after the collapse of the band, that there's no animosity between us.'

'There never was between *us* three,' murmured Todd.

'No, I suppose not. Anyway, I presume from the chats I've had with you over the telephone that you're all prepared to perform at the concert.'

'Yep.'

'Absolutely.'

'It's a wonderful cause.'

'Fine. So your decision isn't dependent on whether or not Mr Daly decides to respond to pleas for his return?'

'No, not at all,' said Todd. 'I mean, we're not re-forming or anything. This is just a one-off to help a good cause.'

'Yeah. In some ways it'd be better if he wasn't found. How would you feel about seeing him again, Todd?' asked Ian.

'Rest assured, I'd cope.' Todd was tight-lipped.

'Well, as the concert is two weeks away and there's not been a sniff of Con reported, I think it's highly unlikely we will be seeing him again. So we must assume he's not coming and make contingency plans. Because of the excitement that's been generated by your possible re-formation, the organisers want you on last to keep the audience watching all the way through. I thought you could start off with "Can Someone Tell Me Where She's Gone?". You shared the melody line with Con on that one anyway, Todd. Then lead into "She Loves You Truly". I was wondering whether at that point we should invite Elton or Rod to join you, plug the Con gap a little, sing an old favourite. A lot of bands are joining forces. Makes the evening more interesting.'

Todd shrugged. 'Whatever,' he said.

'The organisers have suggested the concert should close with Con's last love song.'

'"Losing You"?' Todd asked.

Freddy nodded. 'It's universally known and they hope its poignancy might stir a few more hands to reach deeper into their pockets. All the performers will join you on stage to sing it, hold hands, you know the kind of thing I'm talking about.'

'What about this single that you mentioned?' asked Derek.

'Yeah, they want someone to compose a new song that can be recorded by all the stars taking part, the proceeds obviously going to the charity. Brad at Metropolitan has offered studio time, the factory will press it onto vinyl for free and there's a commitment from most of the stars to record their one or two lines.'

'So it wouldn't just be The Fishermen then?'

'No, Derek. You got the wrong end of the stick there, old chap. With one vital member of the band AWOL, it would be impossible to think of putting out a single,' said Freddy.

'I see.'

'So, are we agreed we work on the premise I've just described?'

Todd and Ian nodded. Derek studied his hands.

'I think you should leave maybe two or three days' space in your diaries for a get-together. I'm sure you're all pretty rusty and even though it's for charity, we want to have some semblance of professionalism. I'll book a studio at Metropolitan to rehearse and try and get whomever we decide on to join the band to come along for a run-through.'

'Sounds fine to me,' said Todd.

'Oh, one last thing. Brad is toying with the idea of issuing a greatest hits LP just around the time of the concert. It may seem mercenary but if you gentlemen are prepared to do your bit to save the starving, then Brad sees no reason not to cash in on any renewed wave of interest in The Fishermen. Anyone got any objections?'

Derek's face brightened considerably. 'No, not at all.'

'Personally, I think it's morally wrong to cash in on what has up to now seemed a completely selfless idea,' commented Ian.

'Don't be pious, Ian, it doesn't become you,' said Todd.

'Well, there's not a lot you can do. Metropolitan can release any of your old songs any time they want. It can only be to your financial benefit anyway. Give the royalties away to Africa if it salves your conscience. Okay, so that's about it, other than announcing the news to the media of course. We'll have to arrange a press conference for some time in the next few days, but I'll be in touch with you all as to the date and time of that.' Freddy smiled. 'I think it'll be fun for you to flex your musical muscles again.'

Todd stood up. 'I'm looking forward to dusting down that old guitar. I gotta run. See you chaps soon.'

'And me,' said Ian. 'Virginia is waiting downstairs. We're taking the kids to the Trocadero for some spaghetti.'

'Cheers, gentlemen,' said Freddy as Ian and Todd left the suite.

'I must be going too,' Derek said feebly.

'How's business, Derek?' asked Freddy.

'Fine, just fine.' He stood up. 'Bye then, Freddy.'

Freddy watched him as he left. By chance he'd seen an article chronicling Morgan Electronics' demise in the *Financial Times*. From every pore in his body, Derek exuded desperation.

It was gone four in the morning. Helen was hunched over her desk, smoking her fifteenth cigarette since midnight, a habit she'd started in prison.

She was certain of only one thing. Sorcha had been murdered by mistake, protecting the man she loved. It was Con the gunman had been after.

The list in front of her was the same as it had been for seventeen years: suspects who would have wanted to harm Con, and were clever enough to set her up too. The fact that Sorcha had obviously known the murderer had been a key point in the prosecution's evidence. That at least narrowed the list down.

Helen studied the names once more.

Derek Longthorne. He'd certainly hated Con at the time, and Helen had always thought him odd. She did not cross his name off the list.

Todd. He'd had every reason to want Con dead, after being publicly cuckolded. She left his name too.

Lulu. Was this a crime of passion? She left the star's name alone.

Ian. Had he discovered Con wanted him out of the band and decided to gun him down in a drug-crazed fit of rage?

Helen's hand hovered over Ian's name. After what had happened to her, anything was possible, but she doubted he had had enough brain cells back then to plan a crime of this complexity. Still . . .

Brad. She crossed his name off. He'd been incarcerated in his drying-out clinic on that Friday night.

Freddy. The only reason she could come up with was that he knew The Fishermen were falling apart. A murder of one of the band's members would have boosted sales. He was clever enough to have planned it and he had access to the building but . . .

Helen sighed. None of it made sense. It never had.

If only she could talk to Con and interrogate him about what Sorcha had *actually* said just before she died. It was his statement alongside DI Garratt's that had persuaded the jury to convict her.

Con was God knows where.

Her only hope was that Garratt – probably retired by now – would see her.

She'd looked up the address in the telephone book and tried the number earlier in the evening. The sound of his voice sent shudders down her spine but at least she knew he was still alive. Helen hadn't said anything – just hung up. She had his address. Tomorrow, after she had visited the library, she would visit him.

Helen pressed the button that ran her through the microfiche to 19 September 1969. The shooting had of course been front-page news in all of the papers. There was a photograph of Con coming out of the hospital after Sorcha had died. His face betrayed such terrible devastation she could hardly bear to look at it.

On the following page, there was a promotional shot of The

Fishermen taken a few weeks before the shooting. Helen slid back again to the picture of Con. Then back to The Fishermen. There was something her brain was registering but not computing.

She looked at both photos again. Finally, she realised what it was.

In the front-page photo, Con was wearing a cardigan. This in itself was odd, but odder still was the fact that it was identical to the one Derek was wearing in the promotional shot.

Probably a coincidence. Helen sighed. It meant nothing, but at least it was a new fact.

She took the photocopies of both photographs and set off to catch a bus to Ealing.

The exterior of the small terraced house was immaculate. Pansies stood in neat rows around the edge of the patch of green grass and, as Helen rang the brass bell, a little fresh polish smeared her index finger.

The door opened.

'Mr Garratt?'

Despite being well into his seventies, Helen knew he recognised her instantly.

'Miss McCarthy. Have you come to murder me on my doorstep?'

'No. I've come to ask for your help.'

'I see.' He studied her warily. 'Forgive me if I feel ill at ease. It's not the first time I've had an ex-con turn up to exact their revenge. I have a panic button wired to the police station for just such a situation as this.'

'The last thing I want is for you to die. I'm trying to clear my name and you are one of the only people that can help me. You can search me for a gun or a knife if you want. Please just give me a few minutes of your time.'

'You have them, right now.'

'Okay. I want to know exactly what Sorcha said before she died.'

'As you know very well, Miss McCarthy, we asked her if it was you she'd seen standing at the door of recording suite one with the gun and she told Mr Daly and myself that it was.'

'And that was all she said?'

'I can't remember her exact wording, but yes, we both heard her confirm it. I wrote every word she spoke down in my notepad.'

'Would you by any chance have the notepad with the exact wording in it?'

'Sorcha's statement was typed up and will be in the police file.'

'I think it's unlikely I'll be given access to that, don't you?'

'Highly. Miss McCarthy, can I give you one word of advice? You were not only convicted of this crime, but you lost two appeals. The evidence against you was beyond reasonable doubt. Now you are a free woman. Let it go.'

'I didn't do it, Inspector Garratt. My God, if I had wanted to kill either Sorcha or Con, I certainly wouldn't have used my own gun, hid it in the cistern and then walked as bold as brass past the security guard! It doesn't make sense. Nothing makes sense.' Helen's shoulders drooped. 'I'm sorry. I shouldn't have come here. I'll go.'

'Look, give me your address. If I can get hold of the statement, I'll send a photocopy to you, but it won't do you any good. Mrs Daly's words are there in black and white and there are two witnesses who heard her.'

Helen scribbled her address on the back of her bus ticket and handed it to him.

'Still the same address. You managed to hang on to the house then.'

'Yes, it's about the only thing I've got left. Goodbye then.'

'Miss McCarthy, just one thing before you go. As you know, past crimes are always inadmissible at a trial, but I've always wondered . . . Did you kill that young man we found in the bath at his flat? Tony . . . er . . .'

'Tony Bryant? No! Of course not! You really do believe I'm a calculating, cold-blooded murderess, don't you?'

'My job was to look at the facts, Miss McCarthy. With your conviction for Sorcha Daly's death and your presence in the flat of another murder victim, it has made me ponder the possibility, especially as Bryant's murder was never solved.'

Helen could feel the tears burning the back of her eyes. 'You see? Until I clear my name everyone will react like you do. I'm guilty until proven innocent.' Helen clenched her jaw. 'And I intend to prove that innocence if it's the last thing I do. Goodbye, Inspector!'

He watched her turn and stride off down the path. She had certainly convinced herself of her innocence, if no one else. He'd seen it before. If he remembered correctly, it had been an open-and-shut case.

Garratt closed the door and went into the small room he used as a library. There on the shelves, filed neatly in alphabetical order, were photocopies of his case notes on crimes he'd investigated that had specifically interested him. One of his only pleasures these days was to look at the unsolved ones again. It kept his brain active.

'Daly . . . Daly . . .' He pulled the file off the shelf and, just for the hell of it, removed Tony Bryant's file too. Moving to his desk, Garratt sat down and opened them up. He found the page that Helen McCarthy had been so interested in, then flicked through the rest of the notes and statements he had taken from all personnel who worked at Metropolitan.

427

No, there was no denying her guilt. His eyes moved across to Bryant's file and read through the contents again.

'Hold on a minute . . .'

Garratt re-examined the Daly file to double-check.

Yes, sure enough, the name was the same.

It was a total coincidence, surely? Garratt had seen many in his time, but one never knew . . .

He took out a sheet of writing paper and an envelope. He enclosed the photocopied page from his notebook, then scribbled down the name he'd just discovered. He presumed Helen knew of the connection, but if she didn't, it might be worth looking into.

Garratt sealed the envelope, addressed and stamped it, then decided it was time for a cup of tea.

53

'Right, chaps, let's see what kind of noise you make,' grinned Freddy as Todd, Derek and Ian settled themselves in the studio. 'Let's start off with "Way Across the River". The riffs are easy on rusty hands. Okay, whenever you're ready.'

Todd gave the signal and they started playing.

Brad stood by the door to the studio, his arms folded. 'Blimey, takes you back, doesn't it?'

'Yeah, those were the good old days,' agreed Freddy.

'Dunno about that – can't remember much about them,' smiled Brad. 'I've got a photographer coming at three thirty to take some shots.'

'Fine.'

'The media interest is big, Freddy. I've given the go-ahead for the compilation CD and LP to be released a week after the concert.'

The telephone rang. Brad moved to the recording console and picked it up. 'Brad here. What? Okay, Melody, I'll be up immediately.' He put the telephone down. 'Gotta go and check out a weirdo who keeps peering into reception. Back in a second.'

Brad took the stairs two at a time.

'There he is.' Melody pointed to the glass doors. 'He's been there for a good twenty minutes. I don't like the look of him.'

Brad stared at the man standing on the other side of the glass doors. He was tall and well built, dressed in a scruffy pair of jeans with a guitar slung over his shoulder. His dark hair was matted and his beard was long and untamed.

'Probably looking for a deal. He'll start playing that ancient guitar the minute I approach him.'

Brad walked towards the front door and pushed it open.

'Can I help you, mate?' The man turned towards him slowly, his eyes a piercing blue in his haggard face. 'I said, can I help you?'

'I don't know, can you?'

'Look, mate, you're scaring our girls loitering around out here. If you have no business here, shove off before I call the police.'

'Brad?'

'Yes?'

The man smiled lazily. 'You really don't recognise me, do you?'

'No, I . . .' Brad studied him again. 'No . . . I . . . Bugger me. Well, bugger me!'

The two receptionists watched in astonishment as their boss threw his arms around the man outside.

'Okay, let's have a bash at "Can Someone Tell Me Where She's Gone?",' said Freddy. 'You take Con's melody line for now, Todd. You'll probably share it with Paul on the night.'

The three started playing the intro.

'*I've travelled far, and still can't find, the woman that I left behind me, I . . .*' Todd's voice petered out as a familiar, slightly husky voice took over.

'*I've searched all corners of the land, over sea and shore and . . . oh, can someone tell me where she's gone?*'

Everyone in the studio turned their heads towards the door.

And watched him as he sang to the end of the verse.

He stopped, and there was silence in the studio.

'Will no one say they're glad to see me?' he asked.

Todd stood up slowly and walked across to him. He held out his hand.

'Hello, Con, welcome home.'

The press photographer who arrived twenty minutes later thought all his Christmases had come at once. There was Con Daly, back from the dead, chatting casually to his old colleagues.

'This'll make the front page of all the tabloids tomorrow,' he assured Brad.

'Good. See that it does. It can only help with the publicity for the concert.'

Con yawned. 'Sorry. I'm knackered.'

'We'll book you a suite at the Ritz, shall we, Con?' Freddy suggested. 'You can chill out and recover for a couple of days. And we'll try and keep the press out of your hair for a while.'

'Don't be silly. Con can come and stay at my house, meet the wife and kids,' said Ian.

'Not sensible, Ian. You'd have to build a six-foot-high wall round the outside to stop the media getting to Con,' Brad put in.

'Come with me, Con. My place is secure,' Todd said gently.

Con looked at him. 'Thanks, Todd. That would be grand.'

They didn't talk much on the drive home. Con stared out of the window at the busy London streets and Todd listened to the news.

'And a story just in: Con Daly, lead singer of the hugely successful sixties rock band The Fishermen, walked into the offices of his old record company, Metropolitan, earlier today. The Fishermen are re-forming to play at the Music for Life concert at Wembley in a week's time. The excitement surrounding

the Irishman's return can only boost interest in the concert, at which The Fishermen will be the star act.'

Todd switched the radio off and looked across at Con. 'I'll do all I can to keep them at bay.'

Con nodded. 'Thanks, Todd.'

Over the next forty-eight hours, Con did no more than eat and sleep. Todd found him curled up on the floor next to the double bed when he took him in breakfast, but he made no comment.

The press camped outside night and day, bringing ladders and even hiring a crane to try to get a shot of the prodigal son returned.

On the third day, as Todd sat in his top-floor attic office, a freshly showered and shaven Con appeared at the door.

'Todd, forgive me.'

He turned round. 'What for?'

'I behaved like a prat, an eejit and an arsehole all those years ago. The apology is seventeen years too late, but I've been wanting to make it anyway.' Todd nodded. 'For what it's worth, and I'm not sure it's worth a lot, nothing ever happened between Lulu and me. She made most of it up.'

'Yeah. I began to figure that out when her flings with all those Hollywood A-listers ended in "*total disaster*" on the front pages of the tabloids.' Todd looked genuinely pained. 'Anyway, it's water under the bridge. Lulu always was flighty.'

'Thanks.' Con's eyes twinkled.

'And let me say how sorry I am about . . . what happened. I still can't believe she's not here.'

'I know.'

'I came round to Hampstead after the trial to see you. The house was shut up so I presumed you'd gone away for some time by yourself. I assumed you'd be back. Why did you stay away so long?'

Con perched on the edge of Todd's desk. He picked up an elastic band and stretched it between his fingers.

'Every time I thought of coming back, I couldn't face it. Sorcha died protecting me from Helen's bullets. Losing her was bad enough, but then to hear she was expecting our child . . . Our baby died with her.' Con looked at Todd, his eyes wet with tears. 'I felt responsible for both their deaths. I still do.'

'Where did you go?'

'Here, there, everywhere. At first I had to keep on the move. Travel numbs the mind. Besides which, people recognised me in those days. Eventually I went home.'

'I don't think your own mother would recognise you today.'

'I realised that when Brad threatened me with the police outside Metropolitan if I didn't move along,' Con smiled.

'Why choose now to come back?'

'I'd been thinking about it for some time. I started to realise I was never going to escape the memories, so I might as well come back and face them. And I'd read about the concert in a newspaper. I liked the thought of our music having a point, doing some good. It was the spur I needed.'

'Did you leave a life behind?'

He shrugged. 'No. Life seems to be about losing the ones you love. Anyway, enough of this melancholy. It's music I've come home to play. When do we get together with the boys for a run-through?'

Helen stared at the photograph of Con Daly in the newspaper, her heart beating hard against her chest.

They had both gone away seventeen years ago and returned within the same week.

Would Con see her? No, he blamed her for Sorcha's death.

She heard the tip of the letter box and went to the hall to collect her post.

There was one white envelope, neatly addressed. She tore it open and saw ex-DI Garratt's name at the bottom of the notepaper. She was surprised and gratified he'd kept his word and written to her. Moving to the dining table, Helen sat down and unfolded the contents.

Dear Miss McCarthy,
    Enclosed is a copy of my notes taken the night Mrs Daly died. You can see for yourself that she implicated you.
    Yours faithfully, T. Garratt

There was a postscript, too.
The name Garratt mentioned within that interested her.
Helen stared out of the window and shook her head.
'So *that's* who it was . . . And I never knew.'
She put the letter to one side and unfolded the page on which were written the last words that Sorcha had spoken.
'I can't . . . remem— the name . . . Yes, Helen . . . ask Helen . . . an old friend . . .'
She took a pen and wrote down the name Inspector Garratt had mentioned in the PS several times. Once more, she studied the words Sorcha had spoken.
Then she stared into space for a long, long time.
She now knew who had murdered Sorcha Daly.
But the question was, why?

54

Todd picked up the post from the mat and went upstairs to the kitchen.

While the percolator did its job, Todd opened his mail. Bills, circulars and a letter addressed to Con. Instinct told him to open it.

YOU'RE BACK, BUT NOT FOR LONG. SATURDAY WILL BE THE LAST TIME YOU SING. THIS TIME THERE'LL BE NO MISTAKES. SEE YOU THEN.

He read it again.

'Shit.' He picked up the telephone. 'Freddy, it's Todd. Listen, I need some advice. You remember Con was receiving death threats through the post? Well, he's had another this morning. I know, I can hardly believe it either. I'll read it to you.'

Freddy uttered an expletive.

'I know, I don't like the sound of it either. Surely it's got to be some creep using the past to frighten him? Should I tell him? You think so? I'm just concerned that if he knows, he might disappear again. Okay, will do. I know we can't take any chances. Catch you later.'

Todd put the receiver down slowly.

'Tell me what?'

Todd turned and saw Con standing in the doorway, arms folded.

'Con, you're not to worry.'

'Tell me what it is, Todd.'

'I'm afraid it's another of those ridiculous letters you used to get years ago.' He handed it to Con.

As he read it, Todd watched Con visibly shudder.

'Don't panic, Con, please. Freddy said we should contact the police immediately. He suggested we let the media know too, broadcast how tight security is going to be at the concert. If this creep is serious, he might be put off if he knows what a huge police presence there'll be. If you agree, I'll call Scotland Yard now. Con?'

Con was holding the letter in his hand, staring out of the window.

'Are you okay?'

Con didn't reply.

'Look, I know how devastating this must be, but there are ways to solve it. Let me call the police, Con. I'm positive this is just a stupid crank letter.'

'Sure. I'll take a shower.'

As the water cascaded over his head, Con wondered if he had been wrong to return.

He dressed and went downstairs. Todd was staring out of the window.

'You called them?'

'Yes. They're sending someone round right now. You'll have immediate twenty-four-hour protection. They're going to liaise with the organisers of the concert this morning to discuss security.'

'Good.'

'Con, there is one other thing you should know.'

'What's that?'

'Helen McCarthy has just been released on parole.'

Helen was running very short of cash. The couple of thousand left in her account was slowly being eaten up. At some point in the next couple of weeks, she would have to take her vintage Porsche out of the garage, replace the starter motor and give it a good wash and brush-up. She'd then try to find a buyer.

But she didn't care if she was left homeless and penniless. Now she knew *who* had ruined her life, it was a case of putting the rest of the jigsaw together, presenting her evidence to the police, and finally clearing her name.

Four telephone calls had secured the information she needed. Anybody who said they were calling from the Inland Revenue was almost always put through, and given the details requested.

And now, at last, Helen was going to meet the person who had set her up so perfectly. She climbed into her rented Mini Metro and drove off.

London's claustrophobic streets gave way to green fields on either side of the motorway, a road that had not been built when she had last travelled this way. It took her a couple of hours of steady driving to reach her destination. She passed through the gates and pulled up outside the crumbling Victorian building. Helen turned off the engine. She took a lipstick out of her handbag and applied it slowly. Then she climbed out of the car, locked it and walked towards the front entrance.

'I'm so sorry you've come all this way for nothing. She left about a month ago. You say you've been abroad yourself?'

'Away, yes,' Helen nodded.

'We always wondered whether she had any family. She never talked about them.'

'No, well, we were never close.'

'You don't look anything like her, if you don't mind me saying. There's no sibling resemblance.'

'Everyone used to say that,' agreed Helen. 'So you can give me her new address?'

'Of course.' The woman opened the file. 'She went to what we call a halfway house. Care in the community is the thing these days, you know. The government doesn't have the money to keep places such as this going any more. Here, I'll write it down for you.'

'How . . . how did she seem when she left?'

'Oh, better than when she arrived. This was the one place she seemed to feel secure. As a matter of fact, she was very excited when she left. She went on and on about this Music for Life concert. As soon as she heard about it, she sent away for a ticket.'

'Really?'

'Yes, it arrived just after she left. I posted it on to her. Oh, she did love her music, but of course you probably know that.'

'After so many years of being out of touch, I don't feel I know her at all. Were there . . . were there any bands or records she liked in particular?'

Helen nodded as the woman gave her the answer she knew she would hear.

'And there was one song in particular she played over and over on that tiny little tape recorder of hers.'

'Which one was it? Maybe I could buy her a new copy as a present for when I see her.'

'Umm, I'm not very good on pop, especially not sixties pop. I prefer country myself. I think it was one of the later ones, just one of them singing. It was different from their earlier stuff.'

'Was it called "Losing You"?'

'Er, yes, I think it was, but I couldn't be sure.'

'Oh well, if you *do* remember, you could always let me know. Listen, I mustn't take up any more of your time.' Helen stood up.

The woman handed her the address printed out on a sheet of paper. 'Send her my love when you see her. After all these years, I've become fond of her. Looking at her, you'd never think . . . well . . . such a tragedy, really. Goodbye, dear.'

Helen stopped at a motorway cafe to eat and mull over the conversation. She bought a newspaper and flicked through it over her bland cheese and lettuce sandwich.

'Plans for tomorrow's concert are going well,' report the organisers. 'As each hour passes we're getting more and more bands offering to turn up and sing for Africa.'

Of course, having so many superstars under one roof is causing a security nightmare, especially as it was reported yesterday that Con Daly, newly returned from his self-imposed exile, has received a death threat, citing the concert as the target point.

'It's probably a crank, but we are taking the threat seriously as Mr Daly has been threatened before,' said a spokesman at Scotland Yard. 'I'd warn anyone out there who is thinking of causing trouble in any way that the security operation will be the tightest seen in years.'

Helen's blood ran cold. She swallowed.
'Oh, God.'

'Testing, testing, one, two, three, four, five, bananas, apples, Bob's balls.'

The voice boomed through the huge loudspeakers as Johnny, the concert organiser, shepherded The Fishermen onto the vast Wembley stage.

'So, guys, Tina will be at the front while your gear is moved into place. When she's finished, you step onto the stage, which will be in complete darkness. I'll announce you to a major dramatic drum roll, then the stage will move forward automatically. When the crowd eventually calms down, which we reckon could take as long as ten minutes, you begin your set. Okay so far? Con?'

Con had wandered to the front of the stage and was looking across the stadium.

'Sure.'

'At the end of the set, the spotlight will fall on you, Con. You begin the first verse of "Losing You" while we organise everyone backstage to come out and join you for the final verse. I'd be prepared for at least three encores. No one will want it to end. We'll eventually bring it to a close by going via satellite to New York. Okay?'

Everyone nodded.

'Good. Now, you're scheduled for three this afternoon. I can only give you forty-five minutes to rehearse; we've thirty bands to give practice time to and you've got fifteen minutes longer than most.'

'That'll be fine, Johnny,' said Todd.

'Good. You must excuse me, but I have a million things to see to. Hang around for as long as you want. There's tea and coffee in the urns over there.'

Johnny waved and set off across the stage.

'What do you want to do?' asked Freddy. 'Go and get a bite to eat? There's a couple of hours until rehearsal time.'

'My tum tells me grub is in order,' said Ian. 'There's a good Indian down the road. It does a mean vegetable curry.'

'Fine,' said Freddy.

'Jesus, he's become precious,' Todd commented to Con as they filed off the stage.

'Derek Longthorne, telephone call for you.' The voice came booming over the loudspeaker.

'This way, Mr Longthorne.' A PA appeared on the stage beside him.

'Catch us up at the Bombay Palace, Derek,' Freddy called.

'Will do.'

Fifteen minutes later Derek practically skipped into the curry house and sat down next to Todd.

'We ordered for you. That is, we ordered most things on the menu. You look happy. Win the pools, did you?'

Derek shook his head. 'No, nothing so exciting, I'm afraid. Just an old friend who wants to come along tomorrow, that's all.'

'Sorry, love, I haven't seen her for two weeks. She's not a prisoner, you know. She can come or go as she pleases.'

It was no more than Helen expected.

'Thank you.'

She walked away from the crumbling terraced house and climbed into her Metro. She felt exhausted. She'd go home, take a shower and try to decide whether she had enough evidence to convince the police.

But there was still no motive . . .

She was turning right into the mews when she saw the police car parked right outside her front door. Heart pounding, she reversed onto the busy road, signalled left into the next street and turned off the engine.

The murder threat on Con's life . . . they suspected her. If she went home now, they'd probably take her in for questioning and keep her in until the concert was over and it was too late.

Helen rubbed her forehead in frustration. The police were obviously not an option.

She'd have to go it alone.

'Oh, Jesus, where to now?' she cried.

There was something she needed from inside her house if she was to stand any chance of finally proving her innocence.

At midnight, Helen saw the police car turn out of the mews. They'd either given up or were changing shifts. She started the engine, reversed the car along the street and backed out dangerously onto the main road, finally pulling into the mews. Leaving her car near the entrance, she climbed out and ran to the front door. She panted upstairs and into her study, rifling through the top drawer until she found what she was looking for. It was old, but the logo hadn't changed and it would help. She grabbed the plastic wallet with her recently gathered information and slipped the pass inside. Throwing the wallet into her handbag, she went to her bedroom and took hold of the smart suit and matching shoes she'd purchased earlier in the week. She grabbed her holdall and threw the clothes in, adding some make-up from the top of her dressing table.

Helen raced downstairs, slammed the front door behind her and ran to the car.

She had driven no more than a hundred yards when she looked in her wing mirror and saw the police car turning back into the mews.

Breathing a sigh of relief, she set off in the direction of central London.

Todd's door buzzer rang at ten past two. Sleepless at the thought of tomorrow, he was up immediately. He ran downstairs to speak through the intercom.

'Yeah?'

'Detective Sergeant Pearson here, Mr Bradley. Sorry to disturb you but can I come in? I need a word with Mr Daly.'

'Sure.'

Con was standing behind him, stark naked.

'We have a copper that wants a word with you. Go and preserve your decency and I'll let him in.'

Todd ushered the policeman up the stairs and into the sitting room. Con emerged in a pair of jeans.

'Sorry about the hour, gentlemen, but we have good news.'

Both men watched him silently.

'This afternoon a woman was noted hanging around outside this house. One of our surveillance team watched her for a while and then questioned her. She became quite obnoxious and refused to show the officer the contents of her handbag. She was arrested and taken down to the station. In her handbag we found this.'

Pearson pulled out a piece of paper, the familiar newspaper lettering filling one side, and placed it on the table.

SEE YOU TOMORROW FOR THE LAST TIME.

'The woman told us that Mr Daly and herself had at one time been lovers, and then Mr Daly had dumped her for his wife.'

'What? Sorcha and I were together from the first moment I arrived in London,' murmured Con.

'Quite, sir. On further investigation, we discovered that the woman in question has been in and out of mental institutions for the past twenty-five years. She's a manic depressive with a history of petty crime. She confessed to sending all those threatening letters to your Hampstead house.'

'So you think this is your woman?'

'Absolutely, Mr Daly. Her fingerprints match up to those on the letter she sent you last week, and on the ones we have on file from seventeen years ago.'

'Do you think she would have tried something tomorrow?'

'Who can tell? Anyway, the point is, she is now safely under lock and key and you can relax.'

'Excellent news, isn't it, Con?' said Todd.

'That it is,' he said.

Pearson stood up. 'Well, I'll say goodbye and let you gentlemen sleep for what's left of the night. And my best wishes for tomorrow.'

'Thank you.' Con stood up and shook his hand. 'And thank you for all your hard work on my behalf. I'm sorry to waste police time.'

'Not at all. It's what we're here for.'

Todd saw the policeman out. Con stood by the window and looked outside into the dark, wondering why he didn't feel more relieved.

55

The Fishermen had been asked to arrive at the stadium by four o'clock. Backstage, the chaos was unbelievable.

'Blimey, listen to that roar.' Todd was peering through a crack in one of the flats backstage, watching a well-known band finish their set.

'The sound of eighty thousand people,' smiled Freddy. 'You've performed to larger audiences in the past.'

'Never with such a great atmosphere, though.'

'Helped by the weather of course.' Ian looked up at the crystal-blue sky. 'Can you imagine if it had pissed down?'

'With the atmosphere that's out there today I think it could have snowed and it wouldn't have mattered.'

'Want to go into the guest box and watch for a while?' Freddy suggested.

'Sure. We have hours yet,' said Con.

'I won't. I'm waiting for someone actually, so I'll hang around here,' replied Derek.

'Okay,' said Todd. 'Join us there.'

'Will do.'

The guest box was crammed with politicians, royalty and a number of the stars taking part in the concert. Champagne was flowing.

'Twenty million pledged so far.' Johnny looked haggard but elated. 'We should easily triple that in the next few hours. New York is just about to kick in.'

'What a day,' enthused Todd. 'It was a dream of an idea, Johnny.'

'But it was you lot giving your support that has really made it come together.'

'Hello, Todd.'

The familiar voice behind him made him shiver. He turned around. 'Lulu.'

She reached forward and kissed him on both cheeks. 'How are you? You look well.'

'I am, very. What brings you here?'

'I had some PR to do in London and thought I'd pop in today to see some old friends.'

'Excuse me. I'll leave you two to it.' Johnny nodded and disappeared.

'This is turning into a real reunion.' Todd tried to maintain his cool.

'It is. How is the one that's newly returned?'

'He's over there talking to the prime minister. I doubt whether he knows who she is,' he smiled.

'Has Con told you where he went?'

'Not in any great detail. Anyway, how are you? You look fantastic.'

'Thanks. I'm fine, just fine.'

'The life of a Hollywood star must be suiting you.'

'Sort of . . . yes . . . It's pleasant. But I really miss . . . London.' Lulu gave him a warm smile.

Todd responded in kind.

'Well, if I say it myself, I've done a good job.'

The hairdresser stood behind her and showed Helen the

back of her head. 'A one-hundred-per-cent improvement, don't you think, duckie?'

Helen smiled. The shiny bob took years off her. Matched with the slimming suit and the carefully applied make-up, no one from prison would recognise her.

'Yes, thank you.'

She went to the desk and handed over some pound notes.

A roar of applause came over the radio.

'Thanks, love,' said the hairdresser. 'Tell you what, I'd rather be at Wembley than sweating it out here today. It sounds fantastic.'

'As a matter of fact, that's where I'm heading.' Helen dug in her bag and pulled out her official Metropolitan Records pass. She pinned it onto her lapel. 'I'm a record company executive.'

'Are you really? Lucky old you. Off to hobnob with the great and the good while I stare at greasy scalps for the afternoon. Have a good time.'

'I will.' She smiled at him and left the salon.

'You came! I was beginning to wonder . . .' He stared at her, eyes agog. Clearly his feelings hadn't changed.

'Of course I did.'

'It's lovely to see you. You look . . . so beautiful.'

'Thank you.'

'Let's go and join the others. I think a glass of champagne is in order.'

He offered her his elbow. She smiled at him, took it and they walked off in the direction of the guest box.

'Excuse me, madam, can I see your pass?'

'Of course.' Helen flashed her lapel badge at the security guard, who shook his head. 'No, madam, your pass for *today*.'

'Oh, that one.' Helen fumbled in her handbag as the guard surveyed her. 'I can't find it.'

'Well, I'm afraid that I can't let you in.'

'What? This is ridiculous! I'm the head of Metropolitan Records! The Fishermen are expecting me.'

'Are they now?' He'd heard every line in the book today.

'Look, I can't find my pass, but I tell you what I do have.' Helen pulled a couple of photos out of her wallet. 'There you go. Me with The Fishermen at Metropolitan after we'd signed the new contract.'

The guard studied them.

'Very nice too, but it doesn't get you through here today.'

Helen stood in an agony of frustration. Short of knocking him out cold with her fists, there was no way she could get past him.

A large limousine pulled up at the entrance to the tunnel. Out of the back spilled several young men dressed in bright Day-Glo tracksuits.

'Blimey, it's the Seven Wonders. My kids love 'em.'

The entrance was suddenly mobbed by a horde of teenage fans.

'This way, gentlemen,' the security guard beamed as the group reached the entrance. 'Excuse me, sir, could I have your autograph for my little girl? She's your biggest fan.' The guard fumbled in his jacket for a piece of paper and a pencil. He handed them to the young man.

'Could you write it to Tracy?' His head bent over as he watched the star scribble on the paper.

It was only as the guard was folding the precious scrap into his wallet that he realised the woman in the blue suit had vanished. He shrugged and thought of Tracy's face when he handed her the autograph.

* * *

Used to being backstage, Helen blended into the general milieu. She was amazed at the number of faces she recognised, and desperately hoped that recognition wouldn't be mutual. She checked her watch. Half past eight. The Fishermen were due on at nine, but she could not see them amongst the crowd. She deposited herself in a chair in the corner of the hospitality tent and waited.

'Come on, chaps. Twenty minutes to go. Time to make a move.' Freddy rounded up his group.

'Right, ladies, are you staying here where you'll get a better view or do you want to come and watch from the side?' Freddy glanced at Ian's wife, Lulu and the attractive blonde who'd attached herself to Derek.

'From the side, I think,' said Virginia.

'Fine. Let's go.'

The Fishermen walked companionably along the tunnel that led backstage.

'You ladies amuse yourself in the hospitality tent while I take the boys for a pep talk,' suggested Freddy. 'We'll come and collect you when it's time. Come on, gentlemen. Follow me.'

Helen saw her as soon as she walked in.

'Jesus,' she breathed. Even now, she couldn't believe she'd been right.

Helen sat and watched them as they laughed and chatted together over a glass of champagne. What to do now? She'd no hard-and-fast plan. She could hardly go up to the nearest security guard and say that there was every chance that the woman over there was about to murder Con Daly.

She watched as Freddy returned and shepherded the women out of the tent. Helen followed, a discreet distance behind. The sky was beginning to darken and, thankfully, it was shadowy backstage.

She saw Con first, then Todd and Derek come up from the dressing room and into the wings. She pressed herself back against one of the flats as she tried to clear her brain, her eyes never leaving the woman only yards from her.

'Two minutes, gentlemen,' said an exhausted PA.

Con moved towards the side of the stage, hands in pockets. Lulu followed him.

Ian drifted towards Con, his arm around his wife.

Helen looked on as she moved with Derek towards the group at the side of the stage.

Only Todd stood alone, staring moodily into the distance just yards from her.

'Ladies and gentlemen, very shortly now, the moment you've all been waiting for.'

It was now or never. She had to do something.

She ran forward towards Todd and grabbed his arm.

'Todd, it's Helen, Helen McCarthy.'

Todd turned around, a mixture of horror and surprise on his face.

'Jesus, Helen! What the fuck are you doing here?'

'Listen, you see that woman over there? She's after Con. I still can't work out why. I think she and Con must have had an affair at some point and she was bitter, but all I know is she killed Sorcha and now she's after Con. I know you think I'm crazy but you *have* to believe me. You have to stop her, Todd.'

'I . . .' Todd looked at her in confusion. 'I don't know what you're going on about, Helen, but now is not the time or the place for this. And as for Peggy having an affair with Con, I—'

Helen stared at Todd. 'Peggy? Did you call that woman Peggy?'

'Yes. She's Derek's old girlfriend. You must have heard him

mooning on about her. She turned up here tonight out of the blue.'

Peggy, Peggy, Peggy . . .

Helen struggled to work it out.

'I'm going to have to have someone remove you, Helen. If Con sees you, he'll blow a gasket.' Todd was looking around nervously for someone official.

Helen watched as the woman moved away from the huddle at the side of the stage and into the shadows. She opened her handbag.

'Oh, Jesus, oh, Jesus,' she breathed.

'Excuse me, mate, this lady has no business here. Can you have her removed?' Todd moved forward, glancing nervously at Helen.

'Madam, would you please come this way?'

In slow motion Helen saw the handgun being drawn out of the bag.

'Thirty seconds, boys.'

'Madam, please. I don't want to have to remove you by force.'

Helen watched her, expecting her to move forward and aim the gun at Con. But she stayed where she was.

Peggy, Peggy, Peggy . . .

'Ten seconds and you're on.'

'Come on, madam.' The security guard reached for her and took her by the elbow.

She lifted the gun and aimed it at the person standing directly in front of her.

'Todd! Todd! It's *not* Con she's after, it's *Derek*!' Helen yelled as the security guard began to pull her towards the exit. 'Derek, move! For God's sake, *move!*'

He couldn't hear her. The screaming from the audience had reached fever pitch.

Wrenching herself out of the security guard's grasp, Helen dived forward, throwing herself between Derek's back and the gun.

'You're on!'

The gun went off.

Helen slumped to the ground.

'Bloody hell!' Todd and Derek turned at the sound of the shot. Con and Ian had already begun walking onto the stage.

'Peggy, what on earth . . .' Derek stared in astonishment as he saw the gun, still smoking in her hand.

'You killed him, you bastard, didn't you?'

Derek's face turned white. 'What?'

'Tony! My darling Tony. If you couldn't have me, then no one else could, isn't that right? You sad little weirdo!'

Todd was signalling to the security guard to alert his colleagues immediately. He pushed Lulu and Virginia out of harm's way, terrified at the sight of the gun now pointed directly at Derek.

'Jesus, what is going on? We need you on stage. I—' Johnny stopped short as he saw Helen on the floor and the gun in the woman's hands.

'Okay, okay, I'll go and talk to Con and the crowd, keep things going for a bit.'

'Peggy, I really don't know what you're talking about.'

'Stop calling me *Peggy!*' she screamed. 'I hate it. That was my stupid little nickname at school. My name is Maggie! *Maggie! Maggie!* Short for Margaret! Do you hear me?!' she screamed.

'Okay, okay, Maggie. I'm sorry.'

Derek watched as she waved the gun around, tears streaming down her cheeks.

'You should be dead. I thought I'd killed you before, but you turned out to be Con. I didn't understand it. But I can kill you now, can't I?'

Derek saw the bunch of burly security guards coming up behind her.

'Maggie . . . I didn't kill your Tony . . . he . . . I . . .' Derek's breathing quickened.

'You did kill him, I know you did. I *know* . . .'

'Duck, Derek!' screamed Todd as the security men grabbed her from behind. Arms flailing, Maggie pulled the trigger and three bullets ricocheted off the flats at the side of the stage.

'Okay, okay, lady.' One of the guards wrestled with her until he had the gun in his possession. 'We'll take her and lock her up until the police arrive.'

'God, oh, God.' Derek was crouching on the floor, head in his hands.

Todd knelt next to Helen. He felt for a pulse. 'Someone better call an ambulance and fast. Lulu, come and stay with her until it arrives.' He moved to Derek. 'You okay, mate?'

Derek knew he needed to remain as calm as possible. 'Yeah, yeah, sure.'

'Look, I don't know what the hell she was talking about, but there's a billion people waiting to see our ugly mugs out there. The show must go on, as they say. Can you make it?'

Derek looked up at Todd and smiled weakly. He had no choice. Act. Normal.

'Sure.'

56

Helen opened her eyes and felt the heaviness of her body. Even turning her head was an effort.

She appeared to be in a hospital ward. A numbness in her leg signalled that she had some sort of injury. She stress-tested her other joints and found to her relief that she could move everything else.

Looking up at the drip entering her arm, she wondered how she could attract a nurse's attention.

Ten minutes later, the door to the room opened. 'Sleeping Beauty has awoken.' The matronly nurse checked the drip.

'What's happened to me?'

'You had an operation to remove a bullet from your left thigh. The anaesthetic has made you drowsy, that's all. You were awake when you came in here, carrying on about Peggy and . . . Desmond or someone. Anyway, you're going to be fine. By tomorrow you should be off the drip and onto food, so I'll leave you a dinner-choice card to fill in when you feel like it. Your friend's still here. I'll let her know you've woken up.'

The nurse bustled out.

Helen wondered who she meant by 'friend'. By her reckoning she didn't have any.

'Hello, how are you?'

Lulu was pale and make-up-less.

'I don't know really. Is everyone else okay?'

'Yes. It was a close-run thing, though. They reckon she would have killed Derek if you hadn't done your heroic dive. How did you get on to her?'

Helen sighed. 'It's a long, long story.'

'Well, everyone wants to hear it. We've pieced some of it together ourselves of course. Maggie was your secretary at the time, which meant she had access to your gun and could move around the building with ease. We think that she must have mistaken Con for Derek that day in the studio.'

'Con was wearing Derek's cardigan and he was in the studio Derek was meant to be using. I always knew it wasn't Sorcha the murderer was after. It turns out it wasn't Con either,' sighed Helen.

'Yeah, well, as I said, when you're feeling a bit stronger, perhaps you can go through it slowly for us idiots who are slow on the uptake. I tell you one thing, Helen, you're off the hook now. She confessed last night to shooting Sorcha, even if it was a mistake. Seventeen years for something you didn't do. God, you must be bitter.'

Helen bit her lip as tears came to her eyes.

'Of course I am. But I'm also relieved that it's over at last.'

'We're all feeling devastated that we thought it was you. I hope you'll be able to forgive us.'

Helen nodded. 'How was last night?'

'Well, apart from the little, er, incident, sensational. Totally sensational. I wish you could have seen the boys. It was like they'd never been away. The crowd went wild, especially for Con, of course. There were ten encores. I think The Fishermen could have a whole new career if they wanted it.'

Helen's eyelids began to droop.

'Look, if you don't mind, I'll leave you for a bit. I could do with getting home and having a shower.'

'Of course. You go home.'

'Can I bring the boys to see you later? I think they all want a word. And Derek is yours any time you want him, he's so grateful.'

Helen smiled and closed her eyes.

By six that evening, she was feeling much better. The drip had been removed and she was sitting upright.

The nurse bustled in, her eyes filled with a sudden look of respect for Helen.

'You, my lady, have a special guest. I was only watching him on TV last night. Shall I show him in?'

Helen nodded.

Con filed in looking tired and sheepish, his arms filled with an enormous bouquet. He put the flowers into Helen's arms. 'From the boys and me.'

'Thank you. Could you put them over there?'

'I'll take them.' The nurse hovered in the background. 'Who's a lucky girl then?' she smiled.

Con sat down. 'The band all wanted to come, Helen, but we decided it might be too tiring for you.'

Helen nodded. 'Probably would be. I do feel a bit exhausted.'

'And . . . I wanted to see you, to say thank you. I hear you told Todd you thought Maggie was after me last night. You were there to try and save me.'

'Well, I was there to try and save myself. It was the only way I could prove my innocence.'

'But it wasn't me after all.'

'No, but I didn't realise right until the last minute who she was after.'

Con stared at her. 'I really came to ask your forgiveness for being so quick to accuse you. I was so devastated about losing Sorcha I wanted someone punished.'

'I understand why you believed it was me, Con. Both you and that Inspector Garratt thought Sorcha said it was me she saw in the studio that afternoon. In fact, reading through Garratt's notes, what Sorcha *actually* said was that she couldn't remember Maggie's name, that you were to ask Helen, that she was an old friend of mine.'

'And was she?'

'Yes. I was at college with her when I first came to London. I had a brief affair with our tutor, Tony Bryant, one summer. He'd told me that his girlfriend was away, that he loved her and that our affair would be over when she came back. I never knew the girlfriend was Maggie until Garratt wrote and told me her name. I suppose they kept their relationship quiet because she was a student and he was a tutor. She must have found out that Tony and I had an affair while she was away. Perhaps that's why she set me up,' she mused.

'And Derek's Peggy and your Maggie turned out to be one and the same woman,' sighed Con.

'Both abbreviations for Margaret,' Helen replied.

Con nodded. 'He was always mad about her. She turned him down because she'd said she was in love with someone else. The someone else must have been this Tony. I remember it well.'

'Obviously Maggie thought Derek was the one who killed Tony.'

Con looked surprised. 'Tony died?'

'Yes. He was murdered. They never discovered who did it.' Helen looked at Con. 'You say that Derek was obsessed with his Peggy, but do you think he was obsessed enough to kill Tony for stealing her from him?'

Con inhaled deeply. 'He did sink into a bad depression . . . but Derek doesn't strike me as a murderer. He's called "Derek", for God's sake.' He rubbed his tired eyes. 'The desperate thing is that Todd doesn't believe Derek and Peggy ever had a proper relationship. He blew it all up in his mind. In any case, Tony's death must have done something screwy to Maggie's head.'

'Oh, it certainly did,' Helen agreed. 'I found out in the last few days that she had a nervous breakdown after Tony's murder. The woman was in a psychiatric hospital for three years.' Helen shook her head. 'I obviously had no idea when I employed her as my secretary at Metropolitan. She was only there briefly, but she always declined invites to gigs and made herself scarce every time The Fishermen were at Metropolitan. Clearly she didn't want Derek or any of you to recognise her. When she came to me asking for a job she must have already been planning this.'

'I was wondering last night why Sorcha said hello to Maggie when she appeared at the door with the gun. I'd no idea they'd ever met. I never saw her at Metropolitan.'

'Maggie delivered an envelope to my house while Sorcha was staying there.'

Con nodded, trying to take it all in. 'So where's she been for the past seventeen years?'

'In and out of institutions. I saw the matron of her most recent one. She said Maggie would play a song over and over. It was "Losing You".'

'Oh. Well, let's hope she'll be staying institutionalised permanently from now on.'

Helen sighed. 'Oh, Con, the worst thing about all of this is that Sorcha died. And none of it was anything to do with her.'

'I know. She must have seen Maggie pointing the gun at me and thrown herself forward to try and protect me. And after all I'd put her through . . . I'll live with that for the rest of my life.'

'So will I. That was one of the hardest things to swallow, thinking that Sorcha had accused me of shooting her. Any acrimony there was between us way back when had disappeared.' Tears pricked the back of Helen's eyes. 'We'd become friends.'

'Well, you can comfort yourself that Derek would have died too, if you hadn't have persevered. Helen, can you forgive me and all the others who were so quick to accuse you?'

'I can understand it, certainly. Forgiveness for seventeen lost years will take longer.'

'I know what you mean,' sighed Con.

'After last night is there talk of the band re-forming?'

'Absolutely. You can imagine how it is.'

'Yes.'

'What about you? You must think of your future. There has to be some kind of compensation for being wrongly jailed for all this time.'

'Probably,' Helen smiled. 'I might consult a lawyer, but I doubt it. I've had money all my life and it's never made me happy. I have my houses in London and Ireland and enough to keep me going for a while until I consider where my future lies.'

Con let out a weary chuckle. 'Your Irish house needs a lick of paint. I've been holed up there for a good while.'

Helen raised an eyebrow. 'So that's where you were. You must be worth untold millions with all those royalty cheques piling up for the past seventeen years. You can buy me a new bathroom.'

'I could probably buy a small island in the Caribbean if the mood so took me,' he grinned. Then he reached for her hand. 'Helen McCarthy, I've known you since you were a small girl. We have a shared history. And I'm thinking now that you have more balls than any man I've ever met. You lost a friend in Sorcha. I'd be honoured if you'd consider me as her replacement.'

Helen's eyes filled with tears. 'Do you know, Con, you've just offered me the one thing that I need more than anything else.'

He put his arms around her shoulders and the two of them embraced.

'So, are we on for this then or what?' Freddy asked as he poured them each a cup of tea in his sitting room. 'It's a hell of a deal. A worldwide tour for six months. A record deal with Metropolitan worth almost twenty million. We need to grab it now, while it's on the table.'

Ian shrugged. 'I dunno. I'd have to either leave the wife and kids behind or drag them around the world for six months.'

'I have commitments to my bands,' said Todd.

'Jesus, guys. You're being offered the deal of the century and you talk about incidentals.' Derek shook his head in frustration. 'Well, you know I'm all for it. Just remember that adrenalin rush in front of all those people ten days ago.'

'What a note to close on,' said Todd.

'And I object to you referring to my wife and kids as incidentals,' put in Ian.

'What about you, Con?'

Con sipped his tea slowly. 'I'd have to think about it for a while.'

'But you've had the past two days. We have to give an answer by tomorrow,' urged Derek.

'If they want us tomorrow, they'll want us the day after, Derek.'

'Con's right. Let's take another forty-eight hours to think about it. With that kind of money, Metropolitan will be wanting one-hundred-per-cent commitment. I want you all to be sure.'

'Okay. We'll reconvene in a couple of days.' Todd put his

cup down. 'Are you coming, Con? I have an appointment at five.'

'Sure. See you, chaps.'

Todd went out for the night. Con paced around his old partner's house, pondering the situation.

The past had been resolved now. It was time at last to look to the future.

Ian went home and discussed the situation with Virginia. They'd miss each other, but with that kind of money, they could buy their organic farm somewhere in the Kent countryside, live a blissful life and never have to think of finances again.

Derek went home and sat up all night. If the rest of the boys didn't agree, there was no doubt he was up shit creek without a paddle. He'd be destitute within six months.

On the other hand, had he not been lucky? He was still a free man. Every day since the concert he'd waited for the police to turn up on his doorstep. If they started reinvestigating . . . Derek broke out in a mucksweat. That night, he had totally lost control. He'd fuelled himself on booze and powder, and . . . The memory of his actions made his stomach churn and bile rise.

If the boys agreed to the tour and he collected his share of the twenty million, then he might move abroad, just to be on the safe side.

That night he prayed for one last chance.

Freddy put down the telephone from Con and punched the air. All four had agreed. Twenty per cent of twenty million was . . . Jesus, an awful lot of money.

The Fishermen were back.

*   *   *

Helen sat on the Aer Lingus Fokker 50 and watched as it banked over the lush green fields of County Cork.

The sight sent a tingle up her spine. It was odd that while she had lain incarcerated night after night, her thoughts had flown not to her London house, or her comfortable office at Metropolitan, but to the clean, clear, wind-drenched beaches and crisp, bracing air of the country in which she had been born.

As the aircraft touched down on the runway of Cork airport, Helen experienced a sense of elation.

She knew she'd made the right decision.

She was coming home.

Epilogue

June 1987

The doorbell rang. Helen wiped her hands on a tea towel, left the kitchen and headed for the front door. It took quite a while. Dust sheets and builders' equipment lay scattered in the hall.

She opened the door.

'Con! My God! What on earth are you doing here?'

'Ah, well, maybe I just had an urge to come back and see the place I used to call home and visit my old friend Helen.' He opened his arms and embraced her awkwardly over the paint pots on the floor by the door.

'Come in if you can,' she smiled.

'Major renovations, eh?'

'Er, that's the plan. The builders started six months ago, promising to be out by the summer. So far I think they've managed to dry-line one damp wall, but then, this is Ireland. I'm beginning to suspect they just use my house to store their equipment until they need it elsewhere. Anyway, it doesn't matter. Moneywise, the longer they take, the better. Come through to the kitchen. It's antique but there is room to sit down.'

Helen brewed some tea and Con sat at the table.

'You look good, Helen. You've lost an awful lot of weight.'

'Ah, 'tis worry, Con Daly. For the first time in my life I'm counting the pennies rather than the pounds.'

'To be honest, I've never seen you look happier.'

Helen brought two steaming mugs of tea to the table. 'You're right. For some cockeyed, unexplainable reason, I am happy. Maybe it's age, my expectations becoming more reasonable. Maybe it's this place. Having hated it as a child, I now love it with a passion. Thank God I never sold it.'

'What are your plans, Helen? You must have some.'

'Of course. In the fullness of time, I plan to open this house as a bed and breakfast. And I want to restock the stables. I always loved horses.'

'I remember.' Con sipped his tea.

'So what about you? How was the tour? I'm afraid I don't read the papers and the picture on the television is chronic. I'm completely out of touch.'

'The tour was grand. Hard work but great fun. I think we all decided at the end it was a one-off. We're all too old to sleep in our seats on tour buses then give one hundred per cent to an audience of forty thousand the following day.'

'And the others? How are they?'

'In good form. Ian is doing a course in organic farming, Derek has decided to move to Spain, and Todd is in the States.'

'Really? On business?'

'Lulu business.'

'I see.'

'She's giving him a hard time as always, but there's no denying he loves every second of it.'

'And you? What are your plans?'

'Well, there were two reasons I flew over. The first was to visit Sorcha's mother. I thought, after all this time, I should.'

'Oh, Con, Mary O'Donovan died last year, just before I came back.' Helen shook her head. 'She went to her grave thinking I murdered her daughter.'

'I know she's passed away. They told me in the village last night. Ah, well, if she's up there, she'll know the truth.'

'Well, I'm afraid I gave up believing in all that a long time ago. Anyway, what's the other reason you came back to Ballymore after all this time?'

'Well now, Helen, as I said when I arrived, I wanted to speak with you.'

'What about?'

He told her.

When he had finished, she stood up to boil the kettle. Halfway through filling it, she stopped. 'Bugger it, how do you fancy a glass of whiskey?'

She fetched the bottle and two glasses and sat down at the table again.

'Now let me see if I've got this clear. You want to start a foundation to give help and assistance to talented young musicians, particularly young Irish musicians. And you want me to run it for you?'

'That would be about the size of the thing, Helen, yes.'

'Why me?'

'Because I know of no better business brain. And I hate to see it going to waste.'

'My choice, Con. Brad offered me my directorship back at Metropolitan a year ago. I didn't want it.'

'I know. Helen, I would hate to interfere with your grand plans for this place, but I can hardly see you rising at dawn and slapping bacon and eggs in a frying pan for the rest of your life.'

'If it does well enough, I'll employ someone to do that for me,' she grinned, taking a sip of her whiskey.

'I was thinking, with grounds of this size, how well a small recording studio would fit into one of the old barns.'

'Were you now?'

'Yes. And with all these bedrooms, how it might be possible to run music masterclasses and seminars, invite professional musicians to come away down to Ballymore to give our young talent the benefit of their experience.'

'Con, it seems you have all the ideas. Why on earth can't you run this project yourself?'

'Well now, Helen, that's because I don't intend on being around. Not on a daily basis anyway. But that's another story. Listen, let's get down to basics. If you're keen on the idea, I'd be prepared to pay to renovate this house from top to bottom, fit out a recording suite in one of the barns and turn the house into a centre of musical learning. You could employ as many staff as you wanted, which would mean involving the village. In fact, it would put Ballymore on the map. And you wouldn't have to search far for your talent. I was in a bar in town last night and I heard a young female singer who has the potential to be the next Alison Moyet.'

Con's eyes were sparkling with excitement.

'This idea really has caught your imagination, hasn't it?'

'Yes. Helen, I've more money than I know what to do with. This would give me a chance to give something back, help the next generation. With our joint experience and connections, we really are in a position to make a difference.'

'Oh, Con.' Helen rubbed her forehead. 'I don't know, really I don't.'

'Then I'll keep talking until you say yes.'

It was past eight in the evening before Con left the house. It had taken a lot of persuasion, but he'd at last got Helen's agreement in principle. The finite details could be worked out in the fullness of time. He wouldn't be around for much longer, but he knew Helen. Once she got the bit between her teeth, she wouldn't need him.

Con strolled down the hill towards the sand dunes. The sun was sitting on the horizon, a mass of orange, picture-postcard perfect. He walked across the dunes and saw his old hut, half the roof missing, the windows boarded up, but still standing in defiance of the weather that assaulted it without mercy.

All Con Daly had ever wanted was to make something of his life, to escape the hut, and Ballymore. He had done that, but at a terrible cost.

He sat down on a dune and gazed out to sea.

'Sorcha, I love you. I always will.'

The wind whipped up around him suddenly. He shivered slightly, sensing her presence strongly. It was time to go. Where? He wasn't exactly sure. But it would be remote.

'Goodbye, Sorcha, my love.'

Con began to gently sing her song. The last love song.

'Losing you, after all these years of loving you,
Is the hardest thing I've ever been through.
And it's true, after all the things I've said to you,
And the way that I've been cruel to you,
What else could I expect you to do?
Losing you, losing you.'

Con stood up and walked away from the beach.

Their future is written in the stars.

The Seven Sisters tells the stories of the D'Aplièse sisters,
all adopted as babies by the enigmatic billionaire
they affectionately call Pa Salt.

When Pa Salt dies suddenly, the bereaved sisters gather
together at their childhood home, a spectacular secluded
castle on the shores of Lake Geneva. Each of them is
handed a tantalising clue to their heritage, and eldest sister
Maia finds herself on a journey across the world
to a crumbling mansion in Rio de Janeiro, Brazil.

Eighty years earlier, Izabela Bonifacio's father has
aspirations for her to marry into the aristocracy. But Izabela
longs for adventure, and convinces him to allow her to first
travel to Paris. In the heady, vibrant streets of the city,
Izabela meets an ambitious young sculptor, and knows
at once that her life will never be the same again.

What links these two young women? In the beautiful city
of Rio, will Maia find the answers she needs to understand
who she truly is?

**Read on for an extract of this epic
tale of love and loss . . .**

Maia

June 2007

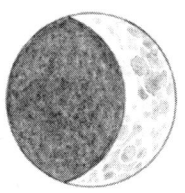

First Quarter

13; 16; 21

1

I will always remember exactly where I was and what I was doing when I heard that my father had died.

I was sitting in the pretty garden of my old schoolfriend's townhouse in London, a copy of *The Penelopiad* open but unread in my lap, enjoying the June sun while Jenny collected her little boy from nursery.

I felt calm and appreciated what a good idea it had been to get away. I was studying the burgeoning clematis, encouraged by its sunny midwife to give birth to a riot of colour, when my mobile phone rang. I glanced at the screen and saw it was Marina.

'Hello, Ma, how are you?' I said, hoping she could hear the warmth in my voice too.

'Maia, I . . .'

Marina paused, and in that instant I knew something was dreadfully wrong. 'What is it?'

'Maia, there's no easy way to tell you this, but your father had a heart attack here at home yesterday afternoon, and in the early hours of this morning, he . . . passed away.'

I remained silent, as a million different and ridiculous thoughts raced through my mind. The first one being that

Marina, for some unknown reason, had decided to play some form of tasteless joke on me.

'You're the first of the sisters I've told, Maia, as you're the eldest. And I wanted to ask you whether you would prefer to tell the rest of your sisters yourself, or leave it to me.'

'I . . .'

Still no words would form coherently on my lips, as I began to realise that Marina, dear, beloved Marina, the woman who had been the closest thing to a mother I'd ever known, would never tell me this if it *wasn't* true. So it had to be. And at that moment, my entire world shifted on its axis.

'Maia, please, tell me you're all right. This really is the most dreadful call I've ever had to make, but what else could I do? God only knows how the other girls are going to take it.'

It was then that I heard the suffering in *her* voice and understood she'd needed to tell me as much for her own sake as mine. So I switched into my normal comfort zone, which was to comfort others.

'Of course I'll tell my sisters if you'd prefer, Ma, although I'm not positive where they all are. Isn't Ally away training for a regatta?'

And as we continued to discuss where each of my younger sisters was, as though we needed to get them together for a birthday party rather than to mourn the death of our father, the entire conversation took on a sense of the surreal.

'When should we plan on having the funeral, do you think? What with Electra being in Los Angeles and Ally somewhere on the high seas, surely we can't think about it until next week at the earliest?' I said.

'Well . . .' I heard the hesitation in Marina's voice. 'Perhaps the best thing is for you and I to discuss it when you arrive back home. There really is no rush now, Maia, so if you'd prefer to continue the last couple of days of your holiday in London, that would be fine. There's nothing more to be done for him here . . .' Her voice trailed off miserably.

'Ma, of *course* I'll be on the next flight to Geneva I can get! I'll call the airline immediately, and then I'll do my best to get in touch with everyone.'

'I'm so terribly sorry, *chérie*,' Marina said sadly. 'I know how you adored him.'

'Yes,' I said, the strange calm that I had felt while we discussed arrangements suddenly deserting me like the stillness before a violent thunderstorm. 'I'll call you later, when I know what time I'll be arriving.'

'Please take care of yourself, Maia. You've had a terrible shock.'

I pressed the button to end the call, and before the storm clouds in my heart opened up and drowned me, I went upstairs to my bedroom to retrieve my flight documents and contact the airline. As I waited in the calling queue, I glanced at the bed where I'd woken up this morning to Simply Another Day. And I thanked God that human beings don't have the power to see into the future.

The officious woman who eventually answered wasn't helpful and I knew, as she spoke of full flights, financial penalties and credit card details, that my emotional dam was ready to burst. Finally, once I'd grudgingly been granted a seat on the four o'clock flight to Geneva, which would mean throwing everything into my holdall immediately and taking a taxi to Heathrow, I sat down on the bed and stared for so long at the sprigged wallpaper that the pattern began to dance in front of my eyes.

'He's gone,' I whispered, 'gone for ever. I'll never see him again.'

Expecting the spoken words to provoke a raging torrent of tears, I was surprised that nothing actually happened. Instead, I sat there numbly, my head still full of practicalities. The thought of telling my sisters – all five of them – was horrendous, and I searched through my emotional filing system for the one I would call first. Inevitably, it was Tiggy, the second youngest of the six of us girls and the sibling to whom I'd always felt closest.

With trembling fingers, I scrolled down to find her number and dialled it. When her voicemail answered, I didn't know what to say, other than a few garbled words asking her to call me back urgently. She was currently somewhere in the Scottish Highlands working at a centre for orphaned and sick wild deer.

As for the other sisters . . . I knew their reactions would vary, outwardly at least, from indifference to a dramatic out-pouring of emotion.

Given that I wasn't currently sure quite which way *I* would go on the scale of grief when I did speak to any of them, I decided to take the coward's way out and texted them all, asking them to call me as soon as they could. Then I hurriedly packed my holdall and walked down the narrow stairs to the kitchen to write a note for Jenny explaining why I'd had to leave in such a hurry.

Deciding to take my chances hailing a black cab on the London streets, I left the house, walking briskly around the leafy Chelsea crescent just as any normal person would do on any normal day. I believe I actually said hello to someone walking a dog when I passed him in the street and managed a smile.

No one would know what had just happened to me, I thought, as I managed to find a taxi on the busy King's Road and climbed inside, directing the driver to Heathrow.

No one would know.

Five hours later, just as the sun was making its leisurely descent over Lake Geneva, I arrived at our private pontoon on the shore, from where I would make the last leg of my journey home.

Christian was already waiting for me in our sleek Riva motor launch. And from the look on his face, I could see he'd heard the news.

'How are you, Mademoiselle Maia?' he asked, sympathy in his blue eyes as he helped me aboard.

'I'm . . . glad I'm here,' I answered neutrally as I walked to the back of the boat and sat down on the cushioned cream leather bench that curved around the stern. Usually, I would sit with Christian in the passenger seat at the front as we sped across the calm waters on the twenty-minute journey home. But today, I felt a need for privacy. As Christian started the powerful engine, the sun glinted off the windows of the fabulous houses that lined Lake Geneva's shores. I'd often felt when I made this journey that it was the entrance to an ethereal world disconnected from reality.

The world of Pa Salt.

I noticed the first vague evidence of tears pricking at my

eyes as I thought of my father's pet name, which I'd coined when I was young. He'd always loved sailing and often when he returned to me at our lakeside home, he had smelt of fresh air and of the sea. Somehow, the name had stuck, and as my younger siblings had joined me, they'd called him that too.

As the launch picked up speed, the warm wind streaming through my hair, I thought of the hundreds of previous journeys I'd made to Atlantis, Pa Salt's fairy-tale castle. Inaccessible by land, due to its position on a private promontory with a crescent of mountainous terrain rising up steeply behind it, the only method of reaching it was by boat. The nearest neighbours were miles away along the lake, so Atlantis was our own private kingdom, set apart from the rest of the world. Everything it contained was magical . . . as if Pa Salt and we – his daughters – had lived there under an enchantment.

Each one of us had been chosen by Pa Salt as a baby, adopted from the four corners of the globe and brought home to live under his protection. And each one of us, as Pa always liked to say, was special, different . . . we were *his* girls. He'd named us all after The Seven Sisters, his favourite star cluster. Maia being the first and eldest.

When I was young, he'd take me up to his glass-domed observatory perched on top of the house, lift me up with his big, strong hands and have me look through his telescope at the night sky.

'There it is,' he'd say as he aligned the lens. 'Look, Maia, that's the beautiful shining star you're named after.'

And I *would* see. As he explained the legends that were the source of my own and my sisters' names, I'd hardly listen, but simply enjoy his arms tight around me, fully aware of this rare, special moment when I had him all to myself.

I'd realised eventually that Marina, who I'd presumed as I grew up was my mother – I'd even shortened her name to 'Ma' – was a glorified nursemaid, employed by Pa to take care of me because he was away such a lot. But of course, Marina was so much more than that to all of us girls. She was the one who had wiped our tears, berated us for sloppy table manners and steered us calmly through the difficult transition from childhood to womanhood.

She had always been there, and I could not have loved Ma any more if she had given birth to me.

During the first three years of my childhood, Marina and I had lived alone together in our magical castle on the shores of Lake Geneva as Pa Salt travelled the seven seas to conduct his business. And then, one by one, my sisters began to arrive.

Usually, Pa would bring me a present when he returned home. I'd hear the motor launch arriving, run across the sweeping lawns and through the trees to the jetty to greet him. Like any child, I'd want to see what he had hidden inside his magical pockets to delight me. On one particular occasion, however, after he'd presented me with an exquisitely carved wooden reindeer, which he assured me came from St Nicholas's workshop at the North Pole itself, a uniformed woman had stepped out from behind him, and in her arms was a bundle wrapped in a shawl. And the bundle was moving.

'This time, Maia, I've brought you back the most special gift. You have a new sister.' He'd smiled at me as he lifted me into his arms. 'Now you'll no longer be lonely when I have to go away.'

After that, life had changed. The maternity nurse that Pa had brought with him disappeared after a few weeks and Marina took over the care of my baby sister. I couldn't understand how the red, squalling thing which often smelt and diverted attention from me could possibly be a gift. Until one morning, when Alcyone – named after the second star of The Seven Sisters – smiled at me from her high chair over breakfast.

'She knows who I am,' I said in wonder to Marina, who was feeding her.

'Of course she does, Maia, dear. You're her big sister, the one she'll look up to. It'll be up to you to teach her lots of things that you know and she doesn't.'

And as she grew, she became my shadow, following me everywhere, which pleased and irritated me in equal measure.

'Maia, wait me!' she'd demand loudly as she tottered along behind me.

Even though Ally – as I'd nicknamed her – had originally been an unwanted addition to my dreamlike existence at Atlantis, I could not have asked for a sweeter, more loveable companion. She rarely, if ever, cried and there were none of the temper-tantrums associated with toddlers of her age. With her tumbling red-gold curls and her big blue eyes, Ally had a natural charm that drew people to her, including our father. On the occasions Pa Salt was home from one of his long trips abroad, I'd watch how his eyes lit up when he saw her, in a way I was sure they didn't for me. And whereas I was shy and reticent with strangers, Ally had an openness and a readiness to trust that endeared her to everyone.

She was also one of those children who seemed to excel at everything – particularly music, and any sport to do with water. I remember Pa teaching her to swim in our vast pool and, whereas I had struggled to stay afloat and hated being underwater, my little sister took to it like a mermaid. And while I couldn't find my sea legs even on the *Titan*, Pa's huge and beautiful ocean-going yacht, when we were at home Ally would beg him to take her out in the small Laser he kept moored on our private lakeside jetty. I'd crouch in the cramped stern of the boat while Pa and Ally took control as we sped across the glassy waters. Their joint passion for sailing bonded them in a way I felt I could never replicate.

Although Ally had studied music at the Conservatoire de Musique de Genève and was a highly talented flautist who could have pursued a career with a professional orchestra, since leaving music school she had chosen the life of a full-time sailor. She now competed regularly in regattas, and had represented Switzerland on a number of occasions.

When Ally was almost three, Pa arrived home with our next sibling, whom he named Asterope, after the third of The Seven Sisters.

'But we will call her Star,' Pa had said, smiling at Marina, Ally and me as we studied the newest addition to the family lying in the bassinet.

By now I was attending lessons every morning with a private tutor, so my newest sister's arrival affected me less than Ally's had. Then, only six months later, another baby joined us, a twelve-week-old girl named Celaeno, whose name Ally immediately shortened to CeCe.

There was only three months' age difference between Star and CeCe, and from as far back as I can remember, the two of them forged a close bond. They were akin to twins, talking in their own private baby language, some of which the two of them still used to communicate to this day. They inhabited their own private world, to the exclusion of us other sisters. And even now in their twenties, nothing had changed. CeCe, the younger of the two, was always the boss, her stocky body and nut-brown skin in direct contrast to the pale, whippet-thin Star.

The following year, another baby arrived – Taygete, whom I nicknamed 'Tiggy' because her short dark hair sprouted out at strange angles on her tiny head and reminded me of the hedgehog in Beatrix Potter's famous story.

I was by now seven years old, and I'd bonded with Tiggy from the first moment I set eyes on her. She was the most delicate of us all, suffering one childhood illness after another, but even as an infant, she was stoic and undemanding. When yet another baby girl, named Electra, was brought home by Pa a few months later, an exhausted Marina would often ask me if I would mind sitting with Tiggy, who continually had a fever or croup. Eventually diagnosed as asthmatic, she rarely left the nursery to be wheeled outside in the pram, in case the cold air and heavy fog of a Geneva winter affected her chest.

Electra was the youngest of my siblings and her name suited her perfectly. By now, I was used to little babies and their demands, but my youngest sister was without doubt the most challenging of them all. Everything about her *was* electric; her innate ability to switch in an instant from dark to light and vice versa meant that our previously calm home rang daily with high-pitched screams. Her temper-tantrums resonated through my childhood consciousness and as she grew older, her fiery personality did not mellow.

Privately, Ally, Tiggy and I had our own nickname for her; she was known among the three of us as 'Tricky'. We all walked on eggshells around her, wishing to do nothing to set off a lightning change of mood. I can honestly say there were moments when I loathed her for the disruption she brought to Atlantis.

And yet, when Electra knew one of us was in trouble, she was the first to offer help and support. Just as she was capable of huge selfishness, her generosity on other occasions was equally pronounced.

After Electra, the entire household was expecting the arrival of the Seventh Sister. After all, we'd been named after Pa Salt's favourite star cluster and we wouldn't be complete without her. We even knew her name – Merope – and wondered who she would be. But a year went past, and then another, and another, and no more babies arrived home with our father.

I remember vividly standing with him once in his observatory. I was fourteen years old and just on the brink of womanhood. We were waiting for an eclipse, which he'd told me was a seminal moment for humankind and usually brought change with it.

'Pa,' I said, 'will you ever bring home our seventh sister?'

At this, his strong, protective bulk had seemed to freeze for a few seconds. He'd looked suddenly as though he carried the weight of the world on his shoulders. Although he didn't turn around, for he was still concentrating on training the telescope on the coming eclipse, I knew instinctively that what I'd said had distressed him.

'No, Maia, I won't. Because I have never found her.'

As the familiar thick hedge of spruce trees, which shielded our waterside home from prying eyes, came into view, I saw Marina standing on the jetty and the dreadful truth of losing Pa finally began to sink in.

And I realised that the man who had created the kingdom in which we had all been his princesses was no longer present to hold the enchantment in place.

The SEVEN SISTERS

The Seven Sisters series is the multimillion-copy bestselling phenomenon by Lucinda Riley, inspired by the mythology of the famous star constellation.

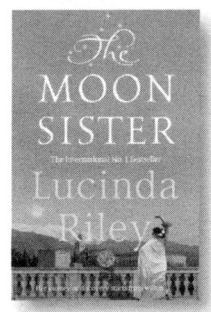

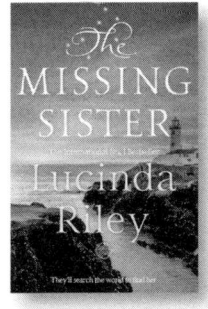

Discover the full series at panmacmillan.com

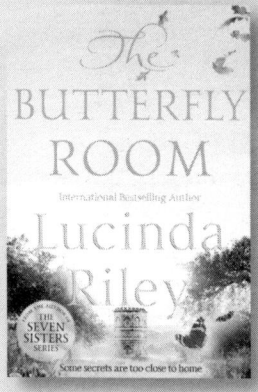
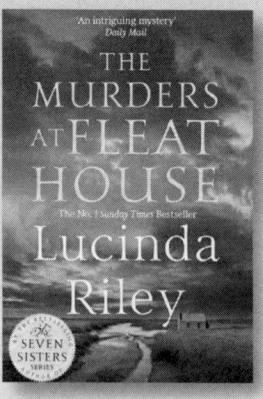

THE
MURDERS
AT FLEAT
HOUSE

A masterful new suspense novel by Lucinda Riley

When a young student is found dead at a private boarding school, its elite reputation is at risk. The headmaster is determined to write the death off as a tragic accident – but Detective Jazz Hunter will soon suspect that a murder has been committed.

Escaping her own problems in London, the isolated, snow-covered landscape of rural Norfolk had felt like the ideal place for Jazz to hide. But when it becomes clear the victim was tangled in a web of loyalties and old vendettas that go far beyond just one student, and the bodies begin to pile up, Jazz knows she's running out of time to find the culprit.

All roads lead back to the closed world of the school. But Fleat House and its residents aren't going to give up their secrets easily – and they're more sinister than Jazz could ever have imagined . . .

Publishing May 2022
Available for pre-order